U0035169

上班族 天天 在用的
工作實況英文

全書MP3一次下載

iOS系統請升級至iOS 13後再行下載，此為大型檔案，
建議使用WIFI連線下載，以免佔用流量，
並確認連線狀況，以利下載順暢

🌐 **國際學村**

本書使用方法

上班族 天天在用的 工作實況英文

這本書的內容看起來好豐富,我該怎麼使用呢?

全書可分為以下幾個部分,只要依次序學習,從此以後各種場合的英文會話再也難不倒你!

輕鬆進入直接用英文對話的5個步驟!

1 CHECK! 瀏覽主題 ⟶ 你在什麼場合?現在是什麼狀況?

2 LOOK UP! 查詢 ⟶ 你會聽到什麼?你會想說什麼?

3 HEAR & SAY! 速聽速答 ⟶ 從對話的一開始到結束的實況會話,讓你快速找到關鍵句!

4 TALK! 暢所欲言 ⟶ 詳列最常用到進階的表達方式,高階的說法也學起來了!

5 LISTEN! 輕鬆聽 ⟶ 特別收錄『用聽的學英文MP3』,『反覆聽』就是讓句子留在腦海裡最有效的方法!

Check! 瀏覽主題
你在什麼場合？現在是什麼狀況？

單元數●
場合●
狀況●

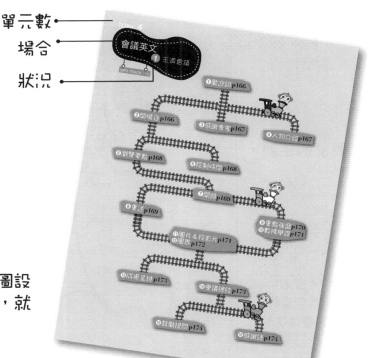

目錄採動線式的流程圖設
計，話題進行到哪裡，就
能夠查詢到哪裡！

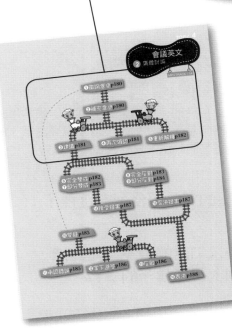

★『場合別』分類，包括六大主題：電話英
文、辦公室事務英文、出差&接待英文、會
議英文、談判英文。

★『狀況別』分類，包括『電話接進來』／
『電話打出去』、『與上級的互動』／『與
同事的互動』／『與廠商的互動』／『與客
戶的互動』／『人事行政與帳務管理』、
『出發到海外』／『海外洽談業務』／『接
待海外賓客』／『廠商參加商展』／『採
購參觀商展』、『主導會議』／『集體討
論』、『主導談判者』／『應對談判者』、
『求職者』／『招募者』等等。

Look up! 查詢

獨創『你可能會聽到什麼？』、『你可能會想說什麼』的分解式學習。每個章節一開始都有逗趣的動物骨頭，一來一往地預演出這個主題中會出現的實況對話，讓你快速掌握關鍵的一句話。

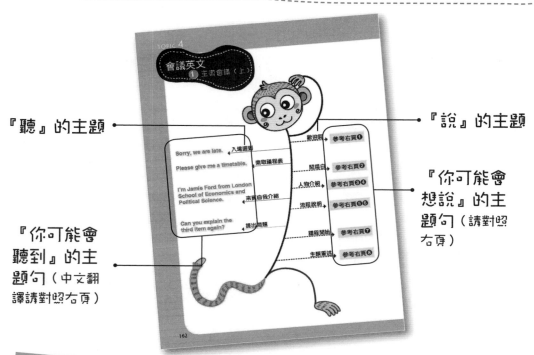

『聽』的主題 ●━━━

『說』的主題 ━━━●

『你可能會想說』的主題句（請對照右頁）

『你可能會聽到』的主題句（中文翻譯請對照右頁）

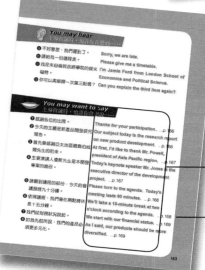

Hear & Say! 速聽速答

把對話的『開始』到『結束』最常用的一句話全面性列出，想知道最簡單、最容易的說法，只要看這兩頁就夠了！

●━━━ 所有想說的句子都條列在這裡了！

●━━━ 想知道這句話的更多進階說法，請翻到上面所標示的頁數。

Talk! 暢所欲言

每個單元的每一句話，都以一個實況對話為基礎，之後詳列出從最簡單常用到進階的表達方式，並標出重點句，讓你不論是口語或繁複的句型都能朗朗上口，競爭力提升200%！

主題句 •

實況對話 •

重點句 •

單字解說 •

特殊說法或
補充說明

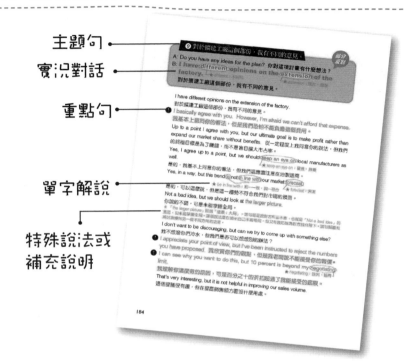

Listen! 輕鬆聽

本書不僅設想好『你可能會聽到什麼』的會話，也特別收錄『用聽的學英文MP3』，上班族沒時間學英文，用聽的最事半功倍！

上班族 天天在用的
工作實況英文

菁英學習 05
ADVANCED

（突破單一層次的）
骨架學習法

國際學村

延伸學習說明

Also need to know

這個單元提供更多中英對照的例句,以及上班族最需要知道的商場禮儀,給你最完整的學習。

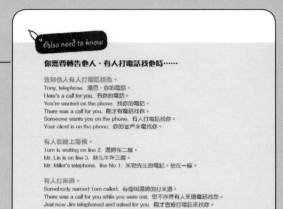

Also need to know

你需要轉告他人,有人打電話找他時……

告知他人有人打電話找他。
Tony, telephone. 湯尼,你的電話。
Here's a call for you. 有你的電話。
You're wanted on the phone. 找你的電話。
There was a call for you. 剛才有電話找你。
Someone wants you on the phone. 有人打電話找你。
Your client is on the phone. 你的客戶來電找你。

有人在線上等候。
Tom is waiting on line 2. 湯姆在二線。
Mr. Lin is on line 3. 林先生在三線。
Mr. Miller's telephone, line No.1. 米勒先生的電話。他在一線。

有人打來過。
Somebody named Tom called. 有個叫湯姆的打來過。
There was a call for you while you were out. 您不在時有人來過電話找你。
Just now Jim telephoned and asked for you. 剛才吉姆打電話來找你。

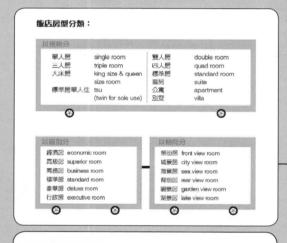

飯店房型分類:

以規格分

單人房	single room	雙人房	double room
三人房	triple room	四人房	quad room
大床房	king size & queen size room	標準房	standard room
		套房	suite
標準房單人住	tsu (twin for sole use)	公寓	apartment
		別墅	villa

以級別分

經濟房	economic room
高級房	superior room
商務房	business room
標準房	standard room
豪華房	deluxe room
行政房	executive room

以朝向分

朝街房	front view room
城景房	city view room
海景房	sea view room
背街房	rear view room
園景房	garden view room
湖景房	lake view room

單字列表

更多實用字彙的整理擴充,查詢時一目瞭然。

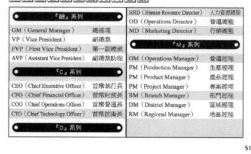

常見主管類職務英文名稱

『總』系列		HRD（Human Resource Director）	人力資源總監
		OD（Operations Director）	營運總監
GM（General Manager）	總經理	MD（Marketing Director）	行銷總監
VP（Vice President）	副總裁	『M』系列	
FVP（First Vice President）	第一副總裁	OM（Operations Manager）	營運經理
AVP（Assistant Vice President）	副總裁助理	PM（Production Manager）	生產經理
『C』系列		PM（Product Manager）	產品經理
CEO（Chief Executive Officer）	首席執行長	PM（Project Manager）	專案經理
CFO（Chief Financial Officer）	首席財務長	BM（Branch Manager）	部門經理
COO（Chief Operations Officer）	首席營運長	DM（District Manager）	區域經理
CTO（Chief Technology Officer）	首席技術長	RM（Regional Manager）	地區經理
『D』系列			

51

CONTENTS

上班族
天天在用的
工作實況英文

Topic 1 　電話英文...... P.26

Topic 2 　辦公室事務英文...... P.42

Topic 3 　出差&接待英文...... P.90

Topic 4 　會議英文...... P.162

Topic 5 　談判英文...... P.190

Topic 6 　面試英文...... P.218

Topic 1 ~ Topic 6 的詳細內容，請翻下一頁

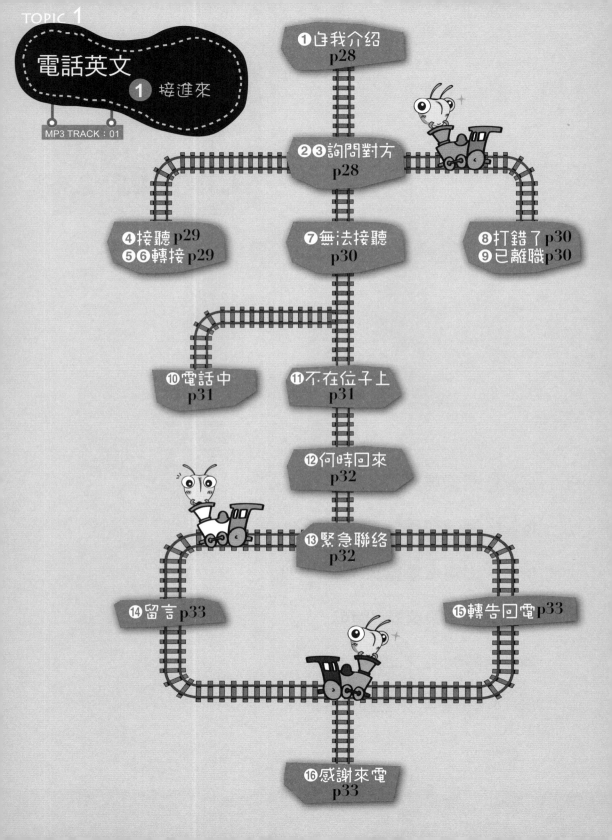

TOPIC 1

電話英文
① 接進來

MP3 TRACK：01

① 自我介紹 p28

②③ 詢問對方 p28

④ 接聽 p29
⑤⑥ 轉接 p29

⑦ 無法接聽 p30

⑧ 打錯了 p30
⑨ 已離職 p30

⑩ 電話中 p31

⑪ 不在位子上 p31

⑫ 何時回來 p32

⑬ 緊急聯絡 p32

⑭ 留言 p33

⑮ 轉告回電 p33

⑯ 感謝來電 p33

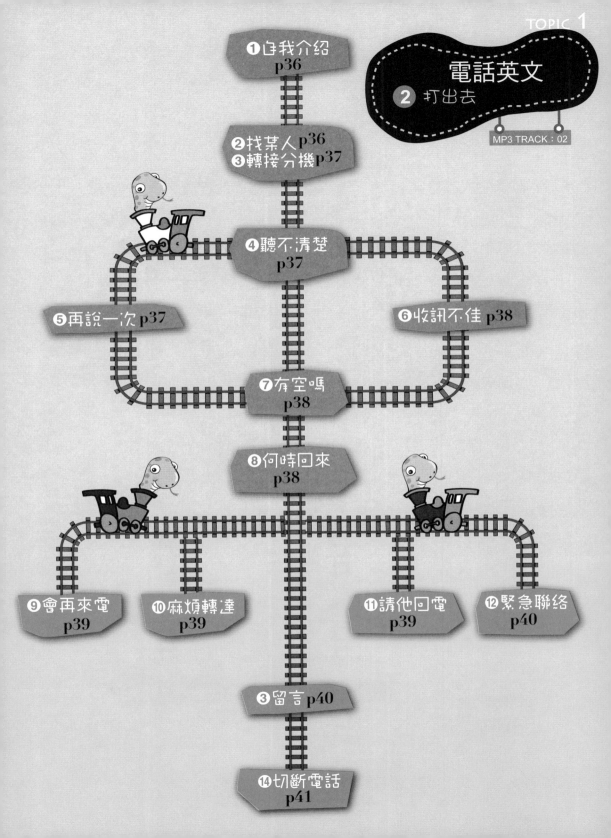

TOPIC 1

電話英文
❷ 打出去

MP3 TRACK：02

❶ 自我介紹
p36

❷ 找某人 p36
❸ 轉接分機 p37

❹ 聽不清楚
p37

❺ 再說一次 p37

❻ 收訊不佳 p38

❼ 有空嗎
p38

❽ 何時回來
p38

❾ 會再來電
p39

❿ 麻煩轉達
p39

⓫ 請他回電
p39

⓬ 緊急聯絡
p40

⓭ 留言 p40

⓮ 切斷電話
p41

辦公室事務英文
1 與上級的互動

MP3 TRACK：03

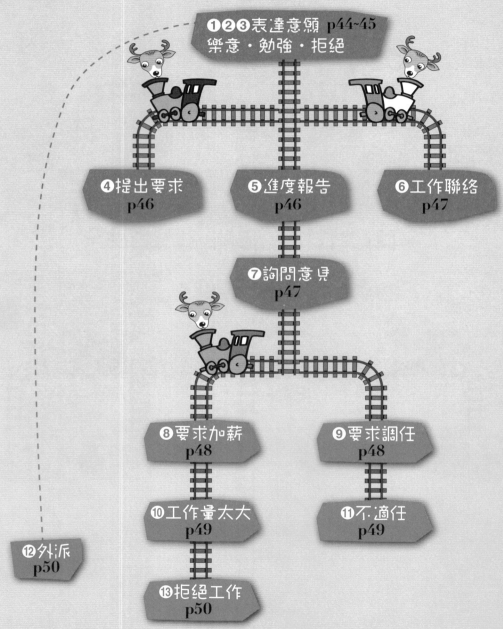

❶❷❸表達意願 p44~45
樂意・勉強・拒絕

❹提出要求 p46

❺進度報告 p46

❻工作聯絡 p47

❼詢問意見 p47

❽要求加薪 p48

❾要求調任 p48

❿工作量太大 p49

⓫不適任 p49

⓬外派 p50

⓭拒絕工作 p50

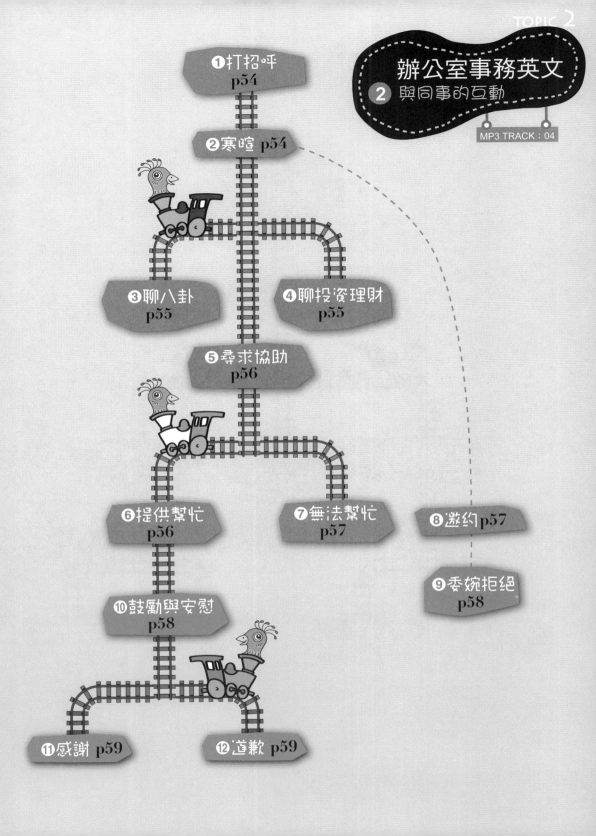

辦公室事務英文
2 與同事的互動

MP3 TRACK : 04

❶打招呼 p54

❷寒暄 p54

❸聊八卦 p55

❹聊投資理財 p55

❺尋求協助 p56

❻提供幫忙 p56

❼無法幫忙 p57

❽邀約 p57

❾委婉拒絕 p58

❿鼓勵與安慰 p58

⓫感謝 p59

⓬道歉 p59

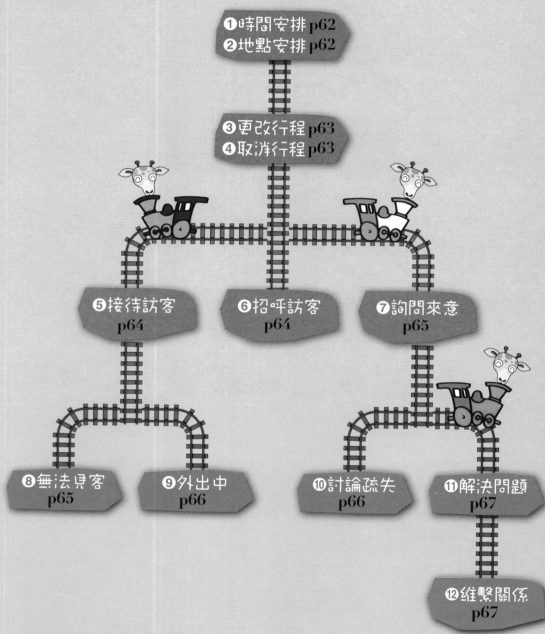

辦公室事務英文
❹ 與客戶的互動
MP3 TRACK : 06

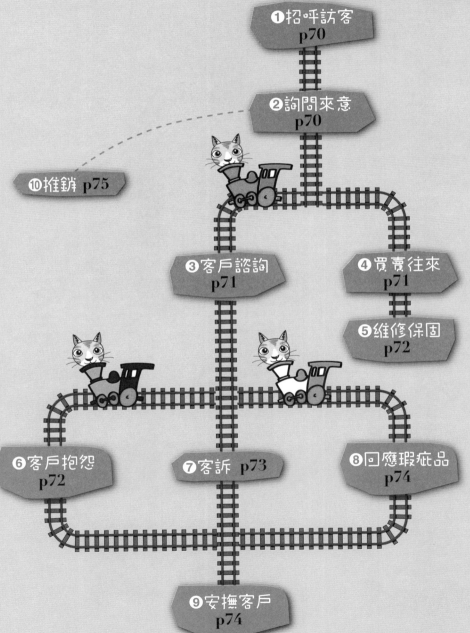

❶招呼訪客
p70

❷詢問來意
p70

❿推銷 p75

❸客戶諮詢
p71

❹買賣往來
p71

❺維修保固
p72

❻客戶抱怨
p72

❼客訴 p73

❽回應瑕疵品
p74

❾安撫客戶
p74

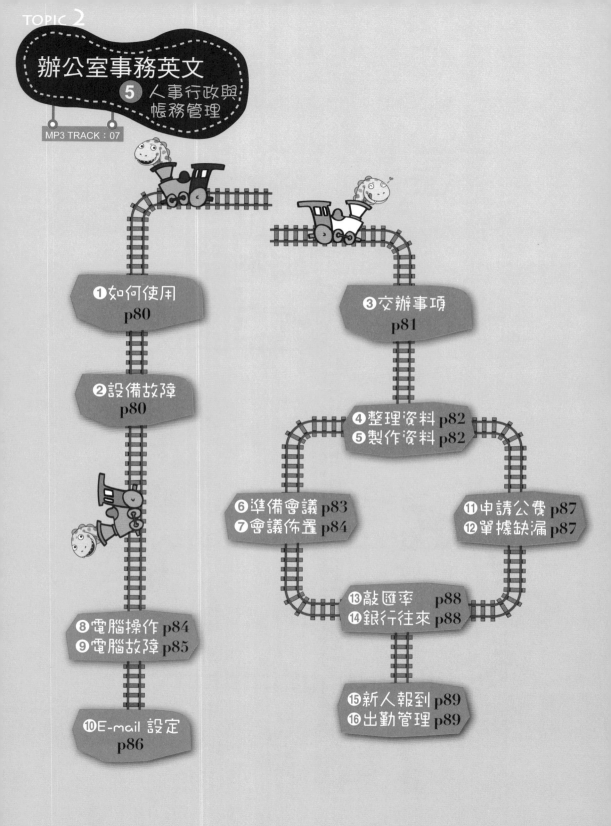

辦公室事務英文
5 人事行政與
帳務管理

MP3 TRACK：07

❶如何使用 p80

❷設備故障 p80

❸交辦事項 p81

❹整理資料 p82
❺製作資料 p82

❻準備會議 p83
❼會議佈置 p84

⓫申請公費 p87
⓬單據缺漏 p87

⓭敲匯率 p88
⓮銀行往來 p88

❽電腦操作 p84
❾電腦故障 p85

⓯新人報到 p89
⓰出勤管理 p89

❿E-mail 設定 p86

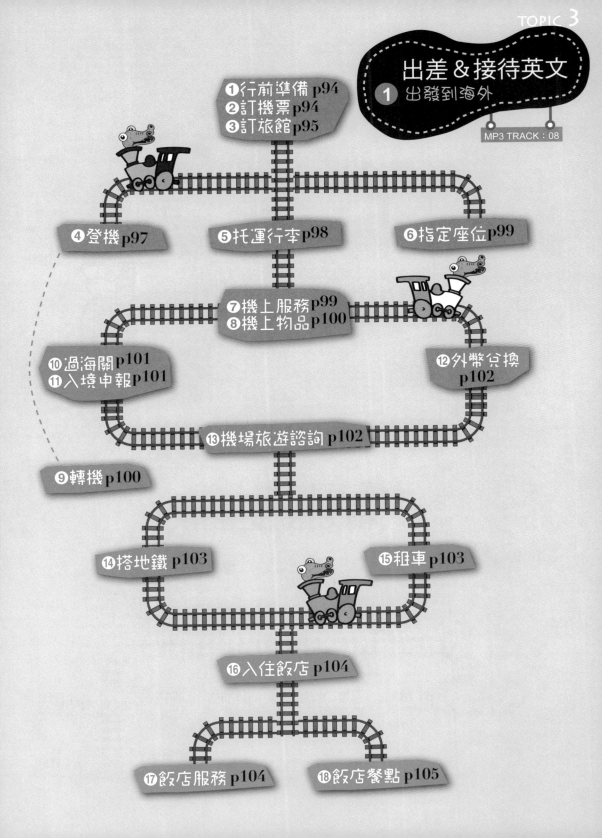

TOPIC 3

出差&接待英文
1 出發到海外

MP3 TRACK：08

❶行前準備 p94
❷訂機票 p94
❸訂旅館 p95

❹登機 p97
❺托運行李 p98
❻指定座位 p99

❼機上服務 p99
❽機上物品 p100

❿過海關 p101
⓫入境申報 p101

⓬外幣兌換 p102

⓭機場旅遊諮詢 p102

❾轉機 p100

⓮搭地鐵 p103
⓯租車 p103

⓰入住飯店 p104

⓱飯店服務 p104
⓲飯店餐點 p105

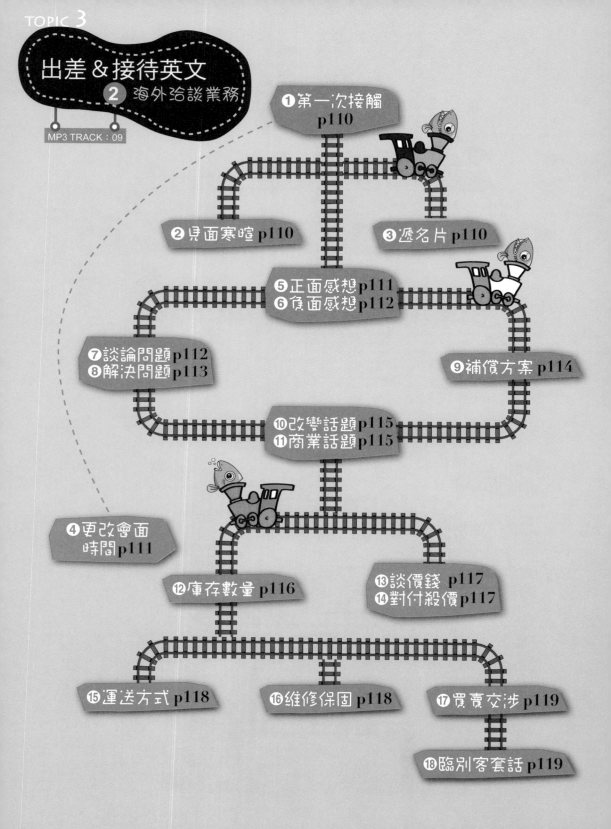

出差&接待英文
② 海外洽談業務

MP3 TRACK : 09

❶ 第一次接觸 p110

❷ 見面寒暄 p110

❸ 遞名片 p110

❺ 正面感想 p111
❻ 負面感想 p112

❼ 談論問題 p112
❽ 解決問題 p113

❾ 補償方案 p114

❿ 改變話題 p115
⓫ 商業話題 p115

❹ 更改會面 時間 p111

⓬ 庫存數量 p116

⓭ 談價錢 p117
⓮ 對付殺價 p117

⓯ 運送方式 p118

⓰ 維修保固 p118

⓱ 買賣交涉 p119

⓲ 臨別客套話 p119

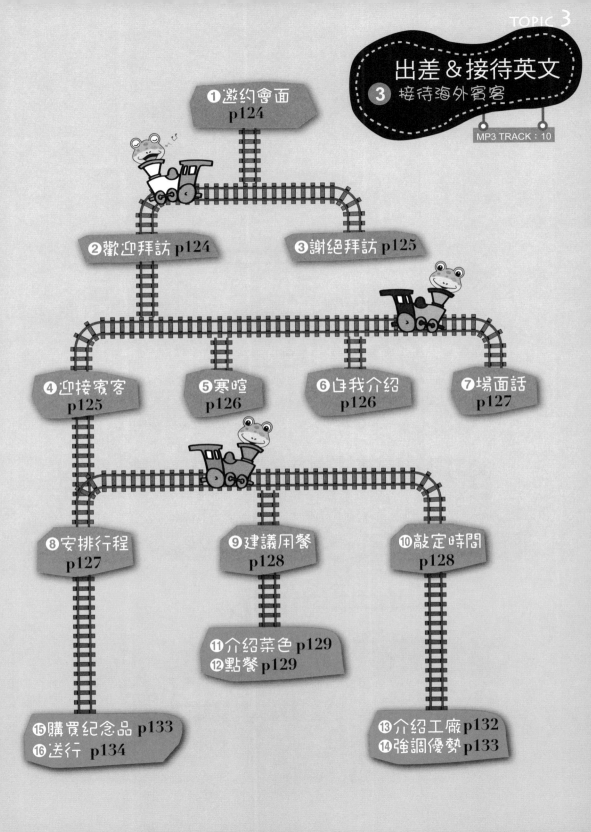

出差 & 接待英文
③ 接待海外賓客

MP3 TRACK：10

❶邀約會面 p124

❷歡迎拜訪 p124

❸謝絕拜訪 p125

❹迎接賓客 p125

❺寒暄 p126

❻自我介紹 p126

❼場面話 p127

❽安排行程 p127

❾建議用餐 p128

❿敲定時間 p128

⓫介紹菜色 p129
⓬點餐 p129

⓭介紹工廠 p132
⓮強調優勢 p133

⓯購買紀念品 p133
⓰送行 p134

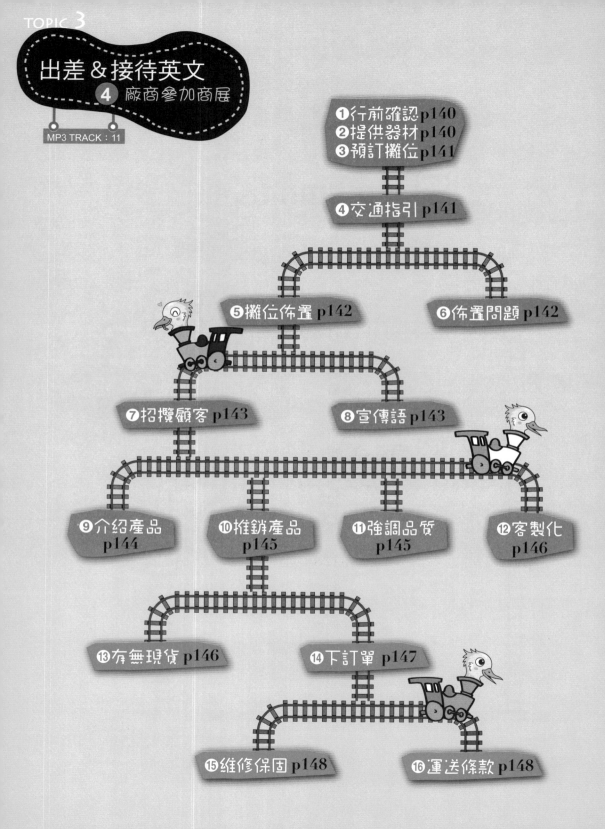

❶行前確認 p140
❷提供器材 p140
❸預訂攤位 p141

❹交通指引 p141

❺攤位佈置 p142

❻佈置問題 p142

❼招攬顧客 p143

❽宣傳語 p143

❾介紹產品 p144

❿推銷產品 p145

⓫強調品質 p145

⓬客製化 p146

⓭存無現貨 p146

⓮下訂單 p147

⓯維修保固 p148

⓰運送條款 p148

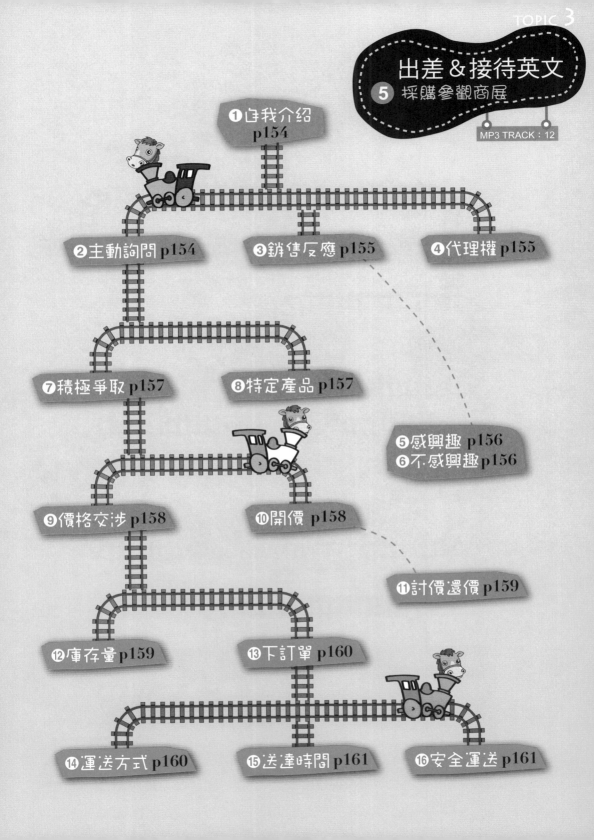

TOPIC 3

出差 & 接待英文
5 採購參觀商展

MP3 TRACK：12

❶自我介紹
p154

❷主動詢問 p154　　❸銷售反應 p155　　❹代理權 p155

❼積極爭取 p157　　❽特定產品 p157

❺感興趣 p156
❻不感興趣 p156

❾價格交涉 p158　　❿開價 p158

⓫討價還價 p159

⓬庫存量 p159　　⓭下訂單 p160

⓮運送方式 p160　　⓯送達時間 p161　　⓰安全運送 p161

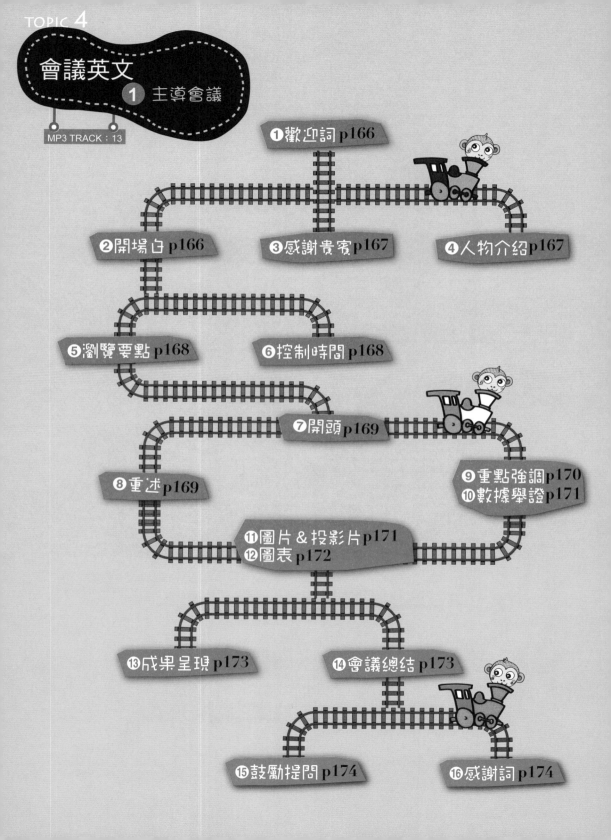

TOPIC 4

會議英文
① 主導會議

MP3 TRACK：13

① 歡迎詞 p166

② 開場白 p166

③ 感謝貴賓 p167

④ 人物介紹 p167

⑤ 瀏覽要點 p168

⑥ 控制時間 p168

⑦ 開頭 p169

⑧ 重述 p169

⑨ 重點強調 p170
⑩ 數據舉證 p171

⑪ 圖片＆投影片 p171
⑫ 圖表 p172

⑬ 成果呈現 p173

⑭ 會議總結 p173

⑮ 鼓勵提問 p174

⑯ 感謝詞 p174

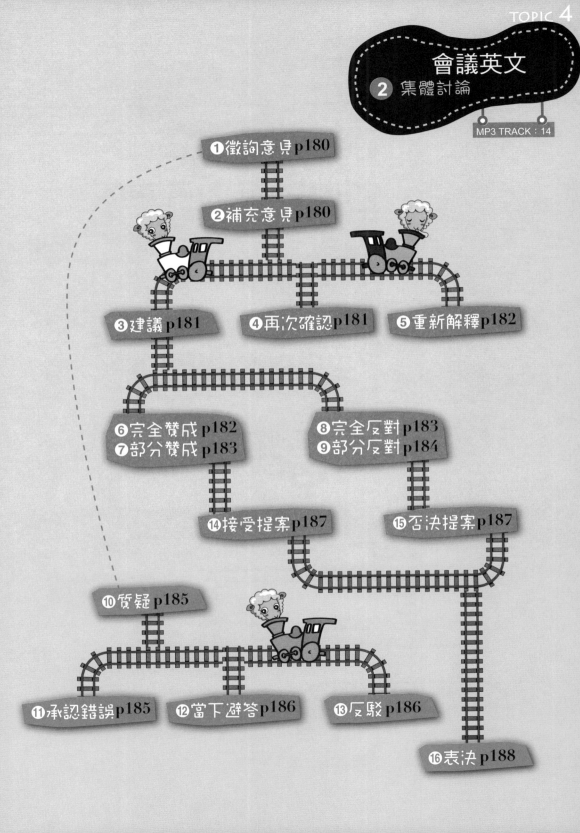

會議英文
❷ 集體討論

MP3 TRACK：14

❶ 徵詢意見 p180

❷ 補充意見 p180

❸ 建議 p181

❹ 再次確認 p181

❺ 重新解釋 p182

❻ 完全贊成 p182
❼ 部分贊成 p183

❽ 完全反對 p183
❾ 部分反對 p184

❿ 質疑 p185

⓫ 接受提案 p187

⓯ 否決提案 p187

⓫ 承認錯誤 p185

⓬ 當下避答 p186

⓭ 反駁 p186

⓰ 表決 p188

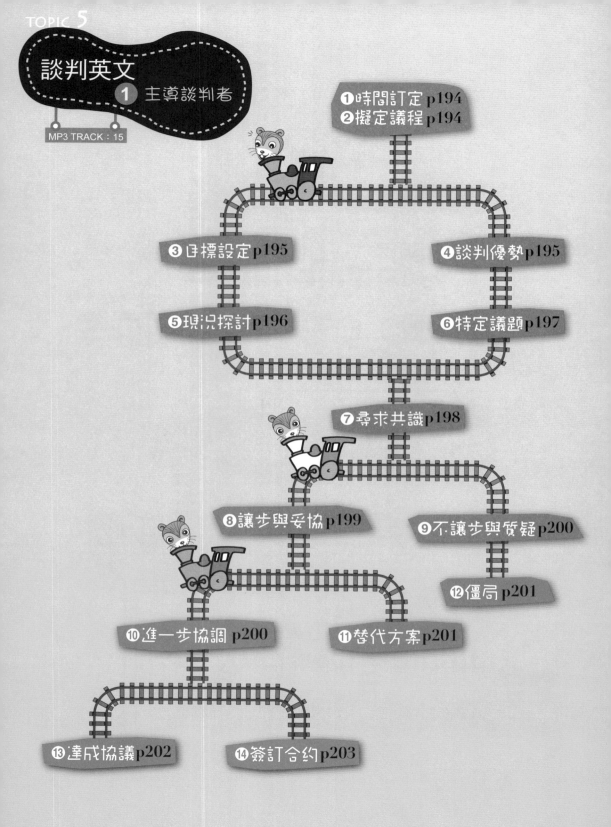

TOPIC 5

談判英文
① 主導談判者

MP3 TRACK：15

❶時間訂定 p194
❷擬定議程 p194

❸目標設定 p195

❹談判優勢 p195

❺現況探討 p196

❻特定議題 p197

❼尋求共識 p198

❽讓步與妥協 p199

❾不讓步與質疑 p200

❿進一步協調 p200

⓫替代方案 p201

⓬僵局 p201

⓭達成協議 p202

⓮簽訂合約 p203

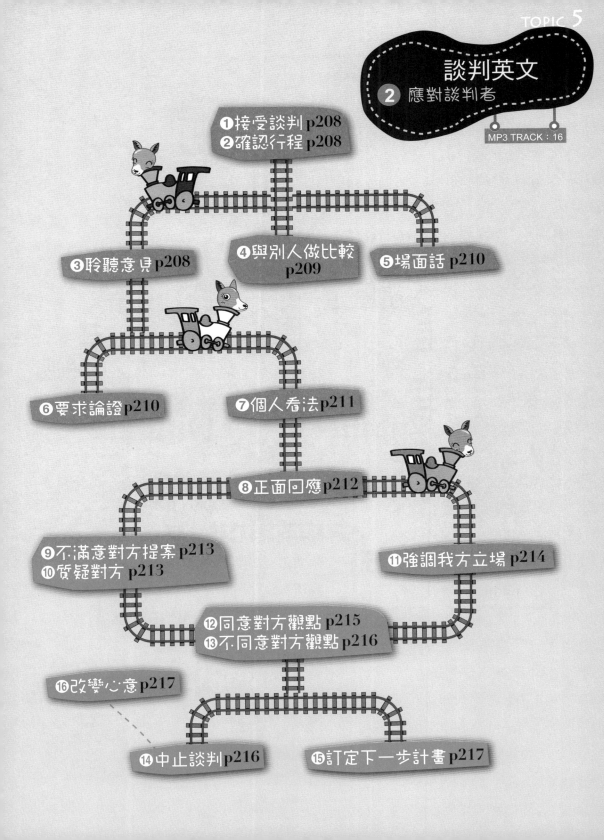

談判英文
❷ 應對談判者

MP3 TRACK：16

❶ 接受談判 p208
❷ 確認行程 p208

❸ 聆聽意見 p208

❹ 與別人做比較 p209

❺ 場面話 p210

❻ 要求論證 p210

❼ 個人看法 p211

❽ 正面回應 p212

❾ 不滿意對方提案 p213
❿ 質疑對方 p213

⓫ 強調我方立場 p214

⓬ 同意對方觀點 p215
⓭ 不同意對方觀點 p216

⓰ 改變心意 p217

⓮ 中止談判 p216

⓯ 訂定下一步計畫 p217

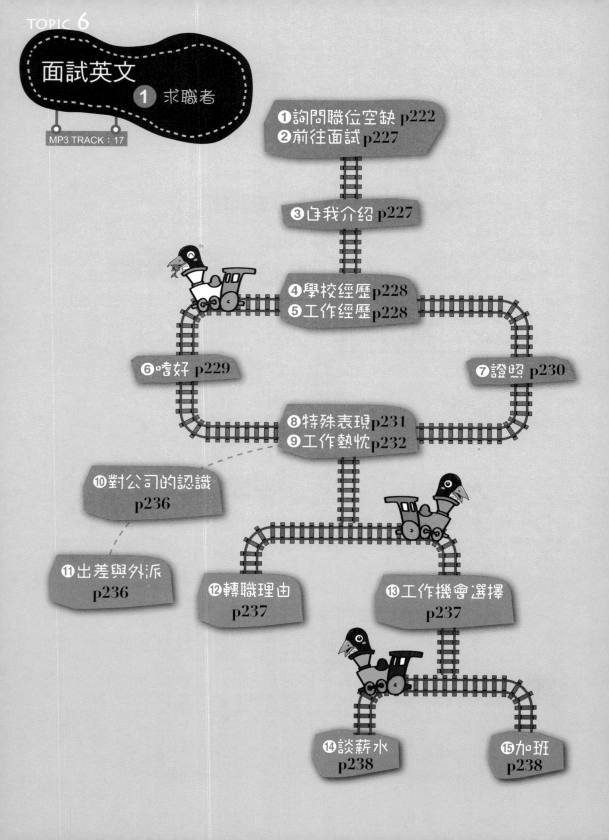

TOPIC 6

面試英文

1 求職者

MP3 TRACK : 17

❶詢問職位空缺 p222
❷前往面試 p227

❸自我介紹 p227

❹學校經歷 p228
❺工作經歷 p228

❻嗜好 p229

❼證照 p230

❽特殊表現 p231
❾工作熱忱 p232

❿對公司的認識 p236

⓫出差與外派 p236

⓬轉職理由 p237

⓭工作機會選擇 p237

⓮談薪水 p238

⓯加班 p238

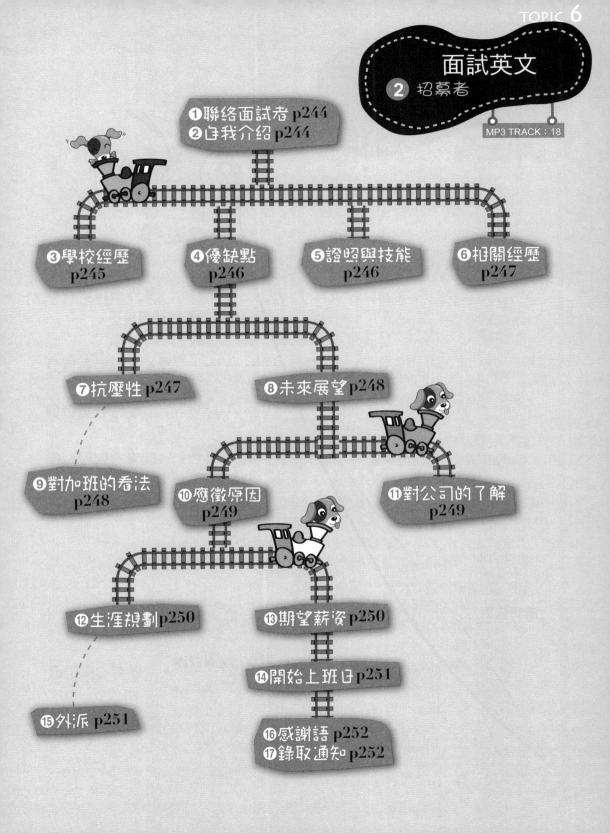

面試英文

2 招募者

❶聯絡面試者 p244
❷自我介紹 p244

❸學校經歷 p245

❹優缺點 p246

❺證照與技能 p246

❻相關經歷 p247

❼抗壓性 p247

❽未來展望 p248

❾對加班的看法 p248

❿應徵原因 p249

⓫對公司的了解 p249

⓬生涯規劃 p250

⓭期望薪資 p250

⓮開始上班日 p251

⓯外派 p251

⓰感謝語 p252
⓱錄取通知 p252

電話英文

1 接進來

MP3 TRACK：01

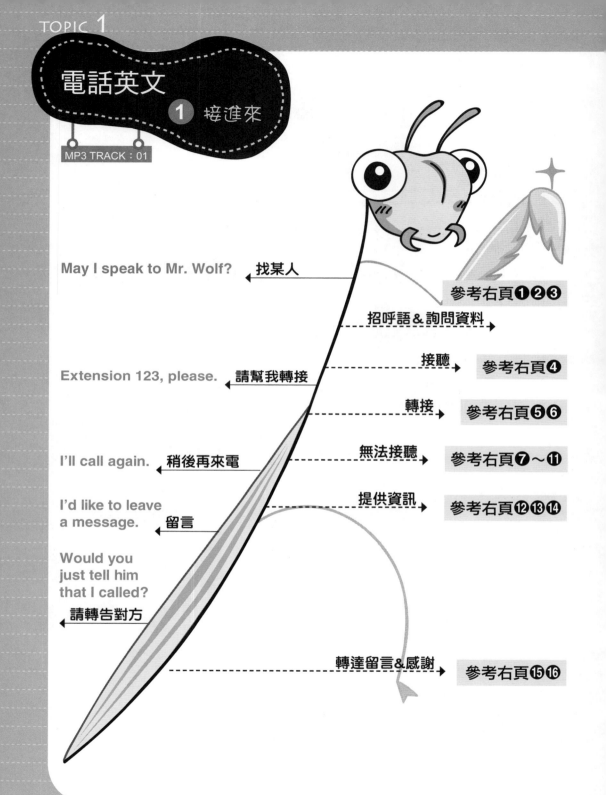

May I speak to Mr. Wolf? ← 找某人

參考右頁 ❶❷❸

招呼語＆詢問資料 →

接聽 →　參考右頁 ❹

Extension 123, please. ← 請幫我轉接

轉接 →　參考右頁 ❺❻

I'll call again. ← 稍後再來電

無法接聽 →　參考右頁 ❼～⓫

I'd like to leave a message. ← 留言

提供資訊 →　參考右頁 ⓬⓭⓮

Would you just tell him that I called?

← 請轉告對方

轉達留言＆感謝 →　參考右頁 ⓯⓰

線上音檔

You may hear
接電話時，也許你會聽到……

ⓐ 我找沃夫先生。　　　　　　May I speak to Mr. Wolf?

ⓑ 麻煩轉接分機 123。　　　　Extension 123, please.

ⓒ 我會再打來。　　　　　　　I'll call again.

ⓓ 我要留言。　　　　　　　　I'd like to leave a message.

ⓔ 可以請你轉告他我打來過嗎？　Would you just tell him that I called?

You may want to say
接電話時，也許你會想說……

❶ 哈囉，我是湯姆。　　　　　Hello, this is Tom. ...p.28

❷ 請問哪裡找？　　　　　　　Who is this? ...p.28

❸ 請問找哪位？　　　　　　　Who are you looking for? ...p.28

❹ 我就是。　　　　　　　　　Speaking. ...p.29

❺ 請稍等。　　　　　　　　　Just a moment, please. ...p.29

❻ 我幫您轉接。　　　　　　　I'll put him through. ...p.29

❼ 他現在無法聽電話。　　　　He's not available right now. ...p.30

❽ 你打錯電話了。　　　　　　You have the wrong number. ...p.30

❾ 他離職了。　　　　　　　　He's no longer with us. ...p.30

❿ 他正在電話中。　　　　　　He's still on the line. ...p.31

⓫ 他現在不在位子上。　　　　He's not at his desk at the moment. ...p.31

⓬ 他大約五點回來。　　　　　He will be back at about 5 o'clock. ...p.32

⓭ 請撥他的手機好嗎？　　　　Could you call his cell phone? ...p.32

⓮ 您可以留言嗎？　　　　　　Would you like to leave a message? ...p.33

⓯ 需要轉告他回電給您嗎？　　Should I get him to call you back? ...p.33

⓰ 謝謝您的來電。　　　　　　Thank you for calling. ...p.33

❶ 哈囉，我是湯姆。

自我介紹

A: **Hello, this is Tom.** 哈囉，我是湯姆。
B: Hello, is Amy there? 哈囉，請問愛咪在嗎？

Hello. / Yes. / Yeah! 哈囉！／喂。
＊「Yeah!」是比較不正式的講法。

❗ Tom Speaking. 我是湯姆。

❗ Hello, this is Tom. 哈囉，我是湯姆。

Tom Lee, may I help you? 湯姆李，需要什麼幫忙嗎？

This is Tom of Banana Sea Publishers. 我是香蕉海出版社的湯姆。

❷ 請問哪裡找？

詢問對方

A: Hello, could I speak to Mr. Parker, please? 哈囉，我找帕克先生。
B: **Who is this?** 請問哪裡找？

❗ Who is this? 請問哪裡找？

❗ Who's calling, please? 請問哪裡找？

Whom am I speaking to? 請問哪裡找？

❗ May I ask who's calling? 可以請問您哪位嗎？

May I tell him who's calling? 我該跟他說是哪位打來的呢？

Whom may / should / shall I say is calling? 請問我該說是誰打來的？
＊最後兩句是很禮貌的說法。

❸ 請問找哪位？

詢問對方

★ in charge of~：負責，照料

A: **Who are you looking for?** 請問找哪位？
B: I don't know. Anyone in charge of the store!
不知道，可以負責這家商店的任何一個人！

★ look for~：尋找

❗ Who are you looking for? 請問找哪位？

Who do you want to speak with? 您要跟哪位說話？

To whom should I put you through? 我應該幫您轉接哪位？
★ put~through：轉接

28

❹ 我就是。 接聽

A: Hello. Is Tom there? 哈囉，湯姆在嗎？
B: **Speaking.** Who's calling? 我就是。請問您哪位？

❗ Speaking. 我就是。

This is he / she. 現在就是他／她接聽。
＊「This is me.」是錯誤的說法。

❗ This is Tom speaking. 現在是湯姆接聽。

❺ 請稍等。 轉接

A: Hello, can I talk to Matt, please? 你好，可以幫我轉接給麥特嗎？
B: Sure, **just a moment, please.** 當然，請稍等。

❗ Hold on. 請不要掛斷電話。

＊「hold on」有「等一下、停住」的意思；而「hang on」除了有「稍等」之意，還有「（打電話）不掛斷」的意思；「hang up」則是掛斷電話。

Just a sec. 請等一下。 ★ sec. = second

❗ Just a moment, please. 請稍等。

Can I put you on hold? 可以請你不要掛斷電話嗎？

❻ 我幫您轉接。 轉接

★ promotion：促銷

A: Is Mr. Wilson from the promotion department available?
請問促銷部的威爾森先生現在有空嗎？
B: You've called the sales department, but **I'll put him through.**
這裡是業務部，我幫您轉接，請稍候。 ★ sales department：業務部

I'll get him for you. 我幫您轉給他。

❗ I'll put him through. 我轉接給他。

I'll connect you with him. 我幫您轉接給他。

❗ I'll transfer your call. 我將轉接您的來電。

I'll switch you to him. 我將把您的電話轉給他。

＊put ~ through、connect A with B、transfer、switch ~ over / to ~ 都是「轉接電話」的意思。

29

❼ 他現在無法聽電話。

A: Can I speak to Mr. Becker? 請問貝克先生在嗎？

B: Sorry, **he is not available right now.** 對不起，他現在無法聽電話。
★ be available：在場的，可找到的

❗ He is not available right now. 他現在無法聽電話。

He is in a meeting right now. 他在開會。（所以無法聽電話）

He is tied up at the moment. 他忙得不能接電話。 ★ be tied up：沒空，有事

He's extremely busy at the moment. 他現在非常忙碌。 ★ at the moment：此刻，現在

He's right in the middle of something. 他現在正在處理事情。
★ in the middle of：某件事情進行到一半

❽ 你打錯電話了。

A: Can I talk to Mr. Nakashima, please? 請問中島先生在嗎？

B: I'm sorry. I think **you have the wrong number.**
不好意思，我想您打錯電話了。

Wrong number. 打錯了。
＊不正式的說法。

❗ You have the wrong number. 你打錯電話了。

You've dialed / got the wrong number. 你撥錯電話了。
★ dial：撥打（電話）

There's nobody here by that name. 這裡沒有叫這個名字的人。

There's no Nakashima here. 這裡沒有姓中島的人。

❾ 他離職了。

A: May I speak to Mr. Becker? 我能和貝克先生通話嗎？

B: I'm sorry to tell you **he is no longer with us.** 對不起，他離職了。

★ no longer：不再

❗ He is no longer with us. 他離職了。

❗ He quit the job. 他辭職了。

He resigned from this company. 他辭職了。

He left the company. 他離開公司了。
★ resign (from)：辭職

⑩ 他正在電話中。

A: Could I have extension 239, please? 請幫我轉接分機 239。

B: I'm sorry, **he's still on the line.** Would you like to wait, or can I take a message? ★ be on the line：在接電話

對不起，他正在電話中。可以請您稍候一下嗎？或者您要留言？

❗ He's still on the line. 對不起，他正在電話中

❗ He is on another line now. 他正在另一支電話線上。

He is talking to someone else now. 他正在跟另一位講話中。

The line is engaged. 這支電話目前忙線中。

He's busy talking to a client. 他正忙於跟客戶談話。
└─★ be engaged：忙於

⑪ 他現在不在位子上。

A: Good morning. I'd like to speak to Jack, please. This is John Smith of Franklin Company. 早安。我找傑克。我是富蘭克林公司的約翰史密斯。

B: I'm afraid **he's not at his desk at the moment.** Would you like to leave a message? 他現在不在位子上。您想要留言嗎？
└─★ leave a message：留言

❗ He's out now. 他外出了。 ─★ step out：走出去，暫時外出

He just went out. / He just stepped out. 他剛出去。

❗ He's out for lunch. 他出去吃飯了。

He's on his lunch break. 現在是他的午休時間。

He's not in right now. 他現在不在。

❗ He's not at his desk at the moment. 他現在不在位子上。

He is away from his desk. 他不在位子上。

He has left for the day. 他今天已經下班了。

He's gone for the day. 他已經離開了。

❗ He's off today. 他今天休假。
＊只用 off 就可以表示休假。

Today's his day off. 今天他休假。

He's on vacation / holiday. 他正在度假中。

He's on a business trip. 他出差去了。

He hasn't shown up yet. 他還沒有來。
└─★ show up：出席，露面

31

⑫ 他大約五點回來。

A: When will he come back? 他什麼時候回來？
B: **He will be back at about 5 o'clock.** 他大約五點回來。

❗ He will be back at about 5 o'clock. 他大約五點回來。

He will be back by 5 o'clock. 他大概五點以前會回來。

He should be back in ten minutes. 他大概十分鐘後回來。

＊「in」指的不是「以內」，而是「之後」，所以是「十分鐘後」的意思。

❗ Would you try again in 10 minutes? 你可以十分鐘後再打來嗎？

He's expected to be back in a couple of hours. 他應該幾個小時後會回來。

He's gone until Friday. 他禮拜五才會來。

⑬ 請撥他的手機好嗎？

緊急
聯絡

A: This is an emergency. I need to get in contact with him right now.
這件事情很緊急。我現在就需要聯絡到他。
B: If it's urgent, **could you call his cell phone?**
如果有急事的話，請撥他的手機好嗎？

Call his cell. 打他的手機。

❗ Could you call his cell phone? 請撥他的手機好嗎？

Why don't you try his cell? 何不試試打他的手機？

You can try his cell phone. 你可以試著打他手機。

Do you have his cell phone number? 你有他的手機號碼嗎？

You can call his cellular phone or use text messaging.
你可以打他的手機或發簡訊。

He is out of the office today, but you can reach him on his cell phone.
他今天不在辦公室，但你可以打他手機聯絡他。

I'll look up his cell phone number for you. 我幫你找找他的手機號碼。

❗ Please take down his cell phone number. It's zero-nine-three-five, zero-six-nine, eight-seven-six. 請記下他的手機號碼，0935-069-876。

★ take down：記下

⑭ 您可以留言嗎？

留言

A: I'd like to speak to Mr. Halley, please. This is Nancy.
　我想和哈雷先生通話。我是南西。
B: I'm sorry, but Mr. Halley is not in at the moment. **Would you like to leave a message?** 對不起，哈雷先生此刻不在。您可以留言嗎？

❗ Would you like to leave a message? 您可以留言嗎？
　Can I take a message for you? 我可以替您留言嗎？
　Do you have any message to pass on to him? 您有任何訊息要我轉告他嗎？
　Do you want me to (relay) a message for you? 您是否要我轉達訊息給他呢？
　　　　　　　　　　★ relay：轉達
　He is in a meeting right now. Is there any message?
　他現在正在開會。要不要留言呢？
❗ Would you like to leave your number? 您可以留下您的電話號碼嗎？

⑮ 需要轉告他回電給您嗎？

轉告
回電

A: **Should I get him to call you back?** 需要轉告他回電給您嗎？
B: Yes, as soon as possible. 好的，請他盡快回電。

❗ Should I get him to call you back? 需要轉告他回電給您嗎？
　Could I tell him to ring you back? 需要我轉告他回電給您嗎？
　I'll have her return your call later. 稍後我會請她回電給您。

⑯ 謝謝您的來電。

感謝
來電

A: Let me call back later again. Thank you. 我稍後再打電話來。謝謝你。
B: **Thank you for calling.** 謝謝您的來電。

❗ Thank you for calling. 謝謝您的來電。
　Thanks for your call. 謝謝您的來電。
　Thanks for calling me about this matter. 謝謝你打電話來告訴我這個問題。
　I (appreciate) your call. Goodbye. 感謝您的來電，再會。
　　★ appreciate：感謝、感激

電話英文
2 打出去

MP3 TRACK：02

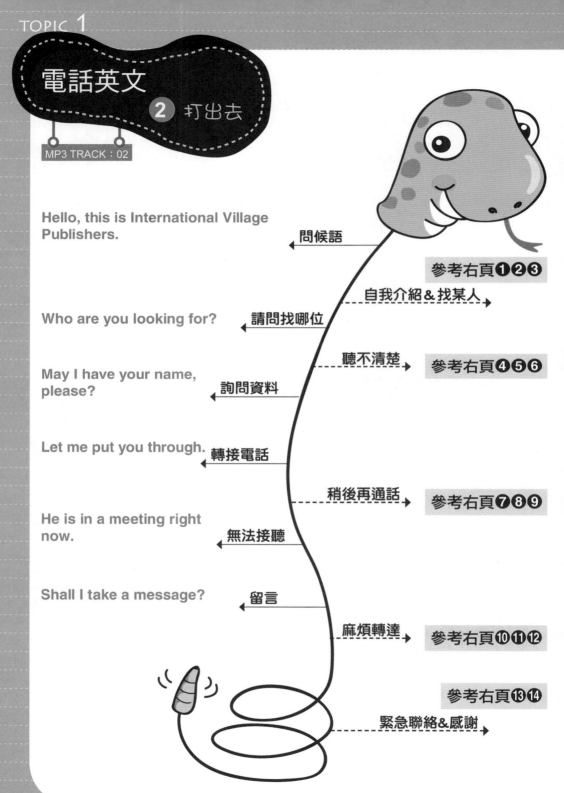

Hello, this is International Village Publishers.

← 問候語

參考右頁 ❶❷❸

自我介紹＆找某人 →

Who are you looking for?

← 請問找哪位

聽不清楚 →

參考右頁 ❹❺❻

May I have your name, please?

← 詢問資料

Let me put you through.

← 轉接電話

稍後再通話 →

參考右頁 ❼❽❾

He is in a meeting right now.

← 無法接聽

Shall I take a message?

← 留言

麻煩轉達 →

參考右頁 ❿⓫⓬

參考右頁 ⓭⓮

緊急聯絡＆感謝 →

You may hear
打電話時，也許你會聽到……

線上音檔

ⓐ 國際學村出版社您好。　　Hello, this is International Village Publishers.

ⓑ 請問找哪位？　　Who are you looking for?

ⓒ 請教您的大名？　　May I have your name, please?

ⓓ 我幫您轉接。　　Let me put you through.

ⓔ 他正在開會。　　He is in a meeting right now.

ⓕ 您要留言嗎？　　Shall I take a message?

You may want to say
打電話時，也許你會想說……

❶ 我是MODE雜誌的凱洛。　　This is Carol of MODE Magazine.　…p.36

❷ 我找沃夫先生。　　May I speak to Mr. Wolf?　…p.36

❸ 麻煩轉接分機 123。　　Extension 123, please.　…p.37

❹ 你可以說大聲一點嗎？　　Could you speak a little louder, please? …p.37

❺ 你可以再說一次嗎？　　Could you repeat that, please?　…p.37

❻ 這裡收訊不是很好。　　We have a bad connection.　…p.38

❼ 你現在方便講電話嗎？　　Is this a good time for you to talk?　…p.38

❽ 他什麼時候回來？　　When will he be back?　…p.38

❾ 我會再打來。　　I'll call again.　…p.39

❿ 請告訴他凱洛打來過。　　Please tell him that Carol called.　…p.39

⓫ 可以請他回電給我嗎？　　Would you just tell him to call me back?　…p.39

⓬ 這件事很緊急，可不可以告　It's urgent. Could you tell me where I can
訴我哪裡可以聯絡得到她？　reach her?　…p.40

⓭ 我要留言。　　I'd like to leave a message.　…p.40

⓮ 謝謝，再見。　　Thank you. Goodbye.　…p.41

❶ 我是MODE雜誌的凱洛。

A: Hello, **this is Carol of MODE Magazine.**
喂，你好。我是 MODE 雜誌的凱洛。
B: Hello, what can I do for you? 你好，請問你有什麼事？

I'm calling from MODE Magazine. 我這裡是 MODE 雜誌。

❗ This is Carol of MODE Magazine. 我是 MODE 雜誌的凱洛。

I'm calling on behalf of MODE magazine. 我代表 MODE 雜誌打來。

＊ A on behalf of B 是「A 代表 B」的意思。

Is this Easy Credit Company? 請問是輕鬆信用公司嗎？
＊這一句是確認所致電的公司是否正確。

This is Carol, and I just called not too long ago. 我是凱洛，剛剛有打來過。

My name's Carol. I was just on the phone with you.

我叫凱洛，剛剛跟您講過電話。
＊最後兩句用於打電話給同一個人第二次以上時使用。

❷ 我找沃夫先生。

A: **May I speak to Mr. Wolf?** 我找沃夫先生。
B: Sure, hold on. 好的，請稍等。
★ hold on：不掛斷電話

❗ Is John available? 約翰有空嗎？

Is John there? 約翰在嗎？

Get me John, please. 請幫我接約翰。

❗ May I speak to Mr. Wolf? 我找沃夫先生。
＊找人時用「May I speak to～」是最普遍的一種說法，另外也可以說「I'd like to speak to～」或「Would you connect me to～」。

Please give me Mr. Wolf in the R&D Department.
★ give：在這裡是轉接電話的意思

請幫我接研發部的沃夫先生。
＊同一個公司可能會有名字相近的人，最好把是什麼部門的人講清楚，以免轉接錯人。

Good morning, I am trying to reach Mr. Wolf, please.

早安，我想找沃夫先生聽電話。
＊「try to」是客氣的說法。

❸ 麻煩轉接分機 123。

A: **Extension 123, please.** 麻煩轉接分機 123。
B: Just a moment, please. 請稍候。

❗ Extension 123, please. 麻煩轉接分機 123。
❗ May I / Could I have extension 123, please? 可以轉接分機 123 嗎？
　 May I speak to Tom, extension 123? 可以幫我轉接分機 123 的湯姆嗎？
　 Please connect me with extension 123. 請幫我轉接分機 123。
　 Could you put me through to the Personnel Department, please?
　 可以請你幫我轉接人事部嗎？ ⌐ ★ Personnel Department：人事部

❹ 你可以說大聲一點嗎？

A: Hello, this is Jim of the Export Department. May I speak to Mr. Wang?
　 你好，我是出口部的吉姆。我找王先生。
B: I am sorry. I can't really hear you. **Could you speak a little louder, please?** 很抱歉，我聽不太清楚。你可以說大聲一點嗎？

❗ Make it louder, please. 請大聲一點。
❗ Could you speak a little louder, please? 你可以說大聲一點嗎？
　 Do you mind speaking up? 你介意說大聲一點嗎？
　 ⌐ ★ speak up：說大聲一點

❺ 你可以再說一次嗎？

A: **Could you repeat that, please?** 你可以再說一次嗎？
B: I'm sorry, what part didn't you get? 不好意思，哪個部份聽不清楚呢？

　 Huh? 什麼？
　 ＊只說「huh?」是很不正式的用法。
❗ Could you repeat that, please? / Could you say that again? 你可以再說一次嗎？
　 I'm sorry. I didn't catch what you said. 抱歉，我沒聽懂你剛剛說的。
　 I'm sorry. I don't understand. Could you say that again?
　 不好意思，我聽不懂。可以請你再說一次嗎？

❻ 這裡收訊不是很好。
收訊不佳

A: I can't hear you well. 我聽不太清楚。
B: I am sorry. I think **we have a bad connection.**
很抱歉，我想這裡收訊不是很好。

❗ We have a bad connection. 電話收訊不好。
There was a lot of echo and I couldn't hear well. 回音太多了，我聽不太清楚。
There's interference on the line. 電話線上有些干擾。
★ interference：干擾，擾亂

❼ 你現在方便講電話嗎？
有空嗎

A: Hello, Tom. This is Andy. **Is this a good time for you to talk?**
湯姆你好。我是安迪。你現在方便講電話嗎？
B: I'm pretty busy now. Can I call you back later?
我現在很忙，可以待會兒再打給你嗎？

❗ Are you available now? 你現在方便講話嗎？
❗ Is this a good time for you to talk? 你現在方便講電話嗎？
What time would suit you best? 什麼時候最適合你？
What time is convenient for you? 你什麼時候有空呢？

❽ 他什麼時候回來？
何時回來

A: **When will he be back?** 他什麼時候回來？
B: In my opinion, he'll be back within two hours.
依我看，他大概兩個小時以內回來。

❗ When will he be back? 他什麼時候回來？
❗ When will Thomas be available? 湯瑪斯什麼時候會有空？
About what time do you think he will be in? 你認為他大概什麼時候會在辦公室？
When is Tom expected to be back? 你認為湯姆什麼時候回來？
Would Sarah be available in 30 minutes? 莎拉半小時後有空嗎？

⑨ 我會再打來。

A: I need to go to a meeting right now. 我現在要去開會。
B: I see. **I'll call again.** 我知道了。我會再打來。

❗ I'll call again. **我會再打來。**
I'll talk to you later. 待會再跟你談。
❗ Let me call you back later. **我等一下回電給你。**
I'll call back in an hour. 我一個小時後會再打來。

⑩ 請告訴他凱洛打來過。

A: He is in a meeting right now. 他現在正在開會。
B: **Please tell him that Carol called.** 請告訴他凱洛打來過。

❗ Please tell him that Carol called. **請告訴他凱洛打來過。**
❗ Would you just tell him that I called? **可以請你轉告他我打來過嗎？**
Could you tell her David rang? 可以告訴她大衛打來過嗎？
Please tell her to call Amy after 4 o'clock. 請她四點以後打給愛咪。

⑪ 可以請他回電給我嗎？

A: **Would you just tell him to call me back?**
可以請他回電給我嗎？
B: Yes. Let me confirm your name and phone number.
好。請留下您的大名和電話號碼。

❗ Would you just tell him to call me back? **可以請他回電給我嗎？**
❗ I'll be going out, but he can get me through my cell phone.
我要出去了，找我的話請他打我的手機。
I'll be in my office if he'd like to get hold of me.
如果他想和我聯絡，我會在我辦公室。
Tell Terry we must touch base later. 告訴泰瑞，晚點我們必須聯絡。

★ touch base：聯絡

⑫ 這件事很緊急，可不可以告訴我哪裡可以聯絡得到她？

A: **It's urgent. Could you tell me where I can reach her?**
這件事很緊急，可不可以告訴我哪裡可以聯絡得到她？
B: Then you can reach her through her cell phone. 你可以打她手機。

❗ It's urgent. Could you tell me where I can reach her?
這件事很緊急，可不可以告訴我在哪裡可以聯絡得到她？

This is an emergency. I need to get in contact with him right now.
我有急事，需要馬上跟他聯絡。

I am afraid I need to talk to him right now. 我想我現在就要跟他說話。

❗ I need to get in touch with him right away.
我需要立刻和他聯繫。

Is there any other way to get hold of him? 有別的方法可以聯絡到他嗎？

I need to talk to him immediately. 我現在就要和他講話。

I have something urgent to consult with him on. 我有急事找他商量。

⑬ 我要留言。

A: He is not available at the moment. 他現在沒有空。
B: That's all right. **I'd like to leave a message.**
沒關係。我要留言。

❗ I'd like to leave a message. **我要留言。**

❗ May / Can I leave a message? **我可以留言嗎？**

Is it possible to leave a message? 允許我留言嗎？

This is important, so please take a message for me.
這很重要，所以請你幫我留言。

Could you take a message for me, please? 可以請你幫我留言嗎？

＊「自己要留言」是leave a message，「請人為我留言」是take a message。

Please give him this message as soon as possible.
請盡快告訴他我的留言。

⑭ 謝謝，再見。

A: **Thank you.　Goodbye.** 謝謝，再見。
B: You are welcome, sir. 不客氣，先生。

❗ Thank you.　Goodbye. 謝謝，再見。
❗ Thanks for your time. 感謝你抽出時間。
　I'll phone again then.　Thanks a lot. 我會再打過來的。多謝。
　Fine.　Thanks for the message. 好。謝謝你的訊息。

"Also need to know

你需要轉告他人，有人打電話找他時……

告知他人有人打電話找他。
Tony, telephone. 湯尼，你的電話。
Here's a call for you. 有你的電話。
You're wanted on the phone. 找你的電話。
There was a call for you. 剛才有電話找你。
Someone wants you on the phone. 有人打電話找你。
Your client is on the phone. 你的客戶來電找你。

有人在線上等候。
Tom is waiting on line 2. 湯姆在二線。
Mr. Lin is on line 3. 林先生在三線。
Mr. Miller's telephone.　Line No.1. 米勒先生的電話。他在一線。

有人打來過。
Somebody named Tom called. 有個叫湯姆的打來過。
There was a call for you while you were out. 您不在時有人來過電話找您。
Just now Jim telephoned and asked for you. 剛才吉姆打電話來找你。

辦公室事務英文
1 與上級的互動

MP3 TRACK：03

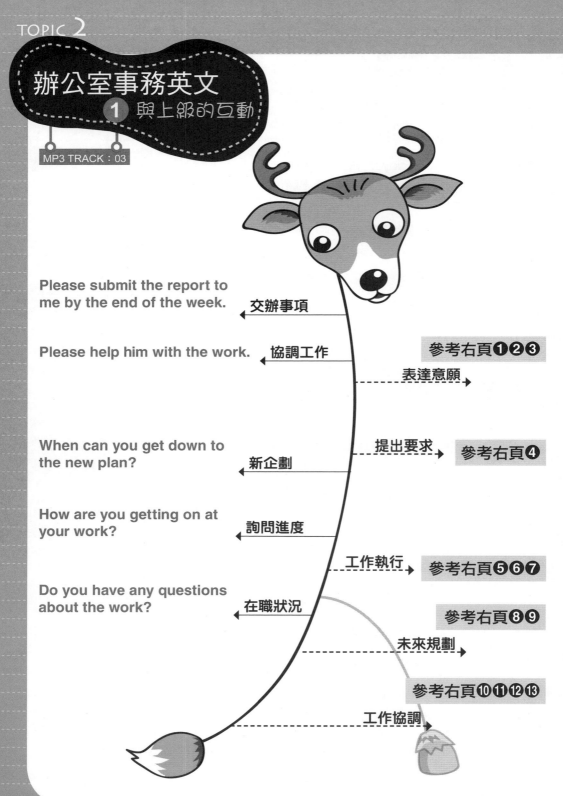

Please submit the report to me by the end of the week.　交辦事項

Please help him with the work.　協調工作　　參考右頁 ❶❷❸

表達意願

When can you get down to the new plan?　新企劃　　提出要求　參考右頁 ❹

How are you getting on at your work?　詢問進度

工作執行　參考右頁 ❺❻❼

Do you have any questions about the work?　在職狀況　　參考右頁 ❽❾

未來規劃

參考右頁 ❿⓫⓬⓭

工作協調

You may hear
與上級互動時，也許你會聽到……

ⓐ 請在本週結束前將這份報告交給我。　Please submit the report to me by the end of the week.

ⓑ 請協助他的工作。　Please help him with the work.

ⓒ 你什麼時候可以著手新的計畫？　When can you get down to the new plan?

ⓓ 你的工作有什麼進展？　How are you getting on at your work?

ⓔ 關於這份工作你有任何問題嗎？　Do you have any questions about the work?

You may want to say
與上級互動時，也許你會想說……

❶ 沒問題，我馬上就做。　No problem. I'll do it right away. ...p.44

❷ 我會設法完成的。　I'll manage to finish it. ...p.44

❸ 但我今天真的抽不出時間。　But I'm really tied up today. ...p.45

❹ 可否將期限延後？　Can you put off the deadline? ...p.46

❺ 我們要提前完工了。　We're way ahead of schedule. ...p.46

❻ 客戶想要親自跟您談談。　The client wants to talk to you in person. ...p.47

❼ 您覺得這個想法如何？　What do you think of this idea? ...p.47

❽ 您認為我過去三個月的表現如何？　What do you think of my performance in the last three months? ...p.48

❾ 我希望轉調到海外事業部。　I'd like to be transferred to the Overseas Business Department. ...p.48

❿ 這件事情我一個人無法負荷。　I can't handle it by myself. ...p.49

⓫ 會計員這份工作不適合我。　The job of accountant is not suitable for me. ...p.49

⓬ 我不想去國外工作。　I'm not willing to work overseas. ...p.50

⓭ 我死也不做這種事。　I'll never agree to do it. ...p.50

① 沒問題，我馬上就做。

A: Could you help me with these files? 你能幫我處理這些文件嗎？
B: **No problem. I'll do it right away.** 沒問題，我馬上做。

❗ Yes, of course. 好的，當然了。

❗ With pleasure. 我很樂意。

❗ By all means. / Certainly. / Sure. 當然了。

I'm quite willing. 我非常願意。

I'm perfectly willing to do so. 我非常願意這麼做。

I'll get that to you by 6 p.m. 我下午六點前交給你。

❗ I'd be happy to do that. 我非常高興這麼做。

❗ No problem. I'll do it right away. 沒問題，我馬上做。

Yes, I don't see why not. 好的，為什麼不願意呢？

Certainly, if you want me to do so. 當然，如果你希望我那麼做的話。

I'm ready to do everything you ask me to do. 你讓我做什麼我都願意。

Is there anything else you'd like me to do? 還有什麼需要我做的嗎？

② 我會設法完成的。

A: Can you help me with the case studies of our projects?
你能幫我做我們計劃的案例分析嗎？
B: **I'll manage to finish it.** 我會設法完成的。

❗ Let me see. 讓我想想。

I'll (manage to) finish it. 我會設法完成的。
 ★ manage to：設法做到

❗ All right, let me have a try. 好吧，讓我試試。

❗ Yes, I understand. 是的，我知道了。

It (involves) a lot of hard work. 那需要很多的辛勤工作。
 ★ involve (in)：需要，包含

I'm sorry, but I'm busy now. Can I do it later?
對不起，我現在很忙，可以過一會兒再做嗎？

I can't at that time, but I'll be happy to help you with something else later.
我那時候沒空，之後有空了我幫你做別的吧。

❸ 但我今天真的抽不出時間。

A: We wouldn't want to stay late this week so we should get it done now.
我們都不想這週加班完成，所以我們現在就要把它做完。

B: **But I'm really tied up today.** 但我今天真的抽不出時間。

I'm sorry I can't. 對不起，我不能做。

! I can't handle it. 我應付不來。

Sorry, I'm afraid I couldn't. 對不起，我恐怕不行。

! I'm really tied up today. 我今天真的抽不出時間。
★ be tied up：沒空，有事

! I'd like to, but I'm not available today. 我願意，但是我今天沒有時間。
★ be available：空閒的

! I am sorry to turn you down. 我很抱歉必須拒絕你。
★ turn down：拒絕

I am really not in the mood. 我真的沒什麼心情。

Sorry, but that isn't my strong suit. 抱歉，這不是我的專長。
★ strong suit：特長

I'm not sure if I could accept your plan. 我恐怕不能接受你的計劃。

I'm sure you will do fine on your own. 我相信你可以自己完成的。

I'm afraid I'm committed to something else. 我另有計劃。

I'm sorry, but I have an emergency to attend to.
抱歉，我有些緊急的事必須要做。 ★ attend to：注意（留意，專注於，照料）

I'm sorry to say I can't be of assistance to you there.
對不起，這件事我幫不了你。

I really want to, but I have an important thing to do just now.
我很想幫你，但我現在有很重要的事要做。

I really want to, but I've got hundreds of things to do.
我真的很想幫你，可是我有好多好多事情要做。

Unfortunately, I've had a few things coming up.
不幸的是，有意外的事情發生了。 ★ come up：開始，發生

I'm trying to focus on finishing up some other things.
我要專心完成一些其它的工作。

＊很多人都不懂得如何拒絕上司指派的工作。其實，在合理範圍內拒絕附加的工作量，是對自己已有工作品質的保證，老闆通常會體諒。因此，當你覺得無法完成工作時，一定要學會拒絕。

45

4 可否將期限延後？

A: **Can you put off the deadline?** 可否將期限延後？
B: I'm sorry, but it is urgent. 不好意思，這件事很緊急。

★ put off：延後
❗ Can you put off the deadline? 可否將期限延後？
❗ Please allow me another three days. 請再寬限我三天時間。

I need ten days, non-working days excluded. 我需要十天時間，不包括非工作日。

It will be next Monday at the earliest. 最快也要到下週一才能完成。

In order to complete the task responsibly, I will ask to postpone it.
為了能更負責的完成任務，我會請求延期。
★ postpone：延期

5 我們要提前完工了。

A: How's the project going? 專案進展得怎麼樣？
B: **We're way ahead of schedule.** 我們要提前完工了。

★ ahead of schedule：提前
We're way ahead of schedule. 我們要提前完工了。
We're right on target. 我們正按計劃進行。
★ on target：正追蹤目標

It's 70% done. 已經完成70%了。

It'll be completed on time. 工作將會準時完成。

❗ It's going on schedule. 一切按計劃進行。
★ on schedule：按預定計劃

❗ So far, everything's been OK. 目前一切順利。

We're just about halfway done. 我們剛做完一半。

❗ Well, frankly, we're running a little behind. 坦白地說，我們有點落後了。

We're behind the eight ball in meeting our sales target. Let's speed things up.
我們的銷售目標遠遠落後。讓我們加快速度吧。
＊behind the eight ball 是「處於非常不利的地位」的意思。

There must be no further delays. The due date / deadline is next Friday's close of
business. 不能再延遲了。最後期限是下週五下班前。
＊due date 相當於 deadline，指「最後期限」、「截止期限」。

We're approaching the critical point for success or failure of this project.
我們正處在關係到整個專案成敗的關鍵時刻。

⑥ 客戶想要親自跟您談談。

A: What's their reply to our quotation? 他們對我們的報價有什麼答覆？
B: **The client wants to talk to you in person.**
客戶想要親自跟您談談。

★ in person：親自

❗ The client wants to talk to you in person. 客戶想要親自跟您談談。

The manager asks me to tell you about the meeting held next week.
經理讓我通知你參加下週的會議。

The secretary of the General Manager called us. 總經理的祕書打過電話給我們。

Mr. White asked you to give him a phone call this afternoon.
懷特先生請你今天下午回電話給他。

⑦ 您覺得這個想法如何？

A: **What do you think of this idea?** 您覺得這個想法如何？
B: It's very good. 非常好。

How do you feel about the policy? 你覺得那項政策如何？

❗ What do you think of this idea? 您覺得這個想法如何？

What do you think about Miranda's report? 你對米蘭達的報告有什麼想法？

What are your thoughts about her proposal? 你對她的提案有什麼想法？

What is your view on the current situation? 你對時局有什麼看法？

What is your take on the retailer's complaints? 你對零售商的抱怨有什麼高見？

★ take：見解，想法　★ retailer：零售商

Tell me more about what you're thinking. 多告訴我一點你的想法。

❗ Am I allowed to make a suggestion? 我可以提個建議嗎？

I think we need to buy a new copier. 我想我們需要買一台新的影印機。
＊說出上句之前，必須說明 our copying machine has broken down again.（我們的影印機又出毛病了）
以作為提案的依據。客氣一些的提議，用 suggest，如 I would suggest we buy a new copier.

Wouldn't it be possible for me to take the day off this Friday?
這個星期五，我可不可以休假一天？

How about attaching a discount coupon? 附上一張折價券怎麼樣？

I think the market investigation and the sales forecasting should be done carefully.
我認為需要仔細地做市場調查和銷售預測的工作。

⑧ 您認為我過去三個月的表現如何？

A: **What do you think of my performance in the last three months?** 您認為我過去三個月的表現如何？

B: Quite good. And I decided to give you a pay raise. 非常好，我決定給你加薪。

❗ I'd like to discuss a pay raise. 我想談一下加薪的事。

❗ What do you think of my performance in the last three months? 您認為我過去三個月的表現如何？

You promised to give me a raise in salary after three months' probation. 你答應過試用期三個月過後給我加薪。 ★ probation：試用期；見習期

I feel quite embarrassed for suddenly having to make this kind of request. 突然提出這個要求，我很不好意思。

＊要求加薪時，要發動一切力量來強調你對公司來說有多大價值，這是重要的第一步。漫天要價是行不通的，如果你的理由不夠有說服力，你也應該問問老闆你還需要加強哪些能力。最後一招就是討價還價了，提起另一家公司在挖角你，是提醒老闆注意你價值的好辦法。不過這一招比較危險，除非對自己很有信心，否則不要用。

⑨ 我希望轉調到海外事業部。

A: **I'd like to be transferred to the Overseas Business Department.** 我希望轉調到海外事業部。

B: Can you tell me the reason? 你可以告訴我原因嗎？

❗ I'd like to talk with you about my transfer. 我想和你談談我調動的問題。 ★ transfer：調任

I'm afraid I'll amount to nothing if I go on like this. ★ amount to：達到

我怕我這樣繼續下去的話，我將一事無成。

❗ I'd like to be transferred to the Overseas Business Department. 我希望轉調到海外事業部。 ★ Overseas Business Department：海外事業部

If I'm transferred, I will make great contributions to our company. 如果我調動職位的話，我會為公司做出巨大的貢獻。

I've worked here as a typist for about 2 years, and I'd like to have a chance of advancement. 我在這裡做打字員大約兩年了，我想有提升自己的機會。

⑩ 這件事情我一個人無法負荷。

A: **I can't handle it by myself.** I suggest you hire an office worker.
這件事情我一個人無法負荷。我建議你再雇用一個員工.
B: I'll make HR do it. 我會讓人力資源部準備。

★ handle：應付，處理
❗ I can't handle it by myself. 這件事情我一個人無法負荷。
❗ We need some temporary staff. 我們需要些臨時工。
Can you arrange more people for us? 你能再安排些人給我們嗎？
❗ We'll have to outsource some of this. 我們得借助外力。

★ outsource：委外製作，外包
I'm always busy with the job. I feel a bit tired. 我一直忙於工作，感到有些疲勞。
No one will get stuck with more work if we quickly find a replacement.

★ get stuck with：無法擺脫，困住
如果我們能夠盡快找到替補人選，工作量就不會增加。
I suggest you hire an office worker so I can get my work done.
我建議你再雇用一個員工，這樣我就可以做自己的工作了。

⑪ 會計員這份工作不適合我。   不適任

★ resign：辭職
A: Can you tell me why you want to resign? 可否告訴我你為何要辭職？
B: **The job of accountant is not suitable for me.**
會計員這份工作不適合我。   ★ suitable for：適當的

❗ To be frank, I don't like this job. 坦白說，我不喜歡這份工作。
The job of accountant is not suitable for me. 會計員這份工作不適合我。
What I do seems so boring and so repetitive. 我做的工作很乏味，老是重複。

★ repetitive：重複的
❗ I need a job that is interesting and challenging, but at the moment I'm doing the same thing day after day.
我想要一份有趣且具有挑戰性的工作，但目前我日復一日做相同的事情。

⑫ 我不想去國外工作。

A: Have you considered my suggestion yesterday?
你考慮過我昨天的建議嗎？

B: Yes, but **I'm not willing to work overseas.**
我考慮過了，但我不想去國外工作。

❗ I'm ready to go anywhere. 我願意配合外派到任何地方。

❗ I'm not willing to work overseas. 我不想去國外工作。

I'm not willing to make trips to local markets. 我不願意到外地出差。

I refuse to be transferred to the branch company. 我拒絕外派到地區分公司。

It's really exciting for me to experience business in an international environment.
如果能在國際舞臺工作的話，那就真的太棒了。

⑬ 我死也不做這種事。

A: **I'll never agree to do it.** It is against my principles.
我死也不做這種事。這有悖我的做人原則。

B: What else can we do? 那我們還能怎麼做？

No way! 不可能！

❗ I'll never agree to do it. 我死也不做這種事。

I can't agree with what you said. 我不同意你說的話。

I can't believe you did this to me. 我不相信你居然對我這麼做。

There is no way I'll agree with this proposal. 我絕不會同意這個提議。

I'm sorry. I just can't. 很抱歉，我不能這麼做。

I can't comply with that request. 我無法遵守這個要求。

★ comply with：遵守

Get someone else to do it. 找別人去做這件事。

常見公司・企業部門英文名稱

營業據點	
總公司	Head Office
分公司	Branch Office
營業處	Business Office

各部門	
人事部	Personnel Department
人力資源部	Human Resources Department
總務部	General Affairs Department
財務部	General Accounting Department
銷售部	Sales Department
促銷部	Sales Promotion Department
事業拓展部	Business Development Department

行銷部	Marketing Department
採購部	Purchasing Department
系統部	System Department
國際部	International Department
出口部	Export Department
進口部	Import Department
公關部	Public Relations Department
廣告部	Advertising Department
企劃部	Planning Department
售後服務部	After-sale Service Department
研發部	Research and Development Department（R&D）
產品開發部	Product Development Department
祕書室	Secretarial Pool

註：Department可簡寫為Dept.

常見主管類職務英文名稱

『總』系列	
GM（General Manager）	總經理
VP（Vice President）	副總裁
FVP（First Vice President）	第一副總裁
AVP（Assistant Vice President）	副總裁助理

『C』系列	
CEO（Chief Executive Officer）	首席執行長
CFO（Chief Financial Officer）	首席財務長
COO（Chief Operations Officer）	首席營運長
CTO（Chief Technology Officer）	首席技術長

『D』系列	

HRD（Human Resource Director）	人力資源總監
OD（Operations Director）	營運總監
MD（Marketing Director）	行銷總監

『M』系列	
OM（Operations Manager）	營運經理
PM（Production Manager）	生產經理
PM（Product Manager）	產品經理
PM（Project Manager）	專案經理
BM（Branch Manager）	部門經理
DM（District Manager）	區域經理
RM（Regional Manager）	地區經理

辦公室事務英文
2 與同事的互動

MP3 TRACK：04

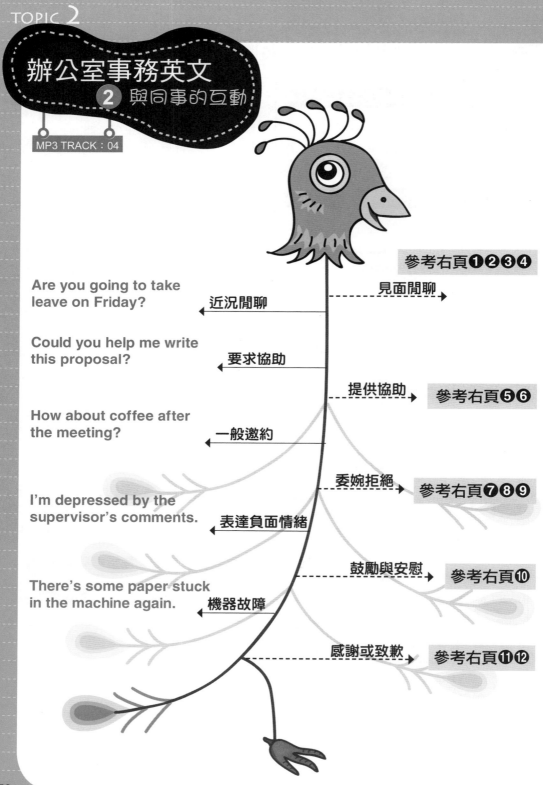

參考右頁 ❶❷❸❹

見面閒聊

Are you going to take leave on Friday? ← 近況閒聊

Could you help me write this proposal? ← 要求協助

提供協助 → 參考右頁 ❺❻

How about coffee after the meeting? ← 一般邀約

委婉拒絕 → 參考右頁 ❼❽❾

I'm depressed by the supervisor's comments. ← 表達負面情緒

鼓勵與安慰 → 參考右頁 ❿

There's some paper stuck in the machine again. ← 機器故障

感謝或致歉 → 參考右頁 ⓫⓬

You may hear
與同事互動時，也許你會聽到……

線上音檔

ⓐ 聽說你禮拜五要休假？　　Are you going to take leave on Friday?

ⓑ 你能幫我寫這個計畫嗎？　Could you help me write this proposal?

ⓒ 會後去喝杯咖啡怎麼樣？　How about coffee after the meeting?

ⓓ 主管的評價讓我很沮喪。　I'm depressed by the supervisor's comments.

ⓔ 影印機又卡紙了。　　　　There's some paper stuck in the machine again.

You may want to say
與同事互動時，也許你會想說……

❶ 早安！　　　　　　　　　Good morning! ...p.54

❷ 週末過得如何？　　　　　How was the weekend? ...p.54

❸ 你知道傑克被降職了嗎？　Have you heard Jack was demoted? ...p.55

❹ 你有在研究基金投資嗎？　Are you considering capital investment? ...p.55

❺ 可以協助我整理這份問卷嗎？　Could you help me sort out the questionnaire? ...p.56

❻ 讓我來幫你吧。　　　　　Let me give you a hand. ...p.56

❼ 我手邊還有更緊急的事情。　I have something more urgent than that. ...p.57

❽ 你會出席潔西卡的婚禮嗎？　Are you going to attend Jessica's wedding ceremony? ...p.57

❾ 我很想去，但恐怕我那天已經有約了。　Much as I would like to, but I'm afraid I'm already booked up for that day. ...p.58

❿ 我對你的企劃有信心。　　I have every confidence in your proposal. ...p.58

⓫ 謝謝你的鼎力相助。　　　Thank you very much for what you have done for me. ...p.59

⓬ 我要為我的疏忽鄭重道歉。　I'd like to apologize for my carelessness. ...p.59

① 早安！ 打招呼

A: **Good morning**, Mr. Bright. 早安！布萊特先生。
B: Good morning, Miss Green. 早安，格林小姐。

❗ Hello! / Hi! 哈囉！／嗨！
＊任何時候都可以使用的招呼語。

❗ Good morning. / Good afternoon. / Good evening. 早安／午安／晚安。

What's up? 近況如何？
＊是較口語的說法。

❗ How are you? / How're you doing? 你好嗎？
＊通常在「Hello.」或「Good morning.」之後就接著問「How are you?」

How do you feel today? 今天感覺怎麼樣？

How is everything? 一切還好吧？

How are things going? 最近如何？

How have you been? 你一直還好嗎？

How are things with you? 你一直還好嗎？

② 週末過得如何？ 寒暄

A: **How was the weekend?** 週末過得如何？
B: Fine, thanks. 很好，謝謝。

❗ How was the weekend? 週末過得如何？

How are you getting along with your work / studies / business?
你的工作／進修／生意如何？

❗ Nice weather, isn't it? 天氣很好，對吧？

What's new? 有什麼新鮮事？

What's happening? 在忙什麼？

You sound busy. 你好像很忙的樣子。

Long time no see. 好久不見。

= I haven't seen you for a long time.

= I haven't seen you for ages.

↙★ for ages：好久一段時間

= We haven't seen each other for a long time.

❸ 你知道傑克被降職了嗎？

A: **Have you heard Jack was demoted?**
你知道傑克被降職了嗎？

B: Really? 真的嗎？

❶ I tell you what, just between you and me, Kelly will quit.
我跟你說，別告訴別人，我聽說凱莉要離職了。

＊just between you and me 是「只屬於我們之間的祕密」的意思。

Have you heard Jack was (demoted)? 你知道傑克被降職了嗎？

He has been dismissed. 他被解雇了。★ demote：降級

＊「解雇」或「失業」的說法：
失業，直接的說法是「unemployed」或「lose one's job」，但較常用的說法是「be downsized」、「be laid off」、「be dismissed」或「be made redundant」。口語的說法還有「I was pink-slipped again!」意思是「I was fired again! 我又被炒魷魚了！」

★ end up：最後（成為）…
Did you know that Stone (ended up) marrying his secretary?
你知道史東最後還是和他的祕書結婚了嗎？

Did you know he was having an affair on his wife?
你知道他有外遇了嗎？

❹ 你有在研究基金投資嗎？

A: **Are you considering capital investment?**
你有在研究基金投資嗎？

B: If you have some spare cash, then why not invest?
如果你手頭有多餘的現金，何不投資呢？

❶ Are you considering capital investment? 你有在研究基金投資嗎？

Did you hear about the latest tech IPO? 你聽說過剛上市的那個科技股嗎？
＊IPO＝Initial Public Offering，是首次公開發行的股票（公司股票首度在股市中公開買賣）。

❶ I wonder which way the (share price) will go. 不知道股價的走勢會如何。

★ share price：股價

I made a ton of cash on my last trade. 上筆交易我賺翻了。

I just opened an online trading account. 我剛剛開了個網上交易帳戶。

I'm thinking about adding some money to my portfolio. 我正考慮再拿些錢去投資。

＊portfolio 在這裡是指投資者持有的全部有價證券或投資組合。

55

❺ 可以協助我整理這份問卷嗎？

A: **Could you help me sort out the questionnaire?**
可以協助我整理這份問卷嗎？
B: With pleasure. 很樂意。

❗ Could you take a look at this? 你能看一下這個嗎？
❗ Would you mind looking at the report? 你能看一下這份報告嗎？

Can you cover for me tomorrow? 你明天能幫我代班嗎？
　　★ cover for：頂替，代替

Could you help me sort out the questionnaire? 可以協助我整理這份問卷嗎？
　　★ sort out：整理某事物

I'm going to ask you to give me a hand. 正想請你幫我忙。
　　★ give a hand：提供幫助

Would you please let the manager know I have called? I want to ask for leave.
你可以告訴經理我打過電話嗎？我想向他請假。
　　★ leave：休假

It would be a big help if you could arrange the meeting.
如果你能安排這個會議的話，就是幫了我大忙。

Could you kindly translate this letter into German for me?
你能幫我把這封信翻譯成德文嗎？

❻ 讓我來幫你吧。

A: I'm expected to finish the work before 5 p.m., but it's already 3:30 now.
I'm afraid I can't manage it.
我必須在五點前完成工作，但現在都三點半了。我恐怕是無法完成了。
B: Don't worry. **Let me give you a hand.** 沒關係，讓我來幫你吧。

❗ Don't worry. Let me give you a hand. 沒關係，讓我來幫你吧。
Can I help you? 需要幫你嗎？
When do you need it done? 你需要什麼時候完成？
Anything I can do for you? 有什麼可以幫忙的嗎？
❗ What can I do for you? 我能為你做什麼嗎？
No sweat. It's a piece of cake. 沒問題，很容易。
　★ no sweat：不費力地，不麻煩。　★ piece of cake：很容易的事

❼ 我手邊還有更緊急的事情。

A: Can you give me a hand? 你可以幫個忙嗎？
B: **I have something more urgent than that.**
我手邊還有更緊急的事情。

★ urgent：急迫的

❗ I have something more urgent than that. 我手邊還有更緊急的事情。
❗ I've got a lot to on my hands. **我手邊還有一大堆事。**

I'm really tired and need a break. 我真的很累，需要休息。

Sorry, I'm afraid I can't help you this time. 對不起，恐怕這次我沒法幫你了。

I didn't take part in your market research and don't know what to write.
我沒有參加你的市場調查，不知道怎麼寫。

❽ 你會出席潔西卡的婚禮嗎？

A: **Are you going to attend Jessica's wedding ceremony?**
你會出席潔西卡的婚禮嗎？
B: Sure. 當然。

Would anyone like to order some drinks? 大家想不想訂飲料？

Are you going to attend Jessica's wedding ceremony?

你會出席潔西卡的婚禮嗎？

There will be a big party at the club. Would you like to come today?

俱樂部有個舞會，你今天要來參加嗎？

What about playing golf this weekend? 週末去打高爾夫怎麼樣？

I'd like to invite you to my new house for a visit. 我想邀請你到我的新家來參觀。

Drop by tomorrow if you have nothing on. 如果你沒事，過來玩玩。

★ drop by：順便拜訪

Why not come to the seaside on Tuesday, Mary? 瑪麗，週二來海邊玩怎麼樣？

❗ How about going to the movies this afternoon? **今天下午去看電影怎麼樣？**

I'd like to invite you to a party next Friday. 我想邀請你參加下週五的晚會。

❗ Do you feel like going to that new restaurant this evening?

今天晚上你想去那家新餐廳嗎？

⑨ 我很想去，但恐怕我那天已經有約了。

A: We're planning to hold a party for Paul to celebrate his promotion this Thursday evening. Would you like to join us?
我們正準備在週四晚上舉行一場慶祝保羅晉升的舞會，你會來嗎？
B: **Much as I would like to, but I'm afraid I'm already booked up for that day.** 我很想去，但恐怕我那天已經有約了。

❗ Let's do it another time. 下次有機會吧。

❗ I have something on. 我有事走不開。

Would you prefer some other time? 你願意再找其他時間嗎？

Much as I would like to, but I'm afraid I'm already booked up for that day.
我很想去，但恐怕我那天已經有約了。

Much to my regret, I have other plans. 太遺憾了，我已經有別的安排了。

❗ Thank you very much for asking me, but some of my friends will come to see me this evening. 謝謝你的邀請，但是今天晚上有朋友來找我。

Unfortunately, I have to take care of my little Tommy. Thank you for thinking of me.
不巧的是，我要照顧我的孩子湯米。謝謝你能夠想到我。

⑩ 我對你的企劃有信心。

A: I'm afraid the manager won't approve it. 我擔心經理不會批准。
B: Don't worry. **I have every confidence in your proposal.**
別擔心。我對你的企劃有信心。

Feel free to try something new. 盡量嘗試新鮮事物吧。

❗ Just do it. You know you can. 放手做吧，你知道你可以的。

I have every confidence in your proposal. 我對你的企劃有信心。

Don't worry. You always come up with great, innovative ideas.

★ come up with：（針對問題等）想出，提供

別擔心，你總能想出絕妙而富有創造性的點子。

Just take it step-by-step. You'll get there.
只要一步一步按照步驟做，你就會完成的。

Consider all your options. You'll come up with the best answer.
想想你所有的選擇，你會想出最佳答案的。

⑪ 謝謝你的鼎力相助。

A: **Thank you very much for what you have done for me.**
謝謝你的鼎力相助。

B: Delighted I was able to help. 很高興我能幫上忙。

I'm very much obliged. 我十分感謝。

★ be obliged：感謝

❗ Thanks a lot. / Thanks a million. 非常感謝。

❗ I appreciate it very much. 深深地感謝。

I would like to express my gratitude. 我想表達我的謝意。

I really can't thank you enough for being so generous.
你如此慷慨我真的感激不盡。

Many thanks for helping me out of the difficulty. 謝謝你幫我走出困境。

Thank you very much for what you have done for me. 謝謝你的鼎力相助。

⑫ 我要為我的疏忽鄭重道歉。

A: **I'd like to apologize for my carelessness.**
我要為我的疏忽鄭重道歉。

B: Don't blame yourself too much. 不要太責備自己。

❗ I'd like to apologize for my carelessness. 我要為我的疏忽鄭重道歉。

❗ Please accept my apologies. 請接受我的道歉。

I can't tell you how sorry I am. 真不知怎麼對你表示歉意。

❗ I really didn't mean that at all. 我不是那個意思。

I've come to apologize. 我是專程來道歉的。

Please forgive me for the incident. 我請求你對此事的諒解。

Forgive me. I'm terribly sorry for having caused so much trouble.
原諒我。我對給你們帶來這麼多的麻煩非常抱歉。

★ oversleep：睡過頭

I'm extremely sorry for being late, but I overslept. 實在對不起，我遲到了，睡過了頭。

Sorry for what I said yesterday. I didn't mean to hurt you.
原諒我昨天所說的話，我不是有意要傷害你的。

★ dispute：爭論，爭執

I do apologize for getting you involved in the dispute. 把你捲入紛爭非常抱歉。

★ involve：連累，牽涉

辦公室事務英文
3 與廠商的互動

MP3 TRACK：05

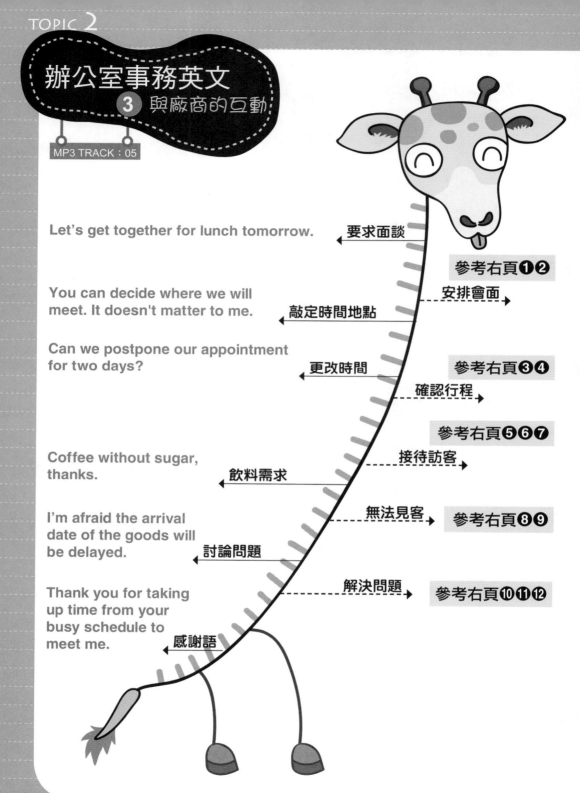

Let's get together for lunch tomorrow.

要求面談

參考右頁❶❷

安排會面 ▸

You can decide where we will meet. It doesn't matter to me.

敲定時間地點

Can we postpone our appointment for two days?

更改時間

參考右頁❸❹

確認行程 ▸

參考右頁❺❻❼

接待訪客 ▸

Coffee without sugar, thanks.

飲料需求

無法見客 ▸　參考右頁❽❾

I'm afraid the arrival date of the goods will be delayed.

討論問題

解決問題 ▸　參考右頁❿⓫⓬

Thank you for taking up time from your busy schedule to meet me.

感謝語

You may hear
與廠商互動時，也許你會聽到……

ⓐ 明天中午一起用餐吧。　Let's get together for lunch tomorrow.

ⓑ 地點您決定就好。　You can decide where we will meet.

ⓒ 可以延後兩天見面嗎？　Can we postpone our appointment for two days?

ⓓ 我的咖啡麻煩不要加糖，謝謝。　Coffee without sugar, thanks.

ⓔ 恐怕這次的到貨時間會延遲幾天。　I'm afraid the arrival date of the goods will be delayed.

You may want to say
與廠商互動時，也許你會想說……

❶ 明天我的行程很滿。　My schedule is tight tomorrow. ...p.62

❷ 到我辦公室談可以嗎？　Can we talk about it in my office? ...p.62

❸ 下午兩點的會面我恐怕無法準時到達。　I'm afraid I won't be able to make it to our appointment at 2 o'clock in the afternoon. ...p.63

❹ 可否約其它的時間？　Would you like to make it another time? ...p.63

❺ 請跟我來。　Come with me, please. ...p.64

❻ 您想喝點什麼嗎？　Would you like something to drink? ...p.64

❼ 先生，請問您有預約嗎？　Have you made an appointment, sir? ...p.65

❽ 茱莉現在正在忙。　Julie is occupied at the moment. ...p.65

❾ 他剛好外出中。　He is out right now. ...p.66

❿ 這些產品的品質都很差。　These products are of bad quality. ...p.66

⓫ 這個錯誤必須改正。　The mistake must be corrected. ...p.67

⓬ 你能保證以後不會再發生類似的事情嗎？　Can you assure such things won't happen again? ...p.67

❶ 明天我的行程很滿。 時間安排

A: I'd like to visit you tomorrow at 12:00. 明天中午我想去拜訪你。
B: I am kind of busy. **My schedule is tight tomorrow.**
我有點忙。明天我的行程很滿。

❗ My schedule is tight tomorrow. 明天我的行程很滿。

I am kind of busy. I have an important meeting tomorrow at lunch time.
我有點忙。明天中午我剛好有個重要會議。

I'm afraid we are really short-staffed this week, Mr. Crandal. I'd like to accommodate
you, but I just don't think I'll have the time. ★ accommodate：照顧到、考慮到
恐怕這星期我們的確人手不夠,克蘭道先生。我很想給您方便,但我恐怕沒有時間。

❗ Sorry. I'm going to be tied up all day. I'll have to take a rain check.
抱歉,我今天一整天都很忙,改天吧。
*take a rain check 是「改期」的意思。原指棒球等露天球賽因下雨改期再賽時,下次進場還可使用的原票根。引申為雙方無法約定日期,改期再約的意思。

Unfortunately, I have plans to travel around that time.
很抱歉,我的日程表中已經安排了出差。

I'm sorry, but I'm really tied up today. 抱歉,我今天的確抽不出時間。

❷ 到我辦公室談可以嗎? 地點安排

A: Where shall we meet tomorrow? 我們明天在哪裡見面?
B: **Can we talk about it in my office? 到我辦公室談可以嗎?**

Let's get something at the hotel restaurant. 我們就到旅館餐廳吃點東西。
If possible, why don't we meet in the hotel tea room at nine?
如果有可能,明天上午九點在飯店茶室會面如何?

❗ Are you in the office tomorrow? 你明天會在辦公室嗎?

❗ Can we talk about it in my office? 到我辦公室談可以嗎?
It's 11 o'clock in Conference Room B at the Hyatt Hotel.
十一點在君悅飯店 B 會議室。

62

❸ 下午兩點的會面我恐怕無法準時到達。

A: **I'm afraid I won't be able to make it to our appointment at 2 o'clock in the afternoon.**
下午兩點的會面我恐怕無法準時到達。

B: Well, actually I can't make it any later, I'm afraid.
事實上我恐怕不能夠再延遲時間了。

❗ Would you mind if we meet at 10 o'clock in the morning?
我們能不能改在上午十點見面？

❗ I'm afraid I have to change our appointment to 10 o'clock.
恐怕我們的約會時間要改到十點。

Can we change our appointment to 10 o'clock? 我們的約會時間能改到十點嗎？

Would it bother you if we changed the time of our next meeting?
如果我們把下次會議的時間變更一下會不會讓你感到麻煩？

I'm afraid I won't be able to make it to our appointment at 2 o'clock in the afternoon.
下午兩點的會面我恐怕無法準時到達。

❹ 可否約其它的時間？

A: I have something urgent to do at the company. **Would you like to make it another time?**
公司突然有緊急的事情要處理，可否約其它的時間？

B: Certainly. 當然。

Would you like to make it another time? 可否約其它的時間？

❗ It's a pity that we must cancel our appointment.
非常遺憾，我們必須取消約會。

I have something urgent tomorrow, so the appointment will have to be cancelled.
我明天有緊急的事，所以約會得取消。

I'm afraid I can't keep my appointment with you this Sunday. I have something important to do. 我週日恐怕不能與你見面了，我有重要的事要做。

❗ Would you mind if we cancelled our meeting tomorrow?
我們取消明天的會議您介意嗎？

⑤ 請跟我來。

A: Good afternoon. I have an appointment with Mr. Sun at 4 p.m..
午安，我與孫先生約好在下午四點見面。

B: Would you please go up to his office? He is waiting for you. **Come with me, please.**
請到他的辦公室吧，他正在等你。請跟我來。

❗ Come with me, please. 請跟我來。

❗ I'll notify Mr. Deng you are here. 我會通知鄧先生你在這裡。

Would you please sign the visitor's book? 請在訪客登記簿上簽個名好嗎？

Would you like to have a seat over there for a moment, please?
請您在那邊坐一會可以嗎？

Mr. Sun will come down to see you in about five minutes.
孫先生大概五分鐘後過來見您。

There are some magazines on the table over there if you'd like to read them.
如果您想看些什麼的話，那邊桌上有一些雜誌。

⑥ 您想喝點什麼嗎？

A: **Would you like something to drink?**
您想喝點什麼嗎？

B: Thank you, coffee, please. 謝謝，我要咖啡。

❗ Would you like something to drink? 您想喝點什麼嗎？

❗ Can I get you anything to drink? 您要喝點什麼？

Do you prefer coffee or tea? 您想要喝咖啡還是茶？

Please help yourself to the food. 這些食物請隨便用。

Could I offer you something to drink? 給您些飲料好嗎？

This is the cream and this is the sugar. If there's anything else you need, please
don't hesitate to tell me. 這是奶油和糖。如果您有什麼需要請盡量說。

★ hesitate：猶豫、有疑慮

64

⑦ 先生，請問您有預約嗎？

A: I am here to see your manager. 我來找你們經理。
B: **Have you made an appointment, sir?**
先生，請問您有預約嗎？

❗ Have you made an appointment, sir？ 先生，請問您有預約嗎？
❗ May I have your name, please？ 請問尊姓大名？

Did you call for an appointment？ 您電話預約了嗎？

Is he expecting you？ 他在等你嗎？

Can I ask what you wish to see him about？ 我可以問您找他有什麼事？

Good morning, can I help you？ 早安，有什麼需要幫忙的嗎？

If you could tell me why you want to see the manager, I'll try to help you.
如果您能告訴我為何要見經理，我可以設法幫您。

⑧ 茱莉現在正在忙。

A: I have something urgent to discuss with Julie.
我有要緊的事要找茱莉商量
B: Would you take a seat and wait for a moment, please？ **Julie is occupied at the moment.**
請您坐下等一會好嗎？茱莉現在正在忙。

❗ Julie is occupied at the moment. 茱莉現在正在忙。

★ be occupied：沒有空

Mr. Bond will soon come down to fetch you up.
龐德先生會下來接您上去。

Would you please have a seat in the meeting room？ I'll let you know as soon as the manager is able to talk with you.
您能到會客室坐一會嗎？經理一有空見您我就告訴您。

I'm afraid Mr. Hu can't meet you at the moment. Would you like to see someone else who can deal with it？
恐怕胡先生暫時沒有空見您。您願意見其他的負責人嗎？

❾ 他剛好外出中。

A: Good morning. I'd like to see the manager. 早安，我想見經理。

B: I'm sorry. **He is out right now** and won't be back until 2:30.
對不起，他剛好外出中，兩點半才會回來。

❗ He is out right now and won't be back until 2:30.
他剛好外出中，兩點半才會回來。

Mr. George is on his way to the office. He just called and asked you to wait a minute. 喬治先生正在來辦公室的路上。他剛打電話來讓您稍等片刻。

I'm afraid that's not possible at the moment. Please leave your card and I'll ask him to get in touch with you himself.
恐怕您現在見不到他。請您將名片留下，我會讓他親自和您聯繫。

❗ I'll tell him as soon as he is back. 等他一回來我就告訴他。

❿ 這些產品的品質都很差。

A: **These products are of bad quality.** 這些產品的品質都很差。

B: Please allow me to express our deepest regret over the unfortunate incident if the fault really lies with our company.
如果責任確實在我們公司的話，請讓我對這件不幸的事情致以最誠摯的歉意。

★ defective：有缺陷的
9 out of 10 items are defective. 十件產品裡有九件劣品。

The goods you sent us do not correspond with the sample we gave you.
你們發過來的貨與我們送過去的樣品不符。 └─ ★ correspond with：符合

❗ The goods we received are not what we ordered.
我們所收到的貨品不是我們所訂購的。

This machine doesn't work. 這台機器壞了。

❗ These products are of bad quality. 這些產品的品質都很差。

The ordered goods are not in conformity with the samples.
訂購的貨品跟樣本並不一樣。

＊be in conformity with 是「一致，符合」的意思。

⓫ 這個錯誤必須改正。

A: **The mistake must be corrected.** 這個錯誤必須改正。
B: We'll do it right away. 我們現在就做。

❗ Can you provide the ⟨solution⟩ for the problem before tomorrow?
你能在明天之前提出解決辦法嗎？ ★ solution：解決辦法

Have you found out yet? 你弄清楚了嗎？

Would you like us to return the goods or hold them for ⟨inspection⟩?
你希望我們退還貨物還是留在這裡檢查？ ★ inspection：檢查，檢驗

❗ The mistake must be corrected. 這個錯誤必須改正。

❗ Please account for this. 請對此做出解釋。

Please make sure this is properly taken care of. 請確保此事得到妥善解決。

This is yet to be improved. 這有待改進。

⓬ 你能保證以後不會再發生類似的事情嗎？

A: **Can you assure such things won't happen again?**
你能保證以後不會再發生類似的事情嗎？
B: This is the first time we've ever encountered such a case.
這是我們第一次遇到這種情況。

Can you assure such things won't happen again?
你能保證以後不會再發生類似的事情嗎？

❗ Do you exchange products under all ⟨circumstances⟩?
在所有情形下你們都可更換產品嗎？ ★ circumstances：情況，環境

❗ Do you provide a guarantee for free service and ⟨parts⟩?
你們保證免費修理嗎？ ★ part：零件

If the car gets into an accident, is it still ⟨under warranty⟩?
如果汽車發生事故，還在保固範圍內嗎？ ★ under warranty：在保固期內

How about repairs after the warranty expires? 在保修期過後的修理怎麼辦呢？

Does your guarantee cover maintenance for both parts and ⟨labor⟩?
你們的保證包括更換零件和免費保養嗎？ ★ labor：勞動

TOPIC 2

辦公室事務英文
④ 與客戶的互動

MP3 TRACK：06

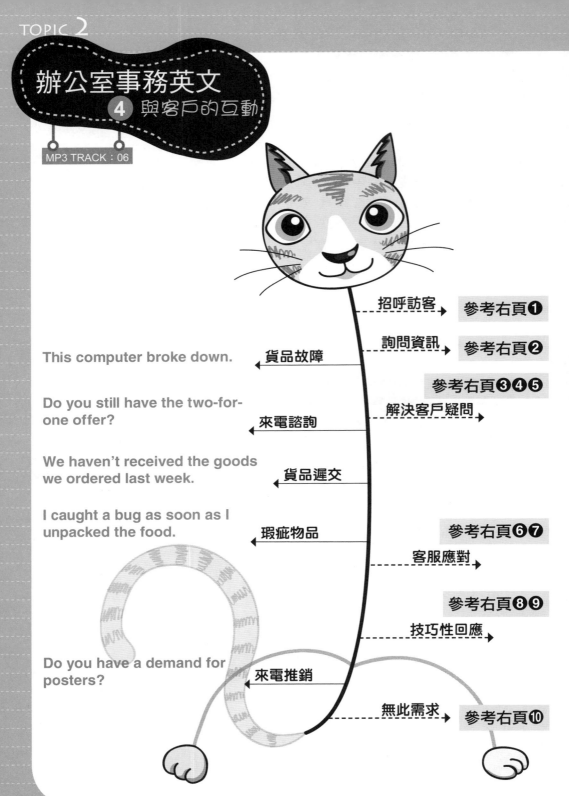

招呼訪客 → 參考右頁❶

詢問資訊 → 參考右頁❷

參考右頁❸❹❺

This computer broke down. ← 貨品故障

解決客戶疑問 →

Do you still have the two-for-one offer? ← 來電諮詢

We haven't received the goods we ordered last week. ← 貨品遲交

I caught a bug as soon as I unpacked the food. ← 瑕疵物品

參考右頁❻❼

客服應對 →

參考右頁❽❾

技巧性回應 →

Do you have a demand for posters? ← 來電推銷

無此需求 → 參考右頁❿

68

You may hear
與客戶互動時，也許你會聽到……

線上音檔

ⓐ 這台電腦出現了故障。　　　　　This computer broke down.

ⓑ 請問買二送一的優惠還有嗎？　　Do you still have the two-for-one offer?

ⓒ 我們上週所訂的商品到現在都還　We haven't received the goods we
　沒收到。　　　　　　　　　　　ordered last week.

ⓓ 我一打開食品包裝就看到小蟲。　I caught a bug as soon as I unpacked
　　　　　　　　　　　　　　　　the food.

ⓔ 你們有製作海報的需求嗎？　　　Do you have a demand for posters?

 ## *You may want to say*
與客戶互動時，也許你會想說……

❶ 請直接進去。　　　　　　　　　Please go right in. ...p.70

❷ 您約的是幾點？　　　　　　　　When are you scheduled to meet? ...p.70

❸ 夏季特賣到八月底為止。　　　　The summer sale will finish by the end
　　　　　　　　　　　　　　　　of August. ...p.71

❹ 我們只與批發商聯絡。　　　　　We deal with wholesalers only. ...p.71

❺ 這項商品的保固期有一年。　　　We'll guarantee this product for one
　　　　　　　　　　　　　　　　year. ...p.72

❻ 非常抱歉，現在立刻為您查詢。　I'm very sorry. I'll inquire about it for
　　　　　　　　　　　　　　　　you right away. ...p.72

❼ 我要為我們的品管道歉。　　　　I apologize for our quality control. ...p.73

❽ 我們所有的產品都經過嚴格的　　All of our products are under strict
　品管。　　　　　　　　　　　　quality control. ...p.74

❾ 我們願意承擔責任。　　　　　　We accept responsibility for this. ...p.74

❿ 我們沒有這筆預算。　　　　　　We have no budget for it. ...p.75

❶ 請直接進去。

A: Mr. Johnson, **please go right in.** Mr. Richards is in his office now.
　強森先生，請直接進去。理查先生正在辦公室。

B: Thank you. 謝謝。

Mr. Johnson, please go right in. 強森先生，請直接進去。

Would you please come with me to Mr. Jordan's office?
請跟我到喬丹先生的辦公室好嗎？

❗ Please come this way. He is waiting for you now.
請往這邊走，他正在等您。

You can take the lift on the left. 您可以搭左邊的電梯。

You just keep walking to the end and turn right, then you'll see it.
你一直往前走再右轉，就會看到了。

❷ 您約的是幾點？

A: **When are you scheduled to meet?**
　您約的是幾點？

B: Four o'clock this afternoon. 今天下午四點。

When are you scheduled to meet? 您約的是幾點？

　★ be scheduled to：預定，計畫

What time are you scheduled for? 您排定的時間是什麼時候？

❗ May I have your name? 能告訴我您的名字嗎？

❗ Do you have an appointment? 您有預約嗎？

Did you call for an appointment? 您電話預約了嗎？

Are you expected? 您約好了嗎？

❗ What do you want to see him about? 你找他有什麼事嗎？

And your name ...? 您的名字是…？

Could you tell me the time of your appointment?
能不能告訴我您約的是幾點？

Could I ask the reason for your visit? 可否請問您來訪的原因？

❸ 夏季特賣到八月底為止。

A: I want to know the ending date of the sale. 我想知道特賣的截止日期。

B: **The summer sale will finish by the end of August.**
夏季特賣到八月底為止。

The summer sale will finish by the end of August. 夏季特賣到八月底為止。

❗ We've adopted universal standards. 我們採用國際通用標準。
　　★ adopt：採取，採用

It's compatible with most of the current systems. 它與目前的大部分系統都能相容。
　　★ compatible：可相容的
　　　　　　　　　　　　　　　　★ catalogue：（圖書、商品的）目錄

❗ You'll find full details on page 6 in the catalogue.
你可以在我們的產品目錄第六頁找到完整說明。

We have service stations all over the country. We are using original parts for all our services. 我們在全國設立了服務站。我們所有的服務都是使用原廠零件。

We have in total 3 types of keyboards. 我們共有三種鍵盤。

❹ 我們只與批發商聯絡。

A: I want to buy some retail goods. 我想購買一些零售物品。

B: **We deal with wholesalers only.** 我們只與批發商聯絡。

Could you shed some light on your intended order size?
　　　　★ shed light on：闡明，解釋
你能透露一下你們要訂的貨物數量嗎？　★ letter of credit：信用狀
Customers should pay by letter of credit. 客戶要用信用狀付款。

❗ We deal with wholesalers only. 我們只與批發商聯絡。

❗ The price depends largely on the amount of your order.
價格主要取決於你們訂購的數量。

This is the maximum quantity we can supply at present.
這是我們目前能夠提供的最大量。

Our standard order is 500 cases at a time. 我們標準的訂貨量是每次五百箱。

You have to pay two thousand dollars in advance as a deposit.
你必須事先付兩千塊美元作為訂金。
　　　　　　　　　　　★ deposit：訂金，保證金

71

⑤ 這項商品的保固期有一年。

A: What are your warranty terms? 你們的保固條款是什麼？
B: **We'll guarantee this product for one year.**
這項商品的保固期有一年。

❶ We'll guarantee this product for one year. 這項商品的保固期有一年。
We'll reimburse all the parts and labor costs to the dealer.
★ reimburse：償還
我們會全額補償給經銷商所需要的零件和手工成本。

❶ Periodic maintenance is included in the price. 價格中包含定期維修費。
Regardless of the causes of the trouble, all repairs are guaranteed within one week.
不管是什麼類型的故障，我們保證在一週之內維修完畢。
The main mechanism carries a 3-year warranty. Any peripheral equipment is
guaranteed for one year. 主要的機器設備三年保修，其他周邊設備保修一年。
★ peripheral equipment：周邊設備

⑥ 非常抱歉，現在立刻為您查詢。

A: I haven't received the goods you sent us.
我到現在還沒收到你寄來的貨物。
B: **I'm sorry. I'll inquire about it for you.**
非常抱歉，現在立刻為您查詢。

I'm sorry. I'll inquire about it for you. 非常抱歉，現在立刻為您查詢。
❶ Hello and thank you for holding. How may I assist you?
您好，抱歉讓您久等了，有什麼可以幫助您的嗎？
Certainly. Can you please explain the problem in detail?
當然，可以請您把問題再講清楚一點嗎？
No problem. We can send you a shipping label so that you can return your
purchase at no extra charge.
沒問題，我們會寄給你一份貨運標籤，你就可以免費退貨了。

❶ I would be glad to help you with that. I will just need a few more details
about your order.
我很樂意為你提供幫助。現在你只需要告訴我有關訂單的一些細節問題。

A: To my great dissatisfaction, what I received is not what I specified at the store. 太讓我失望了，我收到的貨和我在商店裡看到的不一樣。

B: **I apologize for our quality control.**
我要為我們的品管道歉。

❗ We are sorry for the inconvenience it has caused you.
我們為此次帶來的不便表示歉意。

We're grateful for your understanding. 我們感謝您的理解。

I'll call you back after I've finished the investigation. 等我查明後會再回電給您。

We'll find out what has gone wrong. 我們會查明到底是怎麼回事。

❗ I apologize for our quality control. **我要為我們的品管道歉。**

❗ Please accept our compensation. **請接受我們的賠償。**

From our previous transactions you may realize that this sort of problem is quite unusual.
從過去和我們的合作中，你應該知道這次的故障純屬偶然。

How can we best deal with this problem to your satisfaction?
我們該如何做出最完善的處理你才能滿意？

I'd like to make a careful inquiry into the damage once again to make some sense of it. 我需要再次仔細檢查一下看有什麼問題。

❗ We'll complete your order and send replacements for the damaged ones.
我們將會處理您的訂貨並換掉損壞的貨物。

We'll send a serviceman to your region to do any necessary repairs.
我們會派維修人員到貴單位做必要的維修。

If the damage is not serious, I hope you could help us dispose of them at a reduced price. 如果損壞不太嚴重的話，我希望你們能夠幫我們以折扣價處理掉。

Please be assured, I'll solve the problem first thing. 請放心，這件事我會優先處理。

We'll spare no efforts in addressing the matter. 在解決這件事我們會不遺餘力。

└─ ★ spare no efforts：不遺餘力

We'll always try our best to help you. 我們永遠會盡最大的努力幫助您。

Maintenance is under way. 維修正在進行中。

8 我們所有的產品都經過嚴格的品管。

A: The products we ordered have problems with quality.
我們訂的這批貨品質有問題。
B: Impossible. **All of our products are under strict quality control.** 不可能，我們所有的產品都經過嚴格的品管。

The loss is not risen from mistakes on our side. 損失不是我們的過失造成的。
More information is needed before a decision can be made.
我們在作決定之前需要瞭解更多情況。
❗ We assure you that such things won't happen again.
我們保證這種情況下次不會再發生。
❗ All of our products are under strict quality control.
我們所有的產品都經過嚴格的品管。
We don't think your complaint is justified. 我們不認為你的投訴站得住腳。

9 我們願意承擔責任。

A: How is this problem going to be solved? 怎樣解決這一問題？
B: **We accept responsibility for this.** 我們願意承擔責任。

We never expected that this would happen. 我們沒想到會發生此事。
We're shocked by this. 我們很震驚。
❗ We'll find out about it. 我們會調查清楚。
❗ We apologize for this. 我們為此道歉。
We'll get it right away. 我們會立刻處理。
❗ We'll look into the matter right away. 我們會立刻調查此事。
We'll settle it immediately. 我們會立刻解決這件事。
We accept responsibility for this. 我們願意承擔責任。
We admit that it is our fault. 我們承認這是我方的過失。
❗ We regret it as well. 我們對此也非常懊悔。
This is beyond our control. 這已超過我們的控制範圍。
We admit that it is our fault and we'll immediately send you the rest of the goods.
我們承認這是我方的過失，我們會立即補送不足的貨品。

⑩ 我們沒有這筆預算。

A: Are you interested in our new office supplies?
請問您對我們新開發的辦公用品感興趣嗎？
B: **We have no budget for it.** 我們沒有這筆預算。

❗ I'm sorry, but our company has no demand for it at the moment.
抱歉，我們公司現在沒有這項需求。

I'm afraid I don't need it. 我恐怕不需要。

We have no plans to purchase so many calculators.
我們沒有購買大批計算機的計畫。

We have no budget for it. 我們沒有這筆預算。

"Also need to know

學習奉承和讚美主管……

讚美主管的領導能力。
We can certainly achieve it under your leadership. 在您的領導之下，我們絕對辦得到。
I admire your ability to handle the trouble. 我欣賞你處理棘手事物的能力。

誇揚主管的成就非凡。
I expect to become as distinguished as you one day.
我期許有朝一日能像您這樣傑出。
You set the standard that is hard to be followed by others.
你樹立了一個別人無法超越的標杆。

沒有你，我們不知該怎麼辦。
We really don't know how to manage it if you are not in our department.
如果這個部門沒有你，我們不知道該怎麼辦。
We'll be at a disadvantage without your help.
沒有你幫助的話，我們會完全處於劣勢。

＊在自己取得成功時，不要忘記讚美周圍的同事和上司的功勞！

辦公室事務英文
⑤ 人事行政與帳務 管理（上）

MP3 TRACK：07

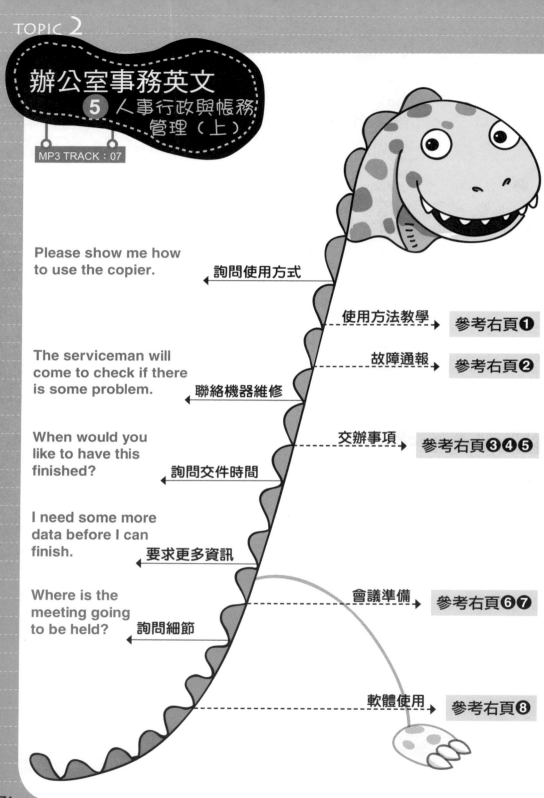

Please show me how to use the copier.

← 詢問使用方式

使用方法教學 → 參考右頁❶

The serviceman will come to check if there is some problem.

← 聯絡機器維修

故障通報 → 參考右頁❷

When would you like to have this finished?

← 詢問交件時間

交辦事項 → 參考右頁❸❹❺

I need some more data before I can finish.

← 要求更多資訊

Where is the meeting going to be held?

← 詢問細節

會議準備 → 參考右頁❻❼

軟體使用 → 參考右頁❽

線上音檔

You may hear
處理行政事務時，也許你會聽到……

ⓐ 請教我影印機的使用方式。　Please show me how to use the copier.

ⓑ 維修員會過來檢查是否有問　The serviceman will come to check if there
　題。　is some problem.

ⓒ 你什麼時候要它完成？　When would you like to have this finished?

ⓓ 我需要更多資訊才能夠完成。　I need some more data before I can finish.

ⓔ 會議將在哪裡舉行？　Where is the meeting going to be held?

You may want to say
處理行政事務時，也許你會想說……

❶ 將原稿面朝下，按下啟動按鈕。　Place the original document face-down, and then press the start button. ...p.80

❷ 這台印表機故障了。　This printer has broken down. ...p.80

❸ 請幫我影印五份這份文件並裝訂好。　Please make five copies for me and have them collated. ...p.81

❹ 請重新整理一次這些文件並歸檔。　Please organize all the documents again and keep them in file. ...p.82

❺ 請幫我將所有的項目分類後做成圖表。　Please classify all the items and then make a chart for me. ...p.82

❻ 今天下午兩點有個緊急會議。　There will be an emergency meeting at 2 o'clock this afternoon. ...p.83

❼ 經理需要使用會議室的投影機。　The manager needs the projector in the meeting room. ...p.84

❽ 我不會使用 Excel 製作財務報表。　I don't know how to make financial statements with Excel. ...p.84

辦公室事務英文

5 人事行政與帳務管理（下）

MP3 TRACK：07

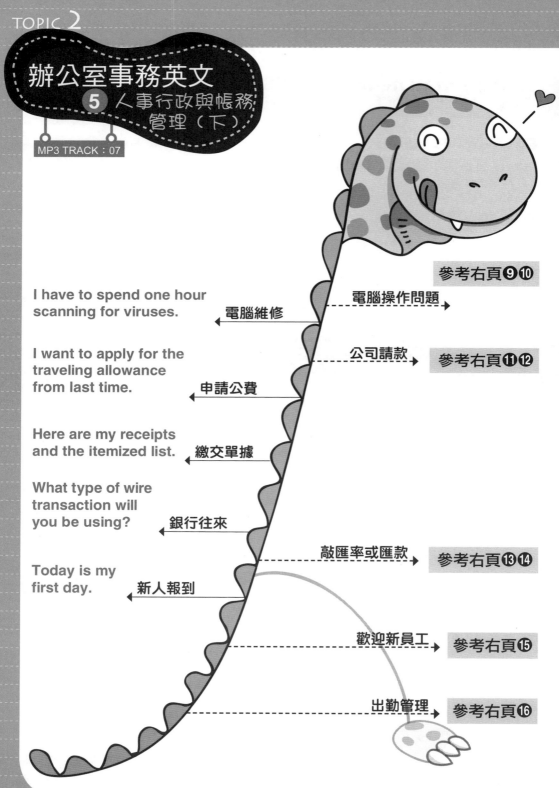

I have to spend one hour scanning for viruses.

電腦維修

電腦操作問題 →

參考右頁 ❾ ❿

I want to apply for the traveling allowance from last time.

申請公費

公司請款 →

參考右頁 ⓫ ⓬

Here are my receipts and the itemized list.

繳交單據

What type of wire transaction will you be using?

銀行往來

敲匯率或匯款 →

參考右頁 ⓭ ⓮

Today is my first day.

新人報到

歡迎新員工 →

參考右頁 ⓯

出勤管理 →

參考右頁 ⓰

f 我需要花一個小時掃描病毒。　I have to spend one hour scanning for viruses.

g 我要申請上次的出差費用。　I want to apply for the traveling allowance from last time.

h 這是我的收據和明細表。　Here are my receipts and the itemized list.

i 你要使用何種方式匯款？　What type of wire transaction will you be using?

j 今天是我第一天上班。　Today is my first day.

You may want to say

處理行政事務時，也許你會想說……（續）

9 我的電腦當機了。　My computer is down. ...p.85

10 請幫我設定垃圾信件匣。　Please help me set up the junk mail box. ...p.86

11 這個月的公關費用已經超支了。　The expenditure on public affairs is already over budget. ...p.87

12 你所附的收據沒有蓋公司章。　The receipt you attached has no company seal on it. ...p.87

13 我們老闆對目前這個匯率很不滿意。　My boss is not satisfied with the current exchange rate. ...p.88

14 我要匯一萬美元到這個帳戶。　I'd like to transfer US $10,000 to this account. ...p.88

15 我帶你稍微參觀一下辦公室。　Let's start a brief tour around the office. ...p.89

16 凱莉今天早上請病假。　Kelly asked for sick leave this morning. ...p.89

① 將原稿面朝下，按下啟動按鈕。

如何
使用

A: We've got a new copier in our office. Can you tell me how to use it?
　我們辦公室新添了一台影印機，你能教我怎麼用嗎？
B: Certainly. **Place the original document face-down, and then press the start button.**
　當然可以。將原稿面朝下，按下啟動按鈕。

★ original document：原稿

❗ Place the original document face-down, and then press the start button.
將原稿面朝下，按下啟動按鈕。

Put the power plug in the socket and switch the power on.
★ plug：插頭　　★ socket：插座
插上電源插頭，打開電源開關。

Lift the copier lid and place the original document face-down, and then close the lid.
掀開影印機蓋，將原稿朝下放置，然後闔上蓋子。

❗ Select the paper size; choose the number of copies.
選擇紙張大小，鍵入影印份數。

Press the start button. 按開始按鈕。

Unplug the printer after you finish. 完成後拔下印表機插頭。
★ unplug：拔去…的插頭

② 這台印表機故障了。

設備
故障

A: **This printer has broken down.** 這台印表機故障了。
B: I suggest we buy a new one. 我建議我們買一台新的。

This printer has broken down. 這台印表機故障了。

❗ It doesn't work now. 它現在無法運轉了。

Well, I thought I've switched on the copier. I pressed the button but nothing came out.
我想我已經開了影印機。我按了按鈕但沒反應。

Let me have a look. Oh, the machine has run out of paper.
讓我看看。哦，機器裡沒紙了。
★ run out of：將…用完

The computer reads, "Please check the connections and try again."
電腦顯示：「請檢查連接並重試」。

There's a disconnection between the printer and the computer.
電腦和印表機之間連接不良。

❸ 請幫我影印五份這份文件並裝訂好。

A: **Please make five copies for me and have them collated.** 請幫我影印五份這份文件並裝訂好。

B: I'll give them to you in ten minutes. 我十分鐘之後交給你。

❗ Please make five copies for me and have them collated.
★ collate：整理，核對

請幫我影印這份文件五份並裝訂好。

Could you draft and type this report for me?
★ draft：起草，設計

請你為我起草並打出這份報告好嗎？

Work without mistakes. / No mistakes are allowed. 不允許有任何錯誤。

Please replace the toner in the copy machine when it runs out.

影印機碳粉用完時請做更換。

Could you please double-space it so that I can make corrections?

請你隔行列印以便我修改。★ double space：空兩倍行距

Can you type it in our company stationery in the usual business letter format?
★ stationery：信紙

你可以用一般商務信函格式把信打到公司信紙上嗎？　　★ reduce：減少，縮小

❗ Could you copy these for me? By the way, could you reduce it?

你可以幫我把它們複印出來嗎？順便說一下，可以縮印嗎？

Do we have a folder that holds 100 B4 sheets?

我們有可以放一百張 B4 尺寸紙張的檔案夾嗎？

Don't waste office supplies. 不要浪費辦公室用品。

Would you please send this document together with the contract terms to Mr. Chang
of Greek Company?
★ contract：契約，合同

你可以將這份文件連同合約條款一起寄給格力克公司的張先生嗎？

❗ The fax is very important, and I really need to send it as soon as possible.

這份傳真非常重要，我需要立刻發送出去。

Could you convert this to digital format for me?

可以請你幫我把這個轉換成數位格式嗎？

❹ 請重新整理一次這些文件並歸檔。

整理資料

A: **Please organize all the documents again and keep them in file.** 請重新整理一次這些文件並歸檔。

B: In which order? 按什麼順序？

★ correspondence：信件　　★ invoice：發票　★ receipt：收據

Outgoing and incoming correspondence is kept in this file, invoices and receipts in this one, and product information, reports and business documents in this one.
收發的信件放在這個檔案裡，發票和收據在這裡，產品資訊、報告和商務文件放在這個檔案裡。

❗ All the files are arranged alphabetically. 所有的檔案都要按字母排序。

└ ★ arrange：整理，安排　　└ ★ alphabetically：照字母順序排列

Please organize all the documents again and keep them in file.
請重新整理一次這些文件並歸檔。

Please arrange them according to main and secondary order.
請把這些按主次順序整理好。

❗ It's arranged according to yearly and monthly order.
把它們按年月順序排好。

❺ 請幫我將所有的項目分類後做成圖表。

製作資料

A: **Please classify all the items and then make a chart for me.** 請幫我將所有的項目分類後做成圖表。

B: I'll give it to you by the end of this week. 我會在本週末之前給你。

❗ Please classify all the items and then make a chart for me.

└ ★ classify：將⋯分類　　　　　　　　　　└ ★ chart：圖表，曲線圖

請幫我將所有的項目分類後做成圖表。

I need you to help me prepare for my presentation on Wednesday morning.
我需要你幫我準備我在週三上午的會報。

Please help me put these cards in order. 請幫我把這些卡片整理好。

We need its English version. 我們需要英文版。

I'd like you to translate something. 我想讓你翻譯一些東西。

❗ Could you type it up as soon as possible? 你能儘快把這個打出來嗎？

❻ 今天下午兩點有個緊急會議。

A: **There will be an emergency meeting at 2 o'clock this afternoon.** 今天下午兩點有個緊急會議。
B: Please tell everybody concerned. 請通知所有相關的人。

There will be an emergency meeting at 2 o'clock this afternoon.
今天下午兩點有個緊急會議。 ┌─★ committee：委員會

The monthly executive committee meeting is planned for next week. Were the members notified? ★ notify：通知，告知
月度執行委員會會議將在下週舉行。委員你都通知過了嗎？

❗ Have you prepared the agenda? 你準備好議程了嗎？
┌─★ agenda：會議議程   ★ charter：憑照，憲章─┐

Have you prepared the minutes book, a copy of the bylaws and the charter, and the draft of the resolutions? └─★ minute：會議記錄   └─★ bylaw：細則，組織章程
你準備會議記錄本、公司施行細則及章程影本和決議草案了嗎？

I've provided all the necessary materials, and I have also prepared a meeting memo. 所有必備的資料我都準備好了，我還準備了一個會議備忘錄。
└─★ memo：備忘錄。

❗ We'll use the conference room on the third floor for the meeting.
我們將使用三樓的會議室開會。

I've arranged an interpreter to be present. 我已安排了一位口譯員出席。

❗ After the report, about 10:00, there will be an interval for rest and refreshments.
└─★ interval：休息時間   └─★ refreshment：茶點，便餐，飲料

在報告後，大概在十點鐘，會有個供應點心的休息時間。

Could you arrange a meeting with the Planning Department?
妳可以籌備與企劃部門的會議嗎？

❗ We have a tentative road map for our discussions.
└─★ tentative：暫時的 └─★ road map：計畫

我們有個暫訂的討論計畫。

I've come up with a rough agenda. Tell me how this sounds to you.
我已經擬出一個大概的議程，告訴我你聽了覺得如何。

7 經理需要使用會議室的投影機。

A: Will you need anything special for the presentation?
你們在報告時需要什麼特殊設備嗎？
B: **The manager needs the projector in the meeting room.**
Please set that up for us. 經理需要使用會議室的投影機。請幫我們安裝。

❗ The manager needs the projector in the meeting room.
經理需要使用會議室的投影機。

❗ Well, I need the display monitor. 我需要顯示螢幕。

I need the whiteboard, a dry-erase marker and an eraser.
我需要白板、白板筆和板擦。

You know what that office is like. You'll have to move some of the desks around to make enough space.
你知道那間會議室裡的樣子。你得挪動一些桌子以騰出足夠的空間。

And I want to set up fold-out chairs too. 我還需要擺上一些折疊椅。
★ fold-out：可折疊的

I will call Martin over there and ask him if they have enough chairs.
我會打電話給那裡的馬丁，詢問他是否他們有足夠的椅子。

8 我不會使用 Excel 製作財務報表。

A: **I don't know how to make financial statements with Excel.** 我不會使用 Excel 製作財務報表。
B: Let me show you. 讓我教你。

The software program asks for a product code, and I don't know the product code.
這個軟體程式需要產品代號，而我不知道。

❗ I don't know how to make financial statements with Excel.
我不會使用 Excel 製作財務報表。

How do you get the toolbar for pictures? 怎樣使用圖片工具欄？

Why do I have to restart every time I install new software?
為什麼我每安裝新的軟體都要重新啟動電腦呢？

Photoshop is good if you want to edit a picture.
如果你要編輯圖像的話，可以用 Photoshop 軟體。

電腦故障

❾ 我的電腦當機了。

A: **My computer is down.** 我的電腦當機了。
B: You have too many applications open. 你應用軟體開得太多了。

❗ My computer is down. / My computer froze (up). 我的電腦當機了。

There is something wrong with my computer. 我的電腦出了些問題。

This server keeps shutting down by itself. 這伺服器老是自動關閉。
∟ ★ server：伺服器 ∟ ★ shut down：停工，關閉

The computer on my desk doesn't work at all! Who can help me fix it?
我桌上的電腦完全不能用！誰可以幫我修理它？

The computer seems to be destroyed. 我好像把電腦弄壞了。

❗ All my documents have been deleted by the computer. What should I do?
電腦把我所有的文件都刪除了，我該怎麼辦？

❗ Our computer is unable to access the Internet. **我們的電腦上不了網。**

We've found that there is a defect in our computer system.
我們發現電腦系統有毛病。

Please help us fix the computer, all right?
幫我們維修一下電腦，好嗎？

I overwrote my document. I mixed up "Save" with "Save as."
我覆寫了很多文件。我把「儲存」和「另存新檔」搞混了。

There's not much room left on the hard disk. 硬碟剩餘的空間不多了。

There's not enough memory. 記憶體不足了。

I forced a restart. 我強制重新開機。

It looks like the printer isn't connected. 印表機似乎沒有連接上。

I wonder if my computer has been infected with a virus.
我懷疑電腦被病毒感染了。

基本電腦配備英文縮寫

CPU (Central Processing Unit)　　　　　中央處理器	ROM (Read-Only Memory)　　　　　唯讀記憶體
RAM (Random-Access Memory)　　　　　隨機存取記憶體	CD-ROM (Compact Disc Read-Only Memory) Drive　　　　　光碟機
HDD (Hard Disk Drive)　　　　硬碟	

⑩ 請幫我設定垃圾信件匣。

A: Anything I can help you with? 有什麼可以幫你的嗎？

B: **Please help me set up the junk mail box.**
請幫我設定垃圾信件匣。

❗ Is the network down? I can't receive any e-mail.
網路斷了嗎？我接收不到郵件。

I can't open my e-mail. 我的電子郵件打不開。

❗ How do I set up my e-mail account in Outlook?
怎樣在 Outlook 上設立我自己的電子郵件帳戶？

How do I set up an e-mail signature in Outlook? 如何在 Outlook 上設置簽名檔？

How do you attach a file to your e-mail? 如何在電子郵件中附加檔案？

★ attatch：附屬，附加

Click on "Attachment", look for the file you want to attach, and click OK.
點擊「附件」，找到你要附加的檔案，然後點擊「確定」。

How often do I need to change the log-in ID?
我要多久更換一次登錄用戶名？

I wonder if I got the e-mail address wrong. 我懷疑我拿到錯誤的電子郵件地址。

I don't know what to do about the junk e-mail I've been getting.
我不知道該怎麼處理一直寄來的垃圾郵件。

My unread e-mail is piling up. 我的未讀信件一直在累積中。

I couldn't send or receive e-mail, since the server was down.
因為伺服器斷線，我無法收發電子郵件。

Could you tell me how to CC it to her? 你可以告訴我如何傳送副本給她嗎？

＊CC：carbon copy，把某份電子郵件的完整副本發送給另一個人。

Please help me set up the junk mail box. 請幫我設定垃圾信件匣。

商用 E-mail 常用標題（Subject:）

Inquiry	詢問	Information	資訊
Information Request	請求給予資料	Announcement	通知
Urgent!	緊急	Quotation	估價單
REQ（=Request）	需求	Order	訂購

⓫ 這個月的公關費用已經超支了。

A: Can I apply for more money? 我可以申請更多預算嗎？
B: But **the expenditure on public affairs is already over budget.** 這個月的公關費用已經超支了。

★ expenditure：支出，經費

The expenditure on public affairs is already over budget.
這個月的公關費用已經超支了。　　★ over budget：超出預算

How is our budget for Adam's project? 亞當負責的專案的預算怎樣？

Last year we went over by 30% on supplies alone. The Finance Department almost lost their head. 去年只算給我們的供貨量就超出 30%。財務部都快被逼瘋了。

❗ Where did the extra money come from to cover expenses?
去哪裡弄額外的經費來補貼開支？

❗ Did you receive the invoice from ABC Company?
你收到 ABC 公司寄來的發票了嗎？ ★ invoice：發票，發貨單

Why do you have to use double-entry accounting? 你為什麼要用複式記帳？

⓬ 你所附的收據沒有蓋公司章。

A: Any problems? 有什麼問題嗎？
B: **The receipt you attached has no company seal on it.**
你所附的收據沒有蓋公司章。

The receipt you attached has no company seal on it.
你所附的收據沒有蓋公司章。

Every item of expenditure must be proved by a petty cash voucher.
每一筆開銷都應有零用現金發票。
＊ petty cash voucher 是「零用現金憑單」或「小額現金收據」的意思。

❗ Whenever cash is paid out, a voucher or receipt should be obtained.
每當支付現金時，就應該拿憑證或收據。

❗ You must keep track of all the incoming money. 你必須記錄所有的收入。
★ keep track of：記錄

These numbers are cross-checked with all expenditure receipts and invoices of accounts receivable. 這些金額都會與支出收據以及應收帳款發票交互查核。

⓭ 我們老闆對目前這個匯率很不滿意。

A: **My boss is not satisfied with the current exchange rate.**
我們老闆對目前這個匯率很不滿意。
B: But we have no other choice.　但我們沒有別的辦法。

❗ What's the exchange rate today?　今天的匯率是多少？

❗ My boss is not satisfied with the current exchange rate.
我們老闆對目前這個匯率很不滿意。

　Could you please tell me why the buying rate is different from what you just quoted?
　Is there any change in the rate?　　　　　　　　　　　★ quote：報價，開價
　可否請你告訴我為什麼現在的買價和剛才你的報價不同？匯率有什麼改變了嗎？
　I'd like to know the rate for this traveler's L/C.　我想知道旅遊信用狀的兌換率。
　　　　　　　　　　　★ L/C：Letter of Credit，（商用）信用狀

⓮ 我要匯一萬美元到這個帳戶。　　　　　　　　　　　　　銀行往來

A: **I'd like to transfer US $10,000 to this account.**
我要匯一萬美元到這個帳戶。
B: Just a moment, please.　請稍等。

❗ I'd like to transfer US $10,000 to this account.　我要匯一萬美元到這個帳戶。
　I'd like to buy a draft of USD 50,000 from your bank.　我要開一張五萬美元的匯票。
　　　　　★ draft：匯票，匯款單

　I'd like to open a savings account.　我要開一個儲蓄存款帳戶。
　Do checking accounts earn interest?　支票帳戶有利息嗎？
　　　　　　　　　　　★ interest：利息

❗ I want to transfer ten thousand Hong Kong Dollars to an account for Mr.
John Li.　我要轉一萬港幣到李約翰先生的帳戶。
　I want to withdraw USD 200 from my deposit account.
　　　★ withdraw：提款

　我要從我的存款帳戶提領兩百美元。
　＊deposit account 是「儲蓄存款帳戶」（相當於 saving account，有別於支票存款帳戶 current account
　或 checking account）。
　What's the interest rate for the savings account?　儲蓄存款帳戶的利率是多少？

⓯ 我帶你稍微參觀一下辦公室。

A: Good morning, Mr. Mo, it's a pleasure to meet you again.
早安，莫先生，很榮幸再見到您。
B: Nice to see you. **Let's start a brief tour around the office.**
很高興見到你。我帶你稍微參觀一下辦公室。

❗ Let's start a brief tour around the office. 我帶你稍微參觀一下辦公室。
Let me show you around and meet some of the staff.
我帶你走走，見見你的一些新同事。

❗ I'll give you a brief introduction to the office work.
我簡單地向你介紹一下辦公室的工作。
Here is your job description. Have a look at it first.
這兒有你的工作職責說明，先看一下吧。
I'll be training you for the position, so if you have any question, I'm the person to ask. 我將對你進行在職訓練，所以如果你有什麼問題，可以來問我。

⓰ 凱莉今天早上請病假。

A: **Kelly asked for sick leave this morning.** 凱莉今天早上請病假。
B: She just called. 她剛剛打過電話。

❗ Kelly asked for sick leave this morning. 凱莉今天早上請病假。
❗ Would it be possible for me to take a day off this Friday?
這個星期五，我是否可以休一天假？
＊take a day off 是請一天假的意思，如果是請兩天以上就用 days off。
Shelly just called in sick. 雪莉剛打電話來請病假。
NTD 500 will be deducted from your pay if you are late for work once.
遲到一次會被扣除新台幣五百元。　　★ deducted：扣款，扣錢
You can have 10 days of paid vacation every year.
每年會有十天帶薪假期。
As a new employee, you get five days of annual vacation.
身為新員工，你有五天特休假。
Working hours are from eight-thirty to five.
工作時間從上午八點半到下午五點。

出差＆接待英文
1 出發到海外（上）

MP3 TRACK：08

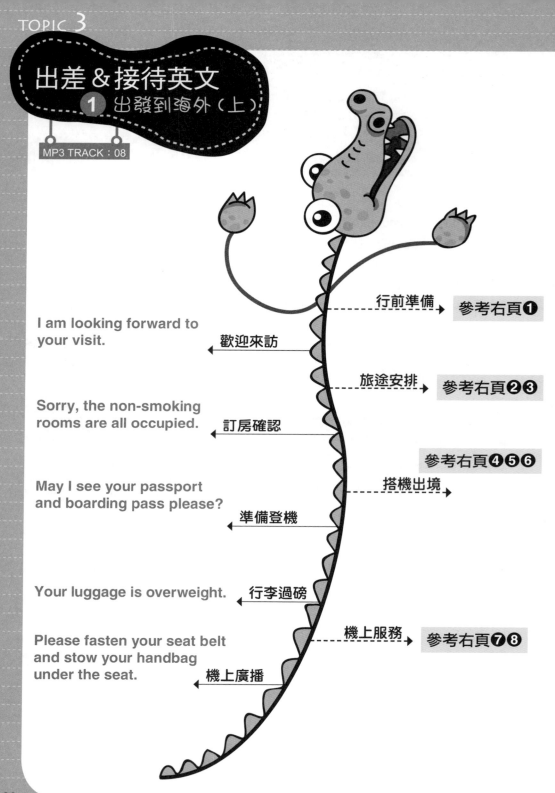

行前準備 ➔ 參考右頁❶

歡迎來訪

I am looking forward to your visit.

旅途安排 ➔ 參考右頁❷❸

訂房確認

Sorry, the non-smoking rooms are all occupied.

參考右頁❹❺❻

搭機出境 ➔

準備登機

May I see your passport and boarding pass please?

行李過磅

Your luggage is overweight.

機上服務 ➔ 參考右頁❼❽

機上廣播

Please fasten your seat belt and stow your handbag under the seat.

You may hear
出發到海外時，也許你會聽到……

ⓐ 衷心期待您的來訪。　　　I am looking forward to your visit.

ⓑ 抱歉，禁煙房已經全部客滿了。　Sorry, the non-smoking rooms are all occupied.

ⓒ 請出示您的護照和登機證。　May I see your passport and boarding pass, please?

ⓓ 你的行李超重了。　　　　Your luggage is overweight.

ⓔ 請繫好您的安全帶，把手提袋放　Please fasten your seat belt and stow
在座椅下方。　　　　　your handbag under the seat.

 You may want to say
出發到海外時，也許你會想說……

❶ 7月11日能去拜訪你嗎？　Can I pay you a visit on the 11th of July?
...p.94

❷ 我要一張7月10日飛往紐約　I'd like a Business Class ticket for the flight
的商務艙機票。　　　　to New York on July 10th. ...p.94

❸ 我要一間位於禁煙樓層的單　I'd like a single room on the non-smoking
人房。　　　　　　　　floor. ...p.95

❹ 可以請你告訴我往紐約的報　Could you tell me where the check-in
到櫃檯在哪裡嗎？　　　counter for the flight to New York is? ...p.97

❺ 我有兩件行李需要托運。　I have two pieces of baggage to check in. ...p.98

❻ 請給我靠走道的座位。　I'd like an aisle seat. ...p.99

❼ 可以麻煩你幫我打開上面的　Could you please help me open the
置物箱嗎？　　　　　overhead bin? ...p.99

❽ 我想要一副耳機。　　　May I have a set of headphones, please? ...p.100

出差＆接待英文
① 出發到海外（下）

MP3 TRACK：08

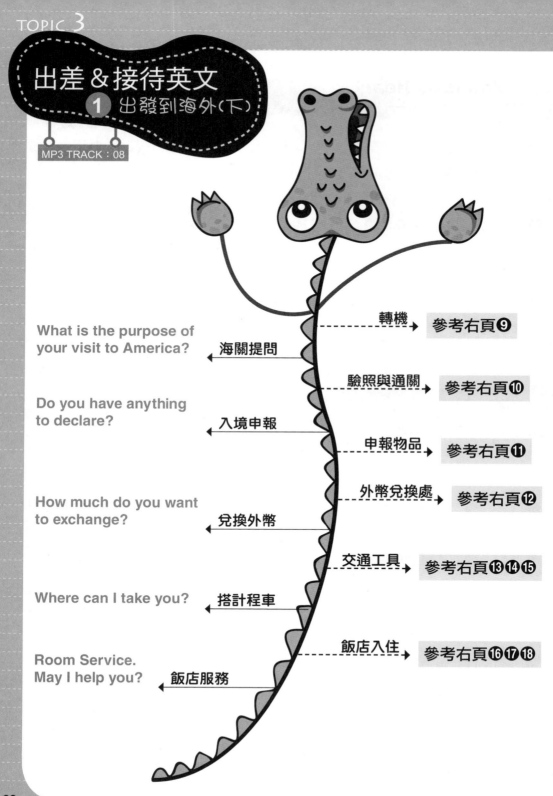

What is the purpose of your visit to America?

海關提問

轉機 → 參考右頁❾

驗照與通關 → 參考右頁❿

Do you have anything to declare?

入境申報

申報物品 → 參考右頁⓫

外幣兌換處 → 參考右頁⓬

How much do you want to exchange?

兌換外幣

交通工具 → 參考右頁⓭⓮⓯

Where can I take you?

搭計程車

飯店入住 → 參考右頁⓰⓱⓲

Room Service. May I help you?

飯店服務

You may hear
出發到海外時，也許你會聽到……（續）

f 你來美國的目的是什麼？　　　What is the purpose of your visit to America?

g 你有什麼東西需要申報的嗎？　Do you have anything to declare?

h 請問你要兌換多少錢？　　　　How much do you want to exchange?

i 我要載你去哪裡？　　　　　　Where can I take you?

j 客房服務。我可以為您效勞嗎？　Room Service. May I help you?

You may want to say
出發到海外時，也許你會想說……（續）

9 轉機要往哪個方向走？　　　Which direction should I go for transit? ...p.100

10 我要到我們的分公司開會。　I'm here to attend the meetings at the branch office. ...p.101

11 我沒有東西需要申報。　　　I have nothing to declare. ...p.101

12 請問外幣兌換處在哪裡？　　Where is the exchange office? ...p.102

13 計程車招呼站在哪裡？　　　Where is the taxi stand? ...p.102

14 地鐵可以直達展覽中心嗎？　Can I get to the exhibition center from here by subway? ...p.103

15 機場裡有租車公司嗎？　　　Is there a car hire company at the airport? ...p.103

16 我預訂了一間單人房，我姓張。　I've booked a single room. My surname is Chang. ...p.104

17 房間裡有無線上網服務嗎？　Do you provide wireless Internet access in the room? ...p.104

18 請問早餐供應到幾點？　　　What are the service hours for breakfast? ...p.105

❶ 7月11日能去拜訪你嗎？

A: **Can I pay you a visit on the 11th of July?**
   7月11日能去拜訪你嗎？
B: Ok. We can meet in my office. 好。我會在辦公室等你。

I'll visit you soon. 我會盡快去拜訪你。

❗ I'd like to visit you tomorrow. **我明天想去拜訪你。**

We'd better meet again soon. 我們應該盡快再見一次面。

❗ I'd like to make an appointment with you. **我想找時間跟你見個面。**

Could we schedule a time to meet next week? 我們下週能約個時間見面嗎？

Can I pay you a visit on the 11th of July? 7月11日能去拜訪你嗎？

I'd like to make an appointment at 2 o'clock on Monday. 我想約星期一下午兩點。

Let's fix a date to talk about supply problems. 我們訂個日子談一下供貨問題吧。

❷ 我要一張7月10日飛往紐約的商務艙機票。

A: This is Phoenix Travel Agency. May I help you?
   這是鳳凰旅行社，需要什麼幫忙呢？
B: **I'd like a Business Class ticket for the flight to New York on July 10th.** 我要一張7月10日飛往紐約的商務艙機票。

❗ I'd like to make a reservation for a flight to New York on September 15th.
   我要訂9月15號到紐約的班機。

I'd like a Business Class ticket for the flight to New York on July 10th.
   我要一張7月10日飛往紐約的商務艙機票。

Could you change my flight date from London to Tokyo?
   請你更改一下從倫敦到東京的班機日期好嗎？

I'd like to reserve a seat to Singapore. 我想預訂去新加坡的機票。

What time does Flight 408 arrive? 408次班機何時抵達？

❗ How much is the airfare? 機票多少錢？

❗ I'd like to reconfirm my plane reservation, please.
   我想再次確認我預訂的機位。

What's the flight number and departure time? 請告訴我班機號碼與起飛時間。

❸ 我要一間位於禁煙樓層的單人房。

A: This is Queen's hotel. May I help you? 這是皇后飯店。需要什麼幫忙？
B: **I'd like a single room on the non-smoking floor.**
我要一間位於禁煙樓層的單人房。

I'd like to make room reservations. 我要預訂房間。

Do you have any vacancies? 請問有空房嗎？

└─★ vacancy：空房

❗ I'd like a suite with an ocean view, please.
我想要一個可以看到海景的套房。

My name is Tom Chang. That is T-O-M, C-H-A-N-G.

我叫張湯姆。T-O-M，C-H-A-N-G。

Have you got any vacancies for the nights of the 12th and the 13th?

請問 12 號和 13 號晚上還有空房間可以預訂嗎？

I'd like to book a presidential suite. 我要預訂一間總統套房。

Have you got one with a view? 你們有景觀房嗎？

It's Mrs. John Brown. It's New York, 341-2877.

我是約翰‧布朗太太。我住紐約，電話是 341-2877。

❗ I'd like a double room / regular room. **我想要一個雙人／標準房。**

I'd like to stay alone in a room for two. 我想一個人住在雙人房。

I'd like a single room on the non-smoking floor.

我要一間位於禁煙樓層的單人房。

What's the earliest time we can check in? 我們最早幾點可以入住？

❗ I'd like to book a room from August 21st to 25th.

我想預訂一個房間，時間從 8 月 21 日到 25 日。

Do you have any conference facilities? 你們有會議設施嗎？

Is that full-board? 這是否包括三餐？

Is breakfast included in the hotel rates? 房價有包含早餐嗎？

❗ What are your rates per night? **你們每晚的收費是多少？**

Can we pay by credit card? 我們可以用信用卡付帳嗎？

飯店房型分類

以規格分

單人房	single room	雙人房	double room
三人房	triple room	四人房	quad room
大床房	king size & queen size room	標準房	standard room
		套房	suite
標準房單人住	tsu (twin for sole use)	公寓	apartment
		別墅	villa

以級別分

經濟房	economic room
高級房	superior room
商務房	business room
標準房	standard room
豪華房	deluxe room
行政房	executive room

以朝向分

朝街房	front view room
城景房	city view room
海景房	sea view room
背街房	rear view room
園景房	garden view room
湖景房	lake view room

特殊房型

不限房型	run of the house	禁煙房	non-smoking room
殘障人士客房	handicapped room	帶廚房客房	room with kitchen
相鄰房	adjoining room		

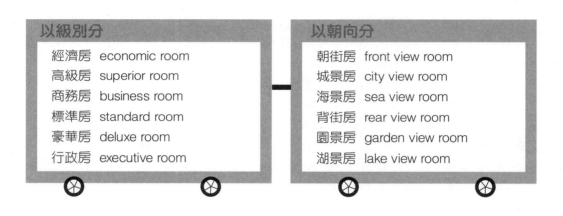

❹ 可以請你告訴我往紐約的報到櫃檯在哪裡嗎？ 登機

A: **Could you tell me where the check-in counter for the flight to New York is?**
可以請你告訴我往紐約的報到櫃檯在哪裡嗎？
B: Go straight and turn left. 向前走然後左轉。

Could you tell me where the check-in counter for the flight to New York is?
可以請你告訴我往紐約的報到櫃檯在哪裡嗎？

Where may I check in for United Airlines Flight no.706?
我該到哪裡辦聯合航空 706 次班機登機手續？

❗ What time will boarding start? 什麼時候開始登機？

＊乘坐國際航班的旅客，應於飛機起飛前至少兩個小時到達機場櫃檯辦理登機手續，否則將有可能被取消原有的訂位。登機門隨時都有可能變更，請注意相關的廣播通知，尤其是到了預計登機時間，沒有航空公司地勤人員提供登機協助時，很有可能自己的登機門有誤，請盡快與工作人員聯繫。

What time do you start check-in? 你們何時開始辦理登機？

I'm connecting with AF123. Where can I get information on a connecting flight?
我要轉接法國航空 123 號班機。 哪裡可以詢問轉接班機的事情？

Is this the right counter to check in for my flight?
我的飛機是在這裡辦理登機手續嗎？

❗ Where can I check in? 在哪裡辦理登機手續？

Where should I pick up my boarding pass? 我該去哪裡領取登機證？

❗ Which way is to Gate 8? 8 號登機門怎麼走？

In which direction is Gate 42? 42 號登機門在哪個方向？

Where can we take a shuttle bus? 我們要在哪裡搭乘機場接駁車？

Where do I board the airport bus? 要在哪裡搭機場巴士？

How do I get to terminal one? 第一航廈要怎麼走？

Am I in the right terminal for my flight? It's CI100 to Tokyo.
我是在正確的航廈嗎？我搭華航 100 號班機往東京。

＊要順利搭上飛機，首先需確定自己的班機在哪個航廈（terminal），並查詢班機時刻表（timetable）該在哪個報到櫃檯（check-in counter）辦理登機手續。拿到登機證（boarding pass）之後，就可以直接前往登機門（gate），或去免稅店（duty-free shop）逛逛。登機門大約會在起飛前 30 分鐘開放。

⑤ 我有兩件行李需要托運。

A: **I have two pieces of baggage to check in.**
　我有兩件行李需要托運。

B: Do you have any carry-on baggage?　您還有手提行李嗎？

★ satchel：小提包

　May I carry this satchel?　我可以帶著這個小提包嗎？

❗ What's the weight limit?　重量限制是多少？

　I hope my bags aren't overweight.　希望我的行李不要超重。

　I have two pieces of baggage to check in.　我有兩件行李需要托運。

　May I take something out of the overweight bag?　There's an overcoat I can carry by hand.

★ overcoat：外套，大衣

　我可以從這個超重的行李裡取出一些東西嗎？裡面的一件外套我可以隨身帶著。

　It's fragile.　Please handle it with care.　這是易碎品。請小心輕放。

"Also need to know

關於行李的各種規定……

托運行李

乘坐國際線航班時，一般免費可托運行李重量為：頭等艙 40 公斤，商務艙 30 公斤，經濟艙 20 公斤。飛美國線為兩件行李，各 23 公斤。但實際情況依各家航空公司規定而略有不同。

隨身行李

1. 乘坐國際線航班頭等艙、商務艙的旅客，每人可攜帶兩件隨身行李；乘坐經濟艙的旅客，每人可攜帶一件行李，每件行李重量皆不得超過 7 公斤。手提行李長寬高的總尺寸不能超過 56 公分×36 公分×23 公分（22 吋×14 吋×9 吋），尺寸包括行李的輪子、手把及側袋。超過規定的部分應作為托運行李運輸。

2. 隨身攜帶物品內不得夾帶易燃、爆炸、腐蝕、有毒、放射性物品、可聚合物質、磁性物質及其他危險物品。旅客乘坐飛機不得攜帶武器、管制刀具、利器和兇器。

免稅品、違例品的規定

以美國為例，可以帶進美國的免稅品有酒 1 瓶，香煙 200 支，另外還有約 100 美元的禮品。如果超過這些，就要課稅。至於個人的隨身用品是不會課稅的。但如果超過恰當的數量，而引起銷售的嫌疑的話，也有可能會被課稅。另外，水果、植物及肉類，因為檢疫上的理由，是禁止攜入的，如果出入境攜帶這些東西，會被海關沒收。

❻ 請給我靠走道的座位。

A: Ticket, please. A window or aisle seat, sir?
請出示機票。您是要靠窗的還是要靠走道的座位，先生？
B: **I'd like an aisle seat.** 請給我靠走道的座位。

❗ I'd like an aisle seat. 請給我靠走道的座位。
＊window seat 是靠窗的座位，aisle seat 是靠走道的座位。

❗ Can I get the seat next to the window? 我可以坐靠窗的座位嗎？

We'd like to have one window seat definitely. 我們一定要一個靠窗的座位。

Can I sit at the back of the plane? 我可以坐在機艙的尾端嗎？

I'd like to sit in the front row of the economy class. 我要坐在經濟艙的前排座位。

I'd prefer to sit next to the emergency exit. 我想要坐在緊急出口旁邊。

Would it be possible to assign me a seat with more legroom?
可以幫我劃個放腳空間較大的位子嗎？

I'd rather not sit so close to the toilets. 我不想坐得靠廁所這麼近。

❼ 可以麻煩你幫我打開上面的置物箱嗎？

A: **Could you please help me open the overhead bin?**
可以麻煩你幫我打開上面的置物箱嗎？
B: With pleasure. 好的。

Could you please help me open the overhead bin?
可以麻煩你幫我打開上面的置物箱嗎？

❗ Could you tell me how to fill out this form? 請告訴我如何填寫這張表格？

Could you tell me our flight number? 麻煩你告訴我班機編號好嗎？

❗ Where is my seat? 我的座位在那裡？

Excuse me, miss. I don't know how to turn on the reading light.
對不起，小姐，我不知道如何開這盞閱讀用的燈。

Can I put my baggage here? 我能將手提行李放在這裡嗎？

Could you change my seat, please? 可否幫我更換座位？

May I smoke? 我是否可以抽煙？

❗ Where is the lavatory? 洗手間在哪裡？

Will this flight get there on time? 這班班機會準時到達嗎？

❽ 我想要一副耳機。

A: How may I help you? 有什麼可以幫助您的嗎？
B: **May I have a set of headphones, please? 我想要一副耳機。**

Scotch and water, please. 請給我加水威士忌。
└─★ Scotch = Scotch Whisky，蘇格蘭威士忌酒

Can I get another drink? 我可以再來一杯嗎？

❗ May I have a set of headphones, please? 我想要一副耳機。

I feel cold, may I have a blanket? 我會冷，請給我一條毯子好嗎？
└─★ blanket：毛毯，毯子

May I have a deck of playing cards? 可不可以給我一副撲克牌？

❗ What kind of drinks do you have? 機上提供那些飲料？

❗ May I have a pillow and a blanket, please? 請給我一個枕頭和毛毯。

I feel a little sick. Can I have some medicine?
我覺得有些不舒服，是否可給我一些藥？

Do you have Chinese newspapers? 你有中文報紙嗎？

I'd like to purchase some duty-free goods. 我想要買一些免稅商品。

❾ 轉機要往哪個方向走？

A: What can I do for you? 有什麼可以幫忙的嗎？
B: **Which direction should I go for transit?**
轉機要往哪個方向走？

Which direction should I go for transit? 轉機要往哪個方向走？

Can you tell me where I can catch my connecting flight?
你能否告訴我要去哪裡轉機？

❗ Is there a layover? 中途要停留嗎？
└─★ layover：旅途中的短暫停留

❗ How long is the layover? 要停留多久？

What time is my next flight? 下一班飛機是什麼時候？

Do I have to change planes? 我需要轉機嗎？

⑩ 我要到我們的分公司開會。 過海關

A: What's the purpose of your visit? 旅行的目的為何？

B: **I'm here to attend the meetings at the branch office.**
我要到我們的分公司開會。

I'm here to attend the meetings at the branch office. 我要到我們的分公司開會。

I will stay in the States for one week. **我會留在美國一個星期。**

I'm just passing through. **我只是過境而已。**

I will stay at Boston Hotel. 我將住在波士頓飯店。

I am leaving for Geneva tonight. 我今晚就會前往日內瓦。

I have a return ticket to Taiwan. 我有臺灣的回程機票。

I have 800 dollars. 我有八百元現金。

Here is a copy of my itinerary. 這是我的行程表。

★ itinerary：旅行計畫；行程表

I'm attending a trade show. 我要來參加商展。

⑪ 我沒有東西需要申報。 入境申報

A: Do you have anything to declare? 您有任何東西要申報嗎？

B: **I have nothing to declare.** 我沒有東西需要申報。

Here is my declaration form. 這是我的申報表。

Which lane should I go through? 我應該走哪一條通道？

I have nothing to declare. **我沒有東西需要申報。**

★ declare：申報（納稅品等）

Do I need to pay duty on this? 我需要為這項物品繳付稅金嗎？

This is a souvenir that I'm taking to Taiwan. 這是我要帶去臺灣的當地紀念品。

Yes, I have two bottles of whisky. 是的，我帶了兩瓶威士忌。

The camera is for my personal use. 這個相機是我私人使用的。

These are for my personal use. **這些是我私人使用的東西。**

These are gifts for my friends. 這些是給朋友的禮物。

＊澳洲的海關相當嚴格，千萬不可帶肉類製品（罐頭）、水果、種子、牛肉、豬肉及蛋類，還有任何食物入境，以免觸犯當地法律。

⑫ 請問外幣兌換處在哪裡？

A: **Where is the exchange office?** 請問外幣兌換處在哪裡？
B: Go straight, and then turn right. 一直往前走，然後右轉。

❗ Where is the exchange office? 請問外幣兌換處在哪裡？

I'd like to change NT$10,000 into U.S. Dollars, please.
我要把一萬元台幣換成美金。

Can you tell me where to change money? 你能告訴我在哪裡兌換外幣嗎？

Can you accept traveler's checks? 你們接受旅行支票嗎？

❗ What's the exchange rate? 匯率是多少？

I'd like to convert this to Japanese Yen. 我想把這些換成日幣。
└─★ convert：兌換

I want to buy 1,500 Euros, please. 我想要買一千五百歐元，麻煩你。

⑬ 計程車招呼站在哪裡？

A: **Where is the taxi stand?** 計程車招呼站在哪裡？
B: It's around the corner. 就在那個轉角處。

Where is the taxi stand? 計程車招呼站在哪裡？

Where is the bus stop? 公車站牌在哪裡？

❗ Where is the tourist information center? 旅遊諮詢中心在哪裡？

❗ Is there an airport bus to the city? 是否有機場巴士可到市區？

Is there a travel agency nearby? 請問附近有沒有旅行社？

Where can I get the limousine for Hilton Hotel?
└─★ limousine：（機場，車站等的）接駁巴士

我在何處可搭乘希爾頓飯店的接駁巴士？

How can I get to Hilton Hotel? 我要如何才能到達希爾頓飯店？

Can I reserve a hotel room (rent a car) here? 我是否可在此預訂飯店（租車）？

❗ How do I get to the metro / subway / underground station?
請問如何前往地鐵站？
＊「地鐵」在歐洲通常用 metro，在北美洲用 subway，在英國則用 underground。

Is there a youth hostel nearby? 請問附近有沒有青年旅館？

⑭ 地鐵可以直達展覽中心嗎？

A: **Can I get to the exhibition center from here by subway?**
地鐵可以直達展覽中心嗎？

B: Yes, you can take the subway. 是的，您可以搭地鐵。

Can I get to the exhibition center from here by subway? 地鐵可以直達展覽中心嗎？

Is it easy to get to Manhattan from here by subway?
從這兒乘地鐵到曼哈頓很方便嗎？

❗ Do you know where the nearest subway station is?
您知道最近的地鐵車站在哪裡嗎？

❗ How much is the fare? 車費是多少？

❗ How long is the ride? 要坐多久？

What should I do with the token? 我該怎麼用這個代幣呢？

★ token：代幣，籌碼

By the way, how do I leave the platform after I get off the train?
順便問一下，我下車後該怎麼出月臺呢？

⑮ 機場裡有租車公司嗎？

A: **Is there a car hire company at the airport?**
機場裡有租車公司嗎？

B: Of course. There are many companies like that. 是的，有很多租車公司。

Is there a car hire company at the airport? 機場裡有租車公司嗎？

Do they hire out vans? 他們出租廂型車嗎？

❗ How much is the rent? 租金是多少？

Can I hire it for this weekend, from Friday afternoon to Sunday evening?
我可以租一個週末嗎？從週五下午到週日晚上。

I'd like to buy full insurance. 我要全部的保險。

❗ Are they in good condition? 車的性能可以嗎？

❗ Can I return the vehicle at another city? 我可以異地還車嗎？

⓰ 我預訂了一間單人房，我姓張。

A: Royal Hotel, can I help you?　皇家飯店，我能為您服務嗎？
B: **I've booked a single room.　My surname is Chang.**
　 我預訂了一間單人房，我姓張。

I've booked a single room.　My surname is Chang.　我預訂了一間單人房，我姓張。

❗ We'll be leaving on Sunday morning.　我們將在星期天上午離開。

❗ Can I pay by credit card?　我可以用信用卡支付嗎？

My name is John Deep.　That is J-o-h-n D-e-e-p.
我叫約翰狄普。J-o-h-n D-e-e-p。

Do I have to leave a deposit?　我需要付押金嗎？

What should I fill in under ROOM NUMBER?　「房間號碼」這一欄我該怎麼填呢？

I'd like to (extend) my stay by three days.　我想在旅館多住三天。

★ extend：延長，延伸

I wonder if it is possible for me to extend my stay at this hotel for another two days.
我想知道是否可以讓我在這兒多待兩天。

I'd like to change my reservation from two nights to three nights.
我想把原先預訂的兩夜改成三夜。

How should the payment be made?　以何種方式付帳？

⓱ 房間裡有無線上網服務嗎？

A: **Do you provide wireless Internet access in the room?**
　 房間裡有無線上網服務嗎？
B: Of course.　And we do not charge for the use of it.
　 當然，並且我們不收任何附加費用。

❗ Do you provide wireless Internet access in the room?
房間裡有無線上網服務嗎？

Do you have any laundry service?
請問有沒有洗衣服務？

I wonder if your hotel has a wake-up call service.
不知道你們飯店是否有晨喚服務？

Is there a swimming pool in your hotel?　你們飯店有游泳池嗎？

⑱ 請問早餐供應到幾點？

A: **What are the service hours for breakfast?**
請問早餐供應到幾點？
B: We serve from seven to ten. 我們從七點供應到十點。

❗ What are the service hours for breakfast? 請問早餐供應到幾點？

By the way, could you tell me about your hotel service?
順便問問，你能不能告訴我飯店服務的情況？

Could you send someone up for my laundry, please?
可以請你們派人來收要洗的衣服嗎？

From what time do you accept laundry tomorrow morning?
明早幾時開始可以送洗衣物？

❗ I would like to request an early wake-up call.
我想請你們明天早上叫醒我。

I'd like to have my hair cut. 我想剪頭髮。

Is there a beauty salon in this hotel? 這家旅館有美容院嗎？

Do you have vegetarian dishes? 餐廳是否有供應素食餐？

★ vegetarian：素食的

"Also need to know

飯店房間的設備出問題時……

There's a strange smell in my room. 我的房間裡有股奇怪的味道。
Can you change the room for me? It's too noisy. 能幫我換房間嗎？這裡太吵了。
The light in this room is too dim. 這房間裡的燈光太暗了。
The toilet doesn't flush. 馬桶沖不下去。
The water tap drips all night long. 水龍頭一整夜都在滴水。
The picture of the TV is wobbly. 電視機的畫面不穩定。
The room is too cold for me. I feel rather cold when I sleep.
這房間太冷了，我睡覺時感到很冷。

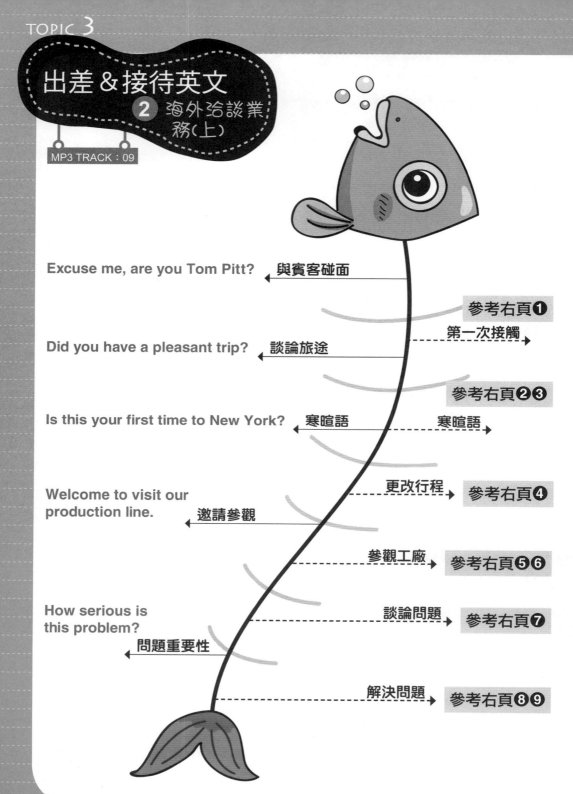

出差&接待英文
2 海外洽談業務(上)

MP3 TRACK：09

Excuse me, are you Tom Pitt?　與賓客碰面

參考右頁❶

第一次接觸

Did you have a pleasant trip?　談論旅途

參考右頁❷❸

Is this your first time to New York?　寒暄語　寒暄語

更改行程　參考右頁❹

Welcome to visit our production line.　邀請參觀

參觀工廠　參考右頁❺❻

How serious is this problem?　談論問題　參考右頁❼

問題重要性

解決問題　參考右頁❽❾

You may hear
海外洽談業務時，也許你會聽到⋯⋯

線上音檔

ⓐ 對不起，請問您是湯姆彼特嗎？　　Excuse me, are you Tom Pitt?

ⓑ 旅途還順利嗎？　　Did you have a pleasant trip?

ⓒ 這是您第一次到紐約嗎？　　Is this your first time to New York?

ⓓ 歡迎您來參觀我們的生產流程。　　Welcome to visit our production line.

ⓔ 這個問題有多嚴重？　　How serious is this problem?

You may want to say
海外洽談業務時，也許你會想說⋯⋯

❶ 我是香蕉海出版社的湯姆。　　This is Tom of Banana Sea Publishers. ...p.110

❷ 能見到你是我的榮幸。　　It's a great pleasure to meet you. ...p.110

❸ 這是我的名片。　　This is my business card. ...p.110

❹ 我恐怕無法準時赴約。　　I'm afraid I won't be able to make it to our appointment on time. ...p.111

❺ 我對新機型的效率印象深刻。　　I was impressed by the efficiency of the new machines. ...p.111

❻ 看來這裡的食品衛生狀況有待加強。　　It seems that you need to improve the food sanitation. ...p.112

❼ 這一批的貨品有一點色差。　　This set of goods is different from the others in the same color. ...p.112

❽ 我們會盡快解決這個問題。　　We'll solve this problem as soon as possible. ...p.113

❾ 我可以向你保證這樣的錯誤不會再發生。　　I can assure you that it won't happen again. ...p.114

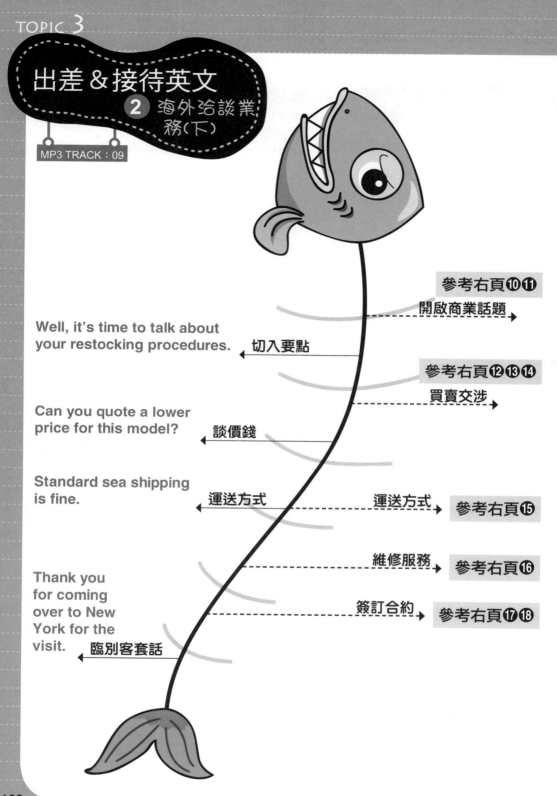

出差＆接待英文
2 海外洽談業務(下)

MP3 TRACK：09

參考右頁⓾⓫
開啟商業話題 ▶

Well, it's time to talk about your restocking procedures.
切入要點

參考右頁⓬⓭⓮
買賣交涉 ▶

Can you quote a lower price for this model?
談價錢

Standard sea shipping is fine.
運送方式　　　運送方式 ▶ 參考右頁⓯

維修服務 ▶ 參考右頁⓰

Thank you for coming over to New York for the visit.
臨別客套話　　　簽訂合約 ▶ 參考右頁⓱⓲

❶ 嗯，該來談談你們的補貨程序了。　Well, it's time to talk about your restocking procedures.

❷ 這個型號的價錢可以再低一些嗎？　Can you quote a lower price for this model?

❸ 一般的海運就可以了。　Standard sea shipping is fine.

❹ 謝謝您專程來到紐約與我們商談。　Thank you for coming over to New York for the visit.

You may want to say
海外洽談業務時，也許你會想說⋯⋯（續）

⑩ 我們可以進行下一個主題了嗎？　Shall we come to the next topic now? ...p.115

⑪ 你在電話裡提到要增加訂單的事。　You told me on the phone you want to increase the order. ...p.115

⑫ 你可以估個數量給我嗎？　Can you give me the estimated number?...p.116

⑬ 請看一下這張價目表。　Please have a look at the price list. ...p.117

⑭ 這個價格已經是最低價了。　This is already the rock-bottom price. ...p.117

⑮ 我們保證物品會在三十天內海運送達。　We can assure you that the goods will be delivered to you by sea within 30 days. ...p.118

⑯ 我們的經銷商會負責所有的維修事項。　Our distributors will be in charge of the maintenance. ...p.118

⑰ 成交！　It's a deal! ...p.119

⑱ 期待下次的見面。　I look forward to seeing you next time. ...p.119

❶ 我是香蕉海出版社的湯姆。

A: **This is Tom of Banana Sea Publishers.**
　我是香蕉海出版社的湯姆。
B: We have been waiting for you. 我們一直在等你。

❗ This is Tom of Banana Sea Publishers.
　我是湯姆，代表香蕉海出版社。
❗ I'm Jackson on behalf of Microsoft Company. 我是傑克遜，代表微軟公司。
　└ ★ on behalf of：代表

　We are agents of Microsoft Company. 我們是微軟公司的代理商。
　I'm Peter Anderson, Manager of Overseas Business Department of IT Investment
　Ltd. 我是彼得安德森，資訊技術有限公司海外業務部的經理。
　This is John Martin, engineer of the R&D Department.
　這是研究開發部的工程師，約翰馬丁。　★ R&D = Research and Development，研究與開發

❷ 能見到你是我的榮幸。

A: **It's a great pleasure to meet you.** 能見到你是我的榮幸。
B: Thank you for your continued support. 謝謝你們的一貫支持。

　I'm glad to do business with you. 很高興能和你們做生意。
　I am pleased / glad to see you here. 見到你非常高興。
❗ It's a great pleasure to meet you today. 今天能見到您非常榮幸。
❗ We've heard a lot about you. 我們久仰您的大名。
❗ It's very nice to see you in person. 能親自見到你很榮幸。

❸ 這是我的名片。

A: **This is my business card.** 這是我的名片。
B: Thank you. 謝謝。

❗ This is my business card. / Here's my business card. 這是我的名片。
　Could I have your business card? 你有名片嗎？

④ 我恐怕無法準時赴約。

A: **I'm afraid I won't be able to make it to our appointment on time.** 我恐怕無法準時赴約。

B: Well, let me check my schedule and see if we can meet next week.
嗯，讓我查一下我的行程表，看看我們下週是否能見面。

❗ Something urgent has come up. I'm going to have to reschedule.
突然有急事。我必須重新安排時間。

Could you move up my appointment from the 25th to the 20th?
可以將會面時間從 25 日提前到 20 日嗎？

I'm afraid I won't be able to make it to our appointment on time.
我恐怕無法準時赴約。

❗ Would you mind if we cancel our meeting tomorrow?
我們取消明天的會議您介意嗎？

I'd like to cancel my appointment with Mr. Chen.
我想取消與陳先生的會面。

⑤ 我對新機型的效率印象深刻。

A: What's your general impression, may I ask? 請問您對公司的印象如何？

B: **I was impressed by the efficiency of the new machines.**
我對新機型的效率印象深刻。

★ be impressed by：被⋯所感動

❗ I was impressed by the efficiency of the new machines.
我對新機型的效率印象深刻。

I was impressed. You have fine facilities and efficient people.
我印象深刻。你們有優良的設備以及高效率的員工。

❗ No one can match you as far as performance is concerned.
就工作表現而言，沒有別的廠商能與你們相比。

I'm impressed by your approach to business.
你們經營業務的方法給我留下了很深的印象。

I didn't know that the information technology in Taiwan had developed so fast these past few years. 我不知道台灣這幾年資訊技術發展的這麼快。

6 看來這裡的食品衛生狀況有待加強。

A: I'm interested to hear your feedback regarding our products.
　　我想聽聽您對我們產品的意見。
B: **It seems that you need to improve the food sanitation.**
　　看來這裡的食品衛生狀況有待加強。

❗ It seems that you need to improve the food sanitation.

★ improve：改進，改善　　★ sanitation：公共衛生，環境衛生

看來這裡的食品衛生狀況有待加強。

❗ Your product quality is terrible. 你們的產品品質很差。

Are you sure you'll be able to handle the quantities we talked about?
你確定你們能應付我們所談的數量嗎？

You had some problems with the price list. 你們公司在價目表上出了問題。

This will have to be sorted out before we can do business.
這必須經過整頓，我們才能做生意。

7 這一批的貨品有一點色差。

A: **This set of goods is different from the others in the same color.** 這一批的貨品有一點色差。
B: We apologize for our mistake. 我們對所造成的錯誤致上歉意。

This set of goods is different from the others in the same color.
這一批的貨品有一點色差。

I'm not sure whether the ordered goods are in conformity with the samples.
我不知道訂的貨是否能跟樣本的品質一樣好。★ in conformity with：一致，符合

The goods you sent us do not correspond with the samples we gave you.
你們給我的貨與我們送給你的樣品不符。★ correspond with：符合

❗ The goods we received are not what we ordered.
我們所收的貨不是我們訂購的商品。

Most of the vases we received are damaged. 我們收到的花瓶大多都破了。

❽ 我們會盡快解決這個問題。

★ lodge：提出（申訴、抗議等）

A: We are lodging a claim for the cotton shirts for inferior quality.

★ claim：索賠

我們要求對這批品質低劣的棉襯衫進行索賠。

B: **We'll solve this problem as soon as possible.**

我們會盡快解決這個問題。

We'll solve this problem as soon as possible. 我們會盡快解決這個問題。

We would like to agree on an out-of-court settlement. 我希望能庭外和解。

*out-of-court settlement 是「庭外和解」的意思。 ★ instruct：指示，吩咐

My home office has instructed me to do my best to remedy it.

我的總公司指示我盡力予以補救。

★ remedy：補救，補償

❗ We will consider compensating partially for your loss.

★ compensate：補償，賠償 ★ partially：部分地

我們會考慮對你們損失進行部分賠償。

I regret very much to get the news. 很遺憾聽到這個消息。

We'll check why the goods are underweight. 我們會調查為什麼貨物會重量不足。

❗ I'm sorry to hear the news, but why don't we figure out what's going on first?

很抱歉聽到這個消息，但為什麼我們不先搞清楚到底是怎麼回事呢？

This is totally due to our negligence in packing, for which we tender our deepest apologies.

★ negligence：疏忽，粗心 ★ tender：提出，提供

這完全是由於我們在包裝上的疏忽所致，為此我致以誠摯的歉意。

I'll send our inspector to check why the packages were broken and the food deteriorated.

★ inspector：檢查員

★ deteriorate：惡化，變質

我們會派檢驗員去調查為什麼包裝會破損和食物會變質。

I understand your anger about the loss. But I advise you to blame the right person.

我理解你對於損失的憤怒。但我建議你應該歸咎於負責的那個人。

In the spirit of good will and friendship, we agree to accept all your claims.

本著誠意和友好精神，我方同意接受您的全部索賠。

We know the problem was caused by us.

我們知道問題是由我方引起的。

We accept the claim and want to know what you want us to do.

我接受你的索賠，並希望瞭解你要我們怎麼做。

❾ 我可以向你保證這樣的錯誤不會再發生。

A: This machine doesn't work. 這台機器壞了。

B: **I can assure you that it won't happen again.**

我可以向你保證這樣的錯誤不會再發生。

★ assure：向…保證，擔保

I can assure you that it won't happen again.

我可以向你保證這樣的錯誤不會再發生。

❗ You can get refunds on any damaged or defective merchandise.

★ refund：退款　　　　★ defective：瑕疵的

任何損壞或瑕疵商品皆可退款。

What could we do to improve our service? 我們能做什麼來改善服務品質？

We can send you a shipping label so that you can return your purchase at no extra charge. 我們會寄給你一張出貨標籤，這樣你就可以免費退貨。

❗ In my opinion, it's evident that the damage must have occurred during transit.

依我看，損壞顯然是在運輸過程中造成的。

★ transit：運輸，運送

So far we haven't had any complaint of this kind. 至今我們沒有過這類投訴。

We regret the loss you have suffered and agree to compensate you with $500.

★ suffer：受損害

我們對你們遭受的損失深表歉意，同意向你們賠償五百美元。

❗ We are not in a position to accept your claim.

★ claim：索賠

我們不能接受你們提出的索賠要求。

If it doesn't work then we can give you a replacement or a refund.

如果不能用的話我們可以幫你換一台或退費。

I can guarantee that the new models won't have the similar problem.

我能保證新機型不會有類似的問題。

I can promise that this solution will work. 我可以承諾這個解決方案會有效。

★ solution：解決辦法

Is it alright if I double-check the data first? 我先把資料再檢查一遍可以嗎？

I will check with the production control department and get back to you immediately.

我會和生產控管部確認，並立刻回覆您。

⑩ 我們可以進行下一個主題了嗎？

A: **Shall we come to the next topic now?**
我們可以進行下一個主題了嗎？

B: If you'll allow me, let me go on to the question of improving sales performance. 如果允許的話，我想接著談談改善銷售的問題。

Shall we come to the next topic now? 我們可以進行下一個主題了嗎？

❗ Now let's turn to the next point. 現在讓我們轉到下一個話題。

Now let's move on to the next issue, which is how to compensate for the loss.
現在我們轉到下一個議題：如何賠償損失。

If you'll allow me, let me go on to the question of improving sales performance.
如果允許的話，我想接著談談改善銷售的問題。

❗ I'm glad we have arrived at a complete agreement on the clauses discussed so far. There remains only the question of packing.
很高興我們各項條款討論取得完全一致意見，剩下就只是包裝問題了。

❗ Next, we'd like to hear the comments by everyone present at the meeting.
接下來我想聽聽各位出席會議貴賓的意見。

Now I'd like to turn to the possible solutions.
現在我想把話題轉向可能採用的解決方法。

⑪ 你在電話裡提到要增加訂單的事。

A: **You told me on the phone you want to increase the order.**
你在電話裡提到要增加訂單的事。

B: Yes, let's discuss the matter in detail. 是的，讓我們討論一下細節。

Earlier, you mentioned that this kind of product is in great demand on the international market.
★ demand：需要，需求
先前你提到這種產品在國際市場上需求量很大。

Did you propose a change in the material of the packaging?
先前你建議改換包裝材料，是嗎？

❗ You told me on the phone you want to increase the order. Will you detail it a bit? 你在電話裡提到要增加訂單的事，能否詳細談談？
★ detail：詳述

115

庫存
數量

⑫ 你可以估個數量給我嗎?

A: I'm afraid we don't have enough products for you.
　恐怕我們沒有足夠的產品提供給你。
B: **Can you give me the estimated number?**
　你可以估個數量給我嗎? ★ estimate:估計,估量

Can you give me the estimated number? 你可以估個數量給我嗎?

What quantity are you looking at? 你要的數量是多少?

We don't have enough material on hand to take care of this.
我們現在手邊的存量不夠你的訂單。 ★ take care of:處理

❗ Yes, we have plenty on hand right now. 可以,我們目前有不少現貨。

❗ In that case, we wouldn't have it in stock. 如果是這樣,我們沒有現貨。
＊「有現貨的」是 in stock,「沒有現貨」是 out of stock。

I'm not sure we have that much on hand. 我不確定現在的存貨有沒有那麼多。

I checked our supply of that material you asked for.
我查過了庫存中你要的那種材料。

We were out of the part you needed. 你要的那種零件我們沒有貨了。

We're out of a lot of the items. 有好幾項都缺貨了。

❗ We're out of one item on your order. 你訂的貨裡有一項我們沒有了。

We can give you a better one at the same price.
我們可以給你更好的一種,價錢一樣。

We should be able to get that off to you right away. 我們應該馬上就可以出貨。

Can we substitute the J-123 for the J-113? 以 J-123 來替代 J-113,可以嗎?
　　　　　　　　　　　★ substitute for:代替

❗ Let's see what we can substitute. 我們來想看看有沒有什麼可以代替的。

Is there any chance that we can substitute this for that? 這個可不可能使用代替品呢?

We may have to back-order three items on this order.
這次訂的貨有三個項目必須要晚點才能交貨。

Can we substitute these things? 這幾項可以用替代品嗎?

We're out of the red adapters. 紅色的接頭沒貨了。
　　　★ adpater:轉接器

I'm not sure when that will be in stock. I will contact you as soon as we have it.
我不確定什麼時候會有貨。只要一進貨,我就會盡快和你聯絡。

⑬ 請看一下這張價目表。 談價錢

A: What is your best price on this item? 你們這個品項的特惠價是多少？
B: **Please have a look at the price list.** 請看一下這張價目表。

Please have a look at the price list. 請看一下這張價目表。

❗ This is the price list, but it serves as a guideline only.
這是價格表，但只供參考。

I'd like to give you our wholesale price if your order exceeds 9,000 sets.
如果你買九千台就可以給你批發價。 ★ exceeds：超過

常見的價格種類

wholesale price	批發價	retail price	零售價
unit price	單價	special price	特別價
discount price	折扣價	net price	淨價
total price	總價	best price	最優惠價

This is our latest price list. 這是我們的最新價格單。
Our standard unit price to wholesalers is 23.5. 我們給批發商的標準單價是 23.5。
★ wholesaler：批發商

⑭ 這個價格已經是最低價了。 對付殺價

A: Could you bring your price down a little bit? 你能再算便宜一點嗎？
B: **This is already the rock-bottom price.**
這個價格已經是最低價了。 ★ rock-bottom：（物價等）最低點

❗ Our price is the lowest. 我們的價格是最低的。
This is already the rock-bottom price. 這個價格已經是最低價了。
We've kept the price close to the cost of production.
這已經把價格壓到生產成本的邊緣了。
It is our lowest possible price. 這是我們的最低價。

❗ This is our best / final price. 這是最終的價格。

❗ I can assure you that our price is the most favorable.
我向你保證，我們的價格是最優惠的。

⑮ 我們保證物品會在三十天內海運送達。

A: When can you effect shipment? I'm terribly worried about late shipment.
你們什麼時候交貨？我非常擔心貨物遲交。

★ deliver by sea：海運

B: **We can assure you that the goods will be delivered to you by sea within 30 days.** 我們保證物品會在三十天內海運送達。

★ consignment：托運貨物

What are the details of this consignment? 交貨的具體要求是什麼呢？

Today let's discuss the mode of transportation of the steel you ordered.
今天我們就談談關於鋼材的運輸方式吧。

We can assure you that the goods will be delivered to you by sea within 30 days.
我們保證物品會在三十天內海運送達。

Shall we have a talk on the date of shipment this afternoon?
今天下午我們要不要談談裝運期的問題？

❗ The goods will arrive to you within 1 week. 貨品在一週內會送到貴公司。

❗ Which means do you prefer for this shipment, by air or by sea?
你覺得這批貨用海運還是空運好？

⑯ 我們的經銷商會負責所有的維修事項。

A: How about repairs after the warranty expires?
在保固期過後的修理怎麼辦呢？

B: **Our distributors will be in charge of the maintenance.**
我們的經銷商會負責所有的維修事項。

❗ We have an extended warranty available at extra cost.
對於額外價錢我們有較長的保證期限。

Our guarantee covers maintenance for both parts and labor.
我們的保證是包括更換零件和免費保養。

Our distributors will be in charge of the maintenance.
我們的經銷商會負責所有的維修事項。

❗ We exchange products under almost all circumstances.
在各種情形下我們都可更換產品。

⑰ 成交！

A: For a good start to our business relationship, we'll make it $11.4 per dozen.
為了我們的交易有個好的開始，就按每打 11.4 美元這個價錢吧。

B: **It's a deal!** Thank you very much for your cooperation.
成交！感謝你的合作。

❗ We're ready to place our order. 我們準備好下訂單了。
   ＊place an order 是「下訂單」的意思。

   I'll make a concession. 我讓步。
   └★ concession：讓步

❗ We accept your offer. 我們接受你們的報價。

   We have come to a full agreement. 我們完全達成了共識。

   I'd like to order your products. 我想訂購你們的產品。

   It seems that we have a deal. 看來我們成交了。

❗ It's a deal! Thank you very much for your cooperation.
成交！感謝你的合作。

⑱ 期待下次的見面。

A: I'm happy to do business with you. 和你們做生意很愉快。

B: **I look forward to seeing you next time.**
期待下次的見面。 └★ look forward to：期待，盼望

   I look forward to seeing you next time. 期待下次的見面。

❗ I look forward to working with you again.
希望能和你們再次合作。

❗ I look forward to another meeting with you. 期待下次的見面。

   I hope our cooperative relationship will continue.
希望我們的合作關係能持續下去。

   I hope you succeed in work. 希望你工作上取得成功。

   Indeed it's necessary to get together again. 確實很有必要再聚聚。

   I see more collaborative projects like this one in the future.
   └★ collaborative：合作的

我預見未來會有更多類似這樣的合作計畫。

出差＆接待英文
3 接待海外賓客（上）

MP3 TRACK：10

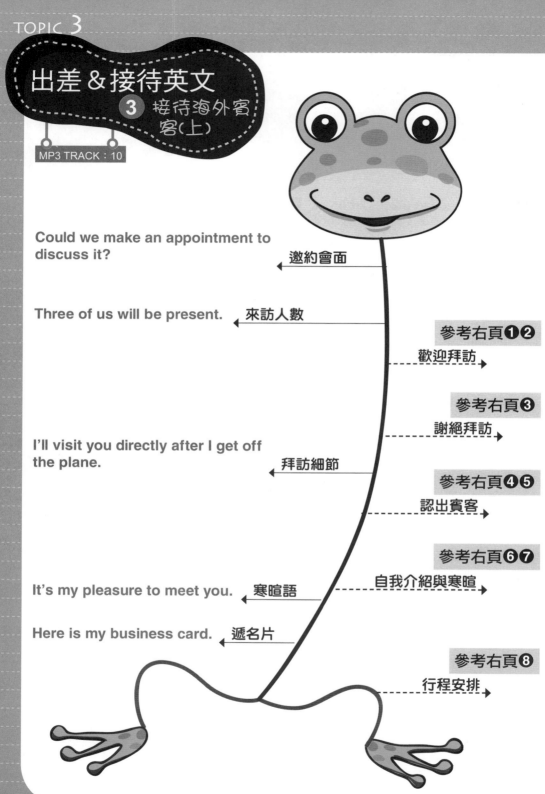

Could we make an appointment to discuss it?
← 邀約會面

Three of us will be present.
← 來訪人數

參考右頁❶❷
歡迎拜訪 →

參考右頁❸
謝絕拜訪 →

I'll visit you directly after I get off the plane.
← 拜訪細節

參考右頁❹❺
認出賓客 →

參考右頁❻❼
自我介紹與寒暄 →

It's my pleasure to meet you.
← 寒暄語

Here is my business card.
← 遞名片

參考右頁❽
行程安排 →

線上音檔

You may hear
接待海外賓客時，也許你會聽到……

ⓐ 我們可以約個時間談談這件事嗎？ Could we make an appointment to discuss it?

ⓑ 我們總共有三個人會出席。 Three of us will be present.

ⓒ 下飛機後我會直接前往拜訪。 I'll visit you directly after I get off the plane.

ⓓ 能夠認識您是我的榮幸。 It's my pleasure to meet you.

ⓔ 這是我的名片。 Here is my business card.

You may want to say
接待海外賓客時，也許你會想說……

❶ 希望我們能當面談一談。 I hope we can have a talk face to face. ...p.124

❷ 我們竭誠歡迎您的來訪。 We cordially welcome your visit. ...p.124

❸ 這段期間總經理不在國內。 Our general manager will be abroad during that period. ...p.125

❹ 請問您是李先生嗎？ Excuse me, are you Mr. Lee? ...p.125

❺ 這是您第一次到紐約嗎？ Is this your first time to New York? ...p.126

❻ 我是凱洛，MODE 雜誌的編輯。 I'm Carol, editor of MODE. ...p.126

❼ 很高興認識您。 I'm pleased to meet you. ...p.127

❽ 計程車會載您到飯店。 The taxi will drive you to the hotel. ...p.127

出差&接待英文
3 接待海外賓客(下)

MP3 TRACK：10

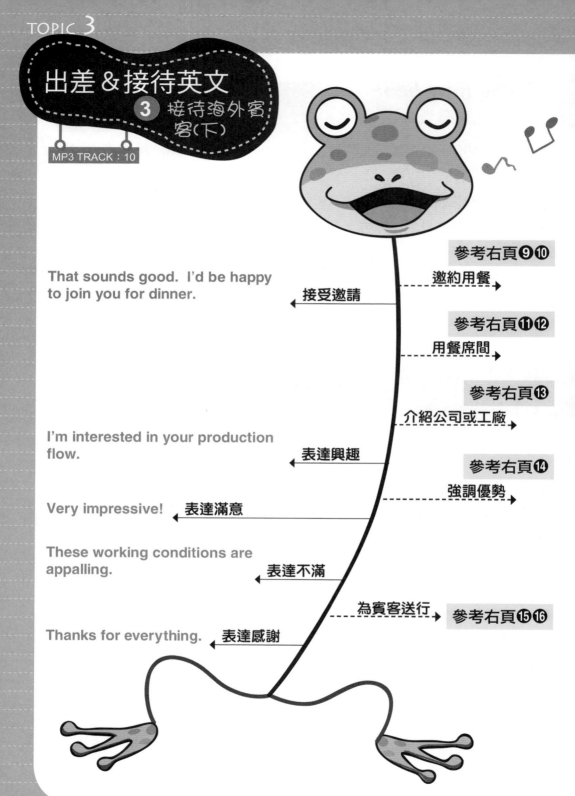

參考右頁 ❾ ❿
邀約用餐 ▶

That sounds good. I'd be happy to join you for dinner.
◀ 接受邀請

參考右頁 ⓫ ⓬
用餐席間 ▶

參考右頁 ⓭
介紹公司或工廠 ▶

I'm interested in your production flow.
◀ 表達興趣

參考右頁 ⓮
強調優勢 ▶

Very impressive!
◀ 表達滿意

These working conditions are appalling.
◀ 表達不滿

為賓客送行 ▶ 參考右頁 ⓯ ⓰

Thanks for everything.
◀ 表達感謝

You may hear
接待海外賓客時，也許你會聽到……（續）

f 聽起來不錯。很高興可以與你們一起用餐。 — That sounds good. I'd be happy to join you for dinner.

g 我對你們的生產流程很感興趣。 — I'm interested in your production flow.

h 真讓人印象深刻！ — Very impressive!

i 這樣的工作環境非常糟糕！ — These working conditions are appalling.

j 謝謝您所做的一切。 — Thanks for everything.

You may want to say
接待海外賓客時，也許你會想說……（續）

9 今天晚上我們在皇后餐廳用餐。 — Let's have dinner together at the Queen's restaurant tonight. ...p.128

10 晚上七點鐘您方便嗎？ — Will 7:00 p.m. be convenient for you? ...p.128

11 這裡的龍蝦很棒。 — The lobster is wonderful here. ...p.129

12 這些菜色還合您的胃口嗎？ — Is the meal to your liking? ...p.129

13 我們是螺絲製造的領導廠商。 — We are the leading manufacturers of screws. ...p.132

14 我們高度重視員工的工作安全。 — We attach great importance to the workers' safety. ...p.133

15 您想買些紀念品回去嗎？ — Do you want to bring some souvenirs back? ...p.133

16 謝謝您的專程來訪。 — Thank you for coming over. ...p.134

❶ 希望我們能當面談一談。

A: **I hope we can have a talk face to face.**
　希望我們能當面談一談。
B: How about some time next week?　下週找個時間怎麼樣？

❗ I'd like to arrange an appointment with you.　我想和你約個時間見面。

Can we talk about it in my office?　到我辦公室談談好嗎？

Can you (spare) some time for me next week?　下週你抽點時間給我好嗎？
　　　└─★ spare：分出，騰出

I hope we can have a talk face to face.　希望我們能當面談一談。

I hope you can come.　我希望你能來。

We'd better have a talk.　我們得找個時間談談。

Shall we meet this week?　這週我們見個面好嗎？

We ought to schedule a meeting.　我們應該安排時間開個會。

We should really get together to talk about the possibility of a joint venture.
我們真的應該碰個面談談共同投資的可能性。

❷ 我們竭誠歡迎您的來訪。

A: I would like to visit you tomorrow.　我明天想去拜訪您。
B: **We (cordially) welcome your visit.**　我們竭誠歡迎您的來訪。
　　　└─★ cordially：誠摯地

❗ We've been looking forward to your visit.　我們一直在等著您來。

I look forward to seeing you then.　我期待著到時候和你見面。

Great. I would also love to talk with you about it.
太好了。我也很願意與你談談這方面的問題。

I'll let my secretary contact you after I confirm my schedule.
我確認日程表後，會請祕書聯絡您。

❗ Let me check my calendar first.　我要先看看我的行程安排。

It's nice to finally meet you.　很高興終於與你見面了。

Could we meet and discuss the matter in a little more detail?
我們能不能碰個面，再討論一下這件事的細節？

❸ 這段期間總經理不在國內。

★ general manager：總經理

A: I'll come to your company to visit your general manager next week.
下週我想去貴公司拜訪你們的總經理。

★ abroad：在國外

B: I'm sorry, but **our general manager will be abroad during that period.** 不好意思，不過這段期間總經理不在國內。

I'm afraid Mr. Baker is away on business at the moment and he won't be back until the 6th of April. 貝克先生正在出差，四月六日才能回來。

Unfortunately, I have plans to travel around that time.
很抱歉，那個時間我已經安排了出差。

❗ My schedule is tight. 我的日程表很滿。

❗ I'm sorry, but I'm really tied up today. 抱歉，我今天的確抽不出時間。

Our general manager will be abroad during that period.
這段期間總經理不在國內。

❹ 請問您是李先生嗎？

A: Excuse me, **are you Mr. Lee?** 請問您是李先生嗎？

B: Yes, I am. And you must be Mr. Takeshita.
是的，我就是，你一定是竹下先生吧。

❗ Excuse me, are you Mr. Lee? 對不起，請問您是李先生嗎？

Pardon me. Are you Ralph Meyers from National Fixtures?
對不起，請問你是從國家裝置公司來的雷夫梅耶斯嗎？

❗ You must be Mr. Chen. 你一定是陳先生吧。

❗ I'm Dennis. I am here to meet you today.
我是丹尼斯，今天我到這裡來接你。

I'm Donald. We met last time you visited Taiwan.
我是唐納德，上次你來臺灣時我們見過面。

I'm Edwin. I'll show you to your hotel. 我是愛德溫，我會帶你去飯店。

It's great to see you again. 再次見到你真好。

⑤ 這是您第一次到紐約嗎？ 寒暄

A: **Is this your first time to New York?** How do you like it?
這是您第一次到紐約嗎？你對它印象如何？
B: I'm happy to be here. 來到這裡我很高興。

Is this your first time to New York? 這是您第一次到紐約嗎？

Have you ever been to Taiwan before? 您以前到過台灣嗎？

Did you have a good flight? 你旅途愉快嗎？

❗ How was your flight? 你的航班怎樣？

Did you get any sleep on the plane? 你在飛機上有睡著嗎？

Mr. Wagner, do you have a hotel reservation? 華格納先生，你有預訂旅館嗎？

❗ Did you have a good trip over? 你旅途還愉快吧？

You must be tired. 您一定累了。

It's a long way from Canada. Did you have a pleasant trip?
您千里迢迢從加拿大來。旅途愉快嗎？

We've been anticipating your arrival. 我們期盼您的到來。
└─ ★ anticipate：期望

I hope your trip was smooth. 希望您旅途還順利。

⑥ 我是凱洛，MODE 雜誌的編輯。 自我介紹

A: **I'm Carol, editor of MODE.** 我是凱洛，MODE 雜誌的編輯。
B: I'm pleased to meet you, Carol. 很高興見到你，凱洛。

❗ I'm Carol, editor of MODE. 我是凱洛。MODE 雜誌的編輯。

I'm Peter Anderson, Manager of Overseas Business Development of IT Investment
Ltd. 我是彼德安德森，資訊技術投資有限公司海外業務部經理。

My name is Frank, Office Manager from the Mayor's Office.
我是法蘭克，市長辦公室的辦公室主任。 └─ ★ mayor：市長

I am Emily, the project manager for your new product.
我是艾蜜莉，貴公司新產品的專案經理。

My name is Jason, a human resources specialist.
我叫傑森，人力資源專員。

126

❼ 很高興認識您。

A: Carol, this is Kathy Chen, our financial officer. Kathy, I'd like you to meet Carol Jacobs.
凱洛，這是凱西陳，我們財務主管。凱西，我想讓你見見凱洛傑柏斯。

B: **I'm pleased to meet you**, Kathy. 很高興認識你，凱西。

❶ I'm pleased to meet you. **很高興認識你。**

I'd like to welcome you all here. 歡迎你們的蒞臨。

Thank you for your visit. 感謝你們的光臨。

❶ Thank you for coming. **謝謝你的光臨。**

I am glad you could come. 對於你們的到來我感到非常高興。

❶ It's our pleasure and honor to see you here.
對於您的到來我們感到非常榮幸。

❽ 計程車會載您到飯店。

A: What do you think we can do now? 你覺得我們現在能做什麼？
B: **The taxi will drive you to the hotel.** 計程車會載您到飯店。

The taxi will drive you to the hotel. 計程車會載您到飯店。

Let's go to the station to get a train into downtown. 我們到火車站去搭車進市中心。

There's a shuttle bus we can take. 我們可以搭乘機場接駁車。

I've brought my car, so I can drive you to your hotel.
我有開車來，所以可以送你到飯店。

I've made a reservation at the hotel you stayed last time.
我已預訂了你上次住過的旅館。

We've booked a Western-style room for you. 我們已為你訂了一間西式的房間。

We'll go and enjoy Beijing Opera after dinner if you like.
★ Beijing Opera：京劇

如果你願意，晚飯後我們一起去欣賞京劇。

❶ I want to talk over the schedule with you. **我想和你們商量一下行程。**

⑨ 今天晚上我們在皇后餐廳用餐。

A: **Let's have dinner together at the Queen's restaurant tonight.** 今天晚上我們在皇后餐廳用餐。
B: Oh, I'd like to very much. 哦，我很想去。

Would you like Chinese food or western food? 你想吃中餐還是西餐？

❗ You must be hungry. Shall we get something to eat?
你一定餓了，我們吃點東西好嗎？

❗ What would you like to eat? 你想吃什麼呢？

Would you like to have some dinner? 你想吃飯嗎？

❗ Can I take you out to dinner? It'll be my treat.
我帶你出去吃飯好嗎？這次我請客。

Have you had breakfast yet? 你吃過早餐了嗎？

Let's get something at the hotel restaurant. 我們就到旅館餐廳吃點東西。

Let's have dinner together at the Queen's restaurant tonight.
今天晚上我們在皇后餐廳用餐。

Let's have dinner together in the evening of the 10th, after Mr. Grant's arrival.
10 號晚上，格蘭特先生來後，我們一起去吃晚飯。

If you're hungry, we can eat dinner now. 如果你餓了，我們現在就去吃飯。

We'd like to treat you to dinner. 我們想請你吃晚餐。

⑩ 晚上七點鐘您方便嗎？

A: **Will 7:00 p.m. be convenient for you?** 晚上七點鐘您方便嗎？
B: No problem. 沒問題。

Let's set an appropriate time to meet. 我們看看什麼時間見面合適。

❗ What time would suit you best? 幾點鐘合適呢？

Is four o'clock okay? 四點鐘怎麼樣？

Will 9:00 a.m. be convenient? 上午九點鐘方便嗎？

❗ When is it convenient for you? 什麼時候您方便呢？

Will 7:00 p.m. be convenient for you? 晚上七點鐘您方便嗎？

⑪ 這裡的龍蝦很棒。

A: **The lobster is wonderful here.** 這裡的龍蝦很棒。

B: I'm glad you like it. 我很高興你能喜歡。

How about a sweet and sour fish and a fried young pigeon with lettuce?

★ sweet and sour fish：糖醋魚

一個糖醋魚和一個萵苣炒乳鴿怎麼樣？

❗ I'd like to recommend you some dishes. **我想推薦您幾道菜。**

What about some vegetables or a salad? 再點點蔬菜或沙拉如何？

The Mongolian Barbecue is nice. 蒙古烤肉味道不錯。

Everything on the menu looks good. 菜單上的菜看起來都不錯。

It's a small steak and a lobster tail. 這是牛小排和龍蝦尾。

Would you like your meat rare, medium or well done?

肉要三分熟、五分熟還是全熟的？

＊點牛排時，服務生通常會詢問你需要幾分熟的牛排。三分熟是 rare，五分熟是 medium，全熟是 well done，至於七分熟則介於五分熟和全熟之間，是 medium well。

⑫ 這些菜色還合您的胃口嗎？

A: **Is the meal to your liking?** 這些菜色還合您的胃口嗎？

B: Yes, I like it very much. 是的，我非常喜歡。

You like vegetables. Please have more. 你喜歡蔬菜，請多吃點。

Anything more? Some more soup perhaps?

還要些別的什麼嗎？或許再多喝一些湯？

More beer perhaps? 或許再喝些啤酒？

Try some fish. 嚐嚐看魚吧！

Try some bread. It's warm. 嚐嚐麵包，趁熱吃。

❗ I'm glad you like it. **很高興你能喜歡。**

❗ Would you like anything else? **還要點什麼其他東西嗎？**

Help yourself to the salad. 沙拉請自己隨便用。

★ help yourself：請自己來、請動手

You must try that home-made apple pie. 你一定要嚐嚐手工蘋果派。

餐廳用餐常用語

人員

waiter	男服務生	waitress	女服務生
cashier	收銀員	chef	廚師

餐具

knife	刀子	fork	叉子
chopsticks	筷子	spoon	湯匙
plate	盤子	bowl	碗
saucer	碟子	cup	茶杯
glass	玻璃杯	toothpick	牙籤

上菜順序

beverage	飲料	appetizer	開胃菜
dish	主菜	dessert	甜食

食物種類

meat	肉類	vegetable	蔬菜
bread	麵包	salad	沙拉

烹調方法

boiling	煮	stewing	煲 / 燉
braising	燒 / 燜 / 燴	frying	煎
stir-frying	炒	deep-frying	炸
smoking	燻	roasting / barbecuing	烤
baking	烘	steaming	蒸

肉類

beef	牛肉	chicken	雞肉
pork	豬肉	mutton	羊肉
turkey	火雞肉	seafood	海鮮

海鮮類

crab	螃蟹	lobster	龍蝦
prawn	蝦子	salmon	鮭魚
sardine	沙丁魚	tuna	鮪魚
shark fin	魚翅	clam	蛤蠣
oyster	生蠔	squid	魷魚
octopus	章魚	abalone	鮑魚

蔬菜類

leek	韭菜	celery	芹菜
spinach	菠菜	lettuce	萵苣
romaine	美生菜	asparagus	蘆筍
hot pepper	辣椒	carrot	胡蘿蔔
cucumber	小黃瓜	tomato	番茄
pumpkin	南瓜	onion	洋蔥
eggplant	茄子	sweet pepper	甜椒
pea	豌豆	corn	玉米
garlic	蒜	green pepper	青椒
mushroom	蘑菇	cabbage	高麗菜
broccoli	花椰菜	scallion	蔥

形容味道、口感

sour	酸的	sweet	甜的
bitter	苦的	hot / spicy	辣的
salty	鹹的	soft / tender	軟的
hard	硬的	crispy	脆的
yummy / tasty / delicious	美味的		

介紹
工廠

A: Welcome to the factory. I'll show you around and explain the operation as we go along. As you know, **we are the leading manufacturers of screws.**

★ leading：領導的

歡迎你到我們工廠來。我陪你到處走走，邊走邊替您講解。如您所知，我們是螺絲製造的領導廠商。　★ manufacturer：廠商，製造公司

B: How much do you spend on advertising every year?
你們每年的廣告投資是多少？

★ stringent：嚴格的

Our production standards are very stringent. 我們的生產標準相當嚴格。

The quality control teams carefully monitor all the equipment.
品管團隊仔細監控所有的設備。　★ yield rate：生產率

Our Vietnam plant has a yield rate of half a million pieces per month.
我們越南廠的生產率是每個月五十萬件。

The output at this facility averages thirty units per hour.
這個工廠平均每小時出產三十件。　★ average：平均達到

We are the leading manufacturers of screws. 我們是螺絲製造的領導廠商。

❗ We've been in the optoelectronics industry for 20 years.
我們在光電產業有二十年的經驗。　★ optoelectronics：光電子學

Our company has been set up for more than 20 years.
我們公司成立有二十多年了。

Our hardware is very reliable. 我們的硬體非常可靠。

We are the leading exporters of meat in Japan. 我們是日本肉類的主要出口商。

We are a well-known lighting brand all over the country.
我們在全國的燈具市場上是非常知名的品牌。

Our corporation has been engaged in medicine for many years.
我們公司從事醫藥生產多年。　★ be engaged in：忙於，致力於

❗ We have an advantage over other companies in price.
我們與其他公司相比有價格優勢。

❗ Our goods are of first-class quality.
我們產品的品質是世界一流的。

Our ceramics are superior in quality to any other brand.
我們陶瓷的品質比其他品牌的陶瓷好得多。　★ reputation：聲望、信譽

We have been established for fifty years and our reputation is second to none.
我們成立都有五十年了，我們的口碑在業內是首屈一指的。　★ second to none：最好的

❹ 我們高度重視員工的工作安全。

A: How many employees do you have? 你們有多少雇員？

B: About 200. And **we attach great importance to the workers' safety.**
大約200人，而且我們高度重視員工的工作安全。

❗ We attach great importance to the workers' safety.
我們高度重視員工的工作安全。
＊attach great importance to 是「非常重視」、「著重於」、「認為…有重要意義」的意思。
This product is doing very well in foreign countries. 這種產品在國外很暢銷。

❗ Our product is competitive in the international market.
我們的產品在國際市場上具有競爭力。
The distinction of our product is its light weight. 我們產品的特點就是它很輕。
Our price is lower than the competitors.
我們的價格比競爭者低廉。── ★ competitors：競爭者
Our service, so far, has been very well-received by our customers.
到目前為止，顧客對我們的服務品質評價甚高。
One of the real pluses of this product is that it is of very high quality and of compact size. 這種產品的真正優點之一就是高品質和小體積。

❺ 您想買些紀念品回去嗎？

A: **Do you want to bring some souvenirs back?**
您想買些紀念品回去嗎？

B: Where can I get them? 在哪裡可以買到？

❗ Maybe you can get some souvenirs for the colleagues back at the office.
也許你可以帶些紀念品回去給你的同事。
There is a counter selling all kinds of souvenirs.
有個櫃檯出售各式各樣的紀念品。
You can buy this bag as a souvenir of your visit to London.
你可以買這個袋子作為訪問倫敦的紀念品。
Please accept this as a souvenir of our friendship.
請接受這個作為我們友誼的紀念品。

⑯ 謝謝您的專程來訪。 送行

A: It's very kind of you to see me off. I really had a very delightful stay here.
很感謝你為我送行。我真的在這裡過得很愉快。
B: **Thank you for coming over.** 謝謝您的專程來訪。

❗ Thank you for your cooperation. 謝謝你們的合作。

❗ It only remains for me to thank you for coming over.
最後感謝你們的到來。

I appreciate your cooperation on these matters. 謝謝你在這些方面的合作。

Your accommodating attitude and cooperation have been most valuable.
我們很看重你大方的態度和合作精神。

I'm very happy with the frank exchange of views.
我很高興我們能坦誠地交換意見。

It's been great talking with you. 跟你談話很高興。

Also need to know

與合作對象的交際應酬……

送禮給客戶。
I'll say thank you by giving you a small gift. 我要用一件小禮物向你表示謝意。
On behalf of everyone here, I'd like to present you with this gift.
我謹代表這裡所有的人,向您呈上這份禮物。

乾杯!
Let's celebrate our new partnership. 讓我們去慶祝一下我們的新合夥關係。
To your health and success in business. 祝你身體健康,生意興隆。

搶付帳。
Let me get it! 我來付錢。
I'll get the bill. 我來買單。
I insist it's my treat. 這一頓當然是我請,沒得商量。

在國外有突發狀況時……

重要物品遺失。

I can't find my baggage. 我找不到我的行李。

I lost my passport. 我的護照不見了。

My wallet is missing. 我的錢包不見了。

My key was lost. I need your help. 我的鑰匙不見了，需要你們幫我開門。

班機取消或延遲。

JAL Flight no.216 tomorrow morning is cancelled. 明天上午的日航 216 號班機取消了。

The storm held up our flight for 40 minutes.

那場暴風雨使我們的航班延誤了四十分鐘。

I regret to inform you that due to the late arrival of my flight, I won't be able to join the meeting.

很抱歉通知您，因航班延誤，我將無法參加會議。

身體不舒服。

I'm not feeling well. 我覺得身體不舒服。

I have a stomachache. 我胃痛。

I have got a bad cold. 我患了重感冒。

My throat is dry and sore. 我的喉嚨又乾又痛。

Please call an ambulance. 請叫救護車。

I have food poisoning. 我食物中毒了。

TOPIC 3

出差＆接待英文
④ 廠商參加商展（上）

MP3 TRACK：11

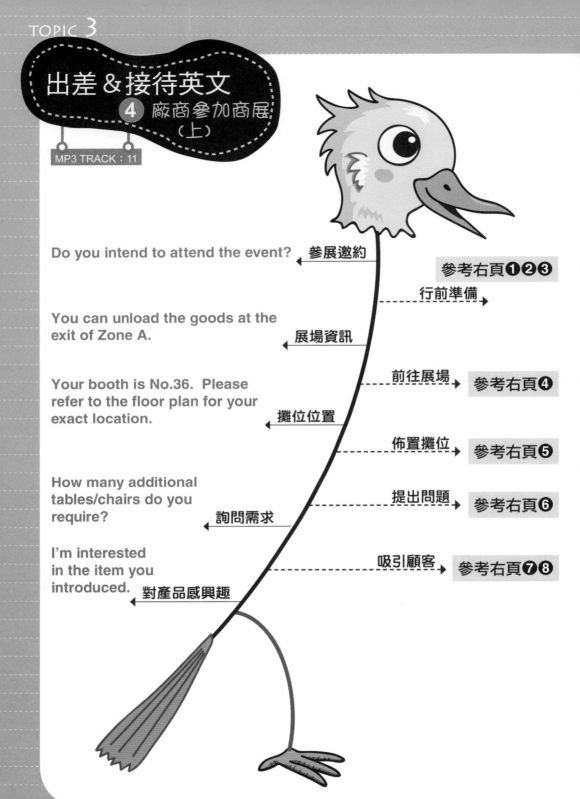

Do you intend to attend the event?　←　參展邀約

參考右頁❶❷❸

行前準備 →

You can unload the goods at the exit of Zone A.　←　展場資訊

前往展場 →　參考右頁❹

Your booth is No.36. Please refer to the floor plan for your exact location.　←　攤位位置

佈置攤位 →　參考右頁❺

How many additional tables/chairs do you require?　←　詢問需求

提出問題 →　參考右頁❻

I'm interested in the item you introduced.　←　對產品感興趣

吸引顧客 →　參考右頁❼❽

136

You may hear
參加商展時，也許你會聽到……

線上音檔

ⓐ 貴公司有意願參加這個活動嗎？ **Do you intend to attend the event?**

ⓑ 你們可以在 A 區出口處卸貨。 **You can unload the goods at the exit of Zone A.**

ⓒ 你們的攤位位於三十六號，請參 **Your booth is No.36. Please refer to** 照這份樓層平面圖。 **the floor plan for your exact location.**

ⓓ 你們還需要多幾張桌子 / 椅子？ **How many additional tables / chairs do you require?**

ⓔ 我對你介紹的這項產品很感興趣。 **I'm interested in the item you introduced.**

You may want to say
參加商展時，也許你會想說……

❶ 預計會有多少人參展？ **How many people are expected to attend the exhibition?** ...p.140

❷ 主辦單位會提供哪些器材？ **What facilities will the organizer provide?** ...p.140

❸ 我想要預訂一個攤位。 **I'd like to reserve a booth.** ...p.141

❹ 請問世貿中心要怎麼走？ **Can you tell me how to get to the World Trade Center?** ...p.141

❺ 把最受歡迎的產品放在顯眼 **Put the most popular products in a** 的位置。 **conspicuous place.** ...p.142

❻ 恐怕我們沒有足夠的電力。 **I'm afraid that we don't have enough power.** ...p.142

❼ 新一季的液晶顯示器有革命 **The LCD of the new season has gained** 性的進步。 **revolutionary progress.** ...p.143

❽ 請拿一份我們的產品目錄作 **Please take a copy of our catalogue for** 為參考。 **your reference.** ...p.143

出差＆接待英文
④ 廠商參加商展
（下）

MP3 TRACK：11

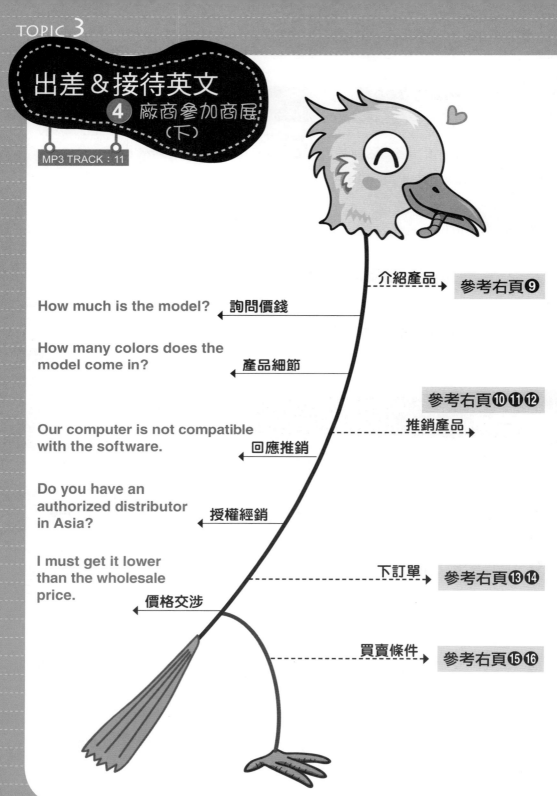

介紹產品 → 參考右頁❾

How much is the model? ← 詢問價錢

How many colors does the model come in? ← 產品細節

參考右頁❿⓫⓬

推銷產品 →

Our computer is not compatible with the software. ← 回應推銷

Do you have an authorized distributor in Asia? ← 授權經銷

I must get it lower than the wholesale price. 價格交涉 ←

下訂單 → 參考右頁⓭⓮

買賣條件 → 參考右頁⓯⓰

f 這個型號多少錢？　　　　How much is the model?

g 這個款式總共有幾種顏色？　How many colors does the model come in?

i 我們的電腦和這種軟體無法相容。　Our computer is not compatible with the software.

j 你們在亞洲地區是否有授權經銷商？　Do you have an authorized distributor in Asia?

k 我必須拿到低於批發價的價格。　I must get it lower than the wholesale price.

9 這本書連續六個月都在暢銷排行榜上。　The book has been on the bestseller list for 6 months. ...p.144

10 我們公司的省電燈泡非常受歡迎。　Our energy-saving bulbs are very popular. ...p.145

11 這種高電量電池是用最新科技生產的。　This high-powered battery is produced with the latest technology. ...p.145

12 新出的考試用書正符合你們的要求。　The newly published exam books can exactly meet your demand. ...p.146

13 我們預計下個月中才會有貨。　We expect the products to be available by the middle of next month. ...p.146

14 單價視你下訂的數量而有不同。　Our price depends on how large your order is. ...p.147

15 所有產品都享有一年的保固期。　We guarantee all our products for a year....p.148

16 我們有幾家長期合作的貨運公司。　We have cooperated for quite a long time with several shipping agents. ...p.148

❶ 預計會有多少人參展？

A: **How many people are expected to attend the exhibition?**
預計會有多少人參展？　　　★ registered：註冊的，登記過的

B: I've no exact number, but there are more than 1,000 registered members.
我沒有確切的數字，但是已經註冊的有一千多人。

❗ I need to get information on fees and payment policies.
我想瞭解相關費用和支付條件的資訊。

How many people are expected to attend the exhibition?
預計會有多少人參展？

Are there some networking events offered? 有沒有提供相互交流的活動？

Where can I download the brochure? 我在哪裡可以下載你們的宣傳冊？

Who should attend the exhibition? 適合參加展覽的人有哪些？

❗ What are the benefits of attendance? 參加此次展覽的好處有哪些？

❗ Can I get the conference schedule? 我可以看一下會議時間表嗎？

❷ 主辦單位會提供哪些器材？

A: **What facilities will the organizer provide?**
主辦單位會提供哪些器材？

B: It depends on what kind of registration fee you pay.
這要看你繳交的是哪一種註冊費。

★ logo：標誌，商標
Can we have our logo in the registration area? 我們可以在簽到處擺放我們的商標嗎？

What facilities will the organizer provide? 主辦單位會提供哪些器材？

❗ Could you provide the basic electricity usage? 基本的用電你們能提供嗎？
★ electricity：電力　★ usage：使用

❗ Are there any pens and writing pads for all attendees?
會給所有的與會者提供紙和筆嗎？　★ attendee：出席者

We'll have company giveaways distributed by a hostess at the entrance.
★ distribute：分發，分配

我們將會派一名女服務員在會場入口發放公司宣傳品。

What you need to prepare is the projector in the meeting room.
你們要準備的就是會議室裡的投影機。 ★ projector：投影機

140

❸ 我想要預訂一個攤位。 預訂攤位

A: Hello, this is Asia Electronic Exhibition and Information Company. Can I help you? 您好！這裡是亞細亞電子會展與資訊傳播有限公司。有什麼可以幫您的嗎？

B: This is ABC Company. **I'd like to reserve a booth.**
這裡是 ABC 公司。我想要預訂一個攤位。
└─ ★ booth：攤位

I'd like to reserve a booth. 我想要預訂一個攤位。

Do we need to pay a deposit in advance if we want to reserve extra space?
如果需要預訂額外的場地，我們需要提前繳納訂金嗎？

Where do I send the registration form? 我要把登記表寄到哪裡？

❶ How large is the space that costs $100? 一百美元的攤位有多大？

A hundred dollar booth is 5 by 6 meters. 五公尺長六公尺寬的攤位要一百美元。

When is the deadline for the registration? 登記的截止日期是什麼時候？

❶ Is there any way that we can have a spot somewhere in the middle?
我們有可能得到靠近中間的攤位嗎？└─ ★ spot：地點，現場

---

❹ 請問世貿中心要怎麼走？ 交通指引

A: **Can you tell me how to get to the World Trade Center?** 請問世貿中心要怎麼走？

B: You can take Bus 5. The driver will tell you where to get off.
你可以搭 5 號公車。司機會告訴你到哪裡下車。

❶ Can you tell me how to get to the World Trade Center?
請問世貿中心要怎麼走？

Excuse me, sir. Can you tell me where the Shanghai New International Expo Center is? 先生能不能告訴我上海新國際博覽中心在那裡？

Could you tell me how I can get to the International Exhibition Center?
請你告訴我去國際展覽中心怎麼走？

Would you please tell me where the Taipei International Convention Center is?
請告訴我台北國際會議中心在哪兒好嗎？

❺ 把最受歡迎的產品放在顯眼的位置。

A: How to set up the booth? 怎樣佈置展位？

B: **Put the most popular products in a conspicuous place.**
把最受歡迎的產品放在顯眼的位置。

❗ Put the most popular products in a conspicuous place.
把最受歡迎的產品放在顯眼的位置。 ★ conspicuous：明顯的，易看見的

❗ Put the catalogues on the desk. 把我們的產品目錄放在桌上。

We'll need to set aside some booth space for product presentations.
★ set aside：留出，撥出

我們需要挪出一些攤位空間做產品展示。

We need to design attractive and informative brochures.
我們需要設計吸引人且內容豐富的手冊。

Please nail two rectangular display shelves here. 在這裡釘兩個長方形展示架。

Here are two table cloths. Put the green one down first and then the white on top.
這裡是兩塊桌布。先把綠色的這塊放在下面，把白色的這塊放在上面。

❻ 恐怕我們沒有足夠的電力。

佈置問題

A: How's everything going? 事情都進展得怎麼樣了？

B: I've got some problems. **I'm afraid that we don't have enough power.** 我遇到一些問題。恐怕我們沒有足夠的電力。

❗ I'm afraid that we don't have enough power. 恐怕我們沒有足夠的電力。

❗ We need an additional electrical outlet for our video display.
為了我們的影像展示，我們還需要一個電源插座。 ★ outlet：電源插座

Please move these three computer display shelves a little more to the left, OK?
請把這三個電腦展示架向左稍微挪一下好嗎？ ★ cord：絕緣電線 ★ extension：延長

It's quite far away from the lights. The cord doesn't reach. We need an extension
cord. 這離燈太遠了，電線拉不到，我們需要一條延長線。

We have a real problem. You're setting up in my booth.
我們有一個問題。你正在佈置的是我的展位。

We don't have any pencils or draw ballots.
我們沒有抽獎用的鉛筆和摸獎券。 ★ ballots：投票用紙

A: What's the difference between the new product and its original version?
這一期的產品和原先的有什麼不同？

B: **The LCD of the new season has gained revolutionary progress.** 新一季的液晶顯示器有革命性的進步。

The LCD of the new season has gained revolutionary progress.
新一季的液晶顯示器有革命性的進步。

This new product is to the taste of the European market. 這種新產品在歐洲很受歡迎。

❗ This is our most recently developed product. **這是我們最近開發的產品。**

This is our latest model. It had a great success at the last exhibition in Paris.
這是我們的最新產品。在上次的巴黎展覽會上獲得很大的成功。

Have a look at this new product. It operates by the touch of a button. It is very flexible. 看一下這款新產品。按一下按鈕就能開始運作，非常靈活。

A: We really need more specific information about your technology.
我們很需要關於你們的技術更進一步的資訊。

B: **Please take a copy of our catalogue for your reference.**
請拿一份我們的產品目錄作為參考。

These are all complementary samples to give out. You may choose any one of them. 這些都是贈送的樣品，請您任意挑選。

❗ We can give you a sample of the product. **我們可以送一個產品樣品給你。**

❗ What about having a look at the sample first? **先看一下樣品怎麼樣？**

You can take some pamphlets for that machine. 你可以拿走那機器的樣本小冊子。

Here are our sales catalog and literature. 這是銷售目錄和說明書。

❗ This is a copy of our catalog. It will give you a good idea of the products we handle.
這是我們的產品目錄。你可以透過它瞭解到我們經營的產品。

★ handle：經營，經銷

Please take a copy of our catalogue for your reference.
請拿一份我們的產品目錄作為參考。

★ construction：構造

We have a video which shows the construction and operation of our latest products.
我們有影片展示我們最新產品的構造與運作方式。

★ operation：運作

143

A: What's the feedback of the readers?　讀者們的反應怎樣？
B: **The book has been on the bestseller list for 6 months.**
這本書連續六個月都在暢銷排行榜上。

The book has been on the bestseller list for 6 months.
這本書連續六個月都在暢銷排行榜上。

This novel was one of last year's best-selling titles.
這本小說是去年最暢銷的書之一。┐★ best-selling：最暢銷的

Our products command a good market both at home and abroad.
我們的產品在國內外市場上都很暢銷。

There's always a ready sale for high-quality furniture.　高檔傢俱總是很暢銷。

The newly developed cell phone sold like hot cakes in America.
那款新研發的手機在美國很暢銷。
＊sell like hot cakes 是「當紅炸子雞」、「十分暢銷」的意思。

❶ Our products are well-received overseas and are always in great demand.
我們的產品在海外十分暢銷，經常供不應求。

❶ This is this year's latest design. It's sold remarkably fast during the domestic trial sale period.　這是今年最新的產品。它在國內試賣期間銷路很好。

Our bicycles find a ready market in the eastern part of our country.
我們生產的腳踏車在我國東部地區銷路很好。

The product is now in great demand and we have on hand many enquiries from other countries.　這產品現在的需求很大，我們收到來自許多國家的產品詢問。

Digital cameras are enjoying fast sales these days.　數位相機最近很暢銷。

Cashmere coats always sell well.　喀什米爾外套一直都賣得不錯。

Our toys are well-received in the European market.
我們生產的玩具在歐洲市場很受歡迎。

❶ Our product is competitive in the international market.
我們的產品在國際市場上具有競爭力。

I can assure you that it'll stand out from the competition.　我敢保證它經得住競爭。
└─★ stand：經得起

❶ Our products have been sold in a number of areas abroad. They are very popular with the users there.
我們的產品已經銷往國外很多地區，並且受到當地使用者的歡迎。

144

⑩ 我們公司的省電燈泡非常受歡迎。

A: Can you introduce some new products to me?
你可以介紹一些新產品給我嗎？ ── ★ bulb：電燈泡

B: **Our energy-saving bulbs are very popular.**
我們公司的省電燈泡非常受歡迎。

Our energy-saving bulbs are very popular. 我們公司的省電燈泡非常受歡迎。

They've met with great favor home and abroad. 這些產品在國內外很受歡迎。

❗ All these articles are best-selling lines. 所有這些產品都是我們的暢銷貨。

Reliability is our strong point. 可靠性正是我們產品的優點。

❗ It has only been on the market for a few months, but it is already very popular. 這款產品上市才幾個月，但已經廣受歡迎。

⑪ 這種高電量電池是用最新科技生產的。　　強調品質

A: What are the product features? 你們這項產品的特色是什麼？

B: **This high-powered battery is produced with the latest technology.** 這種高電量電池是用最新科技生產的。

This high-powered battery is produced with the latest technology.
這種高電量電池是用最新科技生產的。

All products have to go through five checks in the whole process.
所有產品在整個生產過程中都要經過五層品質把關。

Almost every process is computerized. 幾乎每一道程序都是由電腦控制的。
── ★ computerize：使電腦化

❗ All products have to pass strict inspection before they go out.
所有產品出廠前必須要經過嚴格檢查。

No one can match us so far as quality is concerned.
就品質而言，沒有別人能和我們相比。

❗ Our company has strict quality control.
我們公司有嚴格的品質管控。

We always make sure that our products are of standard quality.
我們確信我們的產品達到標準。

⑫ 新出的考試用書正符合你們的要求。

A: **The newly published exam books can exactly meet your demand.** 新出的考試用書正符合你們的要求。

B: Let me have a look at them. 讓我看一下。

I'm sure you'll be pleased with this product. 我保證你會喜歡這種產品的。

I'm really positive that this product has all the features you have always wanted.
我相信這項產品能符合你的各種要求。

The newly published exam books can exactly meet your needs.
新出的考試用書正符合你們的要求。

I strongly recommend this product. 我強力推薦這種產品。

❗ If I were you, I'd choose this product. **如果我是你，我就選擇這種產品。**

❗ Would you be willing to consider our most recently developed product?
你願意考慮我們最新開發的產品嗎？

I think you will do well with this. 我想你很需要這樣東西。

⑬ 我們預計下個月中才會有貨。

A: How soon can you have your product ready?
你們多久才可以把產品準備好呢？

B: **We expect the products to be available by the middle of next month.** 我們預計下個月中才會有貨。

❗ We regret that the goods you inquire about are not available.
很遺憾，你們所詢問的貨物目前沒有現貨。

This is the maximum quantity we can supply at present.
這是目前我們所能提供的最大數量。

We expect the products to be available by the middle of next month.
我們預計下個月中才會有貨。

Our factories are fully committed to business for the third quarter.
我們工廠全心投入第三季的業務。

We certainly expect our product to be available by October 1.
我們當然期望產品可在十月一日前準備好。

⑭ 單價視你下訂的數量而有不同。

★ favorable：有利的

A: If your price is favorable, we can book an order right away.
如果你的價格優惠，我們可以馬上訂貨。

B: To a certain extent, **our price depends on how large your order is.** ★ extent：程度，範圍
在某種程度上，單價視你下訂的數量而有不同。

❗ To a certain extent, our price depends on how large your order is.
在某種程度上，單價視你下訂的數量而有不同。

❗ Could you tell us what quantity you require so that we can work out the ★ work out：制訂出
offer? 為了便於我們提出報價，能否請你談談你們的需求數量？

Will you please tell us the specifications, quantity and packing you want, so that we
can work out the offer ASAP? ★ specification：規格，明細單

請告訴我們貴公司對規格、數量及包裝的要求，以便我們盡快制定出報價。
＊ASAP 是 as soon as possible 的縮略語，「愈快愈好」的意思。

We may reconsider our price if your order is big enough.
如果你們訂貨數量大，價格我們可以再商量。

If you buy 40,000 units, then I can offer a unit price of $19.5.
如果你買四萬件，那麼我可以給你 19.5 元的單價。

★ solve：解決   ★ precise：精確的

I think the discount problem can be solved but you need to be more precise about
numbers. 優惠的問題是可以解決的，但你在購貨量上要更具體一些。

If you want more discount, you must make the order bigger.
如果你想要折扣大一點，那麼你的訂單也要大一些。

❗ If you accept this term, we will agree to make a reduction.
如果你同意這個條件，我們就願意降低價錢。 ★ guarantee：保證

Why don't you pay 20% of the invoice value as a guarantee in advance?
不如你預付 20% 的貨款做為保證吧。 ★ invoice：發票，發貨單

We accept a 10% discount for an order more than 5,000 sets.
訂單超過五千台的話就可以打九折。

You can be offered a discount of 10% if your order exceeds 5,000 sets.
如果你購買五千台以上，就可以得到 10% 的折扣。

⑮ 所有產品都享有一年的保固期。

A: How long is the warranty? 保固期有多長時間？

B: **We guarantee all our products for a year.**
所有產品都享有一年的保固期。

We have long-term quality assurance. 我們有長期的品質保證。

❗ We guarantee all our products for a year.
所有產品都享有一年的保固期。

Normal abrasion is beyond our responsibility. 正常的磨損我們不負責。
★ abrasion：磨損，磨耗

It requires periodical overhaul. 它應該定期檢修。
★ periodical：定期的　★ overhaul：徹底檢修

❗ We offer 5-year and 10-year guarantees. 我們有五年和十年的保固期。

We offer free repair service on equipment. 我們提供設備免費維修的服務。
★ repair：修理，修補

I've offered a 5-year warranty. 我已提供了五年的保固期。
★ warranty：保證書，擔保

⑯ 我們有幾家長期合作的貨運公司。

A: Risks of damage and pilferage still exist no matter where the goods are transshipped. 貨物損壞和被偷的風險依然存在，不管是在哪裡轉船。
★ transship：轉送，轉運　★ pilferage：竊盜

B: **We have cooperated for quite a long time with several shipping agents.** They will take excellent care of our goods.
我們有幾家長期合作的貨運公司，他們會好好照顧我們的貨物。

❗ The goods will arrive to you within 1 week. 我們會在一週之內送達。

We have cooperated for quite a long time with several shipping agents. They will take excellent care of our goods.
我們有幾家長期合作的貨運公司，他們會好好照顧我們的貨物。

Is there any possibility of transporting the goods by train from Berlin to Moscow?
有沒有可能用火車把貨從柏林運輸到莫斯科呢？

❗ What are the details of this consignment? 交貨的具體要求是什麼呢？
★ consignment：委託貨物

"Also need to know

遇到買家殺價時……

價錢沒辦法再更低了。
It is our lowest possible price. 這是我們的最低價。
I'm afraid that I can't take anything off the price. 我恐怕沒辦法再出得更低了。
We have quoted our most favorable price and are unable to entertain any counter offer.
這個報價為最優惠價，恕不能還價。

有條件的降低價錢。
If you accept this term, we will agree to make a reduction.
如果你同意這個條件，我們就願意降低價錢。
If you increase the number in the order, I can accept this price.
如果你可以增加數量，我可以同意這個價錢。

當下避談，之後再答覆。
Let me ask my boss and get back to you. 讓我問過老板再回覆你。
Give me some time, please. 請給我一些時間。
I'll contact you some other time. 改天我會跟你聯繫。
I need to consider that a bit. 我必須考慮一下。

出差＆接待英文
5 採購參觀商展（上）

MP3 TRACK：12

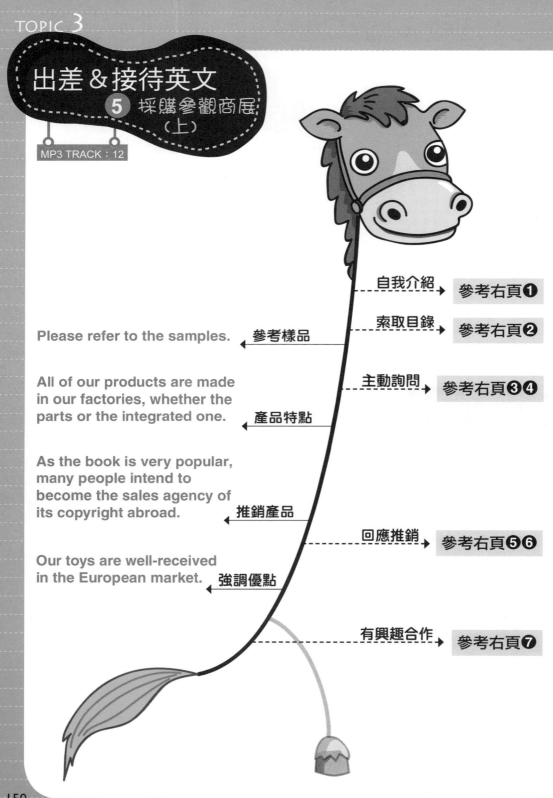

自我介紹 ➜ 參考右頁 **❶**

索取目錄 ➜ 參考右頁 **❷**

Please refer to the samples. ⬅ 參考樣品

All of our products are made in our factories, whether the parts or the integrated one.

主動詢問 ➜ 參考右頁 **❸❹**

產品特點 ⬅

As the book is very popular, many people intend to become the sales agency of its copyright abroad.

推銷產品 ⬅

回應推銷 ➜ 參考右頁 **❺❻**

Our toys are well-received in the European market. 強調優點 ⬅

有興趣合作 ➜ 參考右頁 **❼**

You may hear
參觀商展時，也許你會聽到……

ⓐ 請參考一下這些樣品。　Please refer to the samples.

ⓑ 我們的產品從零件到組裝都是原　All of our products are made in our
廠製作的。　factories, whether the parts or the
integrated one.

ⓒ 這本書很暢銷，有許多業者有意　As the book is very popular, many
願代理國外版權。　people intend to become the sales
agency of its copyright abroad.

ⓓ 我們生產的玩具在歐洲市場很受　Our toys are well-received in the
歡迎。　European market.

 You may want to say
參觀商展時，也許你會想說……

❶ 我們是一家在台灣專門代理　We are a sales agency for Italian leather
義大利皮件的公司。　products in Taiwan. ...p.154

❷ 請問能夠索取產品樣本嗎？　Could I have some samples of your
product? ...p.154

❸ 這項產品的銷售量如何？　What's the sales volume of the product? ...p.155

❹ 可以讓我們獨家代理這個商　Can we become the exclusive agent for
品嗎？　the product? ...p.155

❺ 我對你介紹的那項產品很有　I'm interested in the item you introduced.
興趣。　...p.156

❻ 我必須先跟我們老闆討論一下。　I must first talk to my boss. ...p.156

❼ 我正考慮購買貴公司製造的　I'm considering buying your toys. ...p.157
玩具。

出差&接待英文

5 採購參觀商展（下）

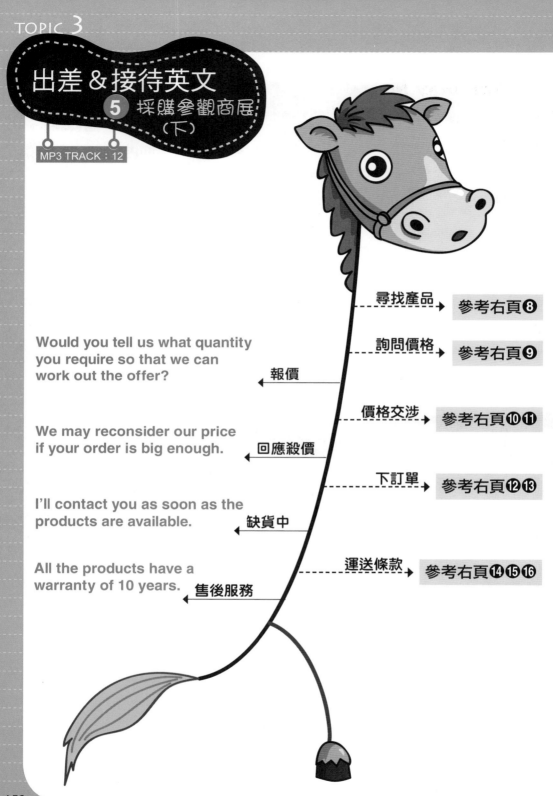

尋找產品 → 參考右頁 ❽

詢問價格 → 參考右頁 ❾

報價

Would you tell us what quantity you require so that we can work out the offer?

價格交涉 → 參考右頁 ❿ ⓫

回應殺價

We may reconsider our price if your order is big enough.

下訂單 → 參考右頁 ⓬ ⓭

缺貨中

I'll contact you as soon as the products are available.

運送條款 → 參考右頁 ⓮ ⓯ ⓰

售後服務

All the products have a warranty of 10 years.

You may hear
參觀商展時，也許你會聽到……（續）

ⓔ 為了便於我們提出報價，能否請你談談你們需求數量？

Would you tell us what quantity you require so that we can work out the offer?

ⓕ 如果你們訂貨數量大，價格我們還可以考慮。

We may reconsider our price if your order is big enough.

ⓖ 只要一進貨，我會盡快與您聯絡。

I'll contact you as soon as the products are available.

ⓗ 所有的產品都有十年的保固期。

All the products have a warranty of 10 years.

You may want to say
參觀商展時，也許你會想說……（續）

⑧ 我正在找某一款在日本熱賣的 mp3 播放器。

I'm looking for a kind of mp3 player that's well- received in Japan. ...p.157

⑨ 這本書的版權費用是多少？

How much is the copyright fee? ...p.158

⑩ 五十美元賣的話，我就買。

If you agree on 50 dollars, I'll buy it. ...p.158

⑪ 我必須拿到低於批發價的價格。

I must get it lower than the wholesale price. ...p.159

⑫ 我需要的量很大，你們的庫存量足夠嗎？

As we will place such a big order, do you have enough product in stock? ...p.159

⑬ 我要預訂一百件八號電纜線。

I'd like to order 100 No.8 cable conductors. ...p.160

⑭ 可以照我希望的方式運送嗎？

Can you deliver the goods as I expect? ...p.160

⑮ 最快何時可以送到？

When is the earliest we can get the goods? ...p.161

⑯ 運送時務必妥善包裝。

Please take the best care to pack the goods before delivery. ...p.161

自我
介紹

A: I've never heard of your company. 我以前從來沒聽說過你們公司。

B: **We are a sales agency for Italian leather products in Taiwan.** 我們是一家在台灣專門代理義大利皮件的公司。

We are a sales agency for Italian leather products in Taiwan.
我們是一家在台灣專門代理義大利皮件的公司。

Our company takes the leading position in the field of electronics.
我們公司在電子工業領域處於領先地位。

❗ Our company is one of the largest companies in this field.
我們公司是該領域中最大的公司之一。

▶ The major business of our company is to develop computer games.
我們的主要業務是開發電腦遊戲。

We started up our business in New York.
我們以紐約為基地展開經營。

▶ Our company has been set up for more than 40 years.
我們公司成立有四十年了。

Our company went on the market 5 years ago. 我們公司是五年前開始上市的。

主動
詢問

A: **Could I have some samples of your product?**
請問能夠索取產品樣本嗎？

B: Here are the samples of packing available now, you may have a look.
這是我們目前用的包裝樣品，你可以看一下。

Could I have some samples of your product? 請問能夠索取產品樣本嗎？

▶ Could I have your latest catalogues or something that tells me about your company? 可以給我一些貴公司最近的商品目錄或相關說明資料嗎？

Could I have some information about your scope of business?
我可以瞭解一下你們的業務範圍嗎？

▶ Would you tell me the main items you export? 你們主要出口什麼產品？

We really need more specific information about your technology.
我們需要關於你們技術更具體的資訊。

154

❸ 這項產品的銷售量如何？

A: **What's the sales volume of the product?**
這項產品的銷售量如何？ ★ volume：（銷售、生產）量
B: We have that right here in this report. 在這份報告書內就有。

❗ What's been the consumer reaction to your product?
消費者對你們的產品有過什麼反應？

How about feedback from your retailers and consumers?
你們的零售商和消費者的反映怎樣？ ★ retailer：零售商

What's the sales volume of the product? 這項產品的銷售量如何？

❗ What about the sale of the new product? 新產品的銷售情況怎樣？

Does this material sell well on the market? 這種材料在市場上暢銷嗎？

Is this style popular among young people? 這種款式年輕人喜歡嗎？

❹ 可以讓我們獨家代理這個商品嗎？

A: **Can we become the exclusive agent for the product?**
可以讓我們獨家代理這個商品嗎？
B: Yes, we would like to appoint you as our sole representative in your territory.
可以的。我們想要指定你為本地的獨家代理商。 ★ sole representative：獨家代理商

We're here to discuss the trademarks of your products.
我們來談談貴產品的商標一事。

Is this material copyrighted? 本資料享有版權嗎？

❗ Can we become the exclusive agent for the product?
可以讓我們獨家代理這個商品嗎？
＊sole agent 和 exclusive agent 都是「獨家代理商」的意思。
★ ingredient：原料
Do we have the right to change the ingredients? 我們有更改配方的權利嗎？

❗ Will those rights be exclusive? How long will they run?
這些是專有權利嗎？期限是多長？

Would it be possible for you to provide us with the details of your technology such
as related laboratory reports in the course of development?
能不能提供給我們你們詳細的技術，比如在研製過程中相關的實驗報告。

❺ 我對你介紹的那項產品很有興趣。

A: This is the price list, but it serves as a guideline only. Is there anything you are particularly interested in?
這是價格表，但只供參考。是否有你特別感興趣的商品？

B: **I'm interested in the item you introduced.**
我對你介紹的那項產品很有興趣。

❶ I'm interested in the item you introduced. 我對你介紹的那項產品很有興趣。

No one can match yours so far as quality is concerned.
就品質而言，沒有別人能和你們相比。

I think we may be able to work together in the future. 我想也許將來我們可以合作。

We are interested in discussing arts and crafts business with you.
我們希望能和你們談談工藝品方面的業務。

We are very much interested in your hardware.
我們對你們的五金器具很感興趣。 ★ hardware：五金器具

❶ I'd like to get some information about the new product.
我想瞭解一些新產品的資訊。

❶ We are very interested in acting as your agent.
我們非常有興趣做你們的代理。

❻ 我必須先跟我們老闆討論一下。

A: **I must first talk to my boss.** 我必須先跟我們老闆討論一下。
B: OK. We look forward to your reply. 好的，我們期待你的答覆。

★ off-hand：未經準備的

❶ I can't say for certain off-hand. 我還不能馬上說定。

I've got to report back to the head office. 我要回去向總部彙報情況。

❶ I must first talk to my boss. 我必須先跟我們老闆討論一下。

❶ I have to report to the head office. 我得報告總公司。

I have to negotiate with the head office.
我必須和總公司好好商量一下。

I'm afraid that the item isn't what we're looking for.
我恐怕這種產品不是我們所要找的。

❼ 我正考慮購買貴公司製造的玩具。

A: **I'm considering buying your toys.**
　我正考慮購買貴公司製造的玩具。
B: This is our most recently developed product. 這是我們最近開發的產品。

★ conclude with：締結

❗ I hope to conclude some business with you.
我希望能與貴公司建立貿易關係。

That sounds like the product we had in mind. 那種產品好像就是我們所想要的。

There is a high demand for cotton textiles in our market. May I have a copy of your catalogues?
　　　　　　　　　　　　　　　↳★ textiles：紡織品
我們的棉紡織品在市場上需求很大。我可以要一份你們的產品目錄嗎？

I'm considering buying your toys. 我正考慮購買貴公司製造的玩具。

❗ The purpose of my coming here is to inquire about the possibilities of establishing trade relations with your company.
我此行的目的正是想探詢與貴公司建立貿易關係的可能性。

❽ 我正在找某一款在日本熱賣的 mp3 播放器。

A: The quality of ours is as good as that of many other suppliers, while our prices are not so high as theirs. By the way, which items are you interested in? 我們的產品品質與其他供應商的一樣好，而我們的價格卻沒有他們高。對了，你對哪個產品感興趣？
B: **I'm looking for a kind of mp3 player that's well-received in Japan.** 我正在找某一款在日本熱賣的 mp3 播放器。

I'm responsible for buying the properties for the television series.
我負責採購電視連續劇所用的道具。

❗ I'm looking for a kind of mp3 player that's well-received in Japan.
我正在找某一款在日本熱賣的 mp3 播放器。
＊表示「受歡迎的」的單字或片語：be popular、be well-received、be hot、sell well、be best-seller。

I'm looking for information about current drug therapies. Can you provide me with recent reports or information?
　　　　　　　　　　　　　　　↳★ therapy：治療，療法
我在找關於目前藥物療法的資訊。你有最新的報告或資訊能夠提供給我嗎？

⑨ 這本書的版權費用是多少？

A: **How much is the copyright fee?** 這本書的版權費用是多少？
B: Please refer to the catalogue. 請參考這本目錄。

How much is the copyright fee? 這本書的版權費用是多少？
★ fee：費用

I hope to get a better discount. 我希望有一個更優惠的折扣。
We have to ask you to cut down your price again. 我們得要求再降一次價。
❗ Is this your lowest possible price? 這是你們的最低價嗎？
Would you review your price again? 你們還能再考慮一下價格嗎？

⑩ 五十美元賣的話，我就買。 開價

A: **If you agree on 50 dollars, I'll buy it.**
五十美元賣的話，我就買。
B: Okay, but that's the rock-bottom price. 好吧，不過那是最低價了。

❗ If you agree on 50 dollars, I'll buy it. 五十美元賣的話，我就買。
50 dollars, OK? 五十美元賣嗎？
I'd like to pay 50 dollars for it. 我願意用五十美元買下來。
Is it acceptable to sell it to us at 50 dollars? 五十美元賣給我們可以嗎？
❗ Would you please give us your wholesale price? 請給我們批發價。
Would you give me a discount? 你可以給我折扣嗎？
I hope to get a better discount. 我希望有一個更優惠的折扣。
Could you bring your price down a little bit? 你還能再便宜一些嗎？
❗ Other suppliers offer it at a much lower price than yours.
其他供應商比你的報價低多了。
Your competitor is offering better terms. 你們的對手提出的條件要更加優惠。
The Japanese quotation is lower. 日本的報價就比較低。
Your price is higher than those we got from elsewhere.
你們的價格比我們從別處得到的報價要高。

❶❶ 我必須拿到低於批發價的價格。

A: What's your expected price? 你期望的價格是多少？

B: **I must get it lower than the wholesale price.**
我必須拿到低於批發價的價格。

I must get it lower than the wholesale price. 我必須拿到低於批發價的價格。

! Could you offer me a 15% discount if we place an additional order of 100 sets?
如果我們再訂一百台，你是不是可以給我們一個八五折？

If we can come to the transaction soon, can you give me a discount?
如果我們能馬上成交，你可以給我打折嗎？

! We expect you to bring your price down another 5%.
我們希望現在的價格再降 5%。

★ margin：利潤，賺頭

I'm ordering in large quantities and I operate on small margins, you see?
我的訂單那麼大，但卻賺不了什麼錢，你也看出來了吧？

We're getting nowhere unless you make a concession.
除非你有所讓步，否則我們就做不成生意了。

! How about if we promise further business-volume sales?
如果我們承諾未來將進行大單交易呢？

❶❷ 我需要的量很大，你們的庫存量足夠嗎？

A: **As we will place such a big order, do you have enough product in stock?** 我需要的量很大，你們的庫存量足夠嗎？

B: We can supply any reasonable quantity of the merchandise.
對此商品，我們能提供任何適當的數量。

! Can you finish the orders in a month? 你能在一個月之內完成訂單嗎？

Can you supply them in different batches? 我們能不能分幾批供應呢？

As we will place such a big order, do you have enough product in stock?
我需要的量很大，你們的庫存量足夠嗎？

If you don't have the book in stock, can we order it?
如果這書你們沒有存貨，我們可以預訂嗎？

As you know, we have been in urgent need of these items as we have only a few in stock. 如您所知，由於本公司存貨已不多，所以對此項貨物的需求極為迫切。

⑬ 我要預訂一百件八號電纜線。

A: **I'd like to order 100 No.8 cable conductors.**
我要預訂一百件八號電纜線。
★ fill out：填寫
B: Great! I'll just fill out the purchase order and have you sign it.
好極了！我馬上寫訂購單並請你簽名。

I'd like to order 100 No.8 cable conductors. 我要預訂一百件八號電纜線。

❗ I'd like to go ahead and place an order for six hundred units.
那我想就先下六百件的訂單。

❗ We'd like to order your products. We'll send our official order today.
我們想訂購你們的產品。今天會送出正式的訂單。

I'm ready to place an order with you, but with one condition that the goods are confined to Finland.
我準備向你們訂貨，但是唯一的條件是，貨物只限賣給芬蘭的公司。

Can we make a change on order No.29734?
我們可以修改一下29734號訂單嗎？

⑭ 可以照我希望的方式運送嗎？

A: **Can you deliver the goods as I expect?**
可以照我希望的方式運送嗎？
B: No problem. 沒問題。

Can you deliver the goods as I expect? 可以照我希望的方式運送嗎？

Since there is no direct vessel, we have to arrange multi-model combined transport by rail and sea. 由於沒有直達船隻，我們只好安排海陸聯運。

It's not reasonable to have the goods unloaded at Hamburg.
把貨卸在漢堡不太合適。
★ unload：卸貨

❗ Do you want the shipment to be by air or by sea?
你覺得這批貨用海運還是空運好？

❗ I think air transportation is the best way to arrive at the destination safely and promptly. 我認為空運是最好的方法，能保證貨物安全快速抵達目的地。

⓯ 最快何時可以送到？

A: **When is the earliest we can get the goods?**
最快何時可以送到？
B: We can ensure the arrival on May 10. 五月十號我們可以送到。

❗ When is the earliest we can get the goods? 最快何時可以送到？

The order is so urgently required that we must ask you to (expedite) shipment.
這批貨物因迫切需要，請貴公司務必加速裝運。　★ expedite：迅速執行

I'm terribly worried about late shipment. 我非常擔心貨物遲交。

The order No.105 is so urgently required that we have to ask you to speed up the shipment. 第 105 號訂單所訂貨物我們要急用，請你們加快貨運速度。

❗ Can you advance the time of delivery? 你們能把交貨期提前嗎？

❗ A timely delivery means a lot to us. 及時交貨對我們很重要。

Time of delivery is a matter of great importance to us.
交貨時間對我們來說是很重要的。

Can't you find some way to convince your producers for an earlier delivery?
你不能想些辦法說服廠家提前一些時候交貨嗎？

⓰ 運送時務必妥善包裝。

A: **Please take the best care to pack the goods before delivery.** 運送時務必妥善包裝。
B: Let's get down to the packing details. 讓我們談談包裝的細節吧。

❗ Please take the best care to pack the goods before delivery.
運送時務必妥善包裝。

Packing in strong wooden cases is essential. 用堅固的木箱包裝是必要的。

Cases must be (battened), nailed and secured with metal straps all over.
木箱必須用板條釘牢，四周用金屬帶固定。　★ batten：在…釘扣板

❗ All cargo is required to be marked and numbered on the outside.
所有的貨物都必須在外包裝上進行標注和標序號。　★ consecutively：連續地

All crates are to be marked as usual, but please number them (consecutively) from No.1 to No. 5. 所有板條箱都依照往例標注，但請按照一到五的順序標明。

會議英文

1 主導會議（上）

MP3 TRACK：13

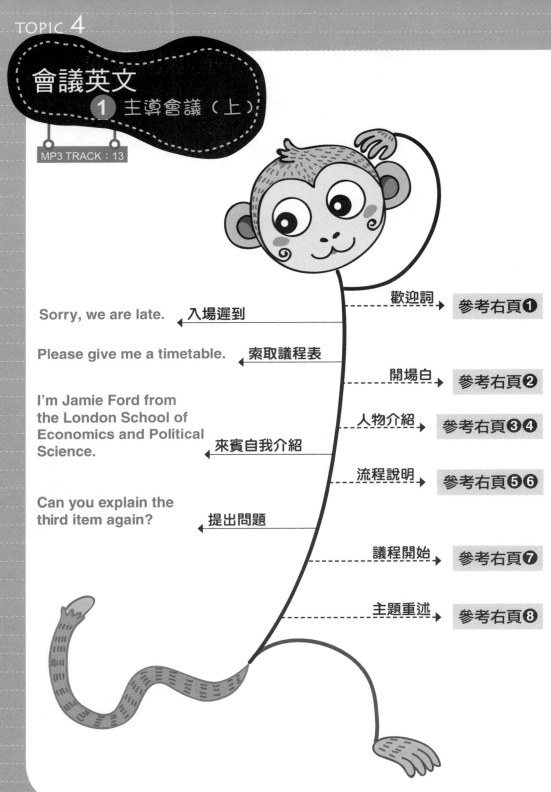

Sorry, we are late.　　入場遲到

Please give me a timetable.　　索取議程表

I'm Jamie Ford from the London School of Economics and Political Science.　　來賓自我介紹

Can you explain the third item again?　　提出問題

歡迎詞 → 參考右頁 ❶

開場白 → 參考右頁 ❷

人物介紹 → 參考右頁 ❸❹

流程說明 → 參考右頁 ❺❻

議程開始 → 參考右頁 ❼

主題重述 → 參考右頁 ❽

You may hear
主導會議時，也許你會聽到……

ⓐ 不好意思，我們遲到了。　Sorry, we are late.

ⓑ 請給我一份議程表。　Please give me a timetable.

ⓒ 我是來自倫敦政經學院的傑米　I'm Jamie Ford from the London School
福特。　of Economics and Political Science.

ⓓ 你可以再解釋一次第三點嗎？　Can you explain the third item again?

 You may want to say
主導會議時，也許你會想說……

❶ 感謝各位的出席。　Thanks for your participation.　...p.166

❷ 今天的主題是新產品開發研究　Our subject today is the research report
報告。　on new product development.　...p.166

❸ 首先要感謝亞太地區總裁伯威　At first, I'd like to thank Mr. Powell,
爾先生的前來。　president of the Asia Pacific region.　...p.167

❹ 主要演講人瓊斯先生是本開發　Today's keynote speaker Mr. Jones is the
專案的總召。　executive director of the development
　project.　...p.167

❺ 請翻到議程的部份，今天的會　Please turn to the agenda. Today's
議歷時九十分鐘。　meeting will last 90 minutes.　...p.168

❻ 依照議程，我們會在兩點時休　We'll take a 15-minute break at two
息十五分鐘。　o'clock according to the agenda.　...p.168

❼ 我們從財務狀況說起。　We'll start with our financial status. ...p.169

❽ 如我先前所說，我們的產品必　As I said, our products should be more
須更多元化。　diversified.　...p.169

會議英文
① 主導會議（下）

MP3 TRACK：13

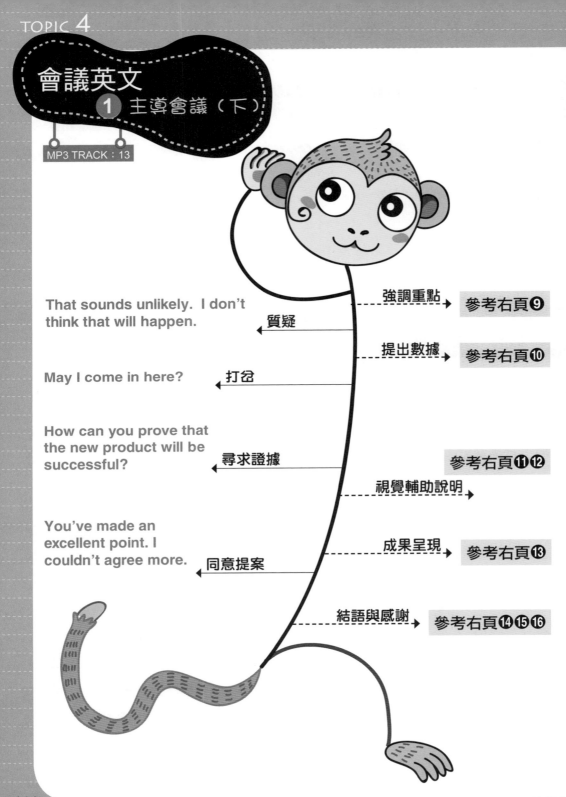

That sounds unlikely. I don't think that will happen.　質疑

強調重點　→　參考右頁❾

提出數據　→　參考右頁❿

May I come in here?　打岔

How can you prove that the new product will be successful?　尋求證據

參考右頁⓫⓬

視覺輔助說明　→

成果呈現　→　參考右頁⓭

You've made an excellent point. I couldn't agree more.　同意提案

結語與感謝　→　參考右頁⓮⓯⓰

ℯ 那聽起來不太可能，我不認為
會發生。

That sounds unlikely. I don't think that
will happen.

f 我可以打個岔嗎？

May I come in here?

g 你如何證明新產品會成功？

How can you prove that the new product
will be successful?

h 你說得非常好，我非常同意。

You've made an excellent point. I
couldn't agree more.

You may want to say
主導會議時，也許你會想說……（續）

❾ 我再強調一次，新款電冰箱可
節省電力達 30%。

Let me emphasize again. The new model
of fridge can save power by as much as
30 percent. ...p.170

❿ 你們可以看到，這項新產品在
美國地區的銷量很好。

You can see that the new product sells
well in the U.S. ...p.171

⓫ 讓我們來看看下一張投影片。

Let's go to the next slide. ...p.171

⓬ 這張圖表上的數據可顯示每個
月的生產成本。

From the chart, we can see the monthly
production cost. ...p.172

⓭ 這項商品會完全改變人們對化
學纖維的成見。

The product will completely change
people's prejudice against chemical
fiber. ...p.173

⓮ 總而言之，我認為這個計劃將
會非常成功。

In conclusion, I think the proposal is very
successful. ...p.173

⓯ 有問題儘管提。

Don't hesitate to ask questions. ...p.174

⓰ 謝謝各位今天的蒞臨指教。

Thanks for your participation. ...p.174

① 感謝各位的出席。

A: Hello, everyone. **Thanks for your participation.** If we are all here, let's get started.
大家好。感謝各位的出席。如果大家都到齊了，會議現在就開始。
B: Ok. Let's start the meeting. 好的，會議現在開始。

! Thank you all for attending. / Thanks for your participation. 感謝各位的出席。
Welcome to our meeting. 歡迎出席此次會議。
Thanks for your participation. 謝謝各位的出席。

! I would like to express my welcome to all of you. 歡迎大家的到來。
I would like to express my welcome to all the participants here. 歡迎各位與會者。

② 今天的主題是新產品開發研究報告。

A: What is our main aim today? ★ aim：目標，目的
我們今天會議的主要目標是什麼？
B: **Our subject today is the research report on new product development.** 今天的主題是新產品開發研究報告。

! Perhaps we'd better get started / get down to business.
會議現在正式開始。
There are a couple of issues we can work on. 我們需要討論這些議題。

! Let me tell you what I believe to be the main issues.
我來說一下今天的主要議題。
Our subject today is the research report on new product development.
今天的主題是新產品開發研究報告。
We're here today to talk about our big proposal of the "Solar City."
我們今天到這兒是為了談論一下我們「太陽城」的大計畫。
Today we have to decide on the distribution in the local market.
我們今天必須敲定在本地市場的分銷事宜。 ★ distribution：分發，分配

★ promote：宣傳，推銷
! I've called this meeting in order to discuss how to promote the sales of our new product. 我今天召開這個會議的目的是討論如何促銷我們的新產品。
Let me bring your attention to the main issues. 讓我們開始關注主要議題。

感謝
貴賓

A: Thank you all for attending. 感謝各位的出席。

B: **At first, I'd like to thank Mr. Powell, president of the Asia Pacific region.** 首先要感謝亞太地區總裁伯威爾先生的前來。

At first, I'd like to thank Mr. Powell, president of the Asia Pacific region.
首先要感謝亞太地區總裁伯威爾先生的前來。

Please join me in welcoming Mr. Robert. 讓我們一起歡迎羅伯特先生的到來。

❗ We're pleased to welcome Mr. Henry. **我們很榮幸地歡迎亨利先生。**

I'd like to extend a warm welcome to Miss Li. 我想熱烈歡迎李小姐。

It's a pleasure to welcome Mr. White. 很榮幸地歡迎懷特先生。

❗ Let's welcome Mr. Smith. **讓我們一起歡迎史密斯先生。**

人物
介紹

A: **Today's keynote speaker Mr. Jones is the executive director of the development project.**
主要演講人瓊斯先生是本開發專案的總召。

B: Nice to meet you. I've heard a lot about you. 很高興認識你,久仰大名。

❗ It is my honor to introduce today's keynote speaker, Mr. Black.

★ keynote speaker:主講人

我非常榮幸地介紹今天主要發言人,布萊克先生。

Today's keynote speaker Mr. Jones is the executive director of the development project. 主要演講人瓊斯先生是本開發專案的總召。

This is Val, the new director of our Export Department.
這是沃爾,我們出口部的新總監。★ Export Department:出口部門

❗ Let's welcome Mr. Smith to say something about this issue.
讓我們歡迎史密斯先生來談談這個問題吧。

Mr. Jones has kindly agreed to give us a report on the technology transfer.
瓊斯先生已經答應為我們做一個有關技術轉讓的報告。

Tom will lead point 1, Maggie point 2, and Angie point 3.
湯姆將帶領大家進行第一點的討論,瑪姬第二點,安姬第三點。

⑤ 請翻到議程的部份，今天的會議歷時九十分鐘。 瀏覽要點

A: All right, I think it's about time we get started. 好吧，我們該開始會議了。
B: **Please turn to the agenda. Today's meeting will last 90 minutes.** 請翻到議程的部份。今天的會議歷時九十分鐘。

To begin with, I'd like to quickly go through the minutes of our last meeting.
首先，讓我先看一下上次的會議紀錄。

❗ Have you all received a copy of the agenda?
你們都拿到一份會議議程了吧？

Please turn to the agenda. Today's meeting will last 90 minutes.
請翻到議程的部份。今天的會議歷時九十分鐘。

There are 3 issues on the agenda. 今天的議程主要有三個事項。

Skip item 1 and move on to item 3. 我們略過第一項和第二項直接討論第三項。

❗ Please turn to page one of the agenda. **請大家翻到議程的第一頁。**

⑥ 依照議程，我們會在兩點時休息十五分鐘。 控制時間

A: When shall we have a break? 我們什麼時候能夠休息？
B: **We'll take a 15-minute break at two o'clock according to the agenda.** 依照議程，我們會在兩點時休息十五分鐘。

❗ We've scheduled one and a half hours for the meeting.
根據我們的安排，這場會議歷時一個半小時。

We'll take a 15-minute break at two o'clock according to the agenda.
依照議程，我們會在兩點時休息十五分鐘。

Let's take a short break at eight. 讓我們八點鐘時休息幾分鐘。

Let's take a rest and get something to drink. 大家休息一下喝點什麼吧。

❗ Let's take a short break. **稍微休息一下吧。**

It's lunch break before 1 o'clock. 一點之前安排的是午休。

Let's dismiss and return in two hours. 現在休會，兩個小時後回來繼續。
★ dismiss：解散

❗ There will be fifteen minutes for each item. **每個項目歷時十五分鐘。**

We will first hear a short report on each point, followed by a discussion of the new company regulations. 我們先聽各要點的簡報，然後就公司新制度進行討論。

168

❼ 我們從財務狀況說起。 開頭

A: Mr. Brown, can we have your report now?
布朗先生，你的報告可以開始了嗎？
B: **We'll start with our financial status.** 我們從財務狀況說起。

First, I'd like Mr. Hunter to briefly introduce the situation.
首先，我想請亨特先生簡要地介紹一下形勢。

❗ We'll start with our financial status. **我們從財務狀況說起。**

Why don't we start with the business mode? 我們先從討論商業模式開始吧？

First let me bring your attention to the market size in East Asia.
首先讓我來談一下東亞的市場規模。

❗ We'll, let me bring your attention to what I see as the main issues.
首先，容我拋磚引玉一下，講講我對主要議題的看法。

❽ 如我先前所說，我們的產品必須更多元化。 重述

A: **As I said, our products should be more diversified.**
如我先前所說，我們的產品必須更多元化。
★ diversify：多樣化
B: You can say that again. 你說得太對了。
★ you can say that again = I couldn't agree more，是「我再同意不過了，你說的沒錯。」的意思。

As I said, our products should be more diversified.
如我先前所說，我們的產品必須更多元化。

I said just now that competition could be very sharp.
我剛剛說競爭可能是極其激烈的。
★ sharp：急劇的，激烈的

❗ Earlier, I mentioned that this kind of product is in great demand in the international market. **先前我提到這種產品在國際市場上需求量很大。**

Correct me if I am wrong, but weren't you suggesting that we put these words down in the contract as a separate clause?
★ clause：（文件的）條款

如果我說的不對請指正，不過你剛剛是否建議這些文字在合約中另列條款？

❗ As I said just now, any money spent now would give you greater savings in the long run. **就像我剛才說的那樣，從長遠看，今天花費的錢會為你以後節省更多的錢。**

❾ 我再強調一次，新款電冰箱可節省電力達 30%。

> A: **Let me emphasize again. The new model of fridge can save power by as much as 30 percent.**
> 我再強調一次，新款電冰箱可節省電力達 30%。
> B: I get your point. 我明白你的意思。

Let me emphasize again. The new model of fridge can save power by as much as 30 percent. 我再強調一次，新款電冰箱可節省電力達 30%。

I must stress that the goods were strictly inspected before shipment with your representative on the spot.
我必須強調，貨物裝船前經過嚴格檢驗，而且你們的代表也在場。

！ Let me emphasize how necessary it is to abide by the contract.
我要強調，遵守合約是十分必要的。　　★ abide by：遵守（堅持）

I can't stress enough the disastrous consequences of breach of contract.
　　★ disastrous：災難性的，悲慘的　　★ breach：裂口，違背

我必須強調，違約會帶來嚴重後果。

And last but not least, there is the question of adequate funding.
最後同樣重要的是要有足夠的資金的問題。

！ We cannot emphasize the importance of good faith too much.
再怎麼強調誠信原則的重要性也不為過。
＊cannot~too much 是「再…也不為過」的意思。

What we really need is a new marketing team in North America to help us launch our products there.
現在我們最需要的是，在北美成立一個行銷團隊，以幫助我們發展新產品。

What we really need are leaders who can motivate and lead our teams to become more productive.
我們最需要的是，能夠激勵以及領導我們團隊的領導者使我們變得更有生產力。

I would like to emphasize that we are aiming for generating new business in the BRICs.
我想要強調，我們正致力於在金磚四國拓展生意。

＊BRICs：金磚四國是指巴西、俄羅斯、印度及中國四個有希望在幾十年內取代七大工業國組織成為世界最大經濟體的國家。這個簡稱來自這四個國家的英文國名開頭字母「BRICs」（Brazil、Russia、India、China）的諧音（意指「磚頭」）。

170

⑩ 你們可以看到，這項新產品在美國地區的銷量很好。

A: Are our new products well-received in international markets?
我們的新產品在國際市場受歡迎嗎？
B: **You can see that the new product sells well in the U.S.**
你們可以看到，這項新產品在美國地區的銷量很好。

You can see that the new product sells well in the U.S.
你們可以看到，這項新產品在美國地區的銷量很好。

❶ Based on past performance, we would normally pick up 40% of this market.
根據以往的業績表現，我們可以佔據百分之四十的市場。

22% of our revenue now comes from there, compared to 9% just 3 years ago.
我們百分之二十二的收入來源於此，而三年前這一部分只占百分之九。

You'll notice from this trend chart that the volume of business in this market is projected to increase by 60% over the next 5 years. 從這張趨勢圖中大家可以注意到，在未來五年內這個市場的業務量預估將會增加百分之六十。

❶ Over the past 3 years, our business in Asia has grown by leaps and bounds.
在過去的三年中，我們在亞洲的業務猛增。
⌐ ★ by leaps and bounds：
  飛快地（突飛猛進地）

Judging from the graph, you can see a marked trend upward on the Japanese stock exchange. 依照這張圖表，你們可以看出日本股市明顯地上漲。

⑪ 讓我們來看看下一張投影片。

A: Let's move on to the next item. 讓我們開始下一個議題。
B: **Let's go to the next slide.** 讓我們來看看下一張投影片。

❶ Let's go to the next slide. 讓我們來看看下一張投影片。
Now, I wonder if you'll direct your attention to the screen. 現在請大家看螢幕。
⌐ ★ direct：將（注意力）指向…

This is the photo of the new site for our factory. 這是我們新廠址的照片。
Please pay attention to the right side of the picture. 請注意這張圖片的右方。
⌐ ★ pay attention to：關心，注意

❶ The next picture can show you the characteristics of our new products.
接下來的圖片可以向大家展示我們新產品的特點。
Allow us, at this point to present some slides. 下面，請大家看幾張幻燈片。

⑫ 這張圖表上的數據可顯示每個月的生產成本。 圖表

A: Can we go to the next slide? Okay.
　我們可以開始下一張投影片了嗎？好的。
B: **From the chart, we can see the monthly production cost.** 這張圖表上的數據可顯示每個月的生產成本。

❗ From the chart, we can see the monthly production cost.
　這張圖表上的數據可顯示每個月的生產成本。　　　　★ flow chart：流程圖
　Let me show you the findings of our project though the flow chart.
　下面我將透過這張流程圖向你們展示一下我們專案的成果。
　From the pie chart you can see our market share in China.
　從這張圓餅圖上你們可以看到我們在中國的市占率。

❗ You'll notice from this trend chart that the volume of business in this market is
　projected to increase by 60% over the next 5 years.　★ volume of business：業務量
　從這張趨勢圖中大家可以注意到，在未來的五年內這個市場的業務量預估
　將會增加百分之六十。
　From the chart, we know that our profits fell by 62 percent to $340 million.
　從這張圖表中，我們可以知道我們的利潤下滑了 62 個百分點，至現在的三億四千
　萬美元。

Also need to know

各種圖表的類型與使用方法……

 **pie chart：圓餅圖** 表示各種事物在總數中所佔的比例。	 **line chart：曲線圖** 表示一種事物的上升或下降趨勢。
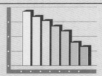 **bar chart：柱型（長條）圖** 表示幾種事物在同一時期上升或下降的情況。	 **organization chart：組織圖** 表示多種事物之間的關係。

⑬ 這項商品會完全改變人們對化學纖維的成見。

A: What do you think of the new product from our vendor?
你對我們供應商的這一新產品看法怎樣？
★ vendor：賣方

B: **The product will completely change people's prejudice against chemical fiber.**
★ fiber：纖維 ★ prejudice：偏見
這項商品會完全改變人們對化學纖維的成見。

The product will completely change people's prejudice against chemical fiber.
這項商品會完全改變人們對化學纖維的成見。

❗ This product has many advantages compared to other competing products.
這項產品與其他同類產品相比有許多優勢。

The demand for this product is steadily on the increase.
對該產品的需求正在穩定增長。

I'm sure that we can sell more this year according to the market conditions.
根據市場情況，我相信今年我們可以賣得更好。

⑭ 總而言之，我認為這個計劃將會非常成功。

★ in conclusion：總之

A: **In conclusion, I think the proposal is very successful.**
總而言之，我認為這個計劃將會非常成功。

B: That wraps up the last item on the agenda.
議程上的項目已全部討論完畢。
★ wrap up = conclude，表示「結束」

❗ Before we close today's meeting, let me just summarize the main points.
在今天結束會議之前，我來總結一下今天的要點。
★ summarize：總結，概括

❗ Let me quickly go over today's main points.
讓我簡短地總結一下今天的要點。

OK, why don't we quickly summarize what we've done today?
好的，我們來總結今天取得的進展。

In conclusion, I think the proposal is very successful.
總而言之，我認為這個計劃將會非常成功。

＊in summary、overall、in conclusion、to sum up 或 to repeat 是做摘要的實用辭彙，通常置於句首。

⑮ 有問題儘管提。

A: **Don't hesitate to ask questions.**
有問題儘管提。
B: Okay. We will interrupt you if we have questions.
好，有問題的話我們會打斷你的。

❗ Any questions? 有什麼問題嗎？
We are going to take questions in order. 我們將按順序聽聽大家的意見。
Do you have any opinions? 你有什麼意見嗎？

❗ Let's leave some time for questions. **我們留一些時間讓大家問問題。**
If you have any questions on the details, feel free to ask.
如果對某些細節有意見的話，請提出來。
Ladies and gentlemen, please feel free to interrupt if you have any questions.
如果各位有什麼問題可以隨時打斷我的講話。

❗ Don't hesitate to ask questions. **有問題儘管提。**
★ hesitate：猶豫

Raise your questions whenever you have one. 有問題請隨時提出來。

⑯ 謝謝各位今天的蒞臨指教。

A: The meeting is finished. We'll see each other next Monday.
會議到此結束，我們下週一再見。
B: **Thanks for your participation.** 謝謝各位今天的蒞臨指教。

❗ Thanks for your participation. 謝謝各位今天的蒞臨指教。
Thanks for listening. 感謝各位的關注。
I'd like to express my thanks for your participation. 謝謝各位的參與。

★ consensus：一致
I think we've reached a consensus. Thanks for your opinions.
我想我們已經達成共識了，感謝大家的意見。
We really appreciate your speech. 我們非常喜歡你的演講。
Thank you, Mr. Black, for your interesting and informative speech.
謝謝你，布萊克先生。謝謝你生動有趣的演講。

174

"Also need to know"

確實掌控會議流程……

處理遲到問題。

Some people are late, but we have no time to wait for them.
有幾個人還沒到，但我們沒時間等遲到的人。

No time left for those who are late. 沒有時間等遲到的人。

Let's not consider the absentees. 我們不要考慮缺席者。

安排休息時間。

We'll have a 20-minute break in an hour. 我們會在一小時後休息二十分鐘。

Let's take a short break. 讓我們休息一下。

Let's take a rest and get something to drink. 大家休息一下喝點什麼吧。

限制各議題的討論時間。

Sorry, but we have to turn to the next item on the agenda.
很抱歉，但我們必須繼續下一項議題。

Now let's turn to the next point on the agenda. 現在讓我們轉到下一個話題。

I think we'd better leave that for the next meeting.
我想我們最好把它留到下次討論。

It's a pity that we're running short of time.
可惜的是，我們沒有足夠的時間談這個了。

會議英文
2 集體討論（上）

MP3 TRACK：14

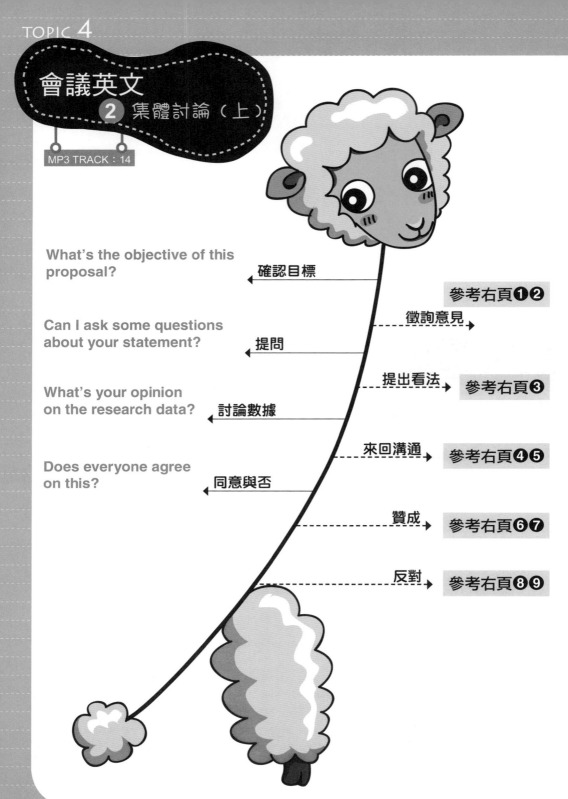

What's the objective of this proposal?

確認目標

參考右頁❶❷

徵詢意見

Can I ask some questions about your statement?

提問

提出看法 參考右頁❸

What's your opinion on the research data?

討論數據

來回溝通 參考右頁❹❺

Does everyone agree on this?

同意與否

贊成 參考右頁❻❼

反對 參考右頁❽❾

You may hear
互動式開會討論時，也許你會聽到……

ⓐ 這個企劃的目標是什麼？　What's the objective of this proposal?

ⓑ 我可以針對你說明的部份提　Can I ask some questions about your
出一些問題嗎？　　　　　statement?

ⓒ 你對研究資料有什麼看法？　What's your opinion on the research data?

ⓓ 是否大家都同意這件事？　Does everyone agree on this?

 You may want to say
互動式開會討論時，也許你會想說……

❶ 歡迎提出各種意見。　　　　I welcome all your ideas. ...p.180

❷ 有任何人要補充什麼的嗎？　Has anyone else got anything to
contribute? ...p.180

❸ 我們必須找個方法改善業績。　We have to find a way to improve
our business performance. ...p.181

❹ 我要釐清你剛剛說的幾個要點。　I need to have a run-through of the
main points you discussed. ...p.181

❺ 讓我試著用另一個方法解釋一遍。　Let me try to put it another way. ...p.182

❻ 我完全同意。　　　　　　I can't agree with you more. ...p.182

❼ 你有幾個觀點我很感興趣。　I'm interested in some of your
viewpoints. ...p.183

❽ 我恐怕不能同意你的看法。　I'm afraid that I can't agree with
you. ...p.183

❾ 對於擴建工廠這個部份，我有不同　I have a different opinion on the
的意見。　　　　　　　　extension of the factory. ...p.184

會議英文
2 集體討論（下）

MP3 TRACK：14

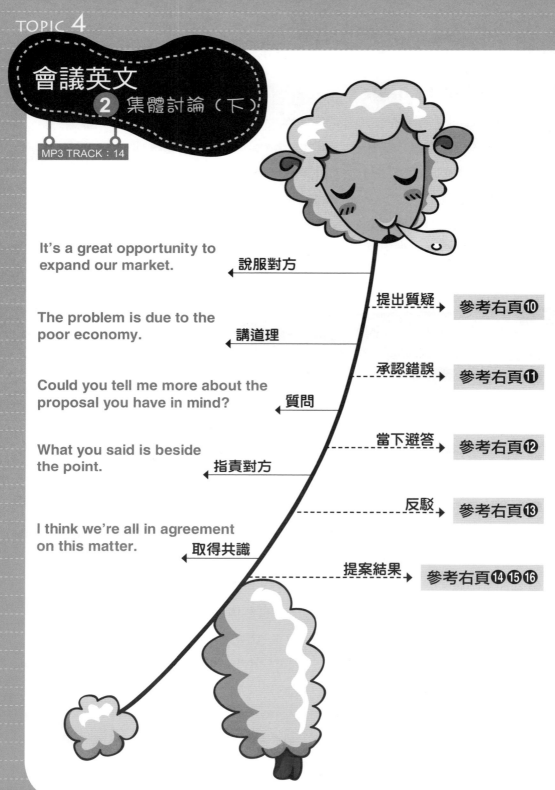

It's a great opportunity to expand our market.
說服對方

提出質疑 → 參考右頁❿

The problem is due to the poor economy.
講道理

承認錯誤 → 參考右頁⓫

Could you tell me more about the proposal you have in mind?
質問

當下避答 → 參考右頁⓬

What you said is beside the point.
指責對方

反駁 → 參考右頁⓭

I think we're all in agreement on this matter.
取得共識

提案結果 → 參考右頁⓮⓯⓰

You may hear
互動式開會討論時，也許你會聽到……（續）

ⓔ 這是我們擴張市場的大好機會。　It's a great opportunity to expand our market.

ⓕ 問題在於經濟不景氣。　The problem is due to the poor economy.

ⓖ 你可以多談談對這個企劃的想　Could you tell me more about the
法嗎？　proposal you have in mind?

ⓗ 你說的不是重點。　What you said is beside the point.

ⓘ 我想我們已就此事達成協議。　I think we're all in agreement on this matter.

You may want to say
互動式開會討論時，也許你會想說……（續）

⓾ 你的論點和先前所說的有矛盾　The argument contradicts your
之處。　original proposal. ...p.185

⓫ 抱歉，我的確沒有考慮到這　I am sorry for not taking it into
一點。　consideration. ...p.185

⓬ 因為手邊沒有相關資料，我現　I'm not able to answer this question as
在沒有辦法回答。　I have no related data in hand. ...p.186

⓭ 即使你不相信，但這就是事　It's a fact even if you don't believe it. ...p.186
實。

⓮ 這個提議很不錯，我們決定　We decided to carry out the proposal
執行。　as it's fairly good. ...p.187

⓯ 這項企劃不夠周密，恐怕無法　The project is not prepared to the last detail.
通過。　I'm afraid it can't be passed. ...p.187

⓰ 是該做決定的時候了。　Better get it settled now while we're at it. ...p.188

❶ 歡迎提出各種意見。

A: That's all for my report. **I welcome all your ideas.**
以上是我的報告，歡迎提出各種意見。　★ loss：損失
B: I think we should get a (policy) for total (loss) only.
我認為我們應該保全損險。　★ policy：保險

❗ I welcome all your ideas. 歡迎提出各種意見。

Are we all in agreement? 大家都同意嗎？

❗ Do we all agree on this? **大家都同意嗎？**

Does everybody agree with it? 大家都同意嗎？

Do I have your support on this? 我能得到大家的支持嗎？

Do we all agree on this plan? 大家都同意這項計畫嗎？

❗ Are we all in favor of this decision? **這項決議大家都同意嗎？**

Does anyone have any (objection) to this proposal? 有人反對這項提議嗎？
★ objection：反對，異議
★ second：贊同　★ motion：（會議上的）動議，提議
Who will (second) the (motion)? 有人要附議嗎？

Are there any more comments? 還有什麼評論嗎？

* be for, be in favor of, agree with, agree to, agree on, be in agreement with 都是表示「同意」、「贊成」的單字或片語。

❷ 有任何人要補充什麼的嗎？

A: **Has anyone else got anything to (contribute)?**
有任何人要補充什麼的嗎？
★ contribute：提供
B: Would you mind talking about the tax (regulations) in Germany?
你介意談一下德國稅收方面的規定嗎？　★ regulation：規定，條例

Has anyone else got anything to contribute? 有任何人要補充什麼的嗎？

Do you have something else to talk about? 你還有什麼要說的嗎？

❗ Do you have any suggestions? **你有什麼建議？**

❗ What do you think about this proposal? **你認為這項提議如何？**

Anything else you want to bring up for discussion? 還有別的問題要討論嗎？

What do you think of this issue? 關於這個議題你有什麼想法？

Would you like to add anything? 你有什麼要補充的嗎？

180

❸ 我們必須找個方法改善業績。

建議

A: **We have to find a way to improve our business performance.** 我們必須找個方法改善業績。
B: I totally agree with you. 我完全同意你的看法。

We have to find a way to improve our business performance.
我們必須找個方法改善業績。

❗ I think it's necessary to move the articles by combined transportation.
我認為聯運貨物十分必要。
★ exaggerate：誇張，擴大

My advice is that you shouldn't try to (exaggerate) the (scope) you cover.
我的建議是你不應該代理超出你能力範圍的區域。 └─ ★ scope：範圍，領域

❗ My proposal is to cut off the share of our technology.
我的建議是降低我們技術出資的比例。

I must point out that the key problem lies in the distribution network.
我不得不指出，最主要的問題是銷售網路的問題。

Would you please consider changing the inner package into small boxes?
你能不能考慮將內包裝改為小盒？

❹ 我要釐清你剛剛說的幾個要點。

再次確認

A: **I need to have a run-through of the main points you discussed.** 我要釐清你剛剛說的幾個要點。
B: Perhaps I haven't made myself clear. Let me try again.
可能我講的不太清楚。我再講一遍。

❗ Let me make sure if I understand you correctly.
讓我確認一下是否正確理解了你的意思。

❗ I'm sorry. Could you explain it? I'm not very clear about that.
對不起，您能解釋一下嗎？我不太懂你的意思。

Can you (elaborate) on it a bit? 你是否能說得更清楚些？
└─ ★ elaborate：詳盡闡述

I need to have a (run-through) of the main points you discussed.
我要釐清你剛剛說的幾個要點。 ── ★ run-through：大綱，概要

I still don't see the point you emphasized. 我仍然弄不清楚你所強調的要點。

⑤ 讓我試著用另一個方法解釋一遍。

A: Sorry. I'm not clear about what you said just now.
對不起，我不太懂你剛才說的意思。

B: **Let me try to put it another way.**
讓我試著用另一個方法解釋一遍。

★ call for：需要

❗ Let me try to put it another way. 讓我試著用另一個方法解釋一遍。

I think that calls for a bit of explanation here. 我想可能要在這裡做點解釋。

Perhaps I haven't made myself clear. 可能我講的不太清楚。

❗ Have I made that clear? 我有沒有解釋清楚？

Do you see what I'm getting at? 你明白我的意思嗎？

Sorry, I think you misunderstood what I said. 我想你誤會了我的說法。

❗ I'm afraid you don't understand what I'm saying.
恐怕你沒理解我正在說的。

⑥ 我完全同意。

★ similar：相仿的

A: You know that our products have the same quality as the similar Japanese ones, but we are selling for half of their price. 你們知道我們的產品可以與日本的同類產品媲美，而價格僅是同類產品的一半。

B: **I can't agree with you more.** 我完全同意。

❗ I'll second that. / I'll go along with that. / I agree with you entirely. / I can't agree with you more. 我同意。

❗ That's a good point. 說的好。

It's a very good idea. 是個好主意。

That's true. I totally agree with you. 說得對，我完全同意你。

I embrace your proposal. 我擁護你的提案。

You made a very good point. / What you said is quite reasonable. / You definitely have a point there. 你說的很有道理。

That's exactly the way I feel. 這正是我的觀點。

I don't think anyone would disagree. 我覺得沒人會不同意。

You and I are on the same wavelength. 你跟我的意見一致。

★ on the same wavelength：我們真有默契

182

❼ 你有幾個觀點我很感興趣。

A: Any comments? 大家有什麼意見？

B: **I'm interested in some of your viewpoints.**
你有幾個觀點我很感興趣。

❗ What you said is quite convincing. But I still have a question.
你所說的很有道理。但我還有一個問題。

   I'm interested in some of your viewpoints. 你有幾個觀點我很感興趣。

   I totally agree with you on this point. But now let's put it more practically.
   在這一點上我完全同意您的看法。但我們現在應當更實際一些。

❗ I agree with what you said, but the price difference should not be so large.
我同意你的說法，但是價格差距應該不會那麼大。

   I see. If the price were less expensive, I would agree with it.
   我明白。如果價格不貴我沒意見。

❽ 我恐怕不能同意你的看法。

A: Qualified staff holding positions who are being laid off will be offered
   retraining for our new positions.
   假如之前被裁掉的職員符合我們的用人要求，我們將向他們提供再培訓的
   機會，以使他們適應我們新職位的需要。

B: **I'm afraid that I can't stand by your side.**
我恐怕不能同意你的看法。
   └ ★ stand by：支持

❗ I can't accept it. 我不能接受。

   I take exception to this question. 我對這個問題有異議。

   I'm afraid that I can't stand by your side. 我不同意你的看法。
   └ ★ stand by one's side：支持，同意

   Unfortunately, I see it differently. 對不起，我不這麼認為。

   I don't agree. The reasons are as follows. 我不同意，理由如下。
   └ ★ as follows：如下

❗ I can't agree with you on this point. / I'm afraid I can't agree with you in this
   respect. 在這一點上，我不太同意你的看法。

   I'm having second thoughts on that. 我有不同的看法。

A: Do you have any ideas for the plan? 你對這項計劃有什麼想法？

B: **I have a different opinion on the extension of the factory.**

★ extension：擴大，增設

對於擴建工廠這個部份，我有不同的意見。

I have a different opinion on the extension of the factory.

對於擴建工廠這個部份，我有不同的意見。

❗ I basically agree with you. However, I'm afraid we can't afford that expense.

我基本上認同你的看法，但是我們恐怕不能負擔這個費用。

Up to a point I agree with you, but our ultimate goal is to make a profit rather than expand our market share without benefits. 從一定程度上我同意你的說法，但我們的終極目標是為了賺錢，而不是盲目擴大市占率。

Yes, I agree up to a point, but we should keep an eye on local manufacturers as well.

★ keep an eye on：留意，照看

是的，我基本上同意你的看法，但我們還應當注意在地製造商。

Yes, in a way, but this trend is not in line with our market forecast.

★ be in line with：和…一致，與…符合　　★ forecast：預測

是的，可以這麼說，但是這一趨勢不符合我們對市場的預測。

Not a bad idea, but we should look at the larger picture.

你說的不錯，可是未能掌握全局。

＊ 「the larger picture」即指「遠景；大局」。這句話是說對方所言不差，也就是「Not a bad idea」的意思，但未能掌握全局。這個說法是在暗示自己不能苟同，但又有技巧地為對方找台階下。這句話還有將討論轉向另一個不同方向的功用。

I don't want to be discouraging, but can we try to come up with something else?

我不想潑你們冷水，但我們是否可以想想別的辦法？

❗ I appreciate your point of view, but I've been instructed to reject the numbers you have proposed. **我欣賞你們的觀點，但是我老闆說不能接受你的報價。**

❗ I can see why you want to do this, but 10 percent is beyond my negotiating limit.

★ negotiating：談判，協商

我理解你這麼做的原因，可是百分之十的折扣超過了我能接受的底限。

That's very interesting, but it is not helpful in improving our sales volume.

這個提議很有趣，但在提高銷售額方面沒什麼用處。

⑩ 你的論點和先前所說的有矛盾之處。

A: Please tell me your opinion frankly. 請坦率直言你的意見。

B: I cannot accept your proposal, since **the argument contradicts your original proposal.**

★ contradict：與…矛盾

我不能接受你的提議，因為你的論點和先前所說的有矛盾之處。

The argument contradicts your original proposal.

你的論點和先前所說的有矛盾之處。

Your interpretation is invalid. 你的理解不正確。

★ interpretation：解釋　★ invalid：無效的

❶ I doubt very much that will happen. 我不覺得那會發生。

That sounds unlikely. 那聽起來不可能。

Are you sure they will lower the price? 你確定他們會降價嗎？

You said the new product will fail. Can you prove that?

你說新產品將會失敗。你能證明這一點嗎？

Who says the plan won't work? 誰說這個計畫不可行？

❶ Some of the figures are apparently not accurate.

這些資料有一些明顯是不準確的。

⑪ 抱歉，我的確沒有考慮到這一點。

A: Nevertheless, some employees may not want to change career paths in midstream, and will probably hand in their notice. 但即便是這樣，可能會有些人不願意中途更換職業，他們仍有可能提出辭呈。

B: **I am sorry for not taking it into consideration.**

抱歉，我的確沒有考慮到這一點。

I am sorry for not taking it into consideration. 抱歉，我的確沒有考慮到這一點。

❶ I'm sorry but I made a mistake. 對不起，我剛才犯了個錯誤。

❶ The methods I used were incorrect. 我用的方法不對。

I misinterpreted your question. 我誤解了你提的問題。

★ misinterpret：誤解

Oh, I'm sorry. I misunderstood you. Then I agree with you.

哦，對不起，我誤解你了。那樣的話，我同意你的觀點。

185

⑫ 因為手邊沒有相關資料，我現在沒有辦法回答。 當下避答

A: Prices depend also on volume. How much quantity do you forecast?
價格也會因數量而有所不同，你預計在第一年銷售多少數量呢？

B: **I'm not able to answer this question as I have no related data in hand.**
因為手邊沒有相關資料，我現在沒有辦法回答。

❗ It all depends. 這得看情況而定。

I am not in a position to say anything about the issue.
我現在不能就這個問題發表任何評論。
＊in a position to 是「處在可以…的位置」、「能夠」、「有能力做…」的意思。

I'm not able to answer this question as I have no related data in hand.
因為手邊沒有相關資料，我現在沒有辦法回答。

❗ I'm afraid that I can't give you a definite reply now.
恐怕我現在無法給你一個明確的答覆。

❗ May I get back to you after I have returned to Japan?
等我回到日本後再回答你好嗎？

I can't make a decision right now. 我現在無法作出決定。

❗ I just need some time to think it over. 我需要時間考慮考慮。

⑬ 即使你不相信，但這就是事實。 反駁

A: To be quite honest, we don't believe this product sold very well in Europe.
說老實話，我們不相信這種產品在歐洲賣得好。

B: **It's a fact even if you don't believe it.**
即使你不相信，但這就是事實。

❗ It's a fact even if you don't believe it. 即使你不相信，但這就是事實。

Don't jump to conclusions so quickly. 不要這麼匆忙下結論。
★ jump to conclusions：輕率得出結論

★ relevance：關聯
I'm not sure what you're saying has any relevance here.
我不知道你所說的和我們的議題有什麼關係。

Despite what you said, my facts are correct. 不管你怎麼說，我的事實是正確的。

It is not clear to us what you had in mind. 我們不清楚您到底是怎麼想的。

⑭ 這個提議很不錯，我們決定執行。

A: **We decided to carry out the proposal as it's fairly good.** 這個提議很不錯，我們決定執行。

B: I've no objection. 我不反對。

We decided to carry out the proposal as it's fairly good.
這個提議很不錯，我們決定執行。

❗ I declare the motion carried. 我宣佈動議獲得通過。
└─★ declare：宣佈　　└─★ carry：（議案等）獲得…的通過

I think this wraps everything up. 我想這樣一來，每件事都圓滿結束了。

I suggest that the capital expenditure program presented to the Board be adopted in its present form. └─★ capital：資本 └─★ expenditure：消費，支出
我提議向董事會介紹的資本支出計畫按它現在的形式被正式通過。

The capital expenditure program is now adopted. 資本支出計畫現在被採用。

⑮ 這項企劃不夠周密，恐怕無法通過。

A: **The project is not prepared to the last detail. I'm afraid it can't be passed.** 這項企劃不夠周密，恐怕無法通過。

B: But I think that we can handle the problem by making a few minor changes.
但是我想我們可以做一些小變動來解決這個問題。

Given the expense of our environment, I have to say sorry to your proposal.
考慮到我們環境所付出的代價，我不得不駁回你的方案。

The project is not prepared to the last detail. I'm afraid it can't be passed.
這項企劃不夠周密，恐怕無法通過。

We are not interested in taking a position in the new project; we don't think there is a market for it. 我們對投資這項新計畫沒有興趣，因為我們不認為它會有市場。

❗ I'm afraid I can't satisfy your requirement at the moment.
您剛才提的要求我們暫時無法滿足。

❗ There's no doubt that this project is unacceptable.
毫無疑問地，這個方案是令人無法接受的.

⑯ 是該做決定的時候了。

A: **Better get it settled now while we're at it.**
是該做決定了。

B: Will those in favor of it please show their hands?
同意的請舉手。 ★ in favor of：贊成，支持

Better get it settled now while we're at it. 是該做決定了。

❗ Are we ready to make a decision? **我們現在可以做決定了嗎？**

Those in favor? Those against? Any abstentions?
有哪些人贊成？有哪些人反對？有人棄權嗎？ ★ abstention：棄權

Who will second this motion? 有人要附議嗎？

Now can I just run over the main areas of agreement and those that are still left
open? ★ run over：很快地把…瀏覽一遍

我現在可以把我們一致同意的和還沒決定的內容瀏覽一遍嗎？

I now make a motion to close the third quarterly meeting of Action Appliances. Is
there a second? 我現在提議結束 Action 家電的第三季會議。有沒有人附議？

會議與議程的相關字彙

場地與人物

hall	會堂，大廳	notice board	佈告欄
rostrum	講臺	speaker	報告人
public gallery	旁聽席		

各種文字記錄

draft resolution	決議草案	minutes / record	記錄
first draft / preliminary draft		summary record	摘要紀錄
	草案初稿	verbatim record	逐字紀錄
whereas	開場白	memorandum	備忘錄
factual report	事實報告		

會議流程

opening	開幕	to place on the agenda	列入議程
standing orders / by-laws	議事程序	closure	閉幕式
rules of procedure	議事規則	closing speech	閉幕詞
constitution / statutes	章程	to convene / to convoke	召開
procedure	程序	to postpone / to adjourn / to put off	推遲，延期
agenda	議程	to adjourn the meeting / to close the meeting	散會
timetable / schedule	日程表，時刻表		
item on the agenda	議程項目		

各種發言、意見、評論

declaration / statement	聲明	to ask for the floor	要求發言
stand	立場，主張	to give the floor to~	同意…發言
consensus	共識	to take the floor / to address the meeting	發言
advisory opinion	顧問意見	to table a proposal	提出建議
proposal	建議	to second / to support	贊成
clarification	澄清	to oppose	反對
comment	評論	to raise an objection	提出異議
decision	決定	to move an amendment	提出修正案
ruling	裁決	to amend	修正
resolution	決議	to reject	拒絕，駁回
motivations	動機		
to make a speech / to deliver a speech	做報告		

談判英文 **1** 主導談判者（上）

MP3 TRACK：15

Thank you for your proposal and we really need to have a talk.

同意談判

前置作業 ▶

參考右頁❶❷

As you know, we are considering other proposals.

提及其他選擇

訂定目標 ▶

參考右頁❸

I'm sure you can see where we stand.

確立立場

我方優勢 ▶

參考右頁❹

We must discuss the following items: price, delivery terms, and the minimum quantity.

主題明確化

談論現況 ▶

參考右頁❺❻

Let's assume things might not go according to the plan.

問題與風險

強調好處 ▶

參考右頁❼

線上音檔

You may hear
找對方談判時，也許你會聽到……

ⓐ 謝謝你的提議，我們的確需要談一談。 Thank you for your proposal and we really need to have a talk.

ⓑ 你們要知道，我們還在考慮其他提議。 As you know, we are considering other proposals.

ⓒ 我相信你可以看出我們的立場為何。 I'm sure you can see where we stand.

ⓓ 我們必須就價錢、運送條款與最小數量這些問題做討論。 We must discuss the following items: price, delivery terms, and the minimum quantity.

ⓔ 我們要假設事情可能不會因計畫而行。 Let's assume things might not go according to the plan.

You may want to say
找對方談判時，也許你會想說……

❶ 我們應該找時間見個面。 I'd like to make an appointment with you. ...p.194

❷ 我們需要討論這些議題。 There are a couple of issues we can work on. ...p.194

❸ 目標是要達到最大利潤。 Our ultimate goal is to maximize our profits. ...p.195

❹ 我們在光電產業有二十年的經驗。 We've been in the optoelectronics industry for 20 years. ...p.195

❺ 液晶螢幕的市場前景看好。 There is a bright market prospect for LCD screens. ...p.196

❻ 油價上漲是現在面臨的最大挑戰。 The explosion in oil prices offers a great challenge. ...p.197

❼ 這樣的結果能讓我們雙方都獲利。 This is a result in which both sides benefit. ...p.198

談判英文
1 主導談判者
（下）

MP3 TRACK : 15

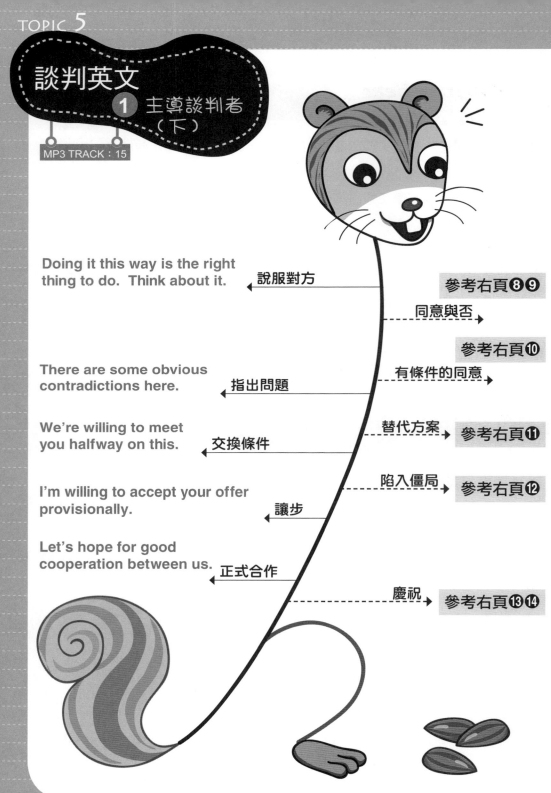

Doing it this way is the right thing to do. Think about it. ← 說服對方 ──── 參考右頁 ❽❾

- - - 同意與否 →

參考右頁 ❿

- - - 有條件的同意 →

There are some obvious contradictions here. ← 指出問題

We're willing to meet you halfway on this. ← 交換條件 ──── 替代方案 - - → 參考右頁 ⓫

- - - 陷入僵局 → 參考右頁 ⓬

I'm willing to accept your offer provisionally. ← 讓步

Let's hope for good cooperation between us. ← 正式合作

- - - 慶祝 → 參考右頁 ⓭⓮

You may hear
找對方談判時，也許你會聽到⋯⋯（續）

f 這麼做才是正確的作法。好好想一想。　Doing it this way is the right thing to do. Think about it.

g 這裡有些明顯的矛盾。　There are some obvious contradictions here.

h 在這一點上，我們願意與你們妥協。　We're willing to meet you halfway on this.

i 我願意暫且接受你的提議。　I'm willing to accept your offer provisionally.

j 我非常期待能夠和你合作。　Let's hope for good cooperation between us.

You may want to say
找對方談判時，也許你會想說⋯⋯（續）

8 你說得很有道理。　You made a very good point. ...p.199

9 我不能接受你們把成本提高一倍。　I cannot accept your doubling the cost. ...p.200

10 如果你同意這個條件，我們就願意降低價錢。　If you accept this term, we will agree to make a reduction. ...p.200

11 來考慮一下其他替代方案。　Let's consider the alternative scheme. ...p.201

12 很遺憾，但我們別無選擇了。　I regret to say that we have no other choice. ...p.201

13 讓我們去慶祝一下我們的新合夥關係。　Let's celebrate our new partnership. ...p.202

14 合約上明訂雙方必須履行的義務。　The contract stipulates the obligations that both parties shall fulfill. ...p.203

❶ 我們應該找時間見個面。

A: **I'd like to make an appointment with you.**
我們應該找時間見個面。
B: Okay. How about next Friday? 好的。下週五我們見一面怎麼樣？

❗ I'd like to make an appointment with you. 我們應該找時間見個面。
When would it be convenient for you? 你們什麼時間有空？
Good, that's settled then. 好的，就這麼定了。
May I arrange the time and the place, please? 能不能讓我安排時間與場所？
❗ My schedule is tight. 我的行程表排得滿滿的。
❗ I'd like to make an appointment at 2 o'clock on Monday.
我想約星期一下午兩點。

❷ 我們需要討論這些議題。

★ come to order：進入議事程序，表示（會議等）即將開始

A: The meeting will now come to order. 會議現在正式開始。
B: **There are a couple of issues we can work on.**
我們需要討論這些議題。

There are a couple of issues we can work on. 我們需要討論這些議題。

❗ Let's get down to business. We've essentially got two items to cover this afternoon. 讓我們直接進入主題吧，今天下午我們有兩項內容要討論。

❗ On the agenda today, we have two items: first, the price clause and second, the payment terms. 按今天的議程，我們有兩個問題要討論，第一是價格條款，第二是付款項目。

I'd like to get the ball rolling by talking about prices. 我們先開始談談價格吧。

★ get down to：著手於　　★ get the ball rolling：開始

❗ Let's get down to the question of price directly.
讓我們直接談談價格的問題吧。

Shall we discuss the means of payment? 讓我們來談談付款方式吧？

The next thing I'd like to bring up for discussion is packing.
下面我想提出來討論的是包裝問題。　★ bring up：提出

We would like to ask you some details of this agreement.
我們想要和你談談這個協議的細節問題。

194

A: Green Company is the main competitor of our company. Their quoted price is 10% lower than ours.
格林公司是我們公司的主要競爭對手。他們打出低於我們10%的價格。

★ quoted price：報價

B: I don't think we should reduce prices. After all, **our ultimate goal is to maximize our profits.**
我認為我們沒必要降價。畢竟我們的目標是要達到最大利潤。

Our ultimate goal is to maximize our profits. 目標是要達到最大利潤。

❗ Our objective is to get the greatest profit. 我們的目標是爭取最大利潤。

❗ The ultimate objective of any negotiation is to gain an agreement.
任何談判最根本的目的是取得一致意見。

I hope this meeting is productive. 我希望這是一次富有成效的會談。

We can work out the details next time. 我們可以下次再來解決細節問題。

We'll focus on maintaining good friendship even when talks break down.
即使談判破裂，我們還是要保持友好。

★ break down：失敗，挫折

A: Our company has a solid reputation for having high quality products in this line of business.

★ line of business：行業

我們公司在本行業內因為產品品質優異而享有盛譽。

B: Sure. **We've been in the optoelectronics industry for 20 years.** 當然。我們在光電行業有二十年的經驗。

★ optoelectronics：光電子學

❗ Our hardware is very reliable. 我們的硬體非常可靠。

Our electrical appliances stand competition well.

★ electrical appliance：電器

我們的電器產品是同業中的佼佼者。

We've been in the optoelectronics industry for 20 years.
我們在光電行業有二十年的經驗。

❗ We have an advantage over other companies in price.
我們與其他公司相比有價格優勢。

195

❺ 液晶螢幕的市場前景看好。

A: Mr. Smith, we expect you to bring your LCD screen price down 5%.
　史密斯先生，我希望你們的液晶螢幕能提供 5% 的折扣。　　★ market prospect：
　　　　　　　　　　　　　　　　　　　　　　　　　　　　市場前景

B: You know, **there is a bright market prospect for LCD
screens.** Taking everything into consideration, including the upward
tendency of the market price, we finally fixed our price at this level.
您知道液晶螢幕的市場前景看好。考慮到各種因素，包括市場價格不斷上
漲，我們最後把價格定在這個層次。

❗ There is a bright market prospect for LCD screens. / The market prospect for
LCD screens is very favorable. 液晶螢幕的市場前景看好。

　LCD screens have very good market potential. 液晶螢幕有很好的市場潛力。

　LCD screens sell well in the U.S. market. 液晶螢幕在美國很暢銷。

　Our toys are well-received in the European market.
　我們的玩具在歐洲市場很受歡迎。

❗ There has been a heavy demand for cell phones. 近來對於手機的需求大增。

　The computer market is bound to advance. 電腦市場被往上帶動。

❗ The market is expanding. 市場在擴大。

　The market has ceased to expand. 市場已經停止了增長。

　There is already no spare space to develop the market.
　市場已經沒有發展的餘地了。　★ spare：多餘的，剩下的

❗ The market has been saturated. 市場已經飽和了。　★ saturate：飽和

　The market is in a slump. 市場真是蕭條啊。
　　　　　　　　　　★ slump：（經濟等）衰落

　There is a strong competition in the market. 這個市場競爭非常激烈。

　The computer business has become more difficult because of the competition.
　由於競爭激烈，電腦生意越來越難做了。

　The real estate market is in recession because of the global financial crisis.
　因為全球金融危機，房地產市場非常不景氣。　★ financial crisis：金融危機，金融海嘯

　This is an area of high unemployment. 這一地區失業率高漲。

❗ The economy has been in recession. 經濟不景氣了。
　　　　　　　　　　　★ recession：蕭條，不景氣

* 表示貨物的英語單字：
goods，merchandise，ware，freight，commodity 這些名詞都可表示「商品，貨物」之意。goods 是一
般生活或商業用詞，指銷售或購入的商品。merchandise 是正式用詞，指商業上銷售或商家擁有貨物的
總稱。ware 指上市待賣的商品或貨物。多用複數形式。freight 指「貨物」時，可與 goods 互換，這是
美式英語；在英國，freight 指船裝貨物。commodity 當「商品」解釋時是經濟學名詞，也可指日用品。

❻ 油價上漲是現在面臨的最大挑戰。 特定議題

★ soar：上升

A: I'm sorry to say that your price has soared. It's almost 20% higher than last year's. 很遺憾，貴公司的價格猛漲，比去年幾乎高出 20%。

B: That's because the price of raw materials has gone up. **The explosion in oil prices offers a great challenge.** 那是因為原材料的價格上漲了。油價上漲是現在面臨的最大挑戰。

The explosion in oil prices offers a great challenge. 油價上漲是現在面臨的最大挑戰。

❗ The biggest issue we are facing is the rise in oil prices.
油價上漲是我們現在面臨的最大問題。

The soaring price of oil is something of a puzzle.
原油價格的不斷飆升讓人感到困惑。

The price of oil has doubled over the past few years.
原油的價格在過去幾年翻了一倍。

The exchange rate is counteracting our profits. 匯率在抵消我們的利潤。

★ counteract：對抗，抵銷

❗ All we can do is to reduce the production cost.
我們能做的就是降低生產成本。

❗ We have kept the price close to the costs of production.
我們已經把價格壓到生產費用的邊緣了。

The dollar is sinking. 美元在貶值。

★ sink：（價格等）降低，減弱

★ devaluation：貶值

To avoid the risk of devaluation of the US dollar, we want to add another clause.
為了避免美元貶值的風險，我們想再增加另外一個條款。

❗ Global economic growth is slowing down. **全球經濟增長正在趨緩中。**

The world economy is worrying about the risks of financial collapse.
全球經濟正擔心金融崩潰。

★ collapse：崩潰，瓦解

The fall in sales affecting the world market is mainly due to the recession.
銷售量減少影響國際市場的主要原因是經濟衰退。

We're finding a difficulty in the turnover in reserve funds for the project.

★ turnover：流動，流通   ★ reserve：儲備

我們發現這個計畫的儲備資金週轉發生困難。

The supplier will be charged a penalty if there is a delay in delivery.
如果供貨商延誤交貨期，將被罰款。

197

❼ 這樣的結果能讓我們雙方都獲利。

A: You increase your order to 2,500 pairs and I increase the discount to 25%. **This is a result in which both sides benefit.**
你加訂到 2500 套，我給你個七五折。這樣的結果能讓我們雙方都獲利。
B: Well, I suppose so. 好吧。

This is a result in which both sides benefit. 這樣的結果能讓我們雙方都獲利。

❗ I'm trying very hard to reach some middle ground.
└─★ middle ground：妥協，中間立場

我盡量讓我們雙方都能找到利益均衡點。

I hope we can find a win-win situation on this.
我希望我們能找到雙贏之處。 └─★ win-win situation：雙贏

❗ How about we both make a concession? / Is it possible for us to make concessions? / How about making some concessions? / How about a compromise? 我們互相讓步怎麼樣？

❗ We can meet each other half way. 我們各讓一步吧。
＊meet someone half way 是「與人妥協」、「遷就某人」的意思。

The market is declining. We recommend your immediate acceptance.
市場在萎縮，我們建議你們馬上接受。

We'll both come out from this meeting as winners. 這次會談的結果將是一個雙贏。

❗ I think we can figure out a way to compromise the interests of both parties, can't we? 我覺得我們可以找出一種方法來中和雙方的利益，不是嗎？

It is unwise for either of us to insist on our own price.
我想我們雙方都堅持自己的價格是很不明智的。

It would leave us only a small profit to accept your proposal.
如果接受你們的建議，我們的利潤就很少了。

The market is bound to advance with the coming season.
隨著旺季的到來，市場狀況會反彈上升。

❗ How about meeting each other half way? In that way the business deal can be concluded. 能不能雙方都讓一步？這筆生意就可以成交。
└─★ conclude：達成協議

Let's make it half way. I agree on your commission rate and you accept the quota I proposed. 我們各讓一步吧。我同意你的傭金比率，你接受我建議的限額。

❽ 你說得很有道理。

讓步與妥協

A: Without the staff proficient in local markets, we might be in a great loss.
沒有熟悉本地市場的人員，我們就有可能受到重大的損失。

B: **You made a very good point.** But I still insist that the flagship is the final form we distribute our products.
你說得很有道理。但我還是堅持旗艦店是我們分銷的最終形式。

❗ You made a very good point. / What you said is quite reasonable.
你說得很有道理。

❗ I'll go along with that. 我贊同。

I'll second that. 我同意。

You and I are on the same wavelength. 你跟我的意見一致。
＊on the same wavelength 是「具有相同觀點，有同感」的意思。

I agree with you entirely. 我完全贊同你。

I don't think anyone would disagree. 我覺得沒人會不同意。

That's a good point. 說的好。

You've been very persuasive. 你很有說服力。

You've made a believer out of me. 你讓我全心信服。

What you have said is quite reasonable and I have to cast my reference to it.
你所說的很有道理，我不得不贊同。

I agree with you in principle, but I should say that the training expense should be included in the total packet.
★ packet：（口語）一大筆錢

我原則上同意你，但我要說，培訓費用應當包括在總價裡。

❗ I agree with you on the whole, but then again the obligations of the two parties should be more specific. ★ on the whole：一般說來，整體而論
我基本上都同意你，但再說一次，雙方的義務應該更具體一點。

You definitely have a point there. 你說的確實有點道理。

❗ I totally agree with you in this point. But now let's put it more practically.
在這一點上我完全同意您的看法。但我們現在應該要更實際一些。

I agree with what you say, but the price difference should not be huge.
我同意你的說法，但是價格差距應該不會那麼大。

Whatever you said sounds reasonable, but one thing you forgot to mention is that we offer the technical support to your first order free of charge.
你說得有道理，但你忘了提到，我們對你們訂的第一批產品提供免費技術支援。

⑨ 我不能接受你們把成本提高一倍。

A: **I cannot accept your doubling the cost.**
我不能接受你們把成本提高一倍。

B: Our price is higher. But the quality of our product is much better.
我們的報價是比較高，但我們的產品品質要好得多。

I cannot accept your doubling the cost. 我不能接受你們把成本提高一倍。

❗ We seem to be talking at cross purposes. 我們好像離題太遠。
★ cross purposes：目的相反，相互誤解

❗ I'm afraid we can't entertain your offer. 很抱歉，我不能接受你的報價。
Unfortunately, we must decline your offer for the following reasons.
抱歉，由於以下的原因我們必須拒絕你的建議。
I'm not being destructive, but I don't see it that way. I just want to emphasize that
the quality is our first priority. ★ destructive：破壞的
我不想打斷，但這件事我並不這麼看。我想強調的是，品質是我們首要考慮的。

⑩ 如果你同意這個條件，我們就願意降低價錢。

A: **If you accept this term, we will agree to make a
reduction.** 如果你同意這個條件，我們就願意降低價錢。

B: How much is the reduction? 降價幅度有多大？

If you accept this term, we will agree to make a reduction.
如果你同意這個條件，我們就願意降低價錢。

❗ If you want a better discount, you must make a larger order.
如果你想要更大的折扣，那你就必須要訂更多的貨。
If you can guarantee that on paper, I think we can discuss this further.
如果你能書面保證的話，我們可以進一步討論這個問題。
If you agree to accept T/T in advance, we can compromise on other terms.
如果你們能夠接受先匯款，我們可以在其他條件上讓步。
＊T/T 是 Telegraph Transfer 的縮略語，也就是「電匯」的意思。

❗ If we can come to the transaction soon, I can give you a discount.
如果我們能馬上成交，我可以給你折扣。

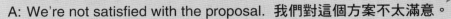

⑪ 來考慮一下其他替代方案。

替代
方案

A: We're not satisfied with the proposal. 我們對這個方案不太滿意。

B: **Let's consider another alternative.**

　　來考慮一下其他替代方案。　★ alternative：可供替代的東西或辦法

❗ Let's consider other alternatives. 來考慮一下其他替代方案。

　 We have another plan. 我們還有一個計畫。

❗ If he wants to make any changes, minor alternations can be made.

　 如果他有什麼意見的話，我們還可以對計畫稍加修改。

　 I think that the second option is the better of the two. 我認為第二個選擇是最好的。

　 There is a way to have the best of both alternatives. / There is a way we can use

　 the best of both options. / There is a way that we can take the best parts from each

　 plan. 有一個兼顧兩種方案的辦法。

⑫ 很遺憾，但我們別無選擇了。

僵局

★ nonnegotiable：不可談判的

A: Do you mean that you are nonnegotiable?

　 你的意思是說咱們沒有商量的餘地了？　★ I regret to say：很抱歉這麼說⋯

B: Our prices are fixed. **I regret to say that we have no other**

　 choice. 我們的價格是固定的。很遺憾，但我們別無選擇了。

❗ I regret to say that we have no other choice. 很遺憾，但我們別無選擇了。

❗ If that's the case, there's not much point in further discussion.

　 如果是這樣的話，那就沒什麼必要再談下去了。　★ incentive：刺激的，鼓勵的

　 Unless you are prepared to offer some kind of incentive, I think we might as well

　 call it a day. 除非你們能提供一些有利的條件，要不然我們倒不如就到這裡吧。

　 ＊call it a day 是「到此為止」的意思。

　 I'm afraid we couldn't give you more preferential conditions. You can choose to

　 terminate. 恐怕我們不能給你更多優惠了。你可以選擇退出。

　 Perhaps we should turn to other suppliers this time.

　 也許我們這次該換其他的供應商了。

　 If that's so, I'm afraid I'll have to walk out of this meeting room disappointed.

　 如果這樣的話，那我恐怕只好退出談判，敗興而歸。

201

⑬ 讓我們去慶祝一下我們的新合夥關係。

A: I think we can call it a day. 我想我們今天就到這裡吧。

★ partnership：合夥（合作）關係

B: **Let's celebrate our new partnership.** It's time to go to the dinner prepared for you by our president. 讓我們去慶祝一下我們的新合夥關係。是時候去吃飯了，我們總裁為你們準備了晚餐。

❗ Let's celebrate our new partnership. 讓我們去慶祝一下我們的新合夥關係。

It's been a very productive meeting. 這是一個非常有成效的會議。

Thank you for coming. 最後感謝你們的到來。

❗ I appreciate your cooperation on these matters.
謝謝你在這些方面的合作。

Your accommodating attitude and cooperation have been most valuable.
我們很看重你大方的態度和合作精神。

I'm very happy with the frank exchange of views. 我很高興我們能坦誠地交換意見。

Thanks for taking time talking to us. 謝謝你花時間和我們談。

It's been great talking to you. 跟你談話很高興。

Let's celebrate the conclusion of the transaction by shaking hands.
讓我們握個手，慶祝生意的談成吧。

❗ The successful conclusion of the transaction certainly calls for some celebration. 生意談成了，一定要來慶祝一下。

It will certainly lead to a better understanding and will most certainly facilitate our discussions. 這會讓我們更深入地相互理解，促進交流。

★ facilitate：促進，幫助

We'll look forward to seeing you here again next Monday, and let's hope we can reach an agreement on everything else.
我們期待著下週一與你們再次會面，希望一切事項都能達成共識。

I suggest we go away and put together a written proposal on these.
我建議我們散會，各自寫一份書面計畫。

❗ I think we can call it a day. We've taken a step in the right direction.
我們今天就到這裡吧。我們已經朝著正確的方向邁進了一步。

I wish a brisk business for you all and a continued development in our partnership!
祝大家生意興隆，生意越做越好！

★ brisk：興旺的，繁榮的

⑭ 合約上明訂雙方必須履行的義務。

簽訂
合約

A: Here is the draft contract. **The contract stipulates the obligations that both parties shall fulfill.**
★ stipulate：規定，約定
★ fulfill：履行，完成
這是合約草案。合約上明訂雙方必須履行的義務。

B: Let's check all the items to make sure that nothing has been overlooked.
讓我們查看一下各項條款，以免疏漏了什麼。
★ overlook：看漏，忽略

❗ The contract stipulates the obligations that both parties shall fulfill.
合約上明訂雙方必須履行的義務。

❗ Can you revise this clause in the contract before we sign it?
在我們簽約前你可以修訂一下這個條款嗎？
★ arbitration：仲裁

In my opinion we should also add a standard arbitration clause.
就我看來，我們應該增加一項標準仲裁條款。

Our sales contract will expire in two years.
我們的銷售合約還有兩年的有效期。

Now, please countersign it. You may keep one original and two copies for yourself.
★ countersign：確認，同意

現在請確認後會簽。你可以保留一份原件和兩份副本。

We renewed the sales contract just now. 我們剛剛續簽了銷售合約。
★ renew：更新，續訂（契約等）   ★ alteration：改變，變更

❗ We can't agree with the alterations and amendments to the contract.
我們無法同意對合約的變動和修改。
★ amendment：修改   ★ duplicate：副本

Please sign a copy of our Sales Contract No.156 enclosed here in duplicate and return it to us for our file.
★ enclose：把…封入

請會簽隨信附寄的第 156 號銷售合約一式兩份，並將它寄回給我們存檔。

Please send a draft of our contract. We will check the contents.
請把合約的草稿寄過來。我們會確認一下內容。

We will send our contract sheets to you today. Please send one of the two copies back to us with your signature.
我們今天會寄合約給貴單位。請簽名後將一式兩份的其中一份寄回。

❗ The two parties involved in a contract have the obligation to execute the contract. **合約雙方有義務履行合約。**
★ execute：執行，履行

Any kind of backing out of the contract will be charged a penalty as it has been stated in the penalty clause. ★ back out：退出（協議、計劃等）

任何背棄合約的行為將處以罰款，這已在處罰條款裡寫得很清楚了。

談判英文
2 應對談判者
（上）

MP3 TRACK：16

Let's go ahead and set up a meeting.

談判邀約

接受談判 ➜ 參考右頁❶❷

Our main objective is to explore the possibility of cooperation.

擬訂目標

參考右頁❸❹

談判前的準備

Who's going to attend from your side?

確認與會人士

寒喧與介紹 ➜ 參考右頁❺

開場策略 ➜ 參考右頁❻❼

Our offer represents a fantastic opportunity for you.

提議

接受提議 ➜ 參考右頁❽

You may hear
對方要求談判時，也許你會聽到……

線上音檔

ⓐ 我們就著手進行並安排個會議吧。　Let's go ahead and set up a meeting.

ⓑ 我們主要的目標是要探尋合作的　Our main objective is to explore the
　可能性。　possibility of cooperation.

ⓒ 你們那邊誰會出席？　Who's going to attend from your side?

ⓓ 我們的提議對你們是個絕佳的機會。　Our offer represents a fantastic
　opportunity for you.

You may want to say
對方要求談判時，也許你會想說……

❶ 我期待著到時候和你見面。　I look forward to seeing you then. ...p.208

❷ 我要先看看我的行程安排。　Let me check my schedule first. ...p.208

❸ 我們想聽聽您的意見。　We would like to hear your
　suggestions. ...p.208

❹ 我們也收到了你們其他競爭對手的　We've also received proposals from
　提案。　your competitors. ...p.209

❺ 久仰大名，我很期待今天的會面。　I've heard a lot about you and have
　been looking forward to today's
　meeting. ...p.210

❻ 你可以舉一個例子來支援你的論點嗎？　Can you give an example to support
　your argument? ...p.210

❼ 對我來說，把成本轉嫁給消費者不　In my opinion, it's not a good idea to
　是個好方法。　transfer the cost to customers. ...p.211

❽ 你的提議的確對我們未來的發展有　Your proposal will be a great help to
　很大助益。　our future development. ...p.212

談判英文
2 應對談判者
（下）

MP3 TRACK：16

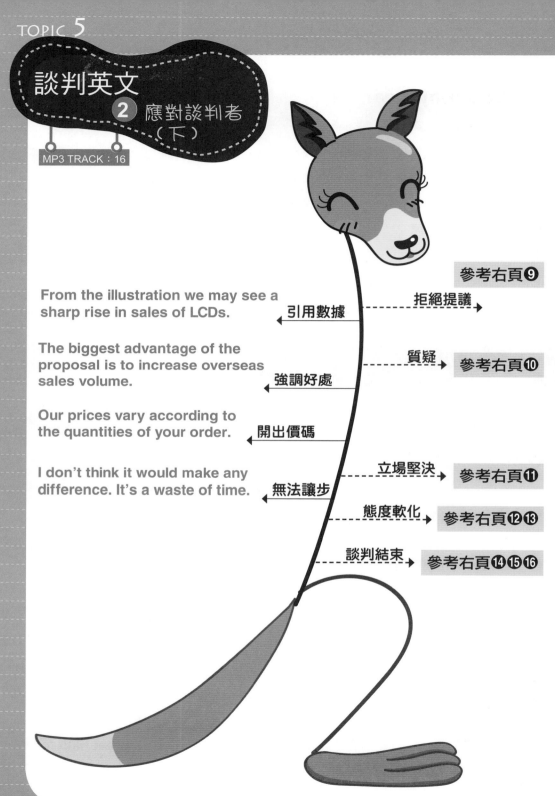

參考右頁❾

From the illustration we may see a
sharp rise in sales of LCDs.

引用數據 ←

拒絕提議 →

The biggest advantage of the
proposal is to increase overseas
sales volume.

強調好處 ←

質疑 →   參考右頁❿

Our prices vary according to
the quantities of your order.

開出價碼 ←

I don't think it would make any
difference. It's a waste of time.

無法讓步 ←

立場堅決 →   參考右頁⓫

態度軟化 →   參考右頁⓬⓭

談判結束 →   參考右頁⓮⓯⓰

🄴 從圖表可以看出，液晶螢幕 | From the illustration we may see a sharp
的銷售量大幅上升。 | rise in sales of LCDs.

🄵 這個提議最大的好處是能夠 | The biggest advantage of the proposal is
提升海外銷售量。 | to increase overseas sales volume.

🄶 我們的價格依訂購數量而有 | Our prices vary according to the quantities
所不同。 | of your order.

🄷 我不認為繼續談下去有什麼 | I don't think it would make any difference.
意義。這是在浪費時間。 | It's a waste of time.

❾ 目前為止你的提議沒有任何吸 | Up till now, your proposal has held few
引我的地方。 | attractions for me. ...p.213

❿ 這裡的數據資料中有些明顯的 | There are several major inconsistencies
矛盾。 | in your data. ...p.213

⓫ 我必須要重申，我們無法增加 | I must repeat that we cannot increase the
廣告預算。 | advertising budget. ...p.214

⓬ 我可以理解你為何這麼說。 | I can understand your position. ...p.215

⓭ 我不認為這是個好辦法，但我 | Although I don't think it is a good idea,
願意考慮。 | I'll take it into consideration. ...p.216

⓮ 我們勢必要錯失這樣的機會了。 | We're sure to lose such an opportunity. ...p.216

⓯ 當務之急是要盡快找到足夠的 | The priority is to find enough advertisers
廣告商。 | as soon as possible. ...p.217

⓰ 我們還有機會跟你談談嗎？ | Is it possible for us to have a talk again? ...p.217

❶ 我期待著到時候和你見面。

A: We need to schedule a time and place to work out the details.
我們約個時間地點，討論一下細節。

B: Sounds great. **I look forward to seeing you then.**
很好。我期待著到時候和你見面。

❗ I look forward to seeing you then. **我期待著到時候和你見面。**

OK. See you at the meeting tomorrow. 好的，明天開會見。

Great. I would also love to talk to you about it.
太好了。我也很願意與你談談這方面的問題。

❷ 我要先看看我的行程安排。

A: I'd like to set up an appointment with you, possibly at the end of April.
How does that sound? 我想與您約在四月底，不知您意下如何？

B: **Let me check my schedule first.** 我要先看看我的行程安排。

I'll let my secretary contact you after I confirm my schedule.
我確認行程表後，會請祕書聯絡您。

Any time this week would be suitable for me. 這週的任何時間我都有空。

❗ Let me check my schedule first. **我要先看看我的行程安排。**

❸ 我們想聽聽您的意見。

A: **We would like to hear your suggestions.**
我們想聽聽您的意見。

B: A 10% discount is beyond my negotiating limit. Any other ideas?
10% 的折扣超出了我能接受的底線。能不能再考慮一下？

❗ We would like to hear your suggestions. **我們想聽聽您的意見。**

Have you got any comments on our proposal? 你對我們的企劃案有何意見呢？

Do you have other suggestions about our quotations? 你對我們的報價有何建議？

Is there anything you would like to change? 有什麼是你們想要改變的？

與別人做比較

★ rock-bottom：最低點

A: This is the most favorable quotation we can make. We consider it a rock-bottom price indeed. 這是我們最優惠的價格了，確實是我們的底價了。

B: We still find no way to accept your quotation. And **we've also received proposals from your competitors.** 我們還是不能接受這個報價。我們也收到了你們其他競爭對手的提案。

❗ Perhaps we should turn to other suppliers this time.
也許我們這次該換其他的供應商了。

We've compared your price with the price from the U.S. and Egypt.
我們把你的報價跟美國和埃及的供應商做了比較。

Other buyers from your neighboring countries have made large quantities at our quoted price. 你鄰國的其他買家按我們的報價進了不少貨。

❗ Other suppliers offer a much lower price compared to yours.
其他供應商比你的報價低。

Your competitor is offering better terms. 你們的對手提出的條件要更加優惠。

❗ Your price is higher than those we got from elsewhere.
你們的價格比我們從別處得到的報價要高。

We are interested in Art. No.HX1115, but we found that your price is much higher than those offered by other suppliers.
我們對你們編號 HX1115 的物件感興趣，但發現你們的報價比其他供應商的報價還要高得多。

We've also received proposals from your competitors.
我們也收到了你們其他競爭對手的提案。

❗ I can show you other quotations that are lower than yours.
我可以把比貴公司報價還低的報價單給你看看。

❗ Don't bother if you are going to tell me about price increases. You'll be wasting your time and I will be forced to speak to your competitors.
如果你是想告訴我要漲價的話就不用了。你是在浪費時間。我也不得不向你的競爭對手尋求合作。

If you don't show your sincerity on this transaction, we may find other investors.
如果你在這筆生意中沒有誠意的話，我們可以找其他投資者。

⑤ 久仰大名，我很期待今天的會面。

A: I'm John Smith from Southern Trading Corporation. I'm glad to have the opportunity to visit your company.
我是南方貿易公司的約翰史密斯。很高興有機會參觀貴公司。

B: **I've heard a lot about you and have been looking forward to today's meeting.** 久仰大名，我很期待今天的會面。

It's been a pleasure to do business with you, Mr. Smith.
史密斯先生，跟你做生意真是我的榮幸。

I'd appreciate your kind consideration in the coming negotiation.
洽談中請你們多加關照。

I've heard a lot about you and have been looking forward to today's meeting.
久仰大名，我很期待今天的會面。

❗ We've been looking forward to your visit and hope we can do business together. 我們一直期待著您的到來，希望我們能夠合作愉快。

⑥ 你可以舉一個例子來支持你的論點嗎？

A: I hope you all agree that we put the location of the new plant in Vietnam.
我希望你們都同意把新廠址定在越南。

B: **Can you give an example to support your argument?**
你可以舉一個例子來支持你的論點嗎？

❗ Could you please explain the premises of your argument in more detail?
你能詳細說明你們的論據嗎？ ↙★ premise：假設，前提

Could you explain what you mean by that? 你能說得更明確點嗎？

Can you explain that in more detail again? 你能更詳細地解釋一下嗎？

Can you give an example to support your argument?
你可以舉一個例子來支持你的論點嗎？

❗ Sounds reasonable. Can you run some numbers for me?
聽起來很合理，您可否給我具體的數字呢？

❗ Has your company done any research in this field?
請問貴公司對此範疇做了任何研究嗎？

個人
看法

❼ 對我來說，把成本轉嫁給消費者不是個好方法

A: Our cost price is $100 for each unit. You can sell at a higher price if you want to get more profit. 我們的成本價是一百元一件。你如果想得到更多利潤的話就需要以更高價出售。

B: **In my opinion, it's not a good idea to transfer the cost to customers** ★ customers：消費者

對我來說，把成本轉嫁給消費者不是個好方法。

In my opinion, it's not a good idea to transfer the cost to customers.

對我來說，把成本轉嫁給消費者不是個好方法

❗ As far as we're concerned, financial staff should be totally appointed by us, including the auditors.
★ appointe：任命，指派

就我們而言，財務人員應該全部由我們任命，包括審計員。

❗ From my point of view, setting up a joint venture to run this project is a win-win situation.
★ win-win：雙贏的，雙方都獲利的

就我看來，建立一個合資企業來經營這個項目對雙方都有利。

I tend to think that the new shop's location on the high street would be costly and ineffective in promoting sales.

我認為，把新開幕的店址定在黃金地段，代價很高卻又無法有效促銷。

I certainly believe that sales through agents would be a wise approach to save our distribution expense.

我確信經由代理商銷售是一個非常明智的方法，能夠節省分銷的成本。

各種企業類型的說法

國營企業	state-run enterprise	國有企業	state-owned enterprise
集體企業	collectively-run enterprise	鄉鎮企業	township enterprise
公營企業	public enterprise	私營企業	private enterprise
合資企業	joint venture	聯合企業	conglomerate
產業複合體	industrial complex	生產型企業	production enterprise

✕   ✕

❽ 你的提議的確對我們未來的發展有很大助益。

A: **Your proposal will be a great help to our future development.** 你的提議的確對我們未來的發展有很大助益。

B: I'm glad to hear that. 很高興聽到你這樣說。

We embrace your proposal. 我們接受你的提案。
★ embrace：欣然接受

I'm satisfied. We have an agreement. 我很滿意。我們達成了共識。

Your proposal will be a great help to our future development.
你的提議的確對我們未來的發展有很大助益。

❗ Looks like we've got ourselves a deal. 看來我們達成協議了。

❗ We found your proposal quite interesting, Mr. Grant.
格蘭先生，本公司對貴公司的提案很有興趣。

Mr. Jackson, I've studied all your reports, and your company is making excellent progress. 傑克森先生，我已經看了貴公司的報告，看來貴公司業績很不錯。

❗ We feel inclined to agree to let you be the agent for our products.
★ incline to：傾向，有意

我們傾向於同意你們做產品代理商。

After considering your proposals and investigating your business standing, we have decided to appoint you as our agent in the district.
經過仔細考慮你們的提議和調查你的業界名望後，我們決定由你們作為我們這一地區的代理商。

各種貿易方式

agency	代理	consignment	寄售
agent	代理人	consignor	寄售人
general agent	總代理	consignee	代銷人
exclusive agent	獨家代理	distribution	經銷
sole agent	獨家代理	distributor	經銷商
commission agent	傭金代理	sole distribution	獨家經銷

❾ 目前為止你的提議沒有任何吸引我的地方。

A: Have you got any comments on our proposal?
你對我們的企劃案有何意見呢？

B: **Up till now, your proposal has held few attractions for me.** 目前為止你的提議沒有任何吸引我的地方。

❗ I don't think that's feasible. 我不認為這可行。

❗ You are not giving us anything really attractive.
你的提案對於我們來說沒有任何吸引力。

Up till now, your proposal has held few attractions for me.
目前為止你的提議沒有任何吸引我的地方。

Given the expense of our environment, I have to say sorry to your proposal.
考慮到我們環境所付出的代價，我不得不駁回你的方案。

We are not interested in taking a position in the new project; we don't think there is a market for it. 我們對投資這項新計畫沒有興趣，因為我們不認為它會有市場。

After weighing the pros and cons, we feel that it would be too expensive to build new offices so close to Taipei.
仔細考慮優缺點後，我們覺得要在臺北附近建新公司，花費太高了。

＊weigh the pros and cons 是「衡量正反意見（得失）」的意思。

❿ 這裡的數據資料中有些明顯的矛盾。

A: What's your opinion of our proposal? 貴公司對我們的提議有什麼看法？

B: We regret that we are unable to accept your proposal as **there are several major inconsistencies in your data.**
我們很遺憾不能接受你們提議，因為這裡的數據資料中有些明顯的矛盾。

❗ Some of the figures are apparently not accurate.
這些資料有一些明顯是不準確的。

There are several major inconsistencies in your data.
這裡的數據資料中有些明顯的矛盾。 ★ inconsistency：前後矛盾

The problem lies in the fact that your numbers don't add up.
問題在於你的數據說不通。

I have some questions about the report. 我對報告有一些疑問。

⑪ 我必須要重申，我們無法增加廣告預算。

A: **I must repeat that we cannot increase the advertising budget.** 我必須要重申，我們無法增加廣告預算。

B: I must first talk to my office. I hope we can find some common ground on this. 我必須向公司彙報，我希望我們能找到共同的立場。

I must repeat that we cannot increase the advertising budget.
我必須要重申，我們無法增加廣告預算。

I regret to say it again that we cannot accept you're doubling the cost.
對不起，我再說一次，我們不能接受你們把成本提高一倍。

What I'm saying makes perfect sense if you think about it logically.
如果你依邏輯來思考，那麼我所說的是非常合理的。

At the risk of repeating myself, there is no way we can agree on that.
雖然我可能是舊話重提，但是我們不可能會同意那一點的。

❗ We'll never be able to come down to your price. The gap is too great.
我們的價格永遠不能降到你們提出的水準，差距太大了。

❗ It is beyond my negotiating limit. **這已經超過了我們談判的底線。**

I'm sorry to repeat it again that this is the best we can do. Please make allowance for our difficulties. 對不起，我重複一次，這是我們的底限了。請體諒我們的難處。
＊ make allowance for 是「考慮到」、「體諒」的意思。

❗ I'm sorry, but I can't go along with that. **對不起，我無法同意這一點。**
└★ go along with：贊同

I'm sorry, but I can't support that position / idea.
對不起，我無法同意這一個觀點。

I don't think it will work. 我認為這不可行。

Can I just run over the main points? 我可否再重複一遍要點?
└★ run over：重溫，匆匆復習

I'm sure there is no room for negotiation. 我肯定沒有商量的餘地。

I don't want to go over the same ground. 在這裡我不想再重複同樣的內容了。
└★ ground：立場，觀點

I think I have covered everything. 我想我已經談及所有內容了。

❗ I don't have anything else to say. **我要說的都說完了。**

214

⑫ 我可以理解你為何這麼說。

A: It is not reasonable if we get a smaller share in the revenue.
如果我們只得到小部分的收益，那就很不合理了。　★ revenue：總收入

B: **I can understand your position.** But we are accountable for
the technical workers as well.　★ accountable：應負責任的
我可以理解你為何這麼說。但是我們也要對技術工人負責。

❗ Now I have a much better understanding. 原來如此啊。

❗ You definitely have a point there. 你說的確實有道理。

We are in complete agreement on this. 我們在這一點上完全一致。

I can understand your position. 我可以理解你為何這麼說。

You've made an excellent point. I couldn't agree more.
你說得非常好，我再同意不過了。

Not a bad idea, but maybe we should look at the larger picture.
不錯的主意，但也許我們應該從大局出發。

Your proposal appears to be acceptable. Let us assume that we agree on that
point, unless I find any objections in it.
你的建議聽上去是可行的。我們同意那一點，除非發現有什麼令人不愉快的地方。

❗ I agree with you in principle, but I would like to add other points sometime
later. 原則上我同意，但稍後我還要補充一下其他觀點。

Concerning the three items we discussed, we agree on item 6 but would like to
consider further whether we can agree on items 4 and 9. 考慮過我們雙方討論的三
件事之後，我們同意第六條。至於第四和第九條，我們還要再進一步考慮。

❗ I can accept your proposal on the scope of the technology, but not the
others. 在技術領域我同意你的建議，但其他方面的我不同意。

I agree with you on the merits of your proposal. But wouldn't it be more practical to
consider handling it in the following manner?
我承認貴公司提案的價值。不過按照以下方法來具體操作是否更為實際？

Let us try to adopt your ideas into a concrete plan satisfactory to both parties.
讓我們嘗試把你的觀點形成一個雙方都滿意的切實計畫。

I agree with some of what you've said, but I still maintain the idea that our customers
are going to notice the difference.　★ maintain：堅決主張
我同意你說的某些話，但是我還是堅決認為我們的客戶會注意到不同之處。

215

⓭ 我不認為這是個好辦法，但我願意考慮。

A: I'd like to propose that we meet each other half way, say a five percent discount instead of ten?
我建議我們雙方各讓一步，比方把九折改為九五折？

B: **Although I don't think it is a good idea, I'll take it into consideration.** 我不認為這是個好辦法，但我願意考慮。

❗ I'm afraid I can't accept that. 我恐怕不能接受。

I'm sorry, but we can't really do that. 對不起，我們不能這麼做。

I'm afraid I'm not very happy about that. 我想我不樂意這麼做。

I'm sorry, but I can't support your proposal. 很抱歉，我不能贊成你的建議。

❗ Although I don't think it is a good idea, I'll take it into consideration.
我不認為這是個好辦法，但我願意考慮。

I'm afraid that it doesn't sound very good to me. 我不太同意。

I'm still not convinced; however, I'm willing to keep listening.
我還是不相信，但是我願意繼續聽下去。

⓮ 我們勢必要錯失這樣的機會了。

A: If you want a big discount, you must make a larger order.
如果你想要更大的折扣，那你就必須要訂更多的貨。

B: Unless you make a concession, **we're sure to lose such an opportunity.**
除非你們有所讓步，否則我們勢必要錯失這樣的機會了。

We're sure to lose such an opportunity. 我們勢必要錯失這樣的機會了。

❗ We're not prepared to accept your proposal at this time.
我們這一次不準備接受你們的建議。

I regret to say that upon scrutinizing your proposal, we found it unacceptable.

★ scrutinize：詳細檢查

很遺憾地說，細看你的提案過後，我們無法接受。

❗ Frankly, we can't agree with your proposal.
坦白講，我無法同意您的提案。

216

⑮ 當務之急是要盡快找到足夠的廣告商。

A: Make a special effort, please. A timely promotion means a lot to us.
請特別加把勁。及時地宣傳對我們很重要。
B: **The priority is to find enough advertisers as soon as possible.** 當務之急是要盡快找到足夠的廣告商。

❗ The priority is to find enough advertisers as soon as possible.
當務之急是要盡快找到足夠的廣告商.

Great. Then let's settle the details of the transfer agreement.
好！那我們來確定有關技術轉移的細節問題。

Let's move on to the issue of equipment and premises.
下面我們來談談設備和廠房問題吧。

I'll contact the home office immediately for instructions on the matter.
我會立刻跟總部聯繫，看看他們在這件事上有什麼指示。

❗ We'll fix the details and get back to you a couple of days later.
我們敲定一下細節問題，兩天以後給你答覆。

We will have the sales contract ready in two days.
兩天後銷售合約就會準備好。

⑯ 我們還有機會跟你談談嗎？

A: **Is it possible for us to have a talk again?**
我們還有機會跟你談談嗎？ ★ adjournment：休會
B: OK, I see. Why don't we have an adjournment and get back to the issue after lunch? 我明白了。我們先休會，吃了午餐再來談好吧？

❗ Is it possible for us to have a talk again? 我們還有機會跟你談談嗎？
Our policy has changed. 我們的政策有了變化。

❗ What happened last week was unacceptable. Shall we move on? 上週的結果是我們無法接受的。現在我們能繼續談一下嗎？
Our supervisor has conducted a reappraisal on your proposal and we find it acceptable to a degree. ★ reappraisal：再評價
我們的上司重新評估了你們的策劃案，發現在一定程度上還是可以接受的。

217

面試英文
① 求職者（上）

MP3 TRACK：17

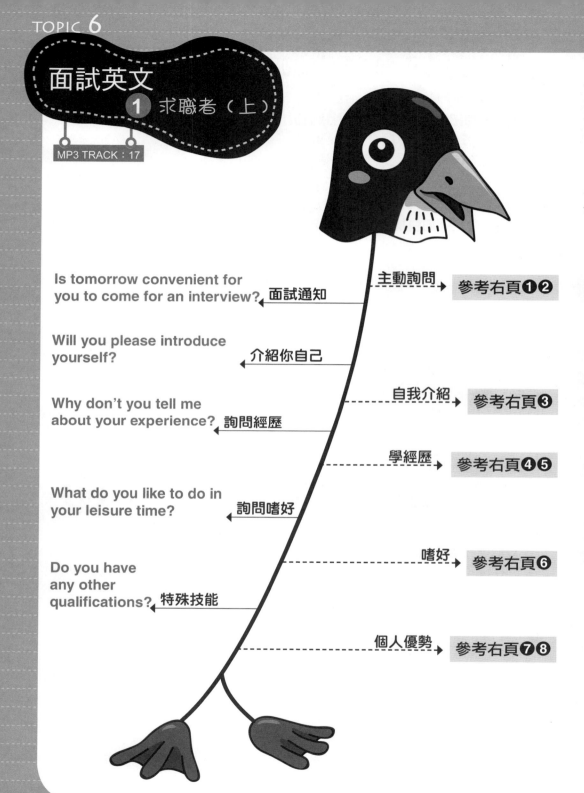

Is tomorrow convenient for you to come for an interview? — 面試通知 — 主動詢問 → 參考右頁 ❶❷

Will you please introduce yourself? — 介紹你自己

自我介紹 → 參考右頁 ❸

Why don't you tell me about your experience? — 詢問經歷

學經歷 → 參考右頁 ❹❺

What do you like to do in your leisure time? — 詢問嗜好

嗜好 → 參考右頁 ❻

Do you have any other qualifications? — 特殊技能

個人優勢 → 參考右頁 ❼❽

線上音檔

You may hear
求職面試時，也許你會聽到……

ⓐ 請問您明天方便過來面試嗎？　Is tomorrow convenient for you to come for an interview?

ⓑ 你可以先自我介紹嗎？　Will you please introduce yourself?

ⓒ 何不談談你的經歷呢？　Why don't you tell me about your experience?

ⓓ 你閒暇時喜歡做些什麼？　What do you like to do in your leisure time?

ⓔ 你還有別的證照嗎？　Do you have any other qualifications?

You may want to say
求職面試時，也許你會想說……

❶ 請問貴公司有任何職位空缺嗎？　Do you have any openings available? ...p.222

❷ 我是來面試祕書職務的，我約兩點。　I've come to apply for the position as an office secretary. We said we'll meet at 14:00. ...p.227

❸ 我是凱莉，台北人，今年二十五歲。　I'm Kelly from Taipei and I'm 25 years old. ...p.227

❹ 大學時期我曾經擔任學生會會長。　I was the president of the Student Union of our university. ...p.228

❺ 目前我在一家科技公司擔任業務經理。　Currently, I serve as a business manager at a technology company. ...p.228

❻ 我喜歡閱讀，尤其是推理小說。　I like reading, especially whodunits. ...p.229

❼ 我擁有國際會計師執照。　I've received my ACCA certificate. ...p.230

❽ 我曾經主導幾項公司的大型計畫。　I was in charge of many large projects for the company. ...p.231

面試英文
① 求職者（下）

MP3 TRACK：17

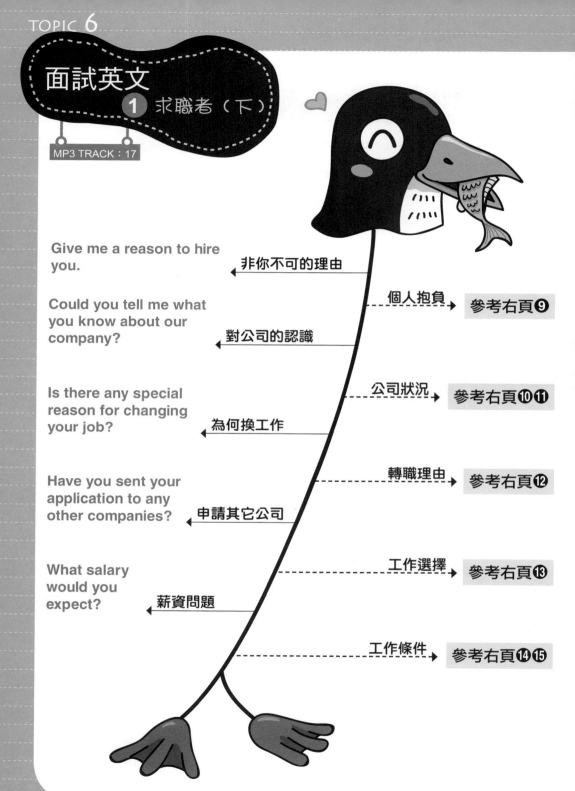

Give me a reason to hire you.
非你不可的理由

Could you tell me what you know about our company?
個人抱負 → 參考右頁❾

對公司的認識

Is there any special reason for changing your job?
公司狀況 → 參考右頁❿⓫

為何換工作

Have you sent your application to any other companies?
轉職理由 → 參考右頁⓬

申請其它公司

What salary would you expect?
工作選擇 → 參考右頁⓭

薪資問題

工作條件 → 參考右頁⓮⓯

You may hear
求職面試時，也許你會聽到……（續）

f 請說出一個我非雇用你不可的理由。　　Give me a reason to hire you.

g 可以談一談你對本公司的認識嗎？　　Could you tell me what you know about our company?

h 你轉換工作有什麼特別原因嗎？　　Is there any special reason for changing your job?

i 你有沒有申請其它公司？　　Have you sent your application to any other companies?

j 你的期望薪資是多少？　　What salary would you expect?

You may want to say
求職面試時，也許你會想說……（續）

❾ 我隨時準備好擔當重任，並且樂於學習。　　I am ready to take responsibility and I'm willing to learn. ...p.232

❿ 貴公司大部分的產品都外銷到日本和南韓。　　The products in your company are mostly marketed in Japan and South Korea. ...p.236

⓫ 我願意配合外派到任何地方。　　I'm ready to go anywhere. ...p.236

⓬ 就收入來說，前一份工作相當不穩定。　　Economically, it's fairly unstable. ...p.237

⓭ 貴公司是我的第一選擇。　　My first choice is your company. ...p.237

⓮ 以我的教育和資格認證，我相信能得到相應的待遇。　　With my education and qualifications, I believe I shall be fairly treated. ...p.238

⓯ 必要的話，即使熬夜或假日工作我也沒問題。　　If necessary, I won't hesitate to work nights or holidays. ...p.238

A: I am looking for a job. **Do you have any openings available?**
　我正在找工作。請問貴公司有任何職位空缺嗎？

B: I might. What kind of experience do you have?
　可能有缺。你有什麼樣的經驗呢？

❗ Do you have any openings available? 請問貴公司有任何職位空缺嗎？

❗ Do you still have that vacancy? 這個職位還空著嗎？

* opening 和 vacancy 在此都指空缺的職位。

What kind of openings do you have? 你們有什麼類型的職位空缺？

Is the job you advertised in the newspaper still vacant?

你們刊登在報紙上的這個職位還有嗎？　　　★ vacant：（職位）空缺的

Do you know if you will have some other openings? 不知道你們其他職位缺不缺人？

❗ I am calling about your advertisement in the newspaper.
　我想詢問關於你們登在報紙上的徵人資訊。

I want to know more about the position. 我希望多了解一下這個職位。

I am calling about the position I saw in the newspaper.
我打電話來詢問報紙上刊登的這個職位。

I'm interested in the job you advertised in the newspaper yesterday.
我對你們昨天在報紙上登的職位感興趣。

"Also need to know

英文履歷表的寫法

最基本的英文履歷表寫法共有五個步驟。原則上先填寫基本資料，接著寫工作經歷與學歷證照等等，並從最新一份的工作內容開始往前填寫（也就是先寫上一份工作經驗，再寫上上一份工作經驗）。

Step 1 → Personal Information（個人資料）。

Step 2 → Employment History（工作經歷）。

Step 3 → Education（學歷、教育程度）。

Step 4 → Skills（特殊技能）。

Step 5 → References（推薦人）。

常見公司・職位中英文對照

公司決策人

執行長・總經理	CEO / GM / President
副總經理	Deputy GM / VP / Management Trainee
總監	Director
合夥人	Partner
總裁・總經理助理	CEO / GM / President Assistant

資訊類

技術總監（經理）	Technical Director (Manager)
資訊技術經理	IT Manager
資訊技術主管	IT Supervisor
資訊技術專員	IT Specialist
專案經理（主管）	Project Manager (Supervisor)
專案執行專員（協調人員）	Project Specialist (Coordinator)
技術支援經理	Technical Support Manager
技術支援工程師	Technical Support Engineer
品質經理	QA Manager
系統管理員	System Manager
網管	Webmaster
網頁設計員	Web Designer
製作	Production
技術員・助理	Technical Clerk / Assistant

業務類

業務總監	Sales Director
業務經理	Sales Manager
區域業務經理	Regional Sales Manager
業務經理	Sales Account Manager
業務主管	Sales Supervisor
業務代表	Sales Representative (Executive)
業務工程師	Sales Engineer
業務助理	Sales Assistant
業務行政經理	Sales Admin. Manager
經銷商	Distributor

市場與財務類

行銷・廣告總監	Marketing / Advertising Director
行銷經理	Marketing Manager
行銷主管	Marketing Supervisor
行銷專員	Marketing Executive
行銷助理	Marketing Assistant
促銷專員	Promotions Specialist
市場分析員	Market Analyst
研究人員	Research Analyst
企業・業務發展經理	Business Development Manager
企業策劃人員	Corporate Planning
財務長	CFO / Finance Director
財務經理	Finance Manager (Supervisor)
會計經理（主管）	Accounting Manager (Supervisor)
會計員	Accountant
出納員	Cashier
財務（會計）助理	Finance (Accounting) Assistant
財務分析經理（主管）	Financial Analysis Manager (Supervisor)
財務分析員	Financial Analyst
成本經理（主管）	Cost Accounting Manager (Supervisor)
成本管理員	Cost Accounting Specialist

審計經理（主管） Audit Manager (Supervisor)	技術・工業設計經理（主管） Technical / Industrial Design Manager (Supervisor)
審計專員　　　　　　Audit Executive	
審計助理　　　　　　Audit Assistant	技術・工業設計工程師
稅務經理（主管） Tax Manager (Supervisor)	Technical / Industrial Design Engineer
稅務專員　　　　　　　Tax Executive	實驗室負責人　　　　　　　Lab Manager
證券經紀人　　　　　　　Stock Broker	工程・設備經理（主管） Engineering / Facility Manager (Supervisor)
投資顧問　　　　　Investment Advisor	工程・設備工程師
投資分析師　Certified Investment Analyst	Engineering / Facility Engineer
進出口・信用證結算人員 Trading / LC Officer	電氣・電子工程師 Electrical / Electronics Engineer
資深客戶經理 Senior Relationship Manager	機械工程師　　　　Mechanical Engineer
	機電工程師
信貸・信用調查人員 Loan / Credit Officer	Electrical & Mechanical Engineer
	維修工程師　　　　Maintenance Engineer
銀行櫃檯出納　　　　　　　Bank Teller	安全・健康・環境工程師
統計員　　　　　　　　　Statistician	Safety / Health / Environment Engineer

● 生產營運類 ●

	工程繪圖員　Project Drafting Specialist
生產・營運・工程人員 Manufacturing / Operations / Engineering staff	機械製圖員　　　　Drafting Specialist
	化驗員　　　　　Laboratory Technician
工廠經理・廠長　Plant / Factory Manager	技工　　　Technician / Engineer Trainee
總工程師　　　　　　　Chief Engineer	電工　　　　　　　　　　Electrician
專案經理（主管） Project Manager (Supervisor)	## ● 人事與行政類 ●
專案工程師　　　　　Project Engineer	人事經理（主管） Human Resources Manager (Supervisor)
營運經理　　　　　Operations Manager	人事專員　Human Resources Specialist
營運主管　　　　Operations Supervisor	人事助理　Human Resources Assistant
生產經理　　　　　Production Manager	招聘經理（主管） Recruiting Manager (Supervisor)
工廠監督　　　　Workshop Supervisor	薪資福利經理（主管） Compensation & Benefits Manager (Supervisor)
生產計畫協調員 Production Planning Executive	
生產主管　　　　Production Supervisor	薪資福利專員・助理 Compensation & Benefits Specialist / Assistant
團隊督導　　　　　　　Team Leader	

培訓經理（主管） Training Manager (Supervisor)	倉庫經理　　Warehouse Manager
	倉管專員　　Warehouse Specialist
培訓專員·助理 Training Specialist / Assistant	運輸經理（主管） Distribution Manager (Supervisor)
行政經理（主管） Administration Manager (Supervisor)	報關專員　　Customs Specialist
	船務專員　　Shipping Specialist
辦公室主任　　Office Manager	快遞員　　Courier
行政專員·助理 Administration Staff / Assistant	倉管人員 Warehouse Stock Management
執行助理　　Executive Assistant	

祕書　　Secretary	**媒體與藝術文化類**
接待員·總機　　Receptionist	編輯　　Editor
後勤　　Office Support	作家　　Writer
資料管理專員 Information (Data) Management Specialist	記者　　Journalist / Reporter
	校對員　　Proofreader
電腦操作員　　Computer Operator	排版設計員　　Layout Designer
打字員　　Typist	創意·設計總監 Creative / Design Director
物流與採購類	導演　　Director
	攝影師　　Photographer
物流經理（主管） Logistics Manager (Supervisor)	音效師　　Recording / Sounds Specialist
	演員·女演員　　Actor / Actress
物流專員·助理 Logistics Specialist / Assistant	模特兒　　Model
	主持人　　MC＝master of ceremonies
物料經理（主管） Materials Manager (Supervisor)	平面·美術設計師 Graphic Artist / Designer
採購經理（主管） Purchasing / Merchandise Manager (Supervisor)	服裝設計師　　Fashion Designer
	工業產品設計師　　Industrial Designer
採購專員　　Purchasing Specialist / Staff	工藝品·珠寶設計師 Artwork / Jewelry Designer
貿易經理（主管） Trading Manager (Supervisor)	**法律類**
貿易專員·助理 Trading Specialist / Assistant	律師　　Lawyer
	法務人員　　Legal Personnel
資深採購　　Senior Merchandiser	律師助理　　Legal Assistant
採購　　Merchandiser	書記員　　Court Clerk
助理採購　　Assistant Merchandiser	

教學類

教學・教務管理人員	
	Education / School Administrator
助教	Teaching Assistant
講師	Lecturer
家教	Tutor

醫學類

醫生（中、西醫）	Medical Doctor
醫學管理人員	
	Healthcare / Medical Management
醫藥技術人員	Medical Technician
藥劑師	Pharmacist
護士・護理人員	
	Nurse / Nursing Personnel
臨床協調員	Clinical Coordinator
臨床研究員	Clinical Researcher
麻醉師	Anesthesiologist
心理醫生	Psychologist / Psychiatrist
臨床實驗室	Clinical Laboratory

顧問類

資深顧問	Senior Consultant
諮詢總監	Consulting Director
諮詢經理	Consulting Manager
諮詢員	Consultant

實習生

培訓生	Trainee / Intern

服務業類

健身教練	Fitness Trainer
餐飲・娛樂經理	
	Banquet Services Manager
接待經理	Reception Manager
領班	Supervisor
服務員	Service Staff
營業員・收銀員	
	Shop Clerk / Cashier
廚師	Chef / Cook
導遊	Tour Guide
司機	Chauffeur / Driver
保全	Security
話務員	Paging Operator

建築類

建築工程師	Architect
結構工程師	Structural Engineer
電氣工程師	Electrical Engineer
排水工程師	Drainage Engineer
工程造價師	Budgeting Specialist
建築工程管理	Construction Management
工程監督人員	
	Engineering Project Supervisor
裝潢師	Decorator
都市規劃與設計師	Urban Designer
電腦製圖員	CAD Drafter
施工人員	Construction Crew
房地產開發・規劃	
	Real Estate Development / Planning
房地產評估	Real Estate Appraisal
房地產仲介	Real Estate Agent
物業管理	Property Management

❷ 我是來面試祕書職務的，我約兩點。

A: Hello. May I help you? 你好。有什麼需要我幫助的嗎？

B: **I've come to apply for the position as an office secretary. We said we'll meet at 14:00.**
   我是來面試祕書職務的，我約兩點。

❗ I've come to apply for the position as an office secretary. We said we'll meet at 14:00. 我是來面試祕書職務的，我約兩點。

I spoke with Miss Chen about a week ago and she told me to come for an interview today. 我一週前和陳小姐通過電話，她讓我今天過來面試。

Excuse me. May I see Mr. Cook, the personnel manager?
打擾了，我想見人事經理酷克先生。

❸ 我是凱莉，台北人，今年二十五歲。

A: Tell me a little about yourself, please? 請介紹一下你自己？

B: **I'm Kelly from Taipei and I'm 25 years old.**
   我是凱莉，臺北人，今年二十五歲。

I'm Kelly from Taipei and I'm 25 years old.
我是凱莉，臺北人，今年二十五歲。

My address is No. 32, Fusing South Road, Taipei.
我的住址是台北市復興南路三十二號。

❗ I was born on January 1, 1985. 我出生於一九八五年一月一日。

I was born into a medium-sized family. 我出生於一個中等家庭。

I was born in Chicago and went to school there, right up through college.
我在芝加哥出生，在那裡直到大學畢業。

My birthplace is Hong Kong. 我的出生地在香港。

We are only three people - my parents and I.
我家只有三個人——父母和我。

❗ My father is a doctor and my mother is a teacher.
我父親是醫生，母親是老師。

❗ I'm not married. I'm still single. 我沒有結婚，還是單身。

❹ 大學時期我曾經擔任學生會會長。

A: Were you in a leadership position when you were a college student?
你讀大學時有沒有擔任過學生幹部？

B: **I was the president of the Student Union of our university.** 大學時期我曾經擔任學生會會長。 └─ ★ Student Union：學生會

I was the president of the Student Union of our university.
大學時期我曾經擔任學生會會長。

❗ English was my best subject. 英文是我最好的科目。

❗ I got a university scholarship in the 2009 academic year.
我在 2009 學年度獲得大學獎學金。

❗ My minor was Business Administration. 我輔修企業管理。
＊minor 是「輔修課程」，major 是「主修課程」。

I did my thesis on "Taiwan's Business Relationship with America."
我的論文題目是「台灣與美國的貿易關係」。

I made many friends by participating in extracurricular activities.
我藉由參加課外活動認識了很多好朋友。 └─★ extracurricular activities：課外活動

❺ 目前我在一家科技公司擔任業務經理。

A: What is your position at present? 你目前的職位是什麼？

B: **Currently, I serve as a business manager at a technology company.** 目前我在一家科技公司擔任業務經理。

Currently, I serve as a business manager at a technology company.
目前我在一家科技公司擔任業務經理。

❗ I used to be a computer engineer. 我曾擔任過電腦工程師。

❗ I worked for a foreign company as a manager. 我在一家外商擔任經理。

I worked as a receptionist for five years at the Gloria Hotel.
我在葛洛莉亞飯店擔任過 5 年大廳接待員。

❗ I have experience of working as a part-time salesman for a company.
我曾當過兼職推銷員。

I have been working as a clerk at the Personnel Department of ABC Company since
I graduated from university. 大學畢業後，我一直在 ABC 公司的人事部當職員。

❻ 我喜歡閱讀，尤其是推理小說。　　　　嗜好

A: What are your hobbies? 你有什麼嗜好？

B: **I like reading, especially whodunits.**

　我喜歡閱讀，尤其是推理小說。　　★ whodunit：（口語）偵探小說或影片

❗ I enjoy rock climbing. **我喜歡攀岩。**

❗ I read books or tidy up my room, or go shopping usually.
　我通常讀書、整理房間或者逛街。

　I like reading, especially whodunits. **我喜歡閱讀，尤其是推理小說。**

　Music and walking are my two great interests in life.
　音樂和散步是我人生中最主要的兩項嗜好。　　★ statesman：政治家

❗ I enjoy reading biographies, especially those about well-known statesmen
　and artists. **我喜歡讀傳記，尤其是著名的政治家和藝術家的傳記。**

❗ My hobbies are hiking, fishing and climbing.
　我的嗜好是遠足，釣魚和爬山。

　My favorite subject is photography. **我最喜歡的的科目是攝影。**

　My type of reading is *Business Weekly*.
　我最喜歡閱讀的書刊是《商業週刊》。

Also need to know

表達興趣愛好的常用句型

I've always liked listening to inspiring speeches.
我一直喜歡聽鼓舞人心的演講。
I enjoy reciting an English passage every day.
我喜歡每天背誦一點英文短文。
I am / get excited about surfing the Internet.
我對上網很感興趣。
I'm crazy about ancient Chinese poetry.
我迷上了中國古代詩詞。
I have a passion for American movies.
我酷愛美國電影。
I have strong interest in visiting historical relics.
我對參觀歷史古跡有濃厚興趣。
Writing articles on my blog is my favorite hobby.
在我的部落格上寫文章是我喜歡做的事。

❼ 我擁有國際會計師執照。 證照

A: Do you have any special skills? 你有什麼特殊才能嗎？
B: **I've received my ACCA certificate.** 我擁有國際會計師執照。

❗ I've received my ACCA certificate. 我擁有國際會計師執照。
　＊CPA = Certified Public Account 註冊會計師
　　ACCA = The Association of Chartered Certified Accountants 英國特許公認會計師協會

❗ I have a good command of secretarial skills. **我熟悉祕書事務。**

　I have a driver's license. 我有駕駛執照。

　I've received a Computer Operator's Qualification Certificate.
　我已取得電腦操作員資格證書。

　I can type at 100 words per minute. 我打字的速度是每分鐘一百字。

❗ I can speak English fluently. **我可以說流利的英文。**

　I can speak not only English, but also French. 我不僅會講英文，還會講法文。

❗ I passed the Advanced Level in the General English Proficiency Test.
　我通過了全民英檢高級測驗。

　I have a Cambridge Business English Certificate. 我有劍橋商務英語證書。

　I can both understand and speak Cantonese. 我聽得懂並且會講廣東話。

　I have taken the exam TOEFL-iBT and received a score of 110.
　我參加了托福考試，得了 110 分的高分。

❗ I'm quite proficient in both written and spoken English.
　我在英語寫與說方面相當熟練。

Also need to know

各類語言考試全稱

TOEFL = Test of English as a Foreign Language 托福測驗，申請美加地區大學或研究所時常用。
IELTS = International English Language Testing System
雅思測驗，申請英澳紐等國家大學或研究所時常用。
GRE = Graduate Record Examinations 美國除商學院、法學院和醫學院研究生之外的研究生考試。
GMAT = Graduate Management Admission Test 美國商學研究所（MBA）入學考試。
TOEIC = Test of English for International Communication 多益測驗，全球通用的商用英語測驗。
GEPT = Genaral English Proficiency Test 全民英檢，台灣自行研發的英語測驗。

❽ 我曾經主導幾項公司的大型計畫。

A: What did you do in your company? 你在以前的公司做過什麼？

B: **I was in charge of many large projects for the company.**
我曾經主導幾項公司的大型計畫。

❗ I was in charge of many large projects for the company.
我曾經主導幾項公司的大型計畫。

★ assort with：和…相配

❗ I can assort with different departments easily.
我能夠確實協調各部門的工作。

I once made a successful case in Shanghai. 我曾在上海完成了一個成功的方案。

I accomplished a commercial advertisement for a well-known company.
我為一家知名公司完成了一則商業廣告。

❗ I established business ties with several firms.
我與幾家公司建立了業務關係。

I've translated various technical materials. 我翻譯過各式各樣的技術資料。

❗ Since I acted as the product manager, I have reduced our production cost
by 35%. 自我擔任生產經理以來，我們的生產成本降低了 35%。

I succeeded in raising our yearly sales volume by 25%.
我成功地把年銷售量提高了 25%。 ★ sales volume：銷售額

I supervised two other female colleagues and also took care of the company's

correspondence ★ correspondence：信件
我督導其他兩位女職員，並處理公司的信件。

I took charge of assigning various subjects of articles and columns to the editors.
我負責指派各種題材的文章和專欄給編輯們去寫。

My former employer told me that my sales skills were an asset to the company.
我之前的老闆說我的銷售技巧對公司很有助益。 ★ asset：有利條件

Because of my work achievements, I have got a lot of praise from my boss,
colleagues and clients.
由於我的工作成就，我得到老闆、同事和客戶的許多稱讚。

At the beginning of the second year after I took that position, our company's share
of the market grew from twenty percent to thirty and the share continues to grow.
在我接任該職務的第二年，我們公司的市場佔有率從百分之二十成長到百分之
三十，而且持續成長。

工作熱忱

A: What's your opinion of the work? 你對工作的觀點是什麼?

B: **I am ready to take responsibility and I'm willing to learn.** 我隨時準備好擔當重任,並且樂於學習。

❗ I am ready to take responsibility and I'm willing to learn.
我隨時準備好擔當重任,並且樂於學習。

★ diligently:勤奮地   ★ supervision:管理,監督

I'm willing and able to work diligently without supervision.
我願意並且能夠在沒有監督的情況下認真工作。

I have an excellent ability to work well with others.
我能夠與他人一起愉快工作。

❗ I can work under pressure with leadership quality.
我能在壓力下工作,並具備領導能力。

I have a stable personality and a high sense of responsibility.
我個性穩重、具高度責任感。

I'm a person with ability plus flexibility. 我是有能力並且適應力強的人。

I'm bright and aggressive. 我反應快、有進取心。

I have a strong determination to succeed. 我有獲得成功的堅定決心。

Professionalism, experience, and attention to details are what I would bring to your firm. 我會為貴公司帶來專業精神、經驗,以及注意小細節的特質。

I can always put things in order. 我做事一向很有條理。

When I work with people of different character, I will adapt my manner to suit them.
當我與個性與自己不同的人共事時,我能改變自己的方式以適應別人。

❗ I can take on jobs that bother other people and work on them patiently until they get done. 我能承擔那些別人嫌麻煩的工作,並能耐心地完成它們。

I'd rather cooperate with other people and get the job done as a team.
我樂於與其他人合作,加入團隊工作。

❗ I think the spirit at work means not only to complete the assignment but also to satisfy one's sense of achievement.
我認為,工作熱忱不只是完成任務,而且要滿足自己的成就感。

形容性格的字彙 A - Z

A

able	有才幹的，能幹的	active	主動的，活躍的
adaptable	適應性強的	adroit	靈巧的，機敏的
aggressive	有進取心的	alert	機靈的
ambitious	有雄心壯志的	amiable	和藹可親的
amicable	友好的	analytical	善於分析的
apprehensive	有理解力的	aspiring	有志氣的，有抱負的
audacious	大膽的，有冒險精神的		

C

capable	有能力的，有才能的	careful	辦事仔細的
candid	正直的	charitable	寬厚的
competent	能勝任的	confident	有信心的
conscientious	認真的，自覺的	considerate	體貼的
constructive	積極的	contemplative	好沉思的
cooperative	有合作精神的	creative	富創造力的

D

dashing	衝勁十足的	devoted	有奉獻精神的
dedicated	有奉獻精神的	diplomatic	老練的，有策略的
dependable	可靠的	discreet	（在行動，說話等方面）謹慎的
disciplined	守紀律的		
dutiful	盡職的	dynamic	精悍的

E

earnest	認真的	well-educated	受過良好教育的
efficient	有效率的	energetic	精力充沛的
enthusiastic	充滿熱情的	expressive	善於表達

F・G

faithful	守信的，忠誠的	forceful	（性格）堅強的
frank	直率的，真誠的	friendly	友好的
frugal	儉樸的	generous	寬宏大量的
genteel	有教養的	gentle	有禮貌的

H

hard-working	勤勞的	hearty	精神飽滿的
honest	誠實的	hospitable	殷勤的
humble	恭順的	humorous	幽默的

I

impartial	公正的	independent	有主見的
industrious	勤奮的	ingenious	有獨創性的
initiative	主動的	intellective	有智力的
intelligent	理解力強的	inventive	有發明才能的，有創造力的

J・K・L・M

just	正直的	kind-hearted	好心的
knowledgeable	有見識的	learned	有學問的
liberal	心胸寬大的	logical	條理分明的
loyal	忠心耿耿的	methodical	有方法的
modest	謙虛的	motivated	目的明確的

O

objective	客觀的	open-minded	虛心的
orderly	守紀律的	original	有獨創性的

P・Q

painstaking	辛勤的，刻苦的	practical	實際的
precise	一絲不苟的	persevering	不屈不撓的
punctual	準時的	purposeful	意志堅強的
qualified	合格的		

R

rational	有理性的	realistic	實事求是的
reasonable	講道理的	reliable	可信賴的
responsible	負責的		

S

self-conscious	自覺的	selfless	無私的
sensible	明白事理的	sincere	真誠的
smart	精明的	spirited	生氣勃勃的
sporting	光明正大的	steady	踏實的
straightforward	老實的	strict	嚴格的

⑩ 貴公司大部分的產品都外銷到日本和南韓。

A: Tell me what you know about our company.
告訴我你對我們公司了解多少。
B: **The products in your company are mostly marketed in Japan and South Korea.**
貴公司大多數的產品都外銷到日本和南韓。

❗ The products in your company are mostly marketed to Japan and South Korea. 貴公司大部分的產品都外銷到日本和南韓。

★ deal in：經營，從事

❗ Your company deals in computer monitors.
貴公司主要經營電腦顯示器。

Your company was founded in Los Angeles in 1987 by John Brown.
貴公司由約翰布朗於 1987 年在洛杉磯建立。

The capital has reached ten billion dollars. 資本總額已達到一百億美元。

The main stockholders are Top Chemical Industrial and Continental Motors.
主要股東是頂尖化學工業和大陸汽車公司。

⑪ 我願意配合外派到任何地方。

A: Would you be willing to work overseas if the office asked you to?
如果公司要你到國外工作你願意嗎？
B: **I'm ready to go anywhere.** 我願意配合外派到任何地方。

❗ I'm ready to go anywhere. 我願意配合外派到任何地方。
I enjoy working abroad. 我喜歡在國外工作。
I'm young and single, so I can go on trips as requested.
我年輕力壯，又沒有結婚，出差沒有問題。

❗ I'm glad to accept any opportunity to travel on business.
我很高興有去外地出差的機會。
It's the reason why I've applied for this job.
我之所以會應徵這份工作就是這個原因。

⑫ 就收入來說，前一份工作相當不穩定。
轉職理由

A: Didn't you like that job? 你不喜歡那個工作嗎？

B: Yes, some of it I enjoyed very much. But economically, it's fairly unstable.

★ economically：在經濟上

★ unstable：不穩固的

是的，有些地方我很喜歡。但就收入來說，前一份工作相當不穩定。

Economically, it's fairly unstable. 就收入來說，前一份工作相當不穩定。

I want to have better opportunities for advancement and that job was not challenging enough.

★ advancement：晉升

我想找到有更多晉升機會的工作，而且原來那份工作挑戰性不夠。

❗ My company is going to lay off a few employees because of the financial crisis. 公司因為金融危機，即將裁掉很多職員。

It would be hard to develop my abilities in such a large company.

在那樣的大公司工作，不容易發揮自己的能力。

My health was quite frail and I couldn't bear the work pressure.

我的健康狀況一直不好，有時無法承受工作上的壓力。

I like that job, but the salary is too low. 我喜歡那份工作，但是薪水太低了。

⑬ 貴公司是我的第一選擇。
工作機會選擇

A: If you are hired by both companies, whose offer will you accept?
如果你同時被兩家公司雇用，你會選擇哪家？

B: Needless to say，**my first choice is your company.**
不用說，貴公司是我的第一選擇。

❗ Needless to say, my first choice is your company.
不用說，貴公司是我的第一選擇。

It's my pleasure to work with you. I'll decline the other offer.
我很榮幸與您共事，我會拒絕其他工作機會的。

❗ Of course I'll accept your offer. I want to work for you.
我當然會接受您的要求，我願意為您工作。

⑭ 以我的教育和資歷，我相信能得到相應的待遇。

A: What starting salary would you expect? 你希望起薪多少？
B: **With my education and qualifications, I believe I shall be fairly treated.**
以我的教育和資歷，我相信能得到相應的待遇。

I expect to be paid according to my abilities. 我希望根據我的能力支付薪資。

❗ I hope the salary will be enough to help me to be independent from my parents economically. 我希望我的薪資能讓我在經濟上獨立，不要依賴父母。

I hope you'll consider my experience and training and will offer me a salary higher than the junior secretary's.
我希望你們能考慮我的經驗和受過的培訓，給我一份高於初級祕書的薪資。

❗ With my education and qualifications, I believe I shall be fairly treated.
以我的教育和資歷，我相信能得到相應的待遇。

加班

⑮ 必要的話，即使熬夜或假日工作我也沒問題。

A: But we do expect you to work overtime when it's necessary.
但必要時我們希望你能夠加班。
B: **If necessary, I won't hesitate to work nights or holidays.** 必要的話，即使熬夜或假日工作我也沒問題。

If necessary, I won't hesitate to work nights or holidays.
必要的話，即使熬夜或假日工作我也沒問題。

❗ If it is necessary to work overtime, I won't be reluctant to do it.
如果有加班的必要，我不會不願意加班的。　★ reluctant：不情願的

❗ It doesn't bother me. I often work overtime and I enjoy it.
我對此完全不介意。我經常加班並樂在其中。

It depends on the situation. 那要視情況而定。

In principle, I'm opposed to overtime work. 原則上我反對加班。

❗ It's a waste of time and money both for employers and employees.
不管對經營者還是員工而言，這都是浪費時間和金錢。

面試時想知道更多公司的特殊規定……

特休假。

How many paid vacation days do I have?
請問一年有幾天特休假？
Do I have to work a whole year before I can take a vacation?
是否要工作滿一年之後才有年假？
I want to know if there's a holiday policy in your company.
我想知道貴公司的休假制度。

晉升機會。

How is your company's promotion policy?
貴公司的晉升制度如何？
I'd like to know if there would be any opportunity to work abroad in the future?
我想知道將來是否有機會到國外工作？
Is there a glass ceiling for women in your company?
在貴公司女性有相同的晉升機會嗎？

試用期規定。

Is there any policy to hire on trial basis?
新人是否有試用期的規定？
Do you have a training program for new employees？
貴公司對新員工有培訓計畫嗎？
How long is my probation?
我的試用期多長？

＊probation 就是求職者必須經歷的「試用期」，也可以說 probation period、probationary period、
probationary employment period 或 trial period。

面試英文
2 招募者（上）

MP3 TRACK：18

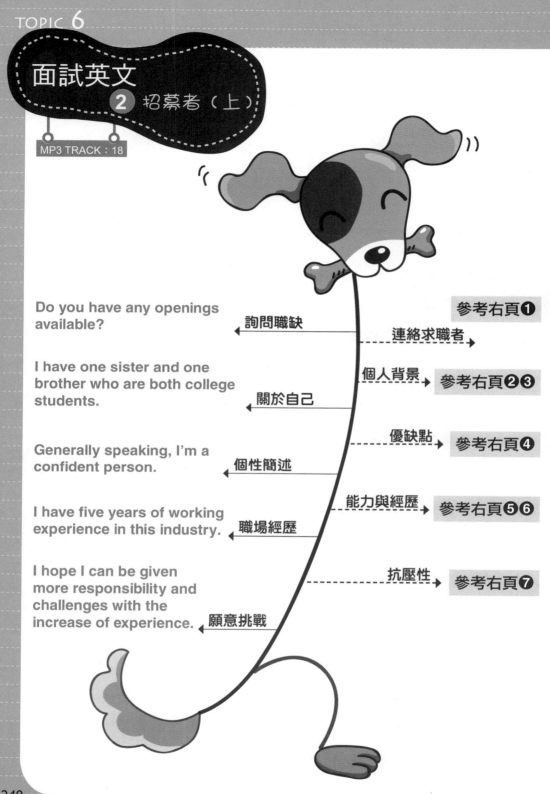

Do you have any openings available?

詢問職缺

連絡求職者

參考右頁❶

I have one sister and one brother who are both college students.

關於自己

個人背景 → 參考右頁❷❸

Generally speaking, I'm a confident person.

個性簡述

優缺點 → 參考右頁❹

I have five years of working experience in this industry.

職場經歷

能力與經歷 → 參考右頁❺❻

I hope I can be given more responsibility and challenges with the increase of experience.

願意挑戰

抗壓性 → 參考右頁❼

You may hear
擔任招募者時，也許你會聽到……

ⓐ 請問貴公司有在徵人嗎？　**Do you have any openings available?**

ⓑ 我有一個妹妹和一個弟弟，　**I have one sister and one brother who are**
　都還在唸大學。　**both college students.**

ⓒ 整體而言，我是一個有自信　**Generally speaking, I'm a confident person.**
　的人。

ⓓ 我擁有五年相同產業的工作　**I have five years of working experience in**
　經驗。　**this industry.**

ⓔ 我希望能隨著經驗的增加被　**I hope I can be given more responsibility and**
　賦予更多的職責和挑戰。　**challenges with the increase of experience.**

 You may want to say
擔任招募者時，也許你會想說……

❶ 請問您什麼時候方便過來面試？　**When will it be convenient for you to come**
　for an interview? ...p.244

❷ 介紹一下你自己。　**Tell me a little about yourself.** ...p.244

❸ 請問你在學時最出色的科目　**What was your strongest subject in college?**
　是哪一項？　...p.245

❹ 你認為你最大的缺點是什麼？　**What do you think your biggest weakness is?**
　...p.246

❺ 請問你有任何技能證照嗎？　**Have you obtained any certificate of**
　technical qualifications? ...p.246

❻ 你有在相同領域工作的經驗嗎？　**Have you had any experience in this field?**
　...p.247

❼ 你如何面對工作上的困難？　**How do you handle difficulty at work?** ...p.247

面試英文
2 招募者（下）

MP3 TRACK：18

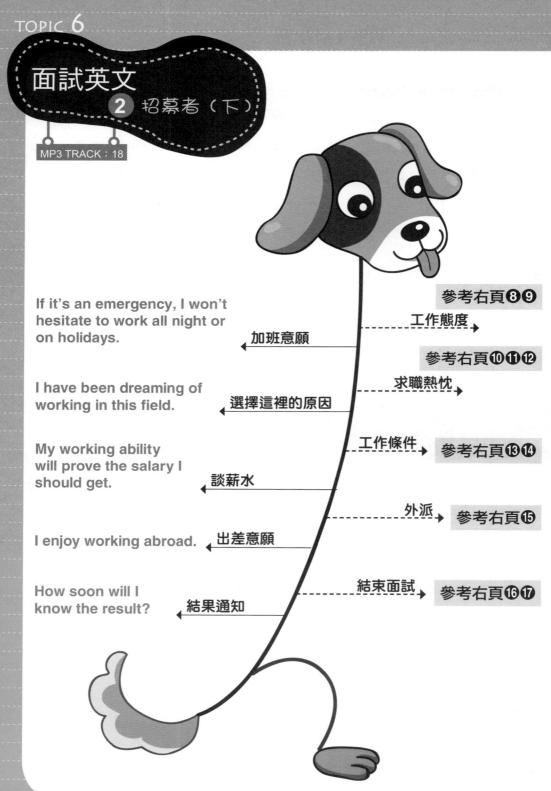

參考右頁 **8 9**

工作態度 →

If it's an emergency, I won't hesitate to work all night or on holidays.

← 加班意願

參考右頁 **10 11 12**

求職熱忱 →

I have been dreaming of working in this field.

← 選擇這裡的原因

工作條件 → 參考右頁 **13 14**

My working ability will prove the salary I should get.

← 談薪水

外派 → 參考右頁 **15**

I enjoy working abroad. ← 出差意願

結束面試 → 參考右頁 **16 17**

How soon will I know the result?

← 結果通知

f 假如狀況緊急，即使熬夜或假日工 作我也會毫不遲疑。 If it's an emergency, I won't hesitate to work all night or on holidays.

g 我一直夢想可以在這個領域工作。 I have been dreaming of working in this field.

h 我的工作能力將會證明我是值得拿 這個薪資的。 My working ability will prove the salary I should get.

i 我喜歡在國外工作。 I enjoy working abroad.

j 什麼時候可以知道結果？ How soon will I know the result?

You may want to say
擔任招募者時，也許你會想說……（續）

8 你期望自己十年後有什麼樣 的成就？ What's your career objective in ten years? ...p.248

9 對於加班你有什麼看法？ How do you feel about working overtime? ...p.248

10 你為什麼來應徵這個工作？ Why did you apply for this job? ...p.249

11 你對我們公司有什麼了解？ What do you know about our company? ...p.249

12 你打算在我們公司工作多久？ How long do you plan to stay here? ...p.250

13 談談你所期望的薪資。 Talk about your salary expectations. ...p.250

14 最快何時可以開始上班？ How soon can you start to work here? ...p.251

15 你願意派駐到其他縣市嗎？ Would you mind relocating? ...p.251

16 謝謝你今天撥空來面試。 Thanks for coming. ...p.252

17 我們會在三天內通知你面試 結果。 We'll notify you in three days. ...p.252

① 請問您什麼時候方便過來面試？

A: **When will it be convenient for you to come for an interview?** 請問您什麼時候方便過來面試？

B: Anytime is okay. 什麼時候都可以。

❗ When will it be convenient for you to come for an interview?
請問您什麼時候方便過來面試？

Do you want to make an appointment at the office tomorrow?
明天你想約個時間來公司談談嗎？

I'd like to make an appointment for an interview at your convenience.
我希望在你方便的時候安排一場面試。

❗ Can you make it Wednesday morning? 星期三上午可以嗎？

We'll contact you to have an interview soon. 不久之後我們會通知你面試的。

❗ We'll need two photographs and a list of advertising projects you have worked on previously.
我們需要你的履歷表、兩張照片，以及你以前做過的廣告企劃。

② 請介紹一下你自己。

A: **Tell me a little about yourself.** 請介紹一下你自己。

B: I'm just leaving school, and I am 18 years old. 我剛畢業，今年18歲。

❗ Tell me a little about yourself. 請介紹一下你自己。

Will you please introduce yourself? 談談你的情況好嗎？

Could you give us a brief introduction of yourself? 能簡單介紹一下你自己嗎？

❗ Will you please introduce yourself to me? 請做一下自我介紹，好嗎？

How would you describe yourself? 你怎樣形容自己？

Would you begin by telling me something about yourself?
請談談你自己的情況好嗎？

Could you tell me something about your present work?
能談談你現在的工作嗎？

Can you sell yourself in three minutes?

★ sell：在這裡有「讓別人了解」的意思。

你能在三分鐘之內介紹你自己嗎？

學校
經歷

❸ 請問你在學時最出色的科目是哪一項？

A: **What was your strongest subject in college?**
　 請問你在學時最出色的科目是哪一項？
B: English was my best subject. I liked it very much.
　 我最好的科目是英語，我很喜歡它。

❗ What was your strongest subject in college?
　 請問你在學時最出色的科目是哪一項？
　 What was your graduation thesis about? 你畢業論文的題目是什麼？

❗ What subject do you like the most? 你最喜歡哪一門課？
　 Could you tell me about the courses of your major subject?
　 能否告訴我你在主修科目上修了哪些課程？

❗ What was your major in university? 你在大學裡主修什麼？
　 Have you received any degrees? 你拿到學位了嗎？
　 What's your minor? 你有輔修什麼課程嗎？
　 How were your grades in college? 你大學時成績如何？

Also need to know

各種學位與證書的說法

certificate 證書
diploma 文憑，畢業證書
degree 學位
bachelor's degree / undergraduate degree 學士學位
master's degree 碩士學位
doctorate 博士頭銜
B.A.＝Bachelor of Arts degree 文學學士學位
B.S.＝Bachelor of Science degree 理學學士學位
M.A.＝Master of Arts degree 文學碩士學位
M.S.＝Master of Science degree 理學碩士學位
M.D.＝Doctor of Medicine 醫學博士
Ph.D.＝Doctor of Philosophy 博士（統稱）
postdoctoral 博士後（研究人員）
honorary degree 榮譽學位

④ 你認為你最大的缺點是什麼？

A: **What do you think your biggest weakness is?**
你認為你最大的缺點是什麼？

B: I'm afraid that I'm a poor talker, and that isn't very good, so I've been studying how to speak.
我恐怕是個不太會說話的人，這不太好，所以我一直在學習如何當眾說話。

❗ What do you think your biggest weakness is?
你認為你最大的缺點是什麼？ ★ weakness：缺點

Are you an outgoing person or more reserved?
你是比較外向還是比較保守的人？ ★ reserved：含蓄的

Could you tell us some of your weaknesses and strengths?
你說說看你有哪些優缺點？

❗ What are your weaknesses? 你不足之處是什麼？

❗ What is your specialty? 你的特長是什麼？

What kind of personality do you think you have? 你認為你有什麼樣的個性？

What do you consider to be your strengths? 你認為你的優點是什麼？

⑤ 請問你有任何技能證照嗎？

A: **Have you obtained any certificate of technical qualifications?** 請問你有任何技能證照嗎？

B: I have received an Engineer's Qualification Certificate.
我獲得了工程師資格證書。

❗ What do you think about your proficiency in written and spoken English?
你認為你的英文寫作和口語熟練程度如何？

What other foreign languages do you speak? 你還會說其他外語嗎？

❗ Have you obtained any certificate of technical qualifications?
請問你有任何技能證照嗎？

Can you tell me what special skills you have? 你能告訴我你有什麼特殊技能嗎？

❗ Have you received any special training in computer programming?
你接受過編寫電腦程式的特殊訓練嗎？

6 你有在相同領域工作的經驗嗎？

A: **Have you had any experience in this field?**
你有在相同領域工作的經驗嗎？

B: Yes, since 2005 I've been employed as a clerk in the ABC Trading Company. 是的，從 2005 年起我就在 ABC 貿易公司做職員。

❗ Have you had any experience in this field?
你有在相同領域工作的經驗嗎？

Have you had any experience with computers? 你對操作電腦有經驗嗎？

❗ Tell me something about your previous (working) experience.
談談你過去的（工作）經驗。

Do you have some experiences in this field? 你在這一行有經驗嗎？

Have you ever done any work in this field? 你曾經做過這行嗎？

❗ Do you have similar job experience? 你有這類工作的經歷嗎？

7 你如何面對工作上的困難？

A: **How do you handle difficulties at work?**
你如何面對工作上的困難？

B: I work well under pressure. 我在壓力下仍可以好好工作。

❗ How do you handle difficulties at work? 你如何面對工作上的困難？
What do you do when you know you're right and others disagree with you?
當你知道自己是正確的，而別人不贊同時你會怎麼做？

❗ Can you work under pressure or tight deadlines?
你能在強大的壓力和嚴格的期限下工作嗎？

Are you good at multi-tasking? 你可以同時承擔多項工作嗎？

How do you get along with co-workers? 你如何和同事們相處？

How do you react to criticism from supervisors that you consider to be unjust?
當你認為主管對你的批評不公平時，你怎麼反應？

❗ How do I know that you can handle the pressure of a job like this?
我怎麼知道你能不能承受這份工作？

Do you work well under pressure? 在強大壓力下你仍可以有效率的工作嗎？

⑧ 你期望自己十年後有什麼樣的成就？

A: **What's your career objective in ten years?**
你期望自己十年後有什麼樣的成就？

★ productive：多產的

B: I'll work hard, and I hope I can be a leader of an energetic and productive sales team.

★ energetic：積極的

我將努力工作，希望成為一個有活力及高生產量的銷售隊伍的主管。

What's your career objective in ten years? 你期望自己十年後有什麼樣的成就？

What's your career objective, particularly your position, in these five years?
這五年中你的事業目標，特別是你想要的職位是什麼？

❗ What would you like to be doing five years from now?
五年後你希望自己在做什麼？

❗ What are your plans for the future? 你對未來有什麼打算？

Where do you see yourself 3 years from now?
從現在三年後你有什麼打算？

What is your aim in going into the field of journalism? 你進入新聞界有什麼目標？

⑨ 對於加班你有什麼看法？

A: **How do you feel about working overtime?**
對於加班你有什麼看法？

B: It doesn't bother me. 我對此完全不介意。

How do you feel about working overtime? 對於加班你有什麼看法？

❗ Will you give up holidays if necessary?
如果有必要的話，你會取消休假嗎？

❗ Will you be able to work overtime? 你可以加班嗎？

What do you think about working overtime if necessary?
必要時我們需要你加班，你認為如何？

Our staff needs to work overtime sometimes. 我們的員工有時需要加班。

❗ You need to understand that the working hours will often be very long.
你要明白，這種工作經常要加班。

❿ 你為什麼來應徵這個工作？

應徵
原因

A: **Why did you apply for this job?** 你為什麼來應徵這個工作？

B: It's because of the journey. Your firm is close to my house within walking distance.
那是因為路程問題。你們公司離我家很近，走路就到了。

❗ Why did you apply for this job? 你為什麼來應徵這個工作？

❗ May I ask why you are interested in working for this company?
告訴我你為什麼想在這家公司工作？

❗ What is it that made you decide to choose this company?
是什麼讓你選擇這家公司？

What made you decide to change jobs? 是什麼讓你決定換工作？

Why should I choose you over the others? 有什麼理由讓我選擇你呢？

What makes you think that you would be successful in this position?
你為什麼認為自己能夠勝任這份工作呢？

⓫ 你對我們公司有什麼了解？

對公司
的了解

A: **What do you know about our company?**
你對我們公司有什麼了解？

B: You are the leading company in the machinery industry.
在機器製造業，貴公司是家重要的公司。

❗ What do you know about our company? 你對我們公司有什麼了解？

❗ What do you know about our major products and our share of the market?
你對我們的主要產品和市場佔有率知道多少？

Do you know who the main stockholders in the company are?
你知道本公司最主要的股東是誰嗎？

What are the advantages and disadvantages of our company?
我們公司的優勢和弱點是什麼？

❗ Tell me what you know about our company. 告訴我你對我們公司知道多少。

When was our company established? 我們公司是什麼時候成立的？

❶❷ 你打算在我們公司工作多久？

A: **How long do you plan to stay here?**
你打算在我們公司工作多久？

★ permanent：固定性的

B: I want to obtain a permanent job.
我渴望擁有一個穩定的工作。

❗ How long do you plan to stay here? 你打算在我們公司工作多久？

What is your goal in life? 你的生活目標是什麼？

❗ Could you tell me what your views on career are?
能談談你對工作的看法嗎？

What kinds of things do you want from your career in the future?
你將來想從工作中獲得什麼？

❶❸ 談談你所期望的薪資。

A: **Talk about your salary expectations.** 談談你所期望的薪資。

B: I expect to be paid according to my abilities.
我希望能根據我的能力支付薪資。

Talk about your salary expectations. 談談你所期望的薪資。

What kind of salary did you get from your previous job? 你上一份工作薪水是多少？

❗ What's your expected salary? 你期望的薪資是多少？

What are your income expectations? 你期望的收入是多少？

❗ What starting salary would you expect? 你希望起薪多少？

薪資單上的英語

Base Salary	基本薪資	Meal Allowance	伙食補貼
OT (Over Time) Allowance	平日加班費	Non-leave Bonus	全勤獎金
Overtime at weekend	週末加班費	Performance Bonus	績效獎金
Overtime at holiday	節日加班費	Quarterly Bonus	季度獎金
Transportation Allowance	交通補貼	Duty Allowance	職務加給

❹ 最快何時可以開始上班？

A: **How soon can you start to work here?**
最快何時可以開始上班？

B: I can start to work in a month. I must go back to Kaohsiung to train my replacement and to go through some necessary procedures.
一個月後我可以開始工作。我要回高雄一趟，移交我的工作，辦理必要的手續。

When can you start the job? 你何時能開始工作？

❗ How soon can you start to work here? 最快何時可以開始上班？

What date can you start to work? 你何時能上班？

How long will it take for you to give a leave notice? 你需要多長時間交接工作？

When will you start working? 你什麼時候能來上班？

❗ If we decide to hire you, when can you start to work?
如果我們錄用你的話，你什麼時候能來上班？

⑮ 你願意派駐到其他縣市嗎？
外派

★ relocate：重新安置

A: **Would you mind relocating?** 你願意派駐到其他縣市嗎？

B: I'm ready to go anywhere, even overseas.
無論什麼地方我都願意去，即使是國外。

Would you mind relocating? 你願意派駐到其他縣市嗎？

Are you willing to make trips to local markets? 你願意到外地出差嗎？

❗ Would you be willing to travel on business? 你願意到外地出差嗎？

If you are hired for this position, you must be prepared to travel abroad frequently.
如果你被錄用，你要有會經常出國的準備。

Would you be willing to work overseas if we ask you to?
如果我們要你去國外工作，你願意嗎？

❗ Can you accept that you would often be on business trips?
你需要經常出差，這一點你能接受嗎？

251

⑯ 謝謝你今天撥空來面試。

A: **Thanks for coming.** 謝謝你今天撥空來面試。
B: Thank you. Goodbye. 謝謝。再見。

This is the end of the interview. Thank you. 面試到此結束，謝謝。

❗ Thanks for coming. 謝謝你今天撥空來面試。
Many thanks for the great interest in this job. 非常感謝你對這份工作的興趣。

❗ That's all for the interview. Please wait for our notification.
面試到此結束，請等候我們的通知。
★ notification：通知

It's been nice talking with you. We'll inform you very soon.
與你談得非常開心。我們會盡快通知你結果。

⑰ 我們會在三天內通知你面試結果。

A: When can I know whether I'm accepted or not?
我什麼時候才能知道我是否被錄取了呢？
B: **We'll notify you in three days.**
我們會在三天內通知你面試結果。

We'll notify you in three days. 我們會在三天內通知你面試結果。
We'll announce the results in a few days. 我們會在幾天後公佈結果。
We'll send you a letter then, if you're hired. 我們如果決定雇用你，就會寄信給您。

❗ We hope to give you good news probably by next Tuesday.
我們大概會在下星期二讓您知道，我希望給您正面的答覆。
I think we'll send you a letter by early next week, if you are wanted.
我想，如果你被錄用，我們將在下週初寄信給你。

❗ We'll notify you next Thursday at the latest. Shall I telephone you?
我們最慢下週四就會通知你。我打電話給您可以嗎？
If we decide to hire you, we will notify you by mail.
如果我們決定錄用你，就寫信通知你。

台灣廣廈 國際出版集團
Taiwan Mansion International Group

國家圖書館出版品預行編目（CIP）資料

上班族天天在用的工作實況英文 / 周梅、溫建平 著；-- 初版. --
新北市：國際學村，2020.06
　　面；　　公分
ISBN 978-986-454-127-0
1. 英語學習　2. 商務英文

805.188　　　　　　　　　　　　　　　　109004920

 國際學村

上班族天天在用的工作實況英文

作　　　者／周梅・溫建平　　　　編輯中心／第六編輯室
　　　　　　　　　　　　　　　　編輯長／伍峻宏・編輯／許加慶
　　　　　　　　　　　　　　　　封面設計／曾詩涵・內頁排版／菩薩蠻數位文化有限公司
　　　　　　　　　　　　　　　　製版・印刷・裝訂／皇甫・秉成

行企研發中心總監／陳冠蒨　　　整合行銷組／陳宜鈴
媒體公關組／陳柔彣　　　　　　綜合業務組／何欣穎

發　行　人／江媛珍
法律顧問／第一國際法律事務所 余淑杏律師・北辰著作權事務所 蕭雄淋律師
出　　　版／台灣廣廈 國際學村 語研學院
發　　　行／台灣廣廈有聲圖書有限公司
　　　　　　地址：新北市235中和區中山路二段359巷7號2樓
　　　　　　電話：（886）2-2225-5777・傳真：（886）2-2225-8052

代理印務・全球總經銷／知遠文化事業有限公司
　　　　　　地址：新北市222深坑區北深路三段155巷25號5樓
　　　　　　電話：（886）2-2664-8800・傳真：（886）2-2664-8801
　　　　　　網址：www.booknews.com.tw（博訊書網）
郵政劃撥／劃撥帳號：18836722
　　　　　　劃撥戶名：知遠文化事業有限公司（※單次購書金額未達500元，請另付60元郵資。）

■出版日期：2020年06月
ISBN：978-986-454-127-0　　　版權所有，未經同意不得重製、轉載、翻印。